MW01503566

Other Books and Writings by David H. Brandin

The Horns of Moses, A Novel
iUniverse, Lincoln, 2007

The Miracle of Alvito (And Other Short Stories)
xLibris, Bloomington, 2008

The Lodge-A Tale of Corruption
iUniverse, New York, 2009

The Technology War (co-authored with Michael A. Harrison)
J. Wiley & Sons, New York, 1987
TBS Britannica, Tokyo, 1989 (Japanese ed.)

The Internet Definition (co-authored with Daniel C. Lynch)
Encyclopedia of Computer Science (4th ed.)
Nature Publishing Group, Oxford, 2000

The Earthquake Prophet

• • •

And Other Stories

David H. Brandin

iUniverse, Inc.
Bloomington

The Earthquake Prophet
And Other Stories

iUniverse books may be ordered through booksellers or by contacting:

iUniverse
1663 Liberty Drive
Bloomington, IN 47403
www.iuniverse.com
1-800-Authors (1-800-288-4677)

ISBN: 978-1-4620-3254-9 (sc)
ISBN: 978-1-4620-3256-3 (hc)
ISBN: 9781-4620-3255-6 (e)

Printed in the United States of America

iUniverse rev. date: 7/18/2011

To
The Greenspan Cousins

"Oh when I die and go to hell to hear the devil's laughter,
O Satan, doom me not to speak, the barren truth hereafter.
When I'm buried, dead and gone, 'tis then my poetry shall speak
Greater truths o gentle reader, if your tongue is in your cheek."
—Reuben Greenspan
(1904 - 1988)
The Earthquake Prophet

"You have ignored the comedy
Of swift, pretentious praise and blame,
and smashed a tavern where they sell
the Harlot's wine that men call fame."
—Maxwell Bodenheim
(1892 - 1954)
President, Ravens Writing Circle of Greenwich Village

Citations

The Miracle of Alvito (And Other Stories)©2008 David H. Brandin, Revised and reprinted by permission of author

Illegals©2008 Cigar Magazine, Reproduced by permission. First published as Illegals: A Chapter in the Life of a Trafficked Cubano Family

Quotation in The Elephant Queen
Horton Hatches the Egg, Dr. Seuss

Photos
Author, Back Cover: Ellen Brandin
Jack, Reuben, and Dave in Death Valley, 1972: Jack Greenspan

Contents

Part IV Fantasy, Science Fiction, and Witchcraft

Preface

I've written fiction for six years; this book represents the collected work of my short stories. All thirty-nine stories are fiction although some might be classified as "creative non-fiction," a category of writing with an elusive definition. Some stories have been previously published under the title *The Miracle of Alvito (And Other Short Stories),* xLibris, Lincoln, 2007. Those stories have been updated and revised.

My favorite writer of short stories is O. Henry. I admire his penchant for ending his pieces with an unusual twist. One can find an infinite number of ideas for stories, but the field narrows when an unexpected ending must be provided. All the stories in this collection end with that "O. Henry" twist.

The work is organized in four parts. The first, entitled *The Earthquake Prophet,* chronicles events in the life of a real person, Reuben Greenspan. He was labeled a "prophet" by the *New York Times, Time* magazine, and the national and international press during one glorious week in July 1935. The first story documents Greenspan's rise to fame; the second relates a bizarre World War II experience in which he played a prominent part; and the third represents my experience in 1972 with him—my uncle Reuben. Points of view in the three stories are varied so that each story may be read independently. The non-fiction result of each episode is noted at the end of each story. Still, I encourage the reader to take them in sequence.

Part II is entitled *Historical Fiction and Political Madness.* Political decisions often are driven by historical events. One might argue that history is influenced as well by politically incorrect decisions. Stories in this section range over such topics as federal spending, illegal immigration, the Middle East, government secrecy, homeland security, global warming, and the World War II battle for Rome. For example, *No-Fly* speculates on TSA procedures; *Sanctuary City* examines the question of how to treat illegal immigrants; *Patient Zero* offers an explanation for the collapse of the American economic system in 2008.

The third part contains stories of general fiction: a strange slot machine, an unusual episode at a shark feed, the relationships between information technology and the law. *The Piano Police* paints the tale of a little boy who struggles with a piano lesson; *Coolidge Said* summarizes some really good advice; and *Street Creds* takes a shot at government duplicity.

Part IV, entitled *Fantasy, Science Fiction, and Witchcraft,* completes the collection. Two stories, *Illegals* and *Special Orders 191*, offers an unusual perspective on America's immigration policy and the Civil War, respectively. *The Elephant Queen* is a political parable and *The Great Race* offer an unusual twist in a classic children's tale. *Gravity*, a science-fiction story, illustrates what happens when unusual materials are used to fabricate a gravity pump.

If readers enjoy these stories, I encourage them to read my novels, *The Horns of Moses*, iUniverse, Lincoln, 2007, and *The Lodge-A Tale of Corruption*, iUniverse, New York, 2009. Both books won awards from the publisher. *The Horns of Moses*, a political thriller, poses the question: Can revenge possibly lead to peace in the Middle East? *The Lodge*, a mystery based on the central coast of California, explores the inept and inane volunteer leadership of a non-profit fraternal order, and ponders whether charity is helpless in the presence of corruption.

David Brandin
California Central Coast
Summer 2011

Part I

The Earthquake Prophet

The Earthquake Prophet

July 10, 1935

Trees trembled, cool still waters turned to scorching caldrons of steam, and lakes and rivers spilled over their banks. Birds exploded from the jungle canopy. The earth rumbled and noxious smoke spewed from a crater.

Thirteen thousand miles away in New York City, a thin, gaunt man stirred in his sleep. As the volcano erupted, he leapt out of bed. *It was happening.* Sleep was out of the question. He reached for a bottle of bourbon and returned to his endless calculations. Perhaps this time, he thought, they'd pay attention.

The volcano, situated on a small island in the Sunda Strait between Java and Sumatra and northeast of Australia, hurled white-hot lava and ash 2,500 feet above its cone. Eruptions occurred every two minutes. The nearby island of Anakrakatau vanished into the sea; tsunami waves thundered across the ocean. Krakatoa, famous for its seismic event in 1883 which killed 36,000 people and blackened the skies for months, had erupted again.

The news of the disaster flashed around the world. Teletypes burst into action. A clerk at the editor's desk of the *New York Times* studied an *Associated Press* (*AP*) dispatch. He frowned and reached into the wastepaper basket to retrieve a letter that had arrived earlier that day. It was one of many written in the past by the same crackpot. The letter's envelope was stained with blots of coffee and reeked of whiskey. The clerk unwound the crumpled paper, re-read it, and ran into the editor's office. He wondered if he could find the previous letters.

• • •

July 12, 1935

Everything was sticky in the garden apartment at 111 West Twelfth Street in Greenwich Village. The humidity was oppressive, palpable, and almost unendurable. Tremendous storms spawned enormous floods and heat lightning throughout the state of New York.

Reuben Greenspan, thirty-one, the man who had dispatched the letters to the editors, brewed coffee in front of a small table fan as sweat beaded on his nose The air moved like distant waves of water, slow and undulating. He heard the public phone ring in the hallway upstairs, and then a neighbor banged on his door. Reuben trudged up the stairs barefooted. He wondered what was next. It seemed like the phone rang continuously since the eruption of Krakatoa.

He listened to the caller, grunted a few times, wiped the sweat off his brow with the back of his hand, and confirmed an appointment for an interview the following week. As he cradled the ear piece of the telephone, he smiled at Miriam, his wife of one month, who watched anxiously from the bottom of the stairs. Miriam, an attractive buxom woman, was on an emotional high from the media attention. Reuben was also excited, but a bit concerned about his wife. Miriam talked too much when she was excited; in her enthusiasm her words outran her thoughts. If he wasn't careful, she might blurt out his secret. He'd made some risky comments the day before on the radio and again to a reporter from the *New York Times*.

Reuben, a serious-faced man, was a merchant seaman who taught classes and tutored navigation mathematics part-time at the Seaman's Institute on Fulton Street. Miriam worked part-time as a piano teacher. They'd met in the Village; Max Bodenheim, the president of the Ravens Writing Circle of Greenwich Village—nicknamed the King of the Bohemians—had introduced them. Reuben had been in his cups when Miriam attracted his attention. She'd laughed at one of her girlfriend's jokes and launched into "Ragtime" by Scott Joplin on the bar's piano. Reuben had pressed Max into service, got his introduction, and wowed Miriam with his tales of the sea. It was love at first sight.

"Another call?" asked Miriam when he came down the steps. "That makes … how many now? This is so thrilling." Miriam, dressed in one of Reuben's old seafaring T-shirts and a pair of panties, poured coffee into mismatched mugs, shoved aside a stack of papers plastered with calculations, and placed the mugs on a worn oilcloth. Reuben's 1918 hand-cranked Rapid calculator, *Betsy*, remained the centerpiece of the table. *Betsy* was Reuben's quintessential tool, a calculator—the prop to impress people, and something to toy with when he was frustrated, bored, or angry.

The Greenspan's two-room apartment was dim and musty, cluttered with Reuben's papers, computational results, and navigation tables of the positions of the heavenly bodies. In the kitchen, Reuben pushed aside an apple crate which housed the portable typewriter to make room for his legs. The tiny room also served as dining room. Space was tight; Miriam's stand-up piano dominated one wall. Reuben sipped his coffee and studied the room with new eyes. If he became famous, he'd get rid of the dump. Even boats had more space.

A small bedroom held a trundle bed and a two-drawer dresser. An old cigar box hosted Miriam's hairbrush and makeup along with Reuben's pocketknife, a few crumpled dollar bills, and loose change. The closet door was missing.

Two windows, tinged with dirt, looked out upon the cracked gray sidewalk and a filthy curb. A police car roared down Twelfth Street. Its siren was muted by windows painted shut. They prevented any cross drafts and contributed to the oppressive humidity. A black 1932 Nash sedan obscured the view of the street and the police car.

"It was *Time* magazine," said Reuben. "They're coming next week to interview me."

"That's wonderful," said Miriam. "Maybe now you can get a job that pays what you're worth—and work in a laboratory with decent equipment."

"Perhaps. But listen, Miriam," he cautioned. "No talk about my dreams."

She nodded, but looked hesitant. Reuben worried if Miriam would keep his secret. It wasn't that he distrusted her. He knew that Miriam loved him. Reuben liked her spirit and playfulness and was amused by her interest in mystical things—she believed in karma and joss. She communed with nature and was almost Buddhist in her thinking. It was possible, he supposed, Miriam found his sixth sense the most exciting thing about him. But he could not let her speculate publicly about his dreams—not after he'd committed himself to a wholly rational explanation for his predictions.

Just yesterday, the *New York Times* had told the world that Reuben forecast the Krakatoa eruption, and he'd been interviewed on national radio. His letters to the metropolitan newspapers throughout the country, sent in increasing numbers since April 1935, had forecast a spate of impending earthquakes. The missives identified specific seismic events by their latitude and longitude, dates, and times. Most of those letters had been dumped in wastepaper baskets; some accumulated in editors' files and collected dust. But Reuben's letter of July 8, 1935, to the *New York Times* caught the attention of the press.

The *Times* had given Reuben front-page billing, above the fold. Before going to press, a reporter interviewed him over the phone. Reuben remembered that conversation vividly:

"Mr. Greenspan? This is the *New York Times.* We're calling to get your reaction to today's eruption of Krakatoa. We just received your letter. Your prediction was quite accurate."

"That's wonderful," gushed Reuben. "I feel vindicated, of course, but I pray for the well-being of the people in that region." Reuben considered his remark a good humanitarian response.

"Can you tell us how you managed to make the prediction?"

Reuben had always dreaded the question. He'd learned, as a teenager and a young adult, that no one believed he could predict earthquakes in his dreams; it was better to let sleeping dogs lie.

"Earth tidal theories," he responded. "I've observed that the highest tides occur when the moon or a large planet align in conjunction with the sun, and thus exert a greater pull on the Earth's crust. I have a mathematical model."

But there was risk. Reuben could be terribly embarrassed. His theory might serve as a public "explanation" for the predictions. But the press might label him a psychic if he couldn't demonstrate his model. Reuben didn't believe in clairvoyance; he was convinced there *was* a rational mathematical basis, based on the movements of heavenly bodies, for his dreams. He was confident he just needed to twiddle the coefficients to produce a coherent set of equations. Then it would be a simple matter, albeit computationally intense, to run the model forward and predict future shakes.

The headline published by the *Times* was startling: "Deadly Krakatoa in Eruption Again." The article reported, "Greenspan, the Mathematician Here who Predicted Earthquakes, Elated Over News." The *Times* acknowledged the timing of the prediction. "… [There was] considerable excitement in the home of … Mr. Greenspan … His letter arrived in newspaper offices about the same time as the cables reporting the Krakatoa eruption."

At last, Reuben reckoned, he'd receive some respect. And with national attention would come a good income and a comfortable life as a distinguished scientist—in contrast to his earlier backbreaking work as a merchant seaman. Not bad, he thought, for a self-educated runaway from a Chicago working-class family, born in White Russia (now Belarus) to peasant Jewish stock.

Thinking of White Russia reminded Reuben of his father. He'd never loved his father, Morris, who'd beat him mercilessly when he got into trouble. But he loved his father's horse. Reuben smiled when he remembered the day the horse had ratted out his father.

Morris had been a milkman who drove a horse-drawn wagon. Morris also had a small gambling habit. As he went about his route, he'd make stops to place bets with the local bookies. After a while, the horse knew all the stops. Sick one day, Morris was replaced by a substitute driver who was confounded by all the extra stops made by the horse—until the man investigated. That, recalled Reuben, was the end of Morris' job.

Reuben shook his head clear. At the moment, he'd reached the first milestone on the road to fame. He smiled at Miriam. "You can make your pound cake when the reporter comes, and I'll show him my calculations."

"Tell me more about your radio interview," said Miriam. "What was it like in Radio City? I thought I was in a dream yesterday. Just think—my husband was on *NBC*!"

Reuben basked in the glow of Miriam's admiration. Under her upswept dishwater blonde hairdo and pencil-thin eyebrows, her eyes flashed mischievously and her pretty face beamed. He smiled as he recollected the adventure.

"When I got on the train to go uptown, I wasn't certain whether I'd tell them about the dreams—but there was this gypsy woman ..."

The gypsy had been at the end of the train. With hand outstretched, she begged a passenger, "Read your fortune for a dime?"

"Get lost," said the man.

With hoots and calls of derision, she worked her way towards Reuben. After a loud "Beat it" and a few angry rejections, the gypsy planted herself in front of Reuben. A transit cop came to his assistance and told her, "Move along."

"It was the way they ridiculed her," Reuben explained to Miriam, "that I resolved to stick to my model."

"She just needed money," said Miriam.

"I know, but I didn't need the distraction—even though it helped push the issue of the dreams out of my mind."

Miriam nodded. "What was Radio City like?"

"Well," he said, "it's a new building, not two years old, and you can still smell the paint in the halls." Reuben slipped into his glib story-telling mode. Reuben had never kissed the Blarney Stone but he was a hypnotic speaker. "They took me up to a studio on the eighth floor ..."

Reuben traversed the hallway in his baggy trousers and an old sport shirt. His good shoes, freshly polished, squeaked. His hip flask, in a back pocket, clinked against his keys and he held his hand on his pocket to stifle the sound. Many of the studios were occupied; red lights blazed above their doors. He encountered two men waiting for him outside Studio 4: Carl Payne Tobey, a renowned astrologer; and William Lawrence, who'd written the first article about Reuben in the *New York Times*.

The men were friendly to Reuben and shook his hand. But as they conversed, the reporter and astrologist treated each other as antagonists. Lawrence rolled his eyes at Tobey's remarks, and Tobey, more obvious, shook his head in disagreement at most of Lawrence's questions and remarks.

Reuben distrusted the motives of both men. The astrologer, Reuben sensed, had his own agenda—to have Reuben confirm that his predictions were based on psychic forces or clairvoyance.

"Tobey's objective was a non-starter," he told Miriam. "I'd already decided that I wouldn't mention the dreams. That's why you got to keep it quiet."

Miriam nodded and refreshed their coffee mugs. "What did the writer for the *Times* say?"

"It was clear to me that Lawrence was a no-bullshit kind of guy. I had to show him a solid scientific method or take a hike." Reuben believed that if Lawrence learned the truth about the predictions, he'd say Reuben sold snake oil.

Reuben had been nervous. He didn't tell Miriam that a few moments before the interview he'd retreated to the rest room. He stepped into a stall, locked the door, and downed a belt of bourbon from his hip flask to steady his nerves. He'd developed a taste for whiskey at sea, and Miriam often criticized Reuben's intense drinking bouts with the Ravens in the Greenwich Village bars.

When Reuben stepped into the *WNBC* broadcast booth, he sealed his reputation as an *Earthquake Prophet.* On the air, Reuben said, with what would prove to be extraordinary accuracy, "… On July 16, 1935, there will be earthquakes in South America on the west coast. There will be recurrences of the earthquakes that are going on down there this afternoon. I predicted these earthquakes to everybody on July 10. Also, on July 16, which is the day of the total eclipse of the moon, the moon will be pulling on one side of the Earth and the sun on another. The area for the quake on this date will be southern China, eastern India, and the northern part of the Philippine Islands, with a possibility of volcanic eruptions in the Philippines … I believe that there will be a serious earthquake … embracing the area near the recent Quetta disaster … on July 29 and July 30. There will be no earthquakes in Montana, Utah and California … up to July 30."

To pander to Lawrence's impressions, Reuben described his experiences as a young Merchant Marine cadet on a Humble Oil vessel, *SS Maravi.* He'd learned how to navigate using sightings of the stars and sun and tables of heavenly bodies to determine the ship's position. He'd read a paper by a scientist, Leo A. Cotton, published in 1922, about earth tides in the lithosphere (the crust and upper mantle of the earth). "That's when I began wondering," said Reuben, "whether earthquakes might be triggered when the planets were aligned."

When the *WNBC* interviewer had asked how Reuben made his predictions, he responded that he had a mathematical model. He explained that it was still in development and required laborious computations that were always prone to error.

Not surprising, after the broadcast, both Tobey and Lawrence continued to ridicule each other in Reuben's presence. It was strange, he mulled, how things had worked out. He was repelled at the idea of support from Tobey, the man most closely aligned with his powers; yet he sought the endorsement of Lawrence, the man most alien to him. But Tobey's interests in metaphysics were just too close to Reuben's method for comfort.

"I was worried," he admitted to Miriam. "There was no doubt in my mind that Tobey's presence would make Lawrence associate my work with astrology."

"Did Mr. Tobey ask you any questions?"

"Not on the air. I'm sure he'd like to know about my dreams. You know, they give me hints," he said. "Then I confirm the earthquakes with my calculations." Reuben grabbed the handle on *Betsy* and spun it. He wagged his finger at Miriam. "Don't forget!" he repeated. "This is damned important. The dreams are just between us."

Reuben reached for his coffee mug. When Miriam retreated to the bedroom to make the bed, he buttressed the brew with a generous shot of bourbon. He began to plan his props for the visit from *Time* magazine. It was unlikely the model would be completed by then. He'd have to finesse it in the meeting. Still, although Reuben was an amateur, he was well-read in mathematics and physics. He expected no problems hoodwinking a mere journalist.

Later that day, Reuben opened the *New York Times*. He read that he'd hit another home run—an earthquake in Japan. The headline read: "Earthquake in Japan Kills 9; Injures 101; Bears out Scientist's Forecast and Theory." The article boosted his credentials. "Support of the theories of young Reuben Greenspan, the amateur scientist who has aroused a large measure of interest by predicting earthquakes a considerable time in advance of their occurrence, came from two sources ... Following today's confirmatory earthquake in Japan, Dr. Clyde Fisher, Curator of Astronomy at the American Museum of Natural History, announced that 'there seems to be considerable scientific basis for this young man's theory. Certainly, the matter deserves to be investigated.'"

Reuben shouted to Miriam, "You've got to read this!" As he waited for her, he turned some pages and found a second headline, in the Radio Section of the newspaper: "64 EARTH TREMORS SUPPORT PROPHET." Based upon his *WNBC* radio interview, the newspaper reported that the "Greenwich Village scientist" predicted an earthquake that rocked a town in Chile; he "FORESAW MANY DISASTERS." The article said, "The earth trembled in far off Copiapo, Chile yesterday, not once, but sixty-four times, as if in response to the bidding of a man in a Greenwich Village apartment. Only last Wednesday the time and place of this earthquake was forecast by Reuben Greenspan ... His prophecies were further borne out by an earthquake that shook the town of Trujillo near Lima, Peru."

Miriam, who'd returned from the bedroom, bent over his shoulder and read the headline. She beamed and jumped into Reuben's arms. "Oh, Reuben, you've done it!"

That evening, at a restaurant in Greenwich Village on Bleeker Street, the

Greenspans celebrated Reuben's new-found notoriety with steaks and a bottle of French wine. Reuben tossed down several bourbons and wondered if he had a tiger by the tail. He really needed those equations.

• • •

July 13, 1935

There was a troubling hiccup, just enough to taint Reuben's infallibility. In his *WNBC* radio interview, he'd reassured America there'd be no earthquake in the nation's fault zones in July. To his dismay, the *United Press International (UPI)* released a wire story that reported that a small earthquake in Southern California had affected Los Angeles, Pasadena, and Hollywood. Almost with glee, brooded Reuben, the article said, "The California Earthquake today was felt also in the east—specifically in the Greenwich Village apartment of Reuben Greenspan, 31, the *earthquake prophet* … The earth by shaking near Los Angeles did Reuben wrong at the moment of his greatest triumph—when newspaper stories here played his 'I told you so' over the tremblors that shivered far-off Copiapo, Chile yesterday."

Reuben fumed.

"Don't be angry, Reuben," urged Miriam. "The *UPI* reporter was just having fun."

Reuben, who'd forecast a flurry of impending shakes in South America and India, was furious. "Damn it. This is nothing to be funny about. I just wish I didn't have these problems with California. I really want to be accurate there. I've got to be more careful with *Betsy*."

On July 16, 1935, the *New York Times* restored Reuben's glory. It reported that an earthquake rocked Managua, Nicaragua, and an aftershock struck Quetta, India. Reuben, characterized in the article as an amateur seismologist and geophysicist, had predicted these shakes, along with tremors on the west coast of South America and elsewhere. Managua matched the longitude of the South American coast; Quetta, however, was on the wrong side of India—the western side (now Pakistan) rather than the eastern.

"Did you make a mistake, Reuben?" asked Miriam. "It's easy to do, isn't it, with *Betsy*?"

Reuben nodded. "All of my work is computationally intense and prone to error. I told them that on the radio, but people don't pay attention. Still, Quetta's important. I said there'd be a big one in Central India at the end of May, and it happened—56,000 lives were lost." But that time, he thought sadly, his prediction had been ignored.

Reuben was relieved when he read a concession from the *New York*

Times. "… It was not until last Wednesday that Mr. Greenspan ceased being a prophet without honor."

"We're flying high!" gloated Reuben. "Let's go to the San Remo tonight."

Miriam smiled, sat at her piano, and played "Happy Days are Here Again."

The next day Reuben struck gold with an earthquake in Formosa (now Taiwan)—which was close enough to agree with his prediction for an event in the northern Philippines. The press swooned. Articles appeared across the country. Small town publications, such as the *Albuquerque Journal, Reno Evening Gazette, Fitchburg Sentinel* (Va.), *and the Evening Huronite* (S.D.) printed stories.

Reuben was ready for his interview with *Time*. But the *AP* beat them to the door. When the reporter made a visit after a short warning telephone call, Reuben was cranking *Betsy*. Miriam was sitting on a chair at the apple crate and typing a letter to her mother. Reuben wore white slacks, an open-necked sport shirt, and a pair of woven straw stuffs. He'd learned that dressing the part of a casual absent-minded professor made one's assertions more credible.

Absent Miriam's pound cake, the Greenspans offered coffee. Reuben first reviewed the general characteristics of his model. After his usual admonishment about "laborious computations" Reuben added, "A university is going to give me a laboratory. It means I can refine my theory and tip prospective victims in advance of a shake."

The reporter was impressed. "Is that another forecast your wife is typing?"

Reuben nodded. "I'm just good with calculations."

"What school is giving you a laboratory?" asked the reporter as he admired Miriam.

"You can say some eastern school—they'll make the announcement next week."

Miriam remained demur and unusually quiet. After the reporter left, Reuben asked her why she was so silent.

"You've been so adamant about the dreams that I decided to just let you talk. Besides, I'm really waiting for that reporter from *Time*."

"Well, thanks. I wonder what this guy will write."

• • •

July 20, 1935

The *Time* magazine reporter was expected. Reuben placed a navigation handbook next to *Betsy* on the kitchen table. Reuben couldn't expose his incomplete model, so he'd ginned up a set of three-dimensional gravitational formulae—just classical Newtonian equations—taught in any freshman physics class. They were fluff. But n-body problems, which involved the gravitational forces of more than two bodies, were complicated. Reuben was certain he could bluff his way through the interview.

Reuben greeted the reporter who looked like some young kid out of journalism school with the brain of a flea. This was a human interest story, not an exciting murder or graft in Tammany Hall. *Time* had sent a cub reporter. Reuben smiled inwardly at his luck. Miriam served coffee and her pound cake. They settled at the table around Reuben's props.

The reporter asked some questions about Reuben's background. Reuben said he was born in Evanston, Illinois, and that his father had owned a fleet of fishing vessels in the Gulf of Mexico. The reporter nodded. "And your education?"

"I went to Armour Institute of Technology in Chicago. Got a PhD in Geophysics."

"So, Dr. Greenspan, can you predict earthquakes?"

"That's right, son," boasted Reuben. "I've developed a mathematical model of earthquakes."

The reporter looked around the table and saw papers covered with computations. The most prominent page displayed several equations with lots of Φ's, Ψ's, X's, Y's, Z's, and large capital F's and M's. The classical trigonometric identities for spherical triangles were scribbled at the bottom.

The reporter picked up the page. "Are these your equations?"

"There're a few lower-order terms missing, but I'm sure you recognize the gravitational force components."

"Uh-huh," mumbled the reporter. After a moment of silence, he added, "That's neat, Dr. Greenspan. When will the next earthquake be?"

"Son, that requires a lot of work. If you look around, you can tell I don't have any fancy equipment. There're lots of computations involved. You know Gauss spent the last twenty years of his life calculating lunar trajectories—a waste of great talent. I don't want to do that."

"I see. Who was Gauss?"

Reuben was convinced the reporter was a gift. "He was the greatest mathematician of all time. He lived a long time ago."

The reporter scribbled in his notebook. "Can you tell me something about your background?"

"As a merchant seaman, I read this paper on tides by Leo Cotton. It gave me an idea. I was already adept at celestial navigation. That enabled me to compute—"

A beaming Miriam interrupted. She rambled on about how Reuben was a genius and how hard he labored. She complained bitterly about the conditions under which he did his research, and spoke indignantly of other scientists whose institutions and positions provided ample numbers of assistants and expensive equipment.

Reuben wasn't sure whether he should get angry or not. Miriam had cut him off in the middle of his exposition. But, when she finished, the reporter thanked them and departed.

The next day, the *AP* published its story under the banner: "Earthquake Prophet to Get Modern Laboratory."

Reuben grinned. "Hey. Miriam, the *AP* reporter must have liked you."

She read, "Mrs. Greenspan, comely piano teacher, wife of 31-year old Reuben Greenspan, who has been calling the earth's seismic shots with astounding accuracy for the last three months, was batting out a fresh forecast on the Greenspan portable typewriter."

"I was typing a letter to my mother," she recalled. "What did you tell him?"

"I just nodded."

• • •

July 22, 1935

Reuben fetched a copy of *Time* magazine from the newsstand. He was delighted. The article was entitled: "Quakes and Prophets." Reuben was described as a "young Jew doing an astonishingly good job of calling them before they happened." The article reported, "Precocious, Reuben graduated from Armour Institute of Technology at 18."

Besides referring to the imaginary fleet of fishing vessels owned by Reuben's father, *Time* went on to quote Miriam. "Reuben is an unsung genius … if they will only listen … they will save a great many lives. When I think of the great scientists who have their million-dollar laboratories while Reuben toils away with only a few charts and instruments, almost junk in comparison, it just burns me up."

In just eleven days, Reuben had become a national phenomenon. Over the next few weeks, news articles around the country consumed gallons of ink raving about the *Earthquake Prophet*. On July 25, the *Fitchburg Sentinel* published: "Forecast Earth Shocks for July 29 and 30." The article said,

"Earthshocks [sic] of serious proportion in the Pacific and Mediterranean areas were forecast for July 29 and July 30 by Reuben Greenspan, whose scientific predictions have been coming true consistently in the past few weeks." Even newspapers around the world joined the party. On July 20, 1935, the *Argus* (Melbourne, Victoria, Australia) referred to Reuben's "uncanny" ability to predict earthquakes.

A reporter from another prominent magazine anointed Reuben. On July 27, 1935, the *Literary Digest* published a full page article: "Home-Made Earthquake Prophet." The *Digest* stressed that Reuben was "no clairvoyant" and suggested that "scientists feel he may be right." The article identified "Fordham University in New York … [as the school that had] … offered him the use of its scientific library and the assistance of its competent staff of seismologists and well-equipped earthquake observatory."

The magazine accepted his "laborious computations" as an explanation for the limited accuracy of his predictions and the need to conduct more research. Citing his marriage to Miriam a month earlier, the *Digest* gave her some space. "'He's a genius,' young Mrs. Greenspan told reporters emphatically, 'and some day the world will own it!'" Reuben was thankful his wife had maintained some semblance of control.

Reuben struggled night and day on his computations. His arm tired from spinning *Betsy*. He was trying to fit the data from several earthquakes to his equations. At the end of the month, he got the coefficients just right. The calculations generated the date and epicenter of a historical shake—a major event that struck Haiyuan, China in 1922 and killed 200,000 people. That earthquake had not been used to construct his model. He'd done it! The equations worked. He made a lazy assumption that the model worked in the general case, and boxed up the equations and latest set of notes. He and Miriam strolled to several cafés near Washington Park, and Reuben drank three bourbons with beer chasers. Later the couple made love and slept well.

• • •

August 1, 1935

Reuben planned to begin calculations for a series of forecasts over the next two years in the western hemisphere. After downing two aspirins and a quart of water, he walked to the newsstand for a copy of the *New York Times*. There were no new earthquakes, but he found a long article by Waldemar Kaempffert, the *Times'* science editor, in the Science Section entitled: "Earthquakes and the Moon." Enchanted, Reuben began to read the article on the street. Kaempffert observed that there were 60,000 earthquakes a year, and that at least 9,000 were tremors or "formidable shocks" that could be felt by people. "With just that as a basis," Kaempffert wrote, "when, therefore, Reuben Greenspan tells us that there will be one on a given day, he is likely to be right."

Reuben sensed a back-handed compliment. His hangover headache began to roar back. He rubbed his eyes and continued to read.

Kaempffert acknowledged the uncanny nature of Reuben's accuracy in predicting the time and place of earthquakes, and that the Quetta prediction was the origin of Reuben's celebrity. But even the great Darwin, noted the science editor, had harbored similar ideas. Kaempffert wrote, "In 1840 Darwin asked: 'On the hypothesis of the crust of the earth resting on fluid matter, would the influence of the moon (as indexed by tides) affect the periods of the shocks, when the force which causes them is just balanced by the resistance of the solid crust?'" Kaempffert further observed it was common knowledge that earthquakes were more frequent at new and full moons than at other times.

Reuben stormed back into the garden apartment. "Where's my bottle of bourbon?"

Miriam, bewildered, pointed at the cupboard under the sink. "What's wrong?"

"This!" Reuben waved the newspaper at her. "It's a disaster." He sat down at the table and fumed while he read on.

Kaempffert had noted that "Other periodic earthquake 'laws' have been discovered." He added, "There are too many [laws] for geological or statistical comfort ... Any good statistician could mimic Reuben's results. When one knew the regions where earthquakes strike, such as the continental shelves, one could correlate the shakes with almost anything." Reuben's blood pressure topped out when he read, "An ingenious manipulator of earthquake records might even correlate them with the rise and fall of U.S. Steel on the New York Stock Exchange."

At the end of the article in which Kaempffert cited numerous examples of correlations, he administered the *coup de grace*. "What Mr. Greenspan gives us is astrology in a new guise."

"Son-of-a-bitch," exclaimed Reuben. His fears that the *New York Times* would associate his work with astrology were realized.

He chugged his bottle of bourbon. Miriam limped into the bedroom, chanting and crying. He stared at Kaempffert's article as he downed gulp after gulp. Reuben trembled. His face turned red and he slammed the bottle down next to *Betsy*. Pages of his computations fluttered to the floor. He grabbed the loose sheets, took the remaining piles, notes, and tables of the positions of the planets and moon, and stuffed them in the box with the equations for his model. He considered throwing *Betsy* in as well, but he was sober enough to realize he needed the calculator if he returned to sea.

He dragged the box into the alley behind Twelfth Street, drenched it with his remaining bourbon, and torched it. As the flames consumed everything, he mumbled, "Fuck 'em. They don't deserve it." He turned and stumbled back into the hallway of his tenement building.

Miriam stared at him with tear-streaked eyes. "Oh, Reuben. All that work wasted."

He glared at her. It was all over, he thought. The rest of the day and evening were spent in a drunken haze.

The next morning Reuben awoke with a start. He realized those equations were all he had. Without them he was nothing; with them he had the basis for a lifetime of recognition. He resolved to reconstruct and thoroughly test his calculations. And this time he'd prove himself and the validity of the model to the scientific establishment. He'd show them—he'd publish his work.

(*N.B.* Reuben Greenspan was a real person. The newspaper and magazine articles are reported accurately. The narrative is imagined. Did Reuben really have equations? Perhaps he did. Kaempffert's criticism was based on a statistical argument—that high correlations in themselves do not mean anything. But sometimes they do. What Kamepffert said failed to rule out Reuben's claims that he'd solved the problem—even though it now is known there were errors in Leo Cotton's assumptions. It was possible, albeit unlikely, that Reuben had fit his earthquake data to a mathematical model. The acid test would have come if, and when, his equations accurately foretold future earthquakes.)

Loose Lips Might Sink Ships

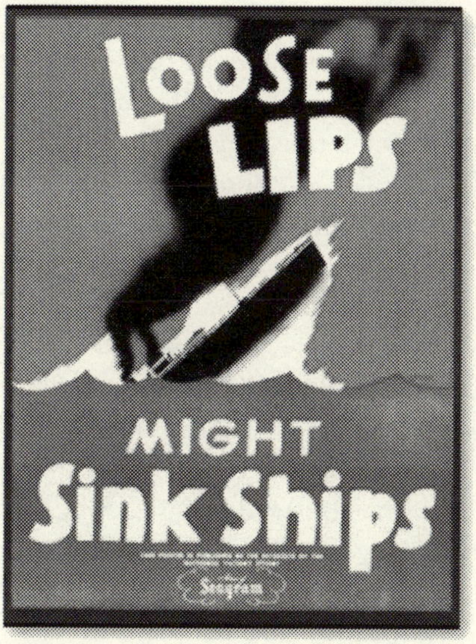

January 1943. The Battle for the Atlantic raged. Rumors filled the airwaves that ninety-five percent of the ships in the last convoy to England were sunk.

Mary Broughton was young, single, lonely, and rich. Since the war began, eligible young men were in short supply. There were soldiers and sailors her age at the clubs, but none who'd make a commitment. Orders were capricious and unpredictable. Men disappeared without warning, shipped off to do battle in strangely-named places like Guadalcanal and New Guinea.

Mary, heiress to the Broughton family construction empire, made her way out of the subway station on Lexington Avenue. She shivered as she walked to the corner of Seventy-Eighth Street. It was a typical January evening in New York City, cold and windy. She wrapped her scarf tightly around her neck and looked forward to her arrival at the Music Box, a small restaurant and bar. GIs hung out there on leave, and she enjoyed dancing with them. Of course, a girl had to be careful. Although most of the men were desperate for a woman's company, some of them had wives at home and were just looking for a one-night stand.

Most of the soldiers that came in were young—kids, really—some with terrible wounds; many had combat fatigue. Mary's throat tightened when she walked into the bar and saw several men with bandages, some with crutches. She handed her coat to the hatcheck girl and went into the restroom to repair the wind damage to her hairdo and to check her makeup.

Mary studied her image in the cracked and cloudy mirror. Acting like a spoiled rich girl either attracted the wrong kind of guy or scared the right guys off, but tonight she'd felt like wearing a full- length red gown. It flattered her slim body and made her look taller than her five foot four. The dress matched her bright red lipstick. Besides, she thought, red was fitting for a club filled with servicemen. It was the color of love and war.

So much war, she mused, but what Mary missed was love. She refreshed her lipstick and went back into the club.

She sat at the bar and ordered a rum and coke. The jukebox in the corner played a Cole Porter tune, "You'd Be So Nice to Come Home To." Mary considered dancing with some of the wounded boys. As she smiled a welcome to two marines nearby, the outer door opened and a naval officer walked into the Music Box. His left arm, bandaged, was in a sling. His topcoat was draped over his shoulders, but Mary identified him as a lieutenant commander. She volunteered at the USO Club near Grand Central Station and knew all the military insignias and ranks.

The officer swung the topcoat off with his right arm, stopped at the hatcheck, and made his way to the bar. When the officer hovered behind Mary as he sought the bartender's attention, the enlisted men looked disappointed.

Mary studied the officer in the mirror behind the bottles lined up along the back counter. She thought the man was handsome, albeit somewhat diminutive, and he had a shy or perhaps bashful look about him. Rather endearing, she fancied.

Mary swiveled on her barstool and smiled. "Good evening, Commander." She nodded at the empty seat next to her. "Please, take a seat."

"Thank you, my dear," replied the commander. "May I buy you a drink?" He moved the stool with his right arm, sat down, and made himself comfortable.

"That would be nice," she replied. "My name's Mary—Mary Broughton." My God, she thought, he looked good.

"Hi, Mary. I'm Reuben Greenspan."

He ordered a bourbon straight with a beer chaser, and she had another rum and coke. He reached for his wallet but fumbled when his left arm in the sling failed to cooperate.

"Commander, let me buy the drinks."

He smiled affably. "Thanks. Please, call me Reuben." He gulped down his bourbon.

"Okay—Reuben. What are you doing on land? Have you been at sea lately?"

"I'm stationed on the *USS Jacob Jones*. It's a destroyer-escort."

"What's that?"

"We escort convoys across the North Atlantic. Sometimes we fight German U-boats."

"Is that how you got your wound?"

"I was wounded in a gunfight with a German *Stuka*. It dive-bombed and strafed my convoy."

"Is it serious? Where were you when it happened?"

Reuben lifted his beer bottle and sipped. "We'd dropped a few ships off at Ponta Delgada, in the Azores, and were headed toward the port of Southampton. I got hit a glancing blow by a machine gun round."

"It's uncomfortable," he added, "but not very painful. It doesn't interfere with my other work, which is quite secret. I'd love to tell you about it but, you know, '*Loose Lips Might Sink Ships.*'" Reuben pointed at a poster with the same words on a wall next to the jukebox. It showed a sinking freighter with black smoke pouring out of its stacks.

When he smiled, Mary felt herself sink into Reuben's large brown eyes. She touched his bandaged left arm in sympathy. They sat there for some time, nursing drinks and talking. She continued to pay. After all, she reasoned, he was a wounded hero, and it seemed so satisfying that she buy.

They danced. Reuben was a little awkward with his arm in a sling, but Mary felt he tried to do his best. They sat down when the music shifted to "Boogie Woogie Bugle Boy" by the Andrew Sisters. During the break, she wondered about his background. "Where are you from, Reuben? I was born on Long Island."

"I was born in Evanston, Illinois. My father owned a small fleet of fishing vessels in the Gulf of Mexico."

"Really? Is that where you got your interest in the sea?"

Reuben grinned. "I loved it. I got really interested in navigation and engineering and earned a math degree at Armour Institute of Technology in Chicago. After school I joined the Merchant Marine."

Mary, who studied classical piano in her free time, was delighted. "That's great. I study piano and love the mathematical nature of music—even though I can't do more than simple algebra."

"It's not difficult," said Reuben, "at least not for me. I can compute the position and the gravitational forces at any spot on the earth. In fact, that's part of my secret work, but I shouldn't say any more about that."

Later, they went to dinner on the West Side. They walked through the park to get to a small café on Central Park West. The temperature had dropped but Reuben's right arm encircled Mary and shielded her from the cold.

At dinner Reuben regaled Mary with tales of the sea. Before the war he'd taught navigation math and astronomy at the Seamen's Institute on Fulton Street.

Reuben smiled. "68.75 North; 33.10 East."

"What's that?" asked Mary.

"That's the latitude and longitude of Murmansk. Want some more? I do it for kicks."

Mary laughed. "When did you join the Navy?"

"They offered me a commission after the Japanese attacked Pearl Harbor."

"That was so sad."

Reuben nodded. "I'm the lead navigator on these convoys. I never know when I'll be called back to sea—departure times are highly confidential and I get little warning. It's the Battle for the Atlantic, you know, and we have to get those ships to England."

To Mary he sounded like an admiral.

He reached for the dinner check, but she stopped him. "Reuben," she declared, "those of us at home don't do enough for our boys. I have a modest inheritance, and your money's no good when you're with me."

He protested, but she was adamant. They caught a cab to her studio apartment in Gramercy Park and made love that night.

• • •

As time went by, they became quite close. Reuben stayed in Mary's apartment whenever he was in town. That wasn't too often; he had to periodically race off to escort another convoy across the Atlantic.

One night in bed, Mary asked Reuben about his secret project. "What can you tell me?" She lit a cigarette and offered him a drag. "Are you making progress?"

"You know I can't talk about that," he cautioned. He took the cigarette, puffed, and stubbed it out. "It's secret, and very important to the war effort."

"Oh come on," she pleaded. "Your secret's safe with me. I would never do anything to threaten our boys at sea. Please, give me a hint. Perhaps I can help." She smiled playfully and slid her hands under the covers to tease him.

"I don't know," he replied. "Let me think about it. I have to leave tomorrow, but if I survive the crossing, I'll tell you—a reward for bringing me and the convoy good luck. And please," he moaned, "keep doing that!"

During his absence Mary, lonely beyond imagination, spent afternoons wandering aimlessly up and down Madison Avenue. Occasionally she'd walk over to Grand Central Station on Forty-Second Street and watch the soldiers and sailors stream through. Once she thought she saw Reuben on the other side of the central hall.

Mary had shouted, "Reuben!" and chased the man all the way to the Lexington Avenue exit before she lost sight of him. But she knew it wasn't him, that she was just fooling herself. She was head over heels in love with Reuben Greenspan and desperate to see him again. To make things worse, the *Loose Lips Might Sink Ships* posters were plastered all over the station. They reminded her of her lover and his secret project.

In early April, Reuben showed up with an old, hand-cranked calculator from his days in the Merchant Marine. He called the machine *Betsy*. The device computed numbers to sixteen decimal places. "*Betsy*'s a fighter, too," he said. "We use her to navigate, and she's been helping me with my secret project."

"Are you going to let me help?" asked Mary. They were drinking wine and Reuben smoked a pipe. She thought he looked dignified but a little silly, too, wearing her dressing gown.

"It's very complicated and requires a lot of engineering. I'm working on a project to detect enemy submarines. If I could just get the damn thing to work—I still have a few problems to work out—it could help our convoys avoid German U-boats and not be torpedoed. You know we've lost hundreds of ships out there?"

She nodded with sympathy but inside she was enthralled. He was telling her his secret! "Can you explain some of it?"

"Let's see if I can offer a layman's explanation." He smiled, relit his pipe, and puffed for a while. "With a calculator like *Betsy*, and a table of heavenly bodies, we can compute the gravitational force at any spot on the surface of the earth. That force varies with the positions of the sun and the moon. So when we're at sea, we compute what the gravity should be at our latitude and longitude. We then measure the gravity, and, if it doesn't agree with the calculations, we assume there's a large mass nearby. If we can't see anything, then it's got to be a submarine."

She looked thoughtful for a while. "But how do you measure the gravity? Isn't that hard to do?"

Reuben looked around the room and put his finger to his lips for emphasis. "That," he whispered, "is the real secret part. I'm working on the detector. It has tubes and parts that require precision milling. I can only work on it when I'm not at sea. That's where I spend my free time when I leave here—at a machine shop in Greenwich Village."

Mary felt a rush of pleasure. A project to protect convoys was the single most important thing she could think of. And, she marveled, he'd shared his secret with her! She basked in the glow of his trust.

• • •

Spring came to New York. Flowers filled the air with sweet scents. The small Victory Gardens behind the brownstones bloomed. Reuben and Mary were together every moment he could spare. They brought in food so they could spend more time in bed. Mary was in love and they spoke of marriage.

One day Reuben seemed pensive when he returned from the machine shop in the Village. "What's wrong?" she asked. "Are you still making progress on the detector?"

"No, damn it, I'm stuck! I need a crucial part and can't afford it. It's a special power klystron tube and it costs $2,000. It's manufactured by the Radio Corporation of America and, until I save enough, the project will have to wait."

He looked dejected. "But Reuben, what about those poor boys on the convoys and the supplies that are needed in England?"

He shook his right hand in a helpless gesture.

Mary poured two shots of bourbon, hoping the whiskey would cheer them up. Later, she took him to dinner in a small café near Washington Park. She was distraught and haunted by the vision of American convoys under attack. It seemed so unnecessary when, as Reuben had said, with his invention ships could be taken safely to their destinations. She considered giving him the $2,000. But he hadn't asked, and she feared he'd feel put off if she offered.

That night they made love. Sometime around 1:00 AM, a little drunk, she was shocked when Reuben began to cry softly. An American hero, a fighting man, she thought, lay in her bed and cried! She held him and rocked gently.

After the tears stopped, she asked what was wrong.

"I hate to admit it. But the thought of losing more convoys is ripping me apart. I just don't know how to speed up the project. It'll take three more months of pay to get enough money for that tube."

"Reuben, stop! Not to worry. I'll give you the money. I have more than enough, and there's more available if needed. I'll do anything I can for our boys."

Reuben frowned. "I don't think I can take your money. It's a lot."

Mary smiled. "Don't be silly. I really can afford it."

"Okay," he said, "but only if you're sure."

Mary wrote a check. Over the next few weeks, Reuben worked on his device. She could tell when he encountered a roadblock; he'd become quiet and sad. She'd have to beg him to take more money for the detector. Mary was certain his pride was wounded, but Reuben cheered up eventually, and most evenings he reported progress.

In mid-May Reuben announced he had to return to sea. "I received orders today. I'm not sure how long I'll be gone, but there's only one problem left on the sensor. I'll do the theoretical work while I'm at sea and finish the project when I return."

"My God, that's wonderful!"

"And there's more. After I demonstrate it to the War Department, I'm sure I'll get a promotion. We can be married. Will you marry me?"

Mary couldn't say "Yes" fast enough. The next day Reuben packed up *Betsy* and departed after the lovers shared a passionate kiss. As he walked out the door he promised, "We'll celebrate the sinking of every U-boat."

• • •

A week later was Mary's twenty-fourth birthday. She celebrated her birthday every year with her mother, Edith Broughton, and her uncle, Judson Broughton, a widower who also lived on the family estate in the Hudson River Valley. Uncle Judson had served under Teddy Roosevelt in the First United States Volunteer Cavalry Regiment, the Rough Riders. He'd charged up San Juan Hill. He was a thoughtful and practical man, and Mary told him about Reuben and her plans to marry.

"Tell me about this man," said Uncle Judson, a civil engineer who built bridges, canals, and dams. "He's a lieutenant commander, you say?"

"Oh, Uncle Judson, he's wonderful. He's a college graduate, a navigator, and his father owned a fleet of fishing vessels."

"Where'd this man go to school?"

"Armour Institute of Technology in Chicago." He's working on a secret project, too." Mary bit her tongue. Darn, she thought, there she was talking about Reuben's project when she should have kept her promise.

Uncle Judson looked at his niece. She was drinking bourbon straight, and he reached for a bottle of Old Forester. He poured two more fingers of whiskey into her glass. Edith Broughton frowned at the sight of her daughter drinking like a sea rat, but Uncle Judson waved his hand at her. "Edith," he commanded, "I'll take care of this. I'm responsible for the reputation of this family."

Mary, nervous, gulped at the whiskey. Time seemed to fly and, before she realized it, she'd explained Reuben's idea for protecting convoys. When she admitted that she gave her lover $9,000, Uncle Judson stormed to his feet.

"God damn it, Edith," he roared. "I told you she's too young to have access to the money. Mary, how could you be so stupid as to believe such nonsense?"

Mary fled the room in tears. She spent the night in misery—torn between love and fear of her uncle, between love of Reuben and fear that he'd manipulated her, and between love of the thought of marrying him and fear that she'd lose him.

The next morning, Mary felt rebellious. As the sun rose, her fears were replaced by an intense desire to hold Reuben again, to be wrapped in his arms, and to marry him.

Mr. Caifano, the family attorney, was at breakfast when Mary came down the stairs. She listened silently as she was told in no uncertain terms this was the end of the affair; the family intended to launch a full scale investigation. They were most concerned about the family reputation and, further, in no way would they accept being swindled out of any money. She was to break off all contact with the man. If Reuben asked for any more money, she was to call Uncle Judson immediately.

As Mr. Caifano talked about swindles and gullible women, Mary became angry. She resolved that she would not stop seeing Reuben. His invention, she knew, was more important than Uncle Judson's silly concern about the family reputation.

• • •

On June 3, 1943, Mary's lover came home from another tour at sea. His bandages were gone. With him spouting tales of the sea, they drank a bottle of wine and talked about his invention.

"I did it," he said. "I solved the last theoretical problem. There were some errors in my assumptions of the moon's orbit."

"Oh, Reuben, I'm so proud of you. When can you show it to the War Department?"

Reuben smiled grimly. "Well, I need to replace that tube you helped me buy with a different model. It'll just be a few more months."

"Don't be ridiculous. Boys are dying—I'll give you the money!"

Reuben hugged her. "I'll purchase the part and complete the gravity detector tomorrow."

In the morning, Reuben surprised Mary. He produced a last will and testament, signed over the rights to his invention and estate to her, and made her the beneficiary of his U.S. Navy life insurance policy. Mary was convinced Uncle Judson was wrong. She gave Reuben another check for $2,000.

"Tomorrow," promised Reuben, "I'll demonstrate the detector to you, and we'll pick up a marriage license at City Hall."

After Reuben left, Mary stared out the window and thought about Reuben's wonderful body—how he'd embraced her and held her close. And then, she remembered—his arm, the left one, as it had caressed her so deliciously—where were the scars? There'd been no wounds! She sat up in bed, startled. Had the whole thing had been an elaborate ruse to gain her sympathy? She asked herself how else she'd been misled. And then it was clear. It was the money, he was after the money! Mr. Caifano and Uncle Judson had spotted it right away. The invention, marriage, the will—it was all a hoax.

Mary wiped the tears from her eyes and climbed out of bed. She washed her face and smoked a cigarette. Over coffee, she resolved to get even. She'd never be fooled again. She walked resolutely to the telephone in the hallway outside her apartment and called Uncle Judson. When he answered, the tears returned. She bawled, "You were right. I was wrong. I'm a fool. Call the police."

• • •

Agents of the FBI arrested Reuben on June 5, 1943. The *International Herald Tribune* reported: "A Fake is Arrested." The newspaper wrote, "[He was] easily the most imaginative and successful of the current crop of Navy officer impersonators." The *New York Times* article was headlined: "Bogus Naval Officer Is Held As Swindler." It reported "[The victim was a] socially prominent New York woman, who was not named by the F.B.I." According to the *Chicago Tribune*, which also published a story, "[She] was only one of a score of gullible women who gave Greenspan unknown sums." All the newspapers said that Reuben had claimed the money was needed to perfect an invention that protected convoys from being torpedoed. Reuben, who'd lived in a three-dollars-a-week furnished room, was arraigned before a United States Commissioner at the Federal Building in New York City. When Reuben could not post $500 bail, he was held in the Federal Detention Center. The Federal Grand Jury for the Southern District of New York indicted him on two counts of impersonation on June 11, 1943. Tried before a federal judge on July 1, 1943, Reuben was found not guilty of both charges.

(N.B. The details of the scam and the Broughton family described herein are fictional. However, other elements of this story are true. Reuben Greenspan was charged with two counts of impersonation and accused of swindling a "woman of social prominence." A Freedom of Information Act (FOIA) demand for details of the trial was served on the United States Department of Justice (DoJ). The documents provided by the government in its response—eleven pages of mostly redacted and illegible information—revealed that Reuben was found not guilty on both counts. One wonders if the complainant failed to appear to protect the family name. Perhaps more puzzling is the fact that the DoJ withheld an additional eleven pages on national security grounds.)

Frenzy

February 5, 1971

John Blackburn, reporter for the *Register*, a Santa Ana, California newspaper, stared at the man on his right. Reuben Greenspan drank sherry instead of his usual bourbon and beer chasers. He was slight, gaunt, and unshaven—but he spoke like a man who had kissed the Blarney Stone.

Newspaper clippings and a *Time* magazine article from 1935 were spread across the bar. Blackburn found the clippings of interest. He was hard up for a feature—a human interest story. Greenspan had a history of accurately predicting earthquakes and looked like he might fill the bill.

Blackburn waved his hand at the bar. "Never mind those past predictions. What about the future predictions?"

"There're going to be two earthquakes," responded Greenspan. "Four days from now a magnitude 6.5 shake in southern California; I figure about 6:03 AM. Then, two years from now at 9:20 AM on January 4, 1973, San Francisco will get hit with a big one. It will probably measure magnitude 7.3 on the Richter scale."

"Maybe I can use the material. But how can you be so sure?"

Reuben Greenspan smiled. "Listen here, John. *Time* magazine called me an earthquake prophet in the '30s. I have a mathematical model. The first shake, on February 9, will hit somewhere near Sylmar. Of course, I could be off a little. All my computations are laborious and subject to error."

Blackburn wasn't certain his editors would be interested. Most of the guys who predicted earthquakes were frauds and charlatans. He wrote the story, but it wasn't published. His editors preferred to wait. If the Southern California prediction proved accurate, they'd reconsider printing the San Francisco prediction.

• • •

February 9, 1971

At 6:00 AM, a magnitude 6.7 earthquake struck near Sylmar in the San Fernando Valley. Sixty-four people died. Damage was estimated at $500 million.

Blackburn was astonished. Reuben Greenspan was three minutes off in his prediction. Six hours later Blackburn tracked down Greenspan in a bar.

The man had another glass of sherry. He was dirty, covered in dust, and surrounded by a collection of cameras. Greenspan, remembered Blackburn, had press credentials as a part-time photographer for the *News Post* in Laguna Beach.

"Reuben, you called it!"

"I guess so. I took a lot of pictures." To Blackburn, Greenspan seemed pleased his forecast was accurate, but not especially joyful.

"I guess we'll be printing your San Francisco forecast."

And so on February 9, 1971, the *Register* published a full-page article entitled: "Laguna Beach Physicist Predicts Killer Quake In Frisco." Wrote John Blackburn, "If the calculations of a Laguna Beach scientist are accurate, at approximately 9 a.m. (PDT) on Jan. 4, 1973, San Francisco will be rocked by an earthquake almost as severe as the devastating 1906 tremors which leveled the city. Skyscrapers will tumble. The Golden Gate Bridge will collapse. And thousands of persons will be left homeless."

Added Blackburn, "This is no scenario from a low-budget science fiction film, but the firm conviction of a physicist-mathematician who has an amazing record for accurately predicting earthquakes. The scientist's name is Dr. Reuben Greenspan, professor at New York (City) University. Dr. Greenspan—he received his doctorate in the physical sciences from Illinois Institute of Technology—claims no clairvoyance. His predictions are made only after laborious computations ..."

Thus the frenzy began—slowly. Impatient for the recognition he felt was due; Greenspan drank excessively, wrote bad checks, and was arrested for DUI. His second marriage had already deteriorated. He abandoned Laguna Beach and moved into a trailer near Death Valley.

For a while, the prediction simmered in the astrological community. On August 8, 1971, Carl Payne Tobey, an astrologer who'd met Greenspan in the '30s, wrote in his column, "Prior to March 27, 1964, Reuben Greenspan using the planets, wrote the N.Y. Times, predicting the Alaskan earthquake (1964) and was within two minutes of being right. His formula was kept secret. If his prediction of a future west coast earthquake comes true, we better take another look."

Sydney Omarr, a prominent astrologer, reported in his syndicated horoscope column on October 14, 1971, that Greenspan had forecast doom for the City by the Bay.

Then the prediction burst anew in the national press. This time in Tucson when, on February 25, 1972, the *Arizona Daily Star* printed an article by John Blackburn. The headline screamed: "Major California Quake Predicted Next Year." Blackburn explained Greenspan's mathematical model, "... strains along fault lines thus paving the way for quakes ... The outside force, Dr. Greenspan thinks, is the gravitational pull of planetary bodies."

The frequency of articles increased. *WGN*, a Chicago radio station, interviewed Greenspan by telephone about his prediction. More time passed.

• • •

March 11, 1972

Dave's phone rang. Dave was a thirty-three-year-old mathematician and computer scientist.

"Dave, it's Cousin Jack. They found Uncle Reuben." Jack was a nuclear physicist, six months older than Dave. Jack's mother was Dave's mother's sister. Uncle Reuben was the sisters' brother.

"Huh?" asked Dave. "I thought he was dead. All I knew about him was that picture on Grandma's dresser—and that he knocked up Cousin Sylvia."

Jack said, "He ran away from home at fourteen, too. Anyway, my mom called. She heard him being interviewed about last year's Sylmar earthquake on talk radio. They said he predicted the time and location of the quake! And get this; *Time* magazine called him an earthquake prophet in 1935."

"Where's he living?"

"Laguna Beach."

"Let's find Uncle Reuben," declared Dave.

The cousins took Dave's red 1966 Porsche 912 and drove from Palo Alto to Laguna Beach. Uncle Reuben wasn't listed in the phone book, but they discovered an old directory at a gas station. It yielded an address. Laguna Beach was pretty snazzy, but the apartment building was a dump, in south Laguna Beach and inland.

When Jack rang the super's bell, an old crone answered the door.

"Yes?" she croaked.

"We're looking for Reuben Greenspan," said Jack.

"Oh, that old fart? His marriage fell apart and he moved out some time ago, to somewhere near Death Valley—some town called Crona or something."

Dave and Jack examined a map. There was a town called Trona forty miles below the southwest portal to Death Valley. The cousins headed east to the Mojave Desert.

That evening, camped in the desert, they made a fire, smoked some weed, and had a few beers.

After they'd crawled into their sleeping bags, headlights and a cloud of dust heralded the approach of a San Bernardino County desert search and rescue team.

"Hey, you guys need help?" asked the driver. "We saw your fire."

Jack said, "Thanks, but we're fine. We're looking for our uncle; his name's Greenspan. He's sixty-five. We think he lives in Trona."

Dave offered joints and beer.

"We don't know him," said the driver. "But there's some old guy caretaking an abandoned gold and antimony mine; he's got a trailer up near Ballarat and Death Valley. The mine's about ten miles below the south portal to the Valley. It might be him. Check with the Post Office. That's Inyo County up there. You should check with their search and rescue squad, too. Thanks for the dope and beer."

In the morning, the clerk in the Trona Post Office said he had a mailbox for Greenspan, but no permanent address. He referred the cousins to the County Recorder's office which, in turn, referred them to Sheriff Johnny Manson.

"Manson, huh?" said Dave rhetorically. "Didn't Charley Manson hang out around here?"

"Yeah, in Panamint Valley," said Jack. "I hope he ain't a relative."

The cousins went to the sheriff's office. Twenty minutes later, Sheriff Manson said, "I'm not sure but it could be the old guy hanging out at a mine up by the Valley." He drew a crude map.

Jack and Dave drove north toward the portal. At a padlocked gate to a mine, they blew the horn. A gray old man came out of the trailer, accompanied by two menacing dogs. He had a beat-up .22 rifle slung over his shoulder. His fly was open, he was thin and shirtless, his boots were ripped, and he bore a striking resemblance to the cousins' grandfather.

"What do you want?" he asked.

"Is your name Reuben Greenspan?"

"Maybe. Why?"

"My name's Jack. My mother's name is Florence Greenspan."

"My name's Dave. My mother's name was Libby Greenspan. We think you're our uncle!"

"I'll be goddamned," said the old man. "My nephews, huh? How are the girls?"

• • •

Greenspan invited the cousins into his trailer for beer. It was hot and musty inside. The sun streamed though a window and spider webs, hung in corners.

Motes of dust hovered in the sunlight. The trailer was littered with papers covered with equations. Handbooks of navigation tables lined the wall. A hand-cranked calculator, an old and dirty globe of the world, pencil stubs, stained dishes, and a tomahawk sat on a wooden table. The sink was cluttered with empty bottles.

"Why'd you look me up?" asked Greenspan.

Jack reported on the conversation with his mother. "She told me *Time* magazine called you an earthquake prophet in 1935."

Greenspan smiled. "So did the *New York Times* and other newspapers."

"As kids," said Dave, "there was just your picture on Grandma's dresser. I think you were wearing a uniform."

"My Merchant Marine outfit. I mailed the photo to her after I joined the Humble Oil Fleet in Baton Rouge. I shipped out on the *SS Maravi*."

"We thought you ran away," said Jack, "because you knocked up Cousin Sylvia."

"Nah," said Greenspan. "I ran away in 1918. That happened in 1929. That was the only time I ever saw the family again."

Nodding, Dave said, "We followed your trail from Laguna to Trona to here. Sheriff Manson drew us a map. Why'd you leave Laguna?"

Greenspan wondered how much he should tell his nephews. He doubted they wanted to hear about his second wife, Beth, and her experiences in Orange County with the John Birch Society—which Greenspan believed had burned down Beth's art studio as an expression of disgust at her hippy background and radical paintings.

"Laguna was intolerable," he complained. "I couldn't work. I felt a profound need to escape into the desert and try to find myself. I've studied under Dr. Omori at the University of Kobe in Japan. He was adept in 'The eightfold path of the compassionate Buddha,' a form of Zen, and I thought living in Death Valley would help me reconstruct my earthquake equations."

"What's this about earthquakes?" asked Jack. With a master's degree in physics, Jack was excited at the prospects of a solution to a classic geophysics problem.

"Later," said Reuben.

Greenspan served up the beer and regaled the nephews with his stories. He'd graduated as an engineer from Armour Institute of Technology, joined the Merchant Marine, and some years later moved to New York City where he taught at the Seaman's Institute and married Miriam.

"What happened to Aunt Miriam?" asked Dave. "We never heard of her."

"It was one of those whirlwind marriages," said Greenspan. "Max Bodenheim—ever hear of him?"

The cousins shook their heads.

"Max introduced me to Miriam. He was the King of the Bohemians in the Village. He was also president of the Ravens Writing Circle of Greenwich Village. I was a member of the Ravens. They had some great writers, and I wrote hundreds of poems. Unfortunately, Miriam ran off with another poet. I guess I wasn't good enough for her. Want to hear one?"

Reuben jumped up and fetched an old notebook. He riffled through some pages and produced *Conformity* (shown here in original form):

"An aged man came up to me
And said I am conformity
I've lived some thousand years or more
I've lived by rote and set great store
on rules and laws which are the norm
And cackled brokenly and "conform"
Conformed to what, I asked this sage
Who prated on in senile rage
Obey, he said, obey the rules
That's what they teach in all our schools
Reject the things you'd like to do,
life will be placid and calm for you
And if you feel the urge to play,
see what the rule book has to say
Conform, conform, it is the norm
The meek obey, risk not the storm
Of fury down upon your head
Which non-conformists have to dread
Is this mad concept really so?
I must find out, I've got to know
And so I made a little plan
To get the truth from this old man
I plied the sage with potent drink
In 'vino veritas' I think
His face contorted with a leer
He said, my friend some truth you'll hear
You're bound to know it in the end
To conform is nonsense, just pretend."

"That's neat," said Jack, "but can we get back to the earthquakes?"

"Later," repeated Greenspan. "After Miriam ran off, I went back to sea. During the war, I got sunk off Murmansk and was repatriated by the Russkies in '43. Then, because I had this engineering background, I spent some time at Los Alamos."

"Really?" Jack's interest was piqued. He'd worked on H-Bomb tests at Christmas Island and studied the effects of nuclear blasts on the atmosphere. "Who'd you work with there?"

"I was just there a short time. Then I went back to New York. My friend Bodenheim introduced me to Ben Hecht."

"I think I heard of him," said Dave.

"Hecht was a playwright and a Zionist. He'd already written several novels and half a dozen books on poetry. He'd just written *Replenishing Aimee,* a novel which was really a platform for his poems, about a young Trotskyite in love with the president of a lady garments workers' union."

"Hey," said Dave, "my mother was an organizer for the ILGWU."

"She was a real radical all right. She always quoted one of those Commies: 'The means of production are in the hands of the workers.' Anyway, Hecht convinced me to help the Jews in Palestine. I spent some time running guns for the Irgun into Palestine from Marseilles, came back, did some engineering work in New York, and then became a professional photographer. I won an award for a picture I took in Resurrection City in 1968."

Greenspan picked up his tomahawk. "This was a gift," he said, "from the Shoshones. During the Poor People's March, I smuggled a Shoshone out of Resurrection City after he shot an FBI informer. The tribe gave me this."

"Uncle Reuben," said Jack, "You have a fascinating background. But, regarding the earthquake stuff, Dave and I are scientists. We went to Illinois Institute of Technology. Armour, where you went, was the precursor to IIT. I think we could understand the basic elements of your model. Can we see the equations?"

"Well, boys, I had this mathematical model which allowed me to forecast the time and latitude and longitude of a shake. It involved laborious computations." Greenspan pointed at the old, hand-cranked calculator on the table. "It was *Betsy* that made it possible."

Dave laughed. He'd begun working with computers in 1959. He programmed some of the most powerful machines in the country. He thought *Betsy* was a toy. "We have computers now—it ought to be a lot less laborious now. Can we see your work?"

"I just need to finish a few terms. A couple of coefficients. Shouldn't be more than a few weeks, and then I'll publish my results."

Dave looked at the scattered papers and tables of the heavenly bodies. "What happened to your original equations?"

Greenspan thought about the night he'd burned his equations. It was after Waldemar Kaempffert, the science editor of the *New York Times*, had likened Greenspan's work to astrology. But Greenspan didn't want to produce the August 1, 1935, article, in which Kaempffert said that any clever manipulator could correlate earthquakes with the rise and fall of U.S. Steel on the New York Stock Exchange.

Greenspan decided to blame another nemesis. "That son-of-a-bitch, Professor Richter. You know, the Richter scale—called me a fraud and a crackpot after the *Time* magazine article." Greenspan was still enraged. "In a drunken fit, I burned my papers. But, I'm close; just a few more weeks and I'll have reconstructed them. I moved to the desert so I could concentrate."

The cousins exchanged looks. They'd gone to the same school as their uncle. Maybe, they thought, the old man really had developed a mathematical model to predict earthquakes. Who knew? Perhaps the wild stories were true. Uncle Reuben rattled off physics equations with ease. His trailer was filled with navigation tables and thousands of pages of computations. Newspapers *had* printed gallons of ink that raved about their uncle. And he'd predicted Sylmar. "If he can do it," Jack mumbled to Dave, "he'll win the Nobel Prize in physics!"

The cousins left the next morning with promises to stay in touch. Dave offered to assist with the computations. Uncle Reuben promised to alert them when he completed his equations. Cranking *Betsy*, he waved good-bye.

• • •

Greenspan went to Tucson, Arizona to visit an old friend, Peggy Hitchcock. Peggy was an heiress and a good friend of Beth, Greenspan's second wife. The couple had married in Peggy's Park Avenue penthouse in the '60s. Peggy's entourage had included Timothy Leary, an advocate of LSD.

Greenspan hung out at Peggy's compound. One day he visited his old acquaintance, Carl Payne Tobey, the astrologist, in Tobey's Tucson home. Tobey had been present at Greenspan's New York radio interview in July 1935; Greenspan had always blamed Tobey for the *Times'* association of him with astrology.

After the recent meeting with Tobey, Greenspan wrote to Beth that Tobey had charted his horoscope. He noted Tobey "discovered my secret … He said my horoscope showed that I was psychic beyond belief and so much psychic that it frightened him … I had pre-cognitive powers and was forced to discover the mathematics of earthquake prediction in order to justify the validity of my scientific beliefs …"

On June 16, 1972, attention in the press heated up. The *Arizona Star* reported on Greenspan's meeting with Tobey: "BIG LOSS OF LIFE FEARED IF QUAKE HITS CALIFORNIA." The *Star* wrote, "Greenspan, now 66, became the boy wonder of the scientific world in 1935 by accurately predicting

17 earthquakes." The article further said that Greenspan worked eighteen hours a day on his predictions, that he claimed that he had automated some calculations, and that it took thirty hours of IBM 1610 [sic—1620] time to "digest his data." Greenspan added he was putting the finishing touches on a scientific paper, "The Breathing Earth as the Causative Mechanism of Earthquakes." He said the missive would be sent to the American Geophysical Union "no later than April." Dr. Charles Richter was called by the reporter who wrote the *Star* article. Richter said, "There is no way you can predict them [earthquakes]. People who make such predictions now are charlatans, fakes, or liars."

Greenspan was not especially happy with Tobey's analysis. He wrote, in another letter to Beth in October, "About Carl Payne Tobey—I try to evaluate his behavior without sitting in judgment upon him. It seems that his intellectual talents are less than mediocre albeit his intuitive processes are better … I know that he wanted me to admit a dependence on astrology in order to shore up and enhance his own posture. However he was totally unaware that the notion of unexplained miracles was repugnant to me …"

• • •

As the news about Uncle Reuben simmered, Dave changed jobs. He took a position as a senior research engineer at the Menlo Defense Research Institute. Uncle Reuben had not made contact with Dave or Cousin Jack. Dave assumed the equations were still incomplete. Dave was working on a transportation simulation problem when William Krauthammer, Sc.D., a distinguished geophysicist, walked into Dave's office. Krauthammer had completed his graduate work at the University of California at Berkeley.

"Do you know a Reuben Greenspan?" he asked.

"Sure, he's my uncle."

"Well," said Krauthammer, "I've been doing a lot of research in earthquake prediction. I heard about his radio interview and wrote to him. I'm interested in his work. He referred me to you. I'm going to visit him next week. I want to learn more and I might bring him back with me."

"Great," said Dave. "If you're interested, his work must be credible. My cousin and I were in Death Valley earlier this year and talked to him, but he wouldn't show us his equations."

"I don't know if he finished his model, but from what I heard, I like where he's going."

"Maybe I can help with the programming. And, he can stay at my house. He's family."

There were more stirrings in the press. On November 1, 1972, just three months before the forecast "big one," the Eureka Springs *Arizona Down Home* newspaper published a large article entitled: "Earthquake." So wrote the newspaper: "Dr. Greenspan, after some forty years, has finally been able to develop a workable mathematical formula (with the aid of a computer) to run a scanning program along the world's fault lines … For the past 14 months or so, he has been working on these equations in Death Valley. The proof of his work is to be presented in early December at the Geophysics convention at Berkeley …"

Wrote the reporter, "As many new ideas are scoffed at, so is the case with Greenspan's theories. Recently Dr. Richter was interviewed about earthquakes and Dr. Greenspan's name was mentioned. Dr. Richter was reported to have said sarcastically, 'You mean that Greenspan is still living?'"

• • •

Krauthammer met Greenspan. He was impressed. Greenspan showed him some formulas and computer listings. The equations weren't complete but, according to Greenspan, they simply needed some fine tuning. "Just a few weeks," he promised. And, noted Krauthammer with interest, Greenspan had worked on the bomb. Berkeley had worked on the bomb, too. Krauthammer wrote a summary of his meeting with Greenspan for Dave: "It was clear right away that Reuben was an unusual fellow, intelligent, inspired, independent, strong in his opinions and beliefs … he was responsive to my request: to learn from him how he made his predictions and to try to verify his system against a catalog of past earthquakes, using a computer. Only in this way, I explained, would his 'theory' be acceptable to the scientific community, something he obviously wanted … he explained his system to me in general terms (earth tides, etc.), well enough to enable me to get started. He described his background as a marine navigator for ocean going ships, so he knew enough spherical trigonometry to calculate the tidal forces."

Krauthammer brought Greenspan back from the desert and stashed him in Dave's house in Palo Alto. Dave's wife wasn't happy; she thought Uncle Reuben was a bum. The couple offered him a small bedroom furnished with a desk and trundle bed. He preferred to sleep on the living room couch. He appropriated Dave's globe, spun *Betsy*, and placed marks on the globe over the continental shelves. Reams of paper covered with trigonometric calculations littered the floor.

On November 23, 1972, just six weeks before the predicted seismic event, Herb Caen, San Francisco's legendary columnist, joined the fray as an antagonist. Wrote Caen, "… As for the other problem we live with all our lives—earthquakes—don't take seriously, as so many seem to be doing, the prediction of that Arizona Geophysicist, Dr. Reuben Greenspan, that we will undergo 'a major earthquake at 9 a.m. on January 4, 1973 …'" Caen went on to repeat Richter's derogatory description: "charlatans, fakes, and liars."

Despite Caen's article, some grass roots interests in Greenspan were triggered. Wrote a science teacher to Paul Harvey, "The people in S.F. have started wondering if possibly the report by Dr. Greenspan is indeed true, after reading an article by Herb Caen … asking why the city fathers are being so apathetic about preparing the city and it's schools for the 'inevitable earthquake.'" He closed with, "Do you suppose that the Dr. feels nobody believes him, thats [sic] why he remains silent and hidden?"

At the same time, the November 1972 issue of *Psychic* magazine published a special report: "The San Francisco Quake." According to the author, Sheldon Ruderman, "Dire warnings of coming earthquakes are not, of course, uncommon. San Francisco and other areas along the San Andreas Fault are popular targets for prognostications of psychics, fame-seekers, and quacks. Dr. Greenspan's work, using a Newtonian physics orientation, is based on a geophysical model published in 1922. And backing his latest prediction is an amazing record for accuracy that can be verified in pages of the *New York Times*, *Time* magazine, and other publications of nearly 40 years ago." Added the author, "The 67-year-old scientist was schooled at the Armour Institute of Technology in Chicago, and later in Gottingen, Germany, where much of the quantum theory in physics was born." Wrote Ruderman to Greenspan on November 26, 1972: "My primary concern is alerting the citizens of San Francisco. My personal friends are going to protect themselves, but the more strategic persons who have access to the media want to talk to you."

Greenspan still was in hiding at Dave's house. Krauthammer and Greenspan collaborated. Dave heard *Betsy* hum day and night. Occasionally Krauthammer would meet with Greenspan into the long hours of the night.

Interest in the predicted earthquake grew. Spots on KGO, KCBS and KANG (Napa) radio asked, "Where is Reuben? We want to interview him?" *The Trona Argonaut*, effectively Greenspan's home-town paper, published: "Man's Quake Prediction Has Bay Area Jittery." The newspaper said, "No one knew where Reuben was. Neighbors report that he left about two weeks ago with a professor from Stanford University to visit the San Francisco or Sacramento areas. There are many who want to interview him when they can find him."

The Bay Area was more than jittery. On December 11, 1972, the venerable *San Francisco Chronicle* published a full page article: "San Francisco, 9 a.m., January 4, 1973: The Man Who Predicts Quakes." Under a photo of Greenspan with the tagline "Reuben Greenspan has predicted the city's doom," the *Chronicle* wrote, "There are few things which make the people of San Francisco more nervous than precise predictions on when the next big earthquake will hit … as usual the Golden Gate Bridge is expected to fall down … What makes Greenspan's forecast unusual is that in past years he has been cloaked in legend in some circles for forecasting earthquakes with an accuracy unusually described as uncanny." The *Chronicle* quoted John Blackburn, who'd launched the latest frenzy with his February 9, 1971, article: "When it happened, I looked at the clock and said, 'My God, Greenspan's done it.' He was accurate to within three minutes. I'll be honest with you, it scared the bejesus out of me and I was a nervous wreck for the rest of the day."

That night Uncle Reuben told Dave that he'd called the local newspapers with an adjusted forecast. The quake now would be magnitude 7.4 and a few miles south of San Francisco. "It's still set for 9:20 AM," he said.

"But Reuben," said Dave, "does Krauthammer agree? I know he wants the prediction to be based on validated equations. Have you guys finished the work, found the missing coefficients?"

"Miriam always said that I had to warn people—that I was responsible for their safety. I called the *San Francisco Chronicle* and the *Oakland Tribune*."

"This is going to crank up the heat," said Dave. "I have visions of TV vans parking in front of the house. Sooner or later, you got to produce the equations. I'll talk to Krauthammer."

The newspapers called the U.S. Geological Survey in Menlo Park, California. The head of the U.S. Office of Earthquake Research and Crustal Studies in Menlo Park agreed that seismologists would "all feel very foolish if this thing proves out."

On December 12, the *Chronicle* published a follow-up article entitled: "Quake Predictor Shook Up the Experts." It cited Ruderman's article in *Psychic* magazine; Leo Cotton's work in 1922; quoted officials at Illinois Institute of Technology who claimed they never heard of Greenspan; and discredited assertions published in 1951 that he'd worked at the Institute for Advanced Studies at Princeton. The newspaper further researched Greenspan's background and reported that he'd had brushes with the law, including a 1950s larceny charges in New York City, a DUI, and an arrest for impersonating a navy officer in 1963 [sic—1943]. But the article closed with a quote from John Blackburn: "To this day … I still don't know what the hell to think of the guy. He might be a charlatan, but he DID hit the Sylmar quake."

People were alarmed. State Farm sold boatloads of earthquake insurance, people planned to leave town, and sales of emergency supplies, first aid kits, blankets, and flashlights increased.

City officials scoffed. Mayor Joseph L. Alioto, in a *UPI* wire report, taunted, "I will be at work at my desk in City Hall at that hour. And I invited Mr. Greenspan to join me for coffee." Added the *Stars and Stripes Southeast Asia*, which had picked up the *UPI* article: "Vicki Settles wishes she had the money to rent a helicopter for a few hours the morning of Jan. 4. She thinks she might witness the destruction of San Francisco in a great earthquake. Word is filtering through this quake-conscious city that the experts say is due—sometime … Residents of some communes where many of the 'hip' people now live, are getting their rusty vans ready for a trek to safer ground …"

The tension was palpable as the entire Bay Area held its collective breath wondering if Greenspan would accept the mayor's challenge. Meanwhile, he was still holed up at Dave's, working on his paper, cranking *Betsy*, sleeping occasionally in a real bed, and eating well. Dave's wife was a great cook. The meetings with Krauthammer intensified.

The *Phoenix Gazette* searched for Greenspan in their article: "Hunt is Staged for Scientist." The newspaper asked, "Is Dr. Reuben Greenspan in the Phoenix area? If he is, would he please contact the Phoenix Gazette for a message?" The message was from a science teacher in the Bay Area who'd searched unsuccessfully for Greenspan. Said the teacher, "[Dr. Greenspan] is a scientist and not a clairvoyant. His predictions are made only after laborious computations … could be the source of saving a lot of lives."

Dave and Krauthammer decided to force Greenspan's hand. It was time to produce the equations. Krauthammer said, "Reuben, you have to hold a press conference. People are scared."

"Okay, schedule one for around the thirtieth."

"We will, but when can we see the equations?" asked Krauthammer.

"Not to worry. I'll give you the whole paper that morning."

Dave and Krauthammer booked a conference room at Ricky's Hyatt House on El Camino Real in Palo Alto. The date was set for Friday, December 29, 1972.

• • •

December 26, 1972

The frenzy spread to New York City. The newspaper that had started it all in 1935, the *New York Times,* added its voice in the article: "Worried San Franciscans Take New Look at Quake Forecaster." Wrote the reporter, "Last week it was all different. Then most of those who lived here in this city that was once destroyed by an earthquake ignored the prediction. Those who did not ignore it chose to laugh at it. And the few who took it seriously kept their concern mostly to themselves. But now, the jokes have disappeared and some persons have begun to quietly take a second look at the prediction that an earthquake will destroy San Francisco at 9. a.m. on Jan. 14 [sic] … Last week as reporters searched for him, he was in hiding but promised to appear in a few days. It is said that when he does he will offer proof of his claim that a quake is about to hit the bay area."

• • •

December 29, 1972

About three dozen members of the media and some seismologists assembled in a conference room at Ricky's Hyatt House as Dave, Greenspan, and Krauthammer finished their breakfast in the hotel café.

"Okay, Reuben," said Dave, "it's time to produce the equations. Do you have your paper?"

"Bill, we need to talk about this conference," said Greenspan.

"Sure, but hurry up. They're waiting for us."

"Bill, I'm afraid I've made a mistake. There's not going to be an earthquake on the fourth."

"What?" exclaimed Krauthammer. "You're telling me that now? Where are the damn equations? So when will the earthquake be?"

Greenspan sighed. "I don't know. Can I tell you a secret? I've always predicted those earthquakes in my sleep. I thought I had an equation that worked, but I've never been able to reconstruct it."

"But that's preposterous. You've been telling us for months you just needed a few more days to get the coefficients."

"I dreamt every one of those shakes. But the magic only came back once, last year. I've been living off those stupid *New York Times* and *Time* magazine articles my whole life."

"The press is expecting you," said Dave. "You have to say something."

"I'll hedge—tell them that I need to double-check some calculations."

Greenspan began the press conference with a statement. "It gives me profound pleasure to announce that the prediction I made two years ago that an earthquake would take place … is not correct." Then, as the *San Francisco Chronicle* reported the next day, "[The] 66-year-old Greenspan was subjected to the most withering cross-examination in the memory of many reporters." The article on the front page above the fold was headlined: "S.F. Quake Called Off." It noted that Greenspan had defended his theory to the last. He refused to apologize for what he called "an honest mistake." Defending his credentials, he refused to confirm where he'd received his PhD. "I am under no more obligation to conform to the idiocy of the fourth estate than nature is obligated to conform to my theories," he said. Near the end of the conference, Greenspan meandered, "It will all come out in the wash … My work will stand on its own … In manual calculations there is always the probability of error."

Carl Payne Tobey, when asked about Greenspan's press conference, was quoted in the *Modesto Bee*. "[He] called Greenspan a 'pathological liar.'"

• • •

The frenzy was over, but the media wasn't finished with Greenspan. The *UPI* wrote: "S.F. quake prediction recanted." Both *Newsweek* and *Time* magazine jumped in as well in their editions published on January 8, 1973. Greenspan had said that "Mayor Alioto would have to eat a little crow when he invited him for coffee," reported *Newsweek*. "… But it was Greenspan who ate crow …" *Time* was gentler in its article headlined: "Gloomy Forecast." It wrote, "… Last week Greenspan delphically [sic] hedged on his prediction saying he wanted to verify the data and didn't mean to upset anyone, but the idea remained quite unsettling."

That evening, Dave called Cousin Jack and said, "Get this putz out of my house before the press finds out where's he's been staying. Take him back to Death Valley. Take him anywhere. Just get him out of here!"

Dave's wife said, "I told you he was crazy!"

• • •

Some years later, Dave and his wife met Uncle Reuben's former wife, Beth, in San Francisco. When Dave's wife asked Beth why she had married a man twenty years her senior, she replied, "He lied about his age, and I was doing a lot of acid at the time."

There was more to her story. Beth had written to an acquaintance on January 1, 1973, after Greenspan's public denouement, "During the time I was with Reuben I was living out the fantasy of being the woman behind the great man who single-handed [sic] had taken on the great corrupt establishment. The tale I was fed included having his bank account confiscated, Eighty [sic] thousand dollars from sale of his family property on Cape Cod confiscated, a law suit for illegal confiscations against the atomic energy commission, winning that suit before privite [sic] hearings with Chief justice [sic] Douglas, delays in payment with further suits and further penaltys [sic] awarded. Great efforts to bring him back into the "Scientific fold" to work on unspeakably awful military projects, great pressure from the military to turn over certain new mathematical systems he had developed and which he steadfastly resisted because it would be like putting guns in the hands of babys [sic]. I [sic] was a good story ... Reuben is a first class story teller, making up scenes and conversational tidbits with the art of a master."

• • •

Uncle Reuben may have been a pathological liar, but in 1935 he accurately forecast seventeen earthquakes. John Blackburn, in 1971, did swear Greenspan had nailed Sylmar.

Not too long ago, Dave had a troubling dream. The earth shook. Buildings tumbled from San Jose to San Luis Obispo as a powerful earthquake struck northern and central California. In his dream, Dave saw the headline of a future *San Francisco Chronicle*: "Massive 9.0 Shake Rocks California." Dave knew better than to write to the newspapers.

(N.B. Some names were changed. Greenspan's poem and Beth's letter were shown in their original form. Newspaper headlines, stories, letters, radio and media quotes, and the bonfire of lies built upon each other, were reported faithfully. Reuben Greenspan never completed his equations or his technical paper. Before he died in 1988, he wrote, "The kiss that was promised the world has been withdrawn.")

Jack, Reuben, and Dave in Death Valley, 1972

Part II

Historical Fiction and Political Madness

Four Stars

★★★★

Lieutenant General Samuel "Beer" Adams, U.S. Army, third in his class at West Point, and director of the super-secret National Security Agency (NSA), snoozed after a large lunch in his office on the ninth floor of the headquarters building. The sun shone through the windows and the TV monitors were mute. Except for a few command and control displays, all was serene.

Suddenly, the door burst open and a host of people barged into the office. Speaker of the House Nancy Girabaldi, the left-wing darling of San Francisco values, led the charge. She was followed by her political advisor, scribe, photographer, hairdresser, cosmetician, and two Secret Service men who'd been detailed to her by the White House.

The general, startled, dropped his feet off the desk. *What the hell?*

"General Adams?" said Speaker Girabaldi. "You'll excuse this unannounced interruption, but it's impossible to get your telephone number—you know, all that silly top secret stuff."

"Madame," responded the general, "this is a classified area! Where are your badges? You need a clearance to be in here." The general swept all the papers on his desk into a drawer.

"Oh, don't be ridiculous, General. We didn't sign in. I make the appointments to the Intelligence committees; I can give myself all the clearances I want. Your badges are so déclassé—as if they really matter. And, please, call me *Speaker*. I worked very hard for that title."

"As you please. But those clearances matter to me."

"All right, big deal!" She turned to her entourage. "You can all leave."

After the herd departed, the general looked at Girabaldi. "What's this about, Madame Speaker?" He reached for his phone intending to call the MPs.

Girabaldi shook her head and pointed her finger at the phone. "General, how would you like a fourth star? Put that down."

Adams cradled the handset. "You barged into NSA headquarters, dragged half of Washington with you, and broke half-a-dozen national security laws to offer me another star? Please, Madame Speaker, this is an Intelligence agency."

"That's what I want to discuss with you." She looked around the room. "These are nice digs, General. You spooks sure have a good thing going. What did that private toilet over there cost—$150,000?"

"I don't know, Madame Speaker."

"Uh-huh. Well, I have a proposition for you. I'd like you to chair my special bi-partisan Intelligence Reorganization Committee."

"I see. Just what are the goals of this lofty committee?"

"Just as it sounds. I want to reorganize the Intelligence community. Let's say that I believe there's enormous waste. The American people need that money for more pressing things."

"Madame Speaker, it sounds to me like you want to do away with Intelligence! And you're offering me a fourth star to sell it down the river?"

"General, your colleagues don't seem to have a problem. I've already secured the participation of Major General Smith of the Army Intelligence Command, Rear Admiral Jones of the Naval Intelligence Service, and Major General Hook of the Defense Intelligence Agency. They all said they'd be pleased to serve on your committee—I took the liberty of telling them you were on-board."

Adams gagged. *This must be how Admiral Kimmel felt when the Japs bombed Pearl Harbor. Those guys must think I'm nuts.*

"Madame Speaker, just what does 'reorganization' mean—precisely?"

"I'm glad you asked. I want to merge all the military Intelligence agencies, NSA and the CIA. I figure we can save about seventy, perhaps $80 billion a year doing that. As Senator Dirksen once said, 'a billion here and a' ... well, you know ... 'after a while it adds up to real money.' If we also retire a few naval carrier groups, we could get to $100 billion. Just think of all the good things we could do with a tenth of a trillion dollars. We could increase the minimum wage!"

The general felt his temperature rise. The speaker might want a tenth of something, but he could use a fifth of something else. He sensed his blood pressure rise. "What does the CIA think about your plan?"

"I haven't talked to them yet. I thought that with your fourth star you could take over the newly integrated agency."

"Madame Speaker, cuts in spending like that will devastate the Intelligence community, not to mention the Navy. You do know, don't you, that President Clinton cut spending drastically on Intelligence in the '90s, and the result was 9/11?"

"Oh, please, you military types—you always mention 9/11. General, the American people don't give a shit about 9/11. They want jobs! Better social security. Government health insurance. And education—they need more money for education."

The general tried to control his temper which moved toward a volcanic eruption. "Listen here, Madame Speaker, every time you politicians throw more money at education, student performance goes in the crapper. What you need to do is reduce spending, and performance will go up."

"General, I didn't come here to argue with you. We have an aggressive legislative agenda, and we're going to save this country. Why should Americans die for those miserable countries in far-away places?"

"Madame Speaker, have you ever read history? Do you know that the British and the French spoke those very same words in 1938? About Czechoslovakia? That one only cost about eighty million lives."

"General, we're making history. Do you want the job or not? I don't have all day. I have to be in Langley in two hours and I need to tell those idiots something."

General Adams pondered the serene face of the speaker for a few moments. "Would you like a cup of coffee, Madame Speaker? I need to think about this."

"Actually I'd prefer tea, if you don't mind. Mango Ceylon decaffeinated tea."

"Yes, of course." The general picked up his phone and ordered the tea and a cup of coffee. There was an awkward moment while they waited. Adams glared out the window.

A few moments later an aide delivered the beverages.

The general stirred some sugar into his coffee. "So Madame Speaker, if I agree, what happens next?"

"We bring in the photographer and take a picture of us shaking hands. Then I go to Langley, dump on them, have my hair done, and call a press conference. The American people will be thrilled with these savings. Just think of all those hot lunches, new educational programs, and free universal health care!"

"That would be nice, Madame Speaker. I'm certain that your party will garner many more votes in the next election. Perhaps you could also include funds for retraining the Intelligence workers that will lose their jobs."

"Of course. Worker retraining is a keystone of any Democratic agenda. I can't tell you how excited I am with this plan. And this tea is wonderful. Let's bring in the photographer."

Adams sighed, grit his teeth, pulled his 1907 Colt .45 service piece out of his desk drawer, and fired two rounds into Speaker Girabaldi's forehead. When the Secret Service detail stormed into his office, he surrendered his weapon.

In response to the bewildered looks, Adams said, "It felt like I was in a Stephen King story. I just saved America."

Le Pigeon

June 7, 1958

Ron Granville, recently appointed Middle East sales representative of the Rocky Mountain Milling and Manufacturing Company (RMM), and his wife Patti were airborne en route to Beirut, Lebanon. The couple had sailed to England and enjoyed London for a week. Then they'd boarded the flight—their first on a jet airplane—a 36-seat Comet flown by British Overseas Aircraft Corp (BOAC).

Ron knew Patti was impressed with her new husband. It was a big assignment for a recent mechanical engineering graduate from Colorado State University. He was such a young man—Ron was only twenty-four. In fact, it was a colossal opportunity. RMM manufactured the new numerically-controlled machine tools which were critical to the cost-effective production of advanced weapons. The Cold War was in full bloom, and American and Soviet treasure flooded the region. All that wealth poured into weapons.

Ron had laughed at those fools at headquarters in Golden, Colorado. They'd actually called Beirut a hardship post. Just more money, Ron mused—combat pay, with no combat. Sure, there was political tension, but the French called it *une longue histoire*, an old story.

The Granvilles shared a bottle of champagne as they joked about their plans. Ron had a two-year assignment, and the couple intended to bank thousands of dollars while they filled their apartment with Middle Eastern art and furnishings. Their basics—books, clothing, cameras and appliances, along with transformers to deal with the erratic and different Middle Eastern power systems, were in containers en route by sea. Ron expected them to arrive in several weeks.

As he smiled at his bride, Ron wondered how Patti would cope in Lebanon. She was an upper-middle-class girl from a ranching family in Cheyenne, Wyoming, pampered and spoiled by a doting father. A Smith graduate, she'd studied Art History and was interested in the early civilizations of the Middle East. It had been easy to talk her into going to Beirut.

But Patti was picky and often not very thoughtful. She changed her table in busy restaurants two or three times, took forever to select a meal from a menu as waiters hovered, walked a diagonal line on a crowded sidewalk indifferent to the chaos behind her, stood in an intersection and blocked traffic while she decided which way to proceed, and planted herself in front of elevator or subway doors. The latter had earned Patti nasty looks from the British who'd always queued up politely. She also was quick to anger against authority. Her fury was manifested by a biting tongue, clenched fists, a red face, and a light stutter.

Ron, a big man who'd played college football and hockey, was attracted by Patti's independence. But he worried how she'd do in Arab lands. He'd reminded her that the cultures were different in the Middle East—that women were expected to be docile, subservient, and less aggressive than in America, and that the last thing she should do was aggravate the local authorities. He remembered the conversation.

"Cool it," he'd counseled. "This ain't Kansas we're going to. It's not the Debutante Ball."

"They better accept the fact that we're Americans. I won't take any crap from those misogynists. I hear they like little boys, too."

"Jesus! Don't say that in public."

As the plane descended towards Beirut's airport, Ron reassured himself that things would be fine in Lebanon. After all, their American passport was the most treasured document in the world. Ron was confident the U.S. would not tolerate the abuse of her citizens' rights by other governments. The United States was the powerhouse in the Middle East—President Eisenhower had even forced the French and the British to pull out of the Sinai Desert when the Israelis fought the Egyptians in 1956.

Still, Ron knew there were some risks. You couldn't make $80,000 a year plus commissions—tax free, with expatriate benefits—without assuming some risk. And the Middle East always had problems.

The main business impediment was the Arab League Boycott. Arab institutions, dealers, agents and individuals were obliged to reject any business dealings with companies that manufactured, sold, or used products based in whole, or in part, on Israeli goods. Companies that sold goods in Israel violated the boycott. To complicate matters, U.S. law prohibited participation in boycotts. Still, Ron had decided the problem should be manageable—RMM sold no products in Israel and used only American-manufactured parts in its equipment. He smiled to himself; the Arabs would buy a lot of machine tools. And, if they bought weapons from the Russians, they'd need even more machines just to fix the junk the Soviets sold.

The BOAC flight from London landed early, and the Granvilles passed quickly through Lebanese immigration and customs. A cab drove them directly to the elegant Riviera Hotel in the swank Riad El Sah neighborhood near the Mediterranean Sea.

In the hotel room, Ron studied a brochure about the city. Beirut was a financial center and sported American and Arab universities. Sixty miles north of the Israeli border, the city occupied the premier coastline on the eastern shore of the Mediterranean Sea. It enjoyed balmy weather—mild dry days, pleasant breezes, and cool evenings. It was a great and sophisticated metropolitan city. Ron couldn't wait to find an apartment, get unpacked, and start work.

• • •

June 17, 1958

Ron and Patti unpacked one of their shipping containers in their new apartment on Roster Basha Street. They expected another container. The delivery man had said it was delayed in customs. The Granvilles both smiled when there was a knock at the door.

"That's probably the other container," said Ron.

"I'll get it." Patti answered the door and was pushed aside by three men—two soldiers in Lebanese army uniforms, and a plainclothes man, who barged into the room. The man in the suit, who was clearly in charge, glanced around the apartment.

"What's going on?" Ron was bewildered and angry.

"Mr. Granville, you're to come with us immediately." The man pointed at Ron and the two soldiers grabbed his arms.

Patti clenched her fists and reddened visibly. "Over my de-dead body! Who-who are you people? We're Americans. You can't arrest us."

"Madame, we do not wish to restrain you. Mr. Granville is under arrest. I recommend you contact your embassy."

"But ... where, where are you ta-taking him?"

"It's okay, Patti," said Ron, who also fumed but sensed it was not the time to offer resistance. "I'm sure it's a mistake."

The plainclothesman pulled a set of handcuffs from the back of his belt. He mumbled something in Arabic.

"Bull-bullshit!" stuttered Patti, as they slapped a pair of handcuffs on Ron. "Leave him a-alone, you assholes. You can't—"

The man in plainclothes pushed Patti into a chair. Tears sprang to her eyes. As they dragged Ron out of the room, she sprang up and held onto him. The man slapped her and brushed her aside.

"Call the embassy and the company in Golden," shouted Ron over his shoulder.

Patti, stung, tears streaking her makeup, watched from the window as they threw Ron into the back seat of a military sedan. The car merged into traffic and headed east into the heart of the city.

Ron asked, "Where we going? Police Headquarters?"

The plainclothes officer, seated next to the driver, ignored Ron and lit a cigarette. The two soldiers, who flanked Ron in the back seat, didn't respond. Ron became scared. These men weren't dressed in police uniforms. The guy in the suit looked angry, like he still bristled at Patti's epitaph. Ron tried to settle back in the seat but his arms hurt, jammed behind his back by the handcuffs.

Thirty minutes later, the car pulled up in front of Lebanese Army Headquarters.

The plainclothes officer turned and looked over his shoulder, "Mr. Granville, you will be our guest here for some time. My name is Azeem Assad. My rank is major."

"Okay, Major. I'm sure this is a mistake. What's the charge?"

"In due time, Mr. Granville," sneered the major.

"Hey, you can't do that. You can't arrest me without charges. I want to contact my embassy."

Assad nodded at the soldiers. They pulled a protesting Ron out of the car and into the building. They dragged him down a flight of stairs into the basement, took his belt and shoelaces, unlocked the handcuffs, and threw a threadbare blanket at him. He was pushed into a dank cell.

Ron looked around. A small barred and dirt-stained window high on one wall was the only source of light; two folding cots stood on the floor. A stench from a bucket in the corner identified the toilet. The walls were blackened limestone with Arabic, French, and Hebrew writings scratched across the surface. An empty cot was filthy and covered with dried blood stains. The other cot, dirty as well, was occupied.

The man in the cot stirred. "*Bienvenue.*"

Ron acknowledged the greeting with a hopeless shrug. "My name's Ron Granville."

"*Américain? Pourquoi êtes-vous ici?*"

"Why am I here? I have no idea. Who are you?"

"*Je m'appelle Claude; Claude Gourdon*. I am French."

"Can we speak English?"

"*Certainement.*"

"What's going on?" blurted Ron. "I haven't been given any charges. Some major named Assad arrested me."

"Assad? That man is a *bête noir*, a monster. Someday, if I live, I will kill him for this."

Gourdon showed Rod his left hand; the fingernails had been ripped out and the wounds oozed blood and pus. The fingers were purple and yellow.

"They did that to you?" Ron was terrified. "When?"

"Last night, they came for me in the dark."

"Why are they torturing you? What did you do?"

"I was sent here to sell aircraft to the Arabs. I work for an equipment trading company owned by the French *Armée de l'Air*. We're selling World War II P-47D fighter-bombers."

"What's wrong with that? Aren't P-47s American-made aircraft?"

"We inherited them at the end of the war," said Gourdon. "Your government prohibited their use in Vietnam and, after Dien Bien Phu fell, the aircraft became obsolete. Sales were slow, perhaps that's why my managing director double-crossed me and tried to sell them to the Israelis."

"Is that your problem—the Arab League Boycott?" Ron shivered. If they could do this to an innocent man, what could he expect? "Were you involved in any way?"

"I am—what do you say—*le pigeon*?"

"We say 'patsy,'" said Ron. "Why hasn't your government got you out?"

"It was my government," spat Gourdon, "and their trading company that put me in here with their double-dealings. The Fourth Republic may still light up the *Tour Eiffel* to prove that Paris is the City of Light, but the time has passed when France would send a warship to rescue a Frenchman. If I were Russian, the Soviets would have shelled Beirut already."

"They left you here to rot?" said Ron. "I hope my government acts quickly. I'm sure my wife is calling the U.S. Embassy. I think I'll go nuts if I stay in here a day."

Gourdon smiled ruefully. "You really don't know why they arrested you?"

"Not an idea. I've only been in Lebanon a week or so and haven't sold anything. What do you think?"

"*Je ne sais pas.* Perhaps it's a mistake. Be happy they haven't beaten you yet."

Ron flinched at the thought. "Is there any water? Food?"

"They feed me once a day as long as I don't trouble the guards. I recommend you try to relax now. Perhaps you can give me some news from the outside. I haven't had a guest in weeks."

"What happened to the last *guest*?"

"He's gone. They suspected he was a spy for the Israelis."

"My God!" Ron sat down and bent his head. Patti would go crazy with fear. But maybe she'd made contact with the embassy.

• • •

For almost four weeks, Ron shared the cell with Claude Gourdon. Major Assad's men appeared from time to time to drag Gourdon out for "interrogation."

Once he returned with two front teeth missing; often there were new blood stains on his filthy T-shirt.

The guards came for Ron three times and locked him for hours in a small room with another guard who stared at Ron with a menacing smile.

The fourth time it was different. Major Assad smoked a cigarette and stood in a corner. The guards dumped Ron in a chair and hovered behind him.

"So, Mr. Granville, you think you can violate our laws with impunity?" demanded Assad.

"I don't know what you're talking about. I want to talk to my embassy." Ron stared defiantly at Assad, but Ron knew he was too tired, dirty, and demoralized to be convincing.

Assad made a dismissive gesture, and a guard ripped Ron's shirt. The other guard strapped Ron facedown on the table and beat him ten times with a cane. The strokes left angry, bloody welts across Ron's back. He'd cried out with the first blow, but the pain emboldened him, and he steeled himself through the rest of the punishment. When the guard released Ron's bonds, he almost collapsed—but he managed to stumble, in handcuffs, back to his cell without assistance.

Gourdon used some of the dinner drinking water to rinse Ron's wounds. The bloodied water dripped and added to the stains on Ron's cot.

"If we ever get out of here, Claude, I'll buy you a drink."

"Ah, that would be nice. I propose we rendezvous someday in Paris."

"When?"

"Who knows how long we'll be in here?" said Gourdon with a sad smile.

Ron grinned. Survival was questionable and they made plans? "Okay, Claude. That's a date."

"*Moi aussi, mon ami.* I will write you."

The men laughed grimly and made plans neither expected to meet. They memorized each other's home address and agreed to communicate, if there were changes, through American Express mail drops in Paris and Denver.

Ron fell into a painful sleep.

• • •

July 15, 1958

Ron was led into a meeting room in handcuffs. An American embassy official, Sam DiPiccioto, introduced himself. Patti was seated while Major Assad stood, smoking a cigarette. A Lebanese army captain also was in the room.

Ron saw Patti try to jump up, but DiPiccioto grabbed her arm and shook his head. "Mrs. Granville," he said, "we're here to hear the charges. Perhaps you can have a private moment with your husband later."

The guards removed the handcuffs and Ron sat at the table, holding Patti's hand. He was filthy and gaunt; there were dried blood stains on his tattered shirt.

"According to our understanding, Major Assad," said DiPiccioto, "you will now explain the charges against Mr. Granville." He turned to the Lebanese officer. "Captain, before we start, I want you to know that the American government deplores the arrest of Mr. Granville and his detention without notice. We've filed a diplomatic *note verbale,* which contains our strongest protest against the Lebanese government."

The captain was silent. He waved his arm at Major Assad.

"This is not a Lebanese matter," interjected Assad. "The charge is violating the Arab League Boycott. This is a military offense, and we are not required to give notice. The United Arab Republic (UAR) and the Syrian Army have the principal responsibility for enforcing the boycott in the region. The American government should be grateful we've permitted this meeting."

"The boycott?" Ron snorted. "How the hell did I violate that? I'd just arrived when you and your thugs arrested me. I didn't sell a thing in Lebanon."

"Patience, Mr. Granville," counseled DiPiccioto. "Major, please explain yourself."

The major lit another cigarette. "We found an electric table fan in Mr. Granville's personal possessions which were shipped to Lebanon. According to the manifest, this fan was manufactured by the Johnson Electric Company of St. Louis, Missouri. That company has a long standing history of violation of the boycott, and conducting business in Israel. Companies that operate in Israel violate the secondary terms of the boycott. It is illegal to import their products into Arab nations."

"A fan? I've been in this rat's nest for four weeks over a fucking fan? So what's the penalty? How much can it cost?" Ron began to shake with anger.

Patti mumbled, "Wh-what do you expect from people that like little boys?"

"Please, Patti—" blurted Ron.

Major Assad's lips curled. He stared intently at Patti. "Mrs. Granville, this is the second time you have insulted me. I ascribe your words to your country's vicious propaganda against the United Arab Republic."

Patti snorted. "You struck me, Major. That's not very civilized. What am I to expect when you arrested Ron over nothing?"

"Nothing? We take this offense very seriously. The Central Boycott Office in Damascus has been especially concerned about the activities of the Johnson Electric Company of St. Louis, Missouri."

"So, big deal," barked Patti. "What's the possible maximum penalty? We have to get Ron out of here."

The major smiled coldly. "As Mr. DiPiccioto knows only too well, Madame, the maximum penalty is ... quite extreme."

"All right, already, get on with it," snapped Patti.

"Yes, well, the maximum penalty is death! There is no leniency in our circles for those that violate the boycott. We cannot permit any activity that benefits the renegade state of Israel. If we cannot drive the Jews out of our holy lands, we will starve them out. Your husband has violated our law."

Patti paled, and Ron grabbed the edge of the table. "A fan? You're going to execute me over a Johnson Electric Company fan?"

DiPiccioto looked at his watch. "Now, now, Major, I know how you like to be dramatic at times. You're quite well known in diplomatic circles for your unusual methods of torture as well—but let's not get carried away. Circumstances change as we speak. It's 9:00 AM. I think it would be useful if you turned on your radio or consulted with your superiors."

The major turned his gaze from Ron to DiPiccioto. "In matters of the boycott there are no—"

Assad was interrupted as the door opened and an aide rushed to him. The man whispered excitedly in Assad's ear and raised a hand in a helpless gesture. The major blanched as he listened and stubbed out his cigarette angrily. He dismissed the aide with a wave of the arm.

After a moment, Assad regained his composure and turned to DiPiccioto. "Yes, perhaps death, in this case, would be a bit harsh. Despite the seriousness of the crime, we've decided to be lenient with Mr. Granville."

"What does that mean, Major?" Ron's hopes were raised but he still felt vulnerable.

To Ron's surprise, the major grinned. "You're free to leave, Mr. Granville. We will, of course, confiscate and destroy the fan."

Ron was incredulous. "That's it? That's all you have to say?"

DiPiccioto gathered his papers and gestured to Ron and Patti to leave. "Let's go, Mr. Granville. You don't want to overstay your welcome."

"Mr. Granville, you are a very lucky man," said Assad. "Have a nice day and enjoy your stay in Lebanon."

It was two flights of stairs down to the street; Ron thought it was the longest stairwell he'd ever seen. At any moment, he expected Assad's men to grab and restrain him. Guards raced around them and down the steps into the basement, but the Granvilles were unopposed.

Outside, DiPiccioto informed Ron and Patti that the United States had launched an amphibious assault. Fourteen thousand U.S. marines and army troops from the Fourth Infantry Division were streaming across the Beirut beaches, intent upon securing the international airport. "This should stabilize the Lebanese government and reduce the influence of the UAR," said DiPiccioto. "Indeed, we expect the unrest in Lebanon to end immediately. I regret we were unable to come to your assistance these past weeks. We've been very busy with the assault plans."

"That's insane," snarled Ron. "The State Department was too busy to assist me? Do these things happen routinely?"

"The Arabs are quite enthusiastic about their boycott," replied DiPiccioto. "But this is the first time I've seen them get hysterical over an electric table fan. I suspect your grandchildren will never believe it. I do apologize for the delay, but you must admit your government has secured your release. In a few days the embassy should be back to normal; let us know if we can be of further assistance. A car will be along to collect you shortly."

Ron and Patti hugged as DiPiccioto departed. They stood in front of the prison and watched as additional prisoners were released. The local authorities responded to the major show of American force by releasing most of their political prisoners. Ron smiled and waved as Claude Gourdon emerged wrapped in a bloodied Lebanese flag. The American embassy car arrived, and as the Granvilles turned to leave, they saw Gourdon and several other prisoners climb into an automobile that sported French Embassy pennants.

• • •

July 12-13, 2008

The haunting notes of the allegretto to Beethoven's *Tempest* piano sonata looped repeatedly on Ron Granville's iPod as he sought to drown out the snoring passengers and screaming children. En route to Paris, he sat in First Class, yet there were children all over the cabin. The bulkhead was behind him, and the crew had stuffed some bags behind his seat; it wouldn't tilt back more than a few inches. A late in-bound aircraft had had mechanical problems and forced the substitution of a smaller, older aircraft. It was crowded, uncomfortable, the toilets stunk, and Ron was repelled by the food.

In Ron's mind, the gate agent had been typical. Delays were announced in fifteen minute intervals. Ron had decided the agent probably didn't even know how to tell the truth. But, Ron admitted, what he disliked most about the man was that his looks reminded him of Major Assad. It was fifty years ago, but memories of the major still gave him nightmares.

Ron tried to stretch. A large man but with an even larger girth after seventy-four years on Earth, he banged his knees on the seat in front of him and surrendered to the discomfort. He turned up the iPod volume on his headset and swallowed a stiff double Scotch—cheap, he noted. Then he twisted awkwardly in his seat and rubbed the old scars on his back.

He looked over at the row on his left. Two attractive American blondes, perhaps a mother and daughter whom he suspected were taking their first-ever trip to Europe, seemed to enjoy the flight. They were surrounded by a group of Islamic women and children en route to Bahrain, according to the purser. Yet the American women were oblivious to the chaos in the cabin and were laughing. That stirred an old memory. At least Ron's first trip to the Middle East had started nice. He dropped off to sleep as he remembered his trip with Patti. He missed her.

The pilot extended the landing gear, and a rush of air and cabin decompression awoke Ron. The aircraft had begun its descent towards Paris's Roissy Charles DeGaulle Airport. As the plane slowed over Paris and entered its final approach, Ron wondered how this trip would turn out. It was the reunion with Claude Gourdon, the Frenchman who'd been tortured by Major Assad. Fifty years ago, they'd made plans to meet someday. But Ron had never really expected to see Gourdon again. He wondered how Gourdon had occupied his time. Except for a single postcard, sent via the Denver American Express office two months earlier, Ron had had no contact with Gourdon since they'd been released from the Lebanese rat hole. In fact, over the years Ron had forgotten the pledge to meet again in Paris.

Checking into Le Grand Intercontinental Hotel at Place de L'Opera, Ron picked up a copy of *Le Monde*, the French newspaper of the left. He walked to a table on the Boulevard des Capucines and ordered a coffee. Ron had learned enough French while he worked in Lebanon to make his way through the headline: "*Barack Obama est le candidat qui préfere la reste du monde.*" Ron smiled; the French believed that Obama was preferred by the entire world. The newspaper called it "Obamania," a planetary phenomena greater perhaps than "Dianamania." Ron, a political conservative after his experience with Assad, wondered if he ever would understand the French. They were liberal beyond imagination and shrank at the thought of war. Yet they revered Napoleon—who'd glorified conquest and war and brought home more plunder and treasure than any man since Caesar.

A green street-sweeping vehicle rolled down the boulevard toward La Madeleine and captured Ron's attention. He was watching the action of the machine's rotating brushes when someone shouted in his ear, "Monica Lewinsky is pregnant!"

Ron looked up. "What's that?"

A man holding a bunch of *International Herald Tribune*s was smiling at him. "You're American, *n'est pas*? I can tell from your clothes."

"Huh? What's that got to do with Monica Lewinsky?" asked Ron.

The vendor smiled. "I find it's a good way to sell newspapers to tourists. It always gets a laugh. Would you like a newspaper?"

Ron purchased a *Herald Tribune*. It was easier to read than *Le Monde*. The price was two and a half Euros—a small bundle, he thought, almost four dollars at the current exchange rate. He looked at the headline. Someone had murdered a former French deputy minister of transportation in Provence. An international manhunt was underway for the killer who'd also mutilated the left hand and legs of the minister before he was killed. On page 2, Ron discovered France had invited Bashar al-Assad, the president of Syria, to attend the Bastille Day parade scheduled for the next day in Paris. According to the *Reuters* news service, it was a sign of a diplomatic thaw. The old scars on Ron's back began to sting.

The reunion with Gourdon was scheduled for that evening in a restaurant in the 8th Arrondissement. Ron strolled back to his hotel. He climbed into a taxi. It was a magnificent evening in Paris, and the streets were thronged with traffic. The cafés overflowed, and lovers strolled hand in hand around the Place de la Concorde and under the manicured trees along the Seine. Ron admired the trees that marched up and down the river banks. He'd read *Innocents Abroad* and remembered that Mark Twain had marveled at the same sight, remarking that only the French could grow trees to a constant height.

Ron exited his taxi and walked into Chez André, a traditional French restaurant on Rue Marbeuf. Claude Gourdon waited at a table just inside the door. He'd aged considerably more than Ron—his hair had thinned, his jowls sagged, and he looked pale and frail. The men hugged. Gourdon ordered some water and a bottle of a white Burgundy, Le Montrachet, Delagrange-Bachele, 1994.

"The wine is outrageously expensive," said Gourdon. "About €600. But we deserve it. It's been fifty years and I still remember those weeks in prison with you. Besides, I no longer concern myself with money."

Ron raised his eyebrows. "What do you mean? Why would money not matter?"

"Not to worry, *mon ami*. How are you?"

"I'm okay. My wife died a few years ago, and I moved to a small ranch in the mountains near Colorado Springs." He smiled and reached for a glass. "How about you? Did you ever marry? Children? What happened after Lebanon?"

"*Non*, the prison—*comment dit*?—ruined my ability to trust anyone." Gourdon shrugged.

"No one?"

"You, Ron, I trust you."

Ron smiled at the waitress who delivered the wine. "Where are you living these days? Your card was posted from Luxembourg."

Gourdon looked pensive. "I was living in Metz. But I moved out last week. I'm staying at the Hotel Plaza Athenée."

"You're living there? That's terribly expensive." Ron knew the hotel. It was in the same class with the George V and the Ritz—an elegant hotel on Avenue Montaigne.

"I am just staying there. But enough of this small talk." Gourdon handed Ron a Galeries Lafayette shopping bag. "Please accept a small gift to remind you of the bad old days."

As he reached for the bag, Ron noticed that Gourdon's mutilated fingers on his left hand still showed traces of torture.

"What's this?" asked Ron.

"A Lebanese flag. It's stained with blood from 1958. I found it in the prison after they threw open the cell doors. I saved it all these years. But I have other plans now."

"What kind of plans?" asked Ron.

"I promise we will talk of them later."

Ron stared into the bag. It contained a folded flag with two red stripes and a green cedar tree on a white field in the center. "Thanks. I'll treasure it—until I burn it."

Gourdon smiled ruefully.

"Whatever happened," asked Ron, "to Major Assad? I saw a guy who reminded me of him yesterday."

"Assad is still alive. He's here—in Paris."

"How do you know?"

"I received a call from an old friend in Lebanon. My friend's father was murdered by Assad."

"Assad has got to be in his eighties now, old and feeble."

"He is," said Gourdon. "And I'm going to kill him."

"What? Why now?"

"Because I've waited all these years to watch him bleed and die on French soil." Gourdon smiled and wiped his lips. "But before I get into details, let's order our dinner."

Ron was stunned. "But, Claude, this is—"

"I recommend the fish. They do a wonderful sole here." Gourdon waved for the waitress.

Both men ordered *La Belle Sole Meunière* with *frites* and *salade mixte.*

After the waitress left, Gourdon placed his hand on Ron's arm. "This will be my second murder."

"What are you talking about? Are you crazy?"

"Do you remember how my company double-crossed me and sold fighter-bombers to the Israelis when I was in Lebanon?"

"Of course."

"Emmanuel Martineau—he was the managing director of the trading arm of *Armée de l'Air.* He later became a deputy minister of transportation. I murdered him yesterday in Les Baux; I slit his throat."

Ron was aghast. "Claude—"

The waitress interrupted the conversation and served their dinners. Both men were silent while they ate; Gourdon with gusto, while Ron brooded and toyed with his fish.

Later, over coffee and a cognac, Gourdon loosened his tie and stared into Ron's eyes. "Forget Martineau. He was *en cochon*, a pig. Assad is the real target, and you should be grateful."

"What's he doing in Paris?"

"Assad is the uncle of the president of Syria."

"His uncle? There will be security everywhere. All the more reason to forget this nutty idea."

"Ron, I was in that prison far longer than you. I suffered greater indignities. Please, do not try to stop me. My mind is made up and my conscience is clear."

"But Claude, he's not worth it."

"I've waited long enough—how fitting, is it not, that it comes at the time of our reunion?"

Ron swallowed some cognac and thought back to his beating—how Assad had stood there with a cigarette and enjoyed Ron's pain. "All right," conceded Ron. "I won't interfere. In a strange way, I hope you get him. So the old man came with his nephew? I read that the Syrian president was invited to Paris for Bastille Day."

Gourdon nodded. "The monster is part of the president's entourage. I'm going to get him during the parade tomorrow. He's also staying at the Plaza Athenée. He's not too mobile; he will watch the parade on the television in his room. The others will march down the Avenue des Champs Élysées. That is when I will kill him, after I rip out his fingernails and shoot a kneecap or two."

"But then you're no better than him." Ron equivocated; he wasn't sure if he wanted to know any more information, or just be silent.

"I've carried my wounds my entire life. It is not enough to see him dead; he must die a painful death, staring into my eyes. After that, I will find peace.

It will be enough for me. Of course, it's likely they will kill me—that's why I want you to have the flag."

Ron wondered how the Frenchman would pull off an assassination in a secure hotel. His musings were interrupted when four American businessmen were seated at the next table. They were squeezed into a space normally occupied by two people in any restaurant in the states. Ron decided to hold his questions—the other patrons were too close to discuss something as sensitive as an assassination.

Gourdon signaled for the bill. "Let's finish and take a walk to my hotel. It's just a few blocks."

Ron gulped his cognac and reached for his coffee. The Americans began to chat, reviewing their business transaction with Electricité de France, the French power company. Ron gagged when one of the younger men addressed an older man and said, "So, Tom, how do you like running Johnson Electric? We're excited to have the CEO visit—we don't get too many people from the head office. Speaking for the international staff, I want you to know we're one hundred percent committed to support you."

Tom, the CEO, smiled thoughtfully. "Thanks, Jim. I appreciate that. Johnson Electric's a great company. And I know how difficult it can be when management from St. Louis meddles with your accounts. But the team's been very helpful."

Ron shook his head and stared at the older American. He seemed to startle the Johnson CEO, who made eye contact and smiled nervously.

Tom turned back to his men. "Working with the international sales group is rewarding. Our sales meeting this morning was productive. I'm glad we've decided to expand our home appliance business in Israel—it should make a big contribution to the bottom line."

Ron's stomach churned. He flushed and hyperventilated. Johnson Electric? St. Louis? Israel? Sharp pains swept across Ron's back. He saw red. Gourdon was counting his change when Ron put his coffee down, stood, turned slowly towards Tom, clenched a fist, and hit him squarely between the eyes.

"*Mon Dieu*," said Gourdon. "Ron, this is a terrible mistake. I must leave immediately."

Blood splattered out of the Tom's nose, and he went down like a stone. The other Johnson Electric Company employees struggled to get away from the table. Patrons screamed. Gourdon abandoned his change and ran out of the café. When the French police arrived, Ron was seated; the American sprawled below him. Many of the patrons had fled and the restaurant staff stood along the wall, paralyzed with uncertainty. The *maître'd* had rushed to Tom and still kneeled at his side. He dabbed at the blood flowing out of his patron's nose with a napkin. The police arrested Ron for assault and detained him in the Prison de la Santé in the 14th Arrondissement.

• • •

Ron spent Bastille Day alone in a cell on the sixth floor. The next morning he was reflecting on Gourdon's crazy plan when a guard came to escort him to a conference room. An Inspector Henri Kinnert introduced himself. He invited Ron to be seated. Another policeman hovered near the door.

Kinnert looked sternly at Ron. "Monsieur Granville, I inform you that the American whom you assaulted has decided, after consultation with his employer—the Johnson Electric Company of St. Louis, Missouri—not to press charges."

Ron was surprised. "Why not?"

"After your explanation to the arresting officer, and an exchange of cables with St. Louis, the parties decided not to revisit the matter of the Arab League Boycott."

"Does that mean I'm free to go?" asked Ron.

"*Non. Je suis désolé.* You must be detained. There is a continuing investigation. I recommend you seek legal counsel."

"Why, Inspector Kinnert, would I need that?"

"Yesterday afternoon, on Bastille Day, a French national, Claude Gourdon, brutally murdered Azeem Assad, the uncle of the president of Syria in the Hotel Plaza Athenée. Assad's left hand was mutilated, and he also was shot in both knees. Mr. Gourdon was killed by hotel security guards as he sought to escape. Based upon the nature of the crime, we suspect Gourdon also murdered a former deputy minister of France three days ago in a town in Provence."

A shudder of apprehension and fear passed through Ron. "So, what has that to do with me?"

"As you might imagine, this crime has embarrassed France and done irreparable damage to her relationship with the government of Syria. The Syrian government is enraged."

"As far as I can tell, France has always found a way to kiss up to Syria and the other Arab countries," said Ron. "But I repeat, why am I being detained?"

"Perhaps you can explain why you had dinner with the assassin two days ago."

Ron swallowed nervously. It was happening again. "I demand to speak with the American Embassy."

"Yes, of course. But—"

There was a knock at the door. A French policeman entered carrying an envelope. He handed it to Inspector Kinnert who opened it, read a document, and then handed it to Ron.

"What's this? My French is weak."

Kinnert smiled grimly. "I'm afraid it is a notice of intent to extradite you to Syria. It was filed by their attaché. The charges are murder and conspiracy to commit murder."

"Don't they need to conduct an inquiry?" asked Ron, who considered jumping out the window. Such things, he knew, had happened before in French prisons.

"They don't; but we do," said Kinnert. "Perhaps you will be lucky. France is a civilized country. I don't think she will extradite you to a country that executes its criminals. On the other hand, the murder has drawn the ire of the Syrians. Their government may offer assurances that you would not be executed. In that case, you could be their guest for a long time."

Ron shuddered. "I can see how surrendering me to the Syrians might repair that irreparable damage, too. My embassy—when can I contact them?"

"We'll notify them, of course. However, your State Department is often busy dealing with the chaos in the Middle East. It may be some time before they can come to your assistance."

Ron looked at the window again. He wondered what it would be like to jump. Would it be fast? Painful? He steeled himself for the dash to the window. When the inspector turned toward his briefcase, Ron bolted for the window—and then realized it was barred. He stopped, and the French guard slammed him back into his chair.

"Is that a sign of guilt, Monsieur Granville?" asked Kinnert. "I continue to wait for your explanation regarding your dinner with the assassin."

"I'm innocent, Inspector. I've been in France for three days and except for dinner, I last spoke with Claude Gourdon fifty years ago. I don't think I can handle another day in prison. I would rather die than live with the threat of being delivered to the Syrians."

"Perhaps. Sit down, Monsieur Granville. I am not finished."

The guard pushed Ron back in his seat and stood behind him.

Kinnert spoke as he reached into his brief case. "As you know, Lebanon and Syria have been engaged in a serious confrontation since the Syrian Army withdrew from Lebanon." The Inspector retrieved Claude Gourdon's old flag and placed it on the table. "We'd like to know why you had a bloodied Lebanese flag with you."

Ron gulped. An explanation would open the issue of why Gourdon gave him the flag and the conversation at dinner. Ron decided to remain silent.

"No answer, Mr. Granville? I thought so. We're transferring you this afternoon to Gendarmerie Headquarters in the 1st Arrondissement. That is where prisoners are detained during on-going investigations. Perhaps you'll find a window there with no bars. *Bonne journée.*"

Ron wondered who his new cellmate would be. Salvation, this time, would not come from an American amphibious assault.

Four Horses

After the sun set over the Manhattan skyline, two men crept across the roof of the Fire Department of New York Metrotech headquarters building in Brooklyn. They unpacked a microwave transmitter, powered by a Honda motor generator. They connected a Dell XPS laptop computer with a sixteen inch widescreen to the transmitter. They powered up their systems in the dark and linked, across the Metrotech plaza, into the New York Stock Exchange (NYSE) computers that were housed in the Security Industry Automation Corporation datacenter. The men hacked through the firewalls and jammed a sequence of four Trojan Horses into the NYSE computers.

The next day, April 1, dawned sunny on the east coast. Despite the weather, the mood was glum on the floor of the NYSE. The Dow Jones Industrials Average (DJIA) had declined since the inauguration of the new president—the morning open was only 7,750 points, down from 9,000 when the new administration had taken office. Volume was light and the market drifted down another 130 points, launching the first Trojan horse. Suddenly, a jolting message crossed the Big Board: "PRESIDENT SHOT!! AT DEATH'S DOOR."

Traders on the floor paused and looked around. Others grouped in small circles as rumors circulated throughout the NYSE. Everyone watched the numbers on the Board. Slowly, the DJIA began to react to the news: from down 130, it recovered to up five points, spurted to plus fifty, and then continued to rise at a steady pace. When the DJIA reached 8,000, a 250 point gain since the open, programming flags planted in the software tripped the second Trojan horse: "PRESIDENT'S WOUNDS LIFE THREATENING."

The market soared another 250 points in two minutes to 8,250. That triggered the third Trojan horse: "FIRST LADY WOUNDED."

The market rose another two hundred points.

Duncan Webster, the president of the NYSE, was in his office when the phone rang. He picked up the handset.

"Duncan?" said the director of the Securities and Exchange Commission (SEC). "We're going nuts in Washington. All the lines to the White House and the Federal Reserve are busy. The VP's in Zimbabwe and incommunicado. I think the Speaker's drunk, and the Secretary of State's at some UNESCO event in Geneva. Maybe we should close the markets until we can sort out the news. We can't verify anything. The *UPI* says it won't certify the death of the president unless it sees a death certificate."

"I don't know," said Duncan. "We've been looking for a good rally. We're up 700, at 8,450 now. We might get the largest single percentage gain in history. Let's keep it open."

The market was up 1,200 points, to a mind-boggling 8,950, when the fourth Trojan horse flashed the message: "APRIL FOOL!! PRESIDENT AND FIRST LADY OKAY!"

The DJIA plunged to 6,775. The chairman of the Federal Reserve called Duncan. He recommended that the NYSE circuit breakers, which limited daily losses in the DJIA to no more than ten percent of the open, be restored. Duncan Webster notified the director of the SEC that trading was closed for the day.

Top Secret

August 5, 1966

The Soviet Union performed a nuclear test in Eastern Kazakh, and Mao Zedong launched the Cultural Revolution. The United States government was concerned. It wasn't a propitious time to ask the government to share its secrets. I regretted the timing, but I needed the damn clearance for work.

Agent Cararro, who worked for the Defense Investigative Service (DIS), straightened his narrow tie, withdrew several documents from his portfolio—one of those leather ones with the words Department of Defense stamped on its side—and gave me a stern look. We sat in the conference room of the Security Office at Menlo Defense Research Institute (MDRI), where I led a team of experts in anti-missile electronic warfare. The room had a beat-up, old wooden conference table, dirty beige walls, and fluorescent lighting that hissed and popped occasionally. It was cold and I was underdressed—T-shirt, jeans, and sandals.

"So, Mr. Meades," said Cararro, "you're applying for top secret clearance?"

"I need access," I confirmed. "Some of my team's projects could operate at a higher funding level if the application is approved."

I was nervous and I hoped it wasn't apparent. This was my first application at the top secret level, and I worried how the government would deal with my family secret—if it was discovered. There was risk, too; if I didn't get access they could pull my existing lower-level clearance. That would kill my job at MDRI and anywhere else.

"I see." Cararro had a slight sneer. "It must be nice to get government money."

I concluded the man was hostile to my application. It probably went with the job. I decided not to give him any unnecessary information and waited for his questions.

"Mr. Meades, a top secret clearance requires that we investigate your background. We're going to check your past, including your education, friends and family, employment, and present and past residences. Let's review your Personnel Security Questionnaire."

The questionnaire was a multi-page, double-sided government form about two feet long. The government wanted information that included your date of birth, draft board number, your address as well as previous residences for the past seventeen years, and the schools you'd attended.

I wondered what civil libertarians thought of the document which also demanded the disclosure of arrest records, memberships, parentage, personal references, race, and whether any relatives lived outside the country. The government even wanted to know if your spouse had foreign relatives.

The appendix to the questionnaire listed hundreds of organizations designated by the Attorney General, and pursuant to Executive Order 10450, as "Totalitarian, Fascist, Communist, or Subversive, or as having adopted a policy of advocating or approving the commission of acts of force and violence to deny others their rights under the Constitution of the United States, or which sought to alter the form of Government of the United States by unconstitutional means." This included such expected organizations as the Communist Party U.S.A., as well as some surprises like the Committee for the Negro in the Arts, the Congress of American Revolutionary Writers, and the Sakura Kai Patriotic Society, which was composed of veterans of the Russo-Japanese war. You had to certify that you were not now, and had never been, a member of any such group.

The agent looked over my completed questionnaire, folded it, and dropped it into his portfolio. Then he turned on a bright desk lamp, swiveled it around, and pointed it in my face.

"We know that you were granted an earlier lower-level secret clearance," he said, "when you joined the Air National Guard in 1956. Was the application you completed then truthful and complete? Would you like to change any of those answers?" The questions flew out of his mouth like bullets from an automatic weapon.

"I have no changes," I responded. "The answers were complete. Everything I said at that time was true." I'd decided to hedge a little, confident that the intent of my answers in 1956 had been truthful and, after all, I hadn't yet learned the family secret.

"Then let's get down to business."

He walked me through the form and double-checked my answers. Yes, my Air National Guard discharge was Honorable. Yes, I'd belonged to the Boy Scouts of America at a time they wore brown shirts. (Didn't they still wear brown shirts?) Yes, I belonged to an investment club that purchased stock in K-Mart. This, based on the way Cararro raised his eyebrows, was apparently a suspect act.

"Do you object," he asked, "to us contacting your former neighbors?"

"No," I replied grudgingly. After a visit from an investigator, I could picture an ex-neighbor saying "He must be a Commie."

"Mr. Meades, let's talk about your memberships. Do you now, or have you ever, belonged to an organization that advocates the violent overthrow of the Constitution of the United States?"

I was irritated. "Please, sir, I've never belonged to any such organization. We've already checked those questions on the form."

"Thank you. However questions seventeen through twenty-one are quite specific. I'd like to review them again. Of course, none of this would be necessary if you'd volunteer for a polygraph examination." Cararro turned his head up at an angle and raised his eyebrows in an inquisitive and hungry manner.

I had scary visions of an electric chair in a '30s movie. I shook my head and hoped I'd sound indifferent. "Perhaps, Agent Cararro, but I've never taken a lie detector test. I'd like to get some advice first."

"You mean a lawyer, consult with a lawyer, don't you?"

"Why don't you ask your specific questions?" I hoped to steer the agent away from the subjects of the polygraph and the lawyer.

"All right, Mr. Meades. Are you now or have you ever been a member …?"

After we revisited the same questions on the form, I felt I'd done well. Cararro looked as though he were satisfied and stowed the rest of his documents in his case.

"That's very nice, Mr. Meades. You've convinced me that you're a loyal American. That's not easy to do. We'll be in touch about the background investigation with the neighbors."

I smiled with relief as he grabbed his portfolio and rose from his chair.

"Oh, one last question, if you don't mind." He was headed toward the door but paused and turned around. He reached into his pocket and pulled out a three-by-five card. Referring to it, he read, "Do you *know anyone* that has ever been a member of any foreign or domestic organization, association, movement, group, or combination of persons which is Totalitarian, Fascist, Communist, or Subversive, or which has adopted or shows a policy of advocating or approving the commission of acts of force or violence to deny other persons their rights under the Constitution of the United States?"

I gulped. Was it possible the government knew my nasty little secret, the one I'd only learned about last year?

"Er, well," I mumbled. "Does it really matter these days? You're already convinced I'm a loyal American, and I never belonged to any of those organizations."

The agent returned to his chair. He looked at me suspiciously. "Cut the crap, Mr. Meades. Do you know anyone? Your 1956 application states quite clearly that you did not. Were you lying then or are you … Well, you know the question. Do you know anyone that belonged to any such organizations?"

I took a deep breath and looked out the window. Horses grazed on the hills which flanked Sand Hill Road. I wished I was one of them. I figured my job was toast, nodded my head, and whimpered, "Yes, I did know one person that belonged to such an organization."

"Which organization would that be, Mr. Meades?"

"Is this really necessary? Is this legal? Do I have to tell you?" My words sounded like a bleat. I felt weak—and vulnerable.

"What's that you asked, Mr. Meades? Did you say legal?"

"Do I really have to say?"

"Mr. Meades!"

I tried to talk but no sounds came out of my mouth. Then, I steeled myself and croaked, "Communist, the Communist Party U.S.A."

He squinted. I suspected he was anticipating the promotion he'd earn nailing a Red.

"Who was this person?"

I mumbled, "My mother."

"Your mother was a Commie?" Agent Cararro shifted to the edge of his seat. "She carried a card. When? For how long? When did you know? Did you know in 1956? Did you lie on that application? Are you a Communist, too?" That automatic weapon fired again. It seemed like I could smell cordite.

The questions overwhelmed me. I was innocent. I had answers, but I felt hopeless. Growing up in the McCarthy era had conditioned everyone I knew to shun Communists—it was too dangerous to associate with them. Just endorsing a petition could ruin your life. Once tainted, you were a goner. I stared at Agent Cararro.

"Look," I admitted, "my mother was a Communist, but she quit the party when Trotsky was assassinated. That was 1943. Stalin was too brutal for her. I was five at the time, so I wasn't much of a Communist. When I completed that form in 1956, I didn't know she'd been in the party."

Cararro looked perplexed. A five-year-old wasn't much of a catch.

He sat back in his chair and nodded. "I guess that wouldn't have influenced you much. But tell me, when did you learn about your mother's membership?"

"My father had a heart attack in 1965. When I visited him in the hospital, he wanted to talk about my mother. She'd died in 1961. He told me that she'd carried a card. He died just a few days later."

Agent Cararro's eyes flashed. A triumphant smile broke out. "Are you telling me your father made a deathbed confession?"

I was angered by the question but said simply, "I didn't consider it a confession. My father didn't give a shit about Communism; he just wanted me to know about my mother."

"Mr. Meades, this is new information. Is there anything else you think we need to know? What will we discover in the Extended Background

Investigation? You went to Wisconsin. Who were your professors? Were they lefties? How about taking that polygraph?"

My secret was exposed. I didn't see any downside to the polygraph. "I'll have to ask my lawyer, but I think it's likely he'll agree. May I call you to schedule a test?"

Agent Cararro departed. I figured that was the end of it. My nasty little secret was out, so the poly would be a breeze. It was irrelevant, I mused, but if a five-year-old couldn't get a clearance, no one could. Still, to be safe, I called my lawyer, Don Feldman. He suggested that before I call DIS to schedule the poly I take a private examination—for practice.

"You never know," cautioned Feldman. "Once you're in there, they could ask anything. Let's see how you do under pressure—before we place your balls on the block."

"All right," I said. "Schedule one."

"Hey," giggled Feldman, "my Uncle Harry was a Red. Are you sure there isn't anything you need to tell me now?"

I stifled the urge to tell him, "Fuck You."

• • •

The practice polygraph was scheduled for a week later. When I presented myself in Feldman's office, he introduced me to the examiner and left the room. The man hooked me up to a polygraph machine.

"Okay, Mr. Meades," he said. "I'm going to connect several devices—a finger sensor to measure perspiration, a cuff to read your blood pressure, and a halter around your chest that monitors your breathing patterns. Experience tells us these are the variables most likely to change when a person is deceptive."

I wasn't comfortable, but I went along with the routine. Curious, I wanted to learn as much as possible about the methodology.

He explained the procedure. "First, we'll discuss the questions to ensure that you understand them. Each answer during the test must be a simple 'yes' or 'no.' Any ambiguity or uncertainty in the questions must be resolved, before we begin the examination."

"What? You mean I can't explain an answer?"

"We go through all of that before the test. The questions during the test will reflect our discussion."

I wasn't happy, but I nodded.

The examiner assumed a professional mien. He said he'd ask some simple questions to calibrate my responses—I had to be truthful on some and deliberately lie on others.

We began.

"So Mr. Meades, is that your name?"

"Yes." The machine's needles jiggled slightly as they drew more or less straight lines on the recording paper.

"Are you married?"

"No." I lied as instructed and watched the needles jump as they traced zigzag lines on the paper.

We then went into the test in earnest and paper poured out of the machine.

Twenty minutes later, the examiner said, "Mr. Meades, I must tell you that your answers come across as deceptive. Since we're not testing for anything in reality, you must have a guilty personality. You'll fail any test unless you learn how to relax."

I smiled grimly as he removed the monitoring sensors. After I wrote the man a check for $200, he departed. Feldman returned to the room.

"The examiner told me that you probably shouldn't take the DIS test." Feldman smiled, and I didn't like it. His gallows humor came through loud and clear.

"I have to take the test," I moaned. "But now I regret the practice session. How the hell am I going to relax? I've been guilty my whole life. For Christ's sake, I'm a Jew."

• • •

The month before the examination I felt terrible. My job was on the line and I couldn't get the test out of my mind. I noticed more and more articles about Communists in the newspapers. The Soviets landed a probe on the moon. The Red Menace was greater than ever.

To prepare myself for the test, I took no medications and abstained from booze the previous night. In the morning I ran six miles around the hills behind Stanford and chanted Buddhist mantras. I practiced biofeedback techniques in the car on the drive up Highway U.S. 101 to San Francisco.

The exam was in the Federal Building on Golden Gate Avenue. DIS was located on the tenth floor, and the elevator stopped at every floor. On the way up, my shirt saturated with sweat. I considered skipping the test and abandoning my application. Then I reasoned there might not be any sweat left to measure.

Agent Cararro greeted me in the office along with Investigator Ryan, who would administer the test. They were rather distant but professional. After a few moments it was just me and Ryan in the room, but there was a one-way mirror on a wall. I was certain Cararro hovered on the other side.

"Mr. Meades," said Ryan, "have you ever taken a polygraph examination before?"

"No, er ... yes, I have."

"I see. And under what circumstances?"

"Well, I took a practice test last month in my lawyer's office, you know, to see what it's all about?"

I'd thought Ryan was distracted by his machine. As it warmed up, the needles danced all over the paper.

But he was alert. "You took a practice session? To learn how to beat the machine? Is that it, Mr. Meades? Do you have something to hide?"

At that point, it seemed like everything I'd done to get a top secret clearance was futile. The careful answers, the hedging, the practice poly—it was all suspicious. I looked at Ryan sheepishly. "No, it was nothing like that. I was just nervous."

"All right, Mr. Meades. We'll see. Apparently you know the routine. Here are the questions I'm going to ask."

We went through his questions. Was Meades my name? Was I born in Evanston, Illinois in 1938? Did I ever smoke marijuana? Had I gone to Roosevelt High School? Did I graduate from the University of Wisconsin? Had I ever knowingly disclosed classified information to a person not cleared for that information? Did I or my wife have relatives behind the Iron Curtain? On and on it went, but not one of the questions focused on my mother.

I watched the machine during the test and, except for the test questions in which I was directed to lie, not once did the needles jump. I'd begun to relax when Investigator Ryan said, "Thank you, Mr. Meades. Those are all the questions. *Now, is there anything else you want to tell me*?"

Alarm bells went off in my head. The needles exploded, bouncing all over the paper. Twenty-eight years of guilt raced through my mind: stealing a nickel from my grandmother's purse; throwing stones at cars; accidentally hitting a girl in the head with a golf club; cheating on a high school Spanish test; buying a hot TV. My mother never entered my thoughts. Crestfallen, I looked at Ryan.

The investigator smiled. "Relax, Mr. Meades. That question doesn't count. We're just having fun. We do that to everybody. Remember? We have to review the questions first."

• • •

The letter went directly to MDRI. The director of security informed me I'd received my clearance. I was elated and went to the project office for a briefing on the procedures for handling top secret documents. The project administrator took me into a secure facility and gave me the combination to a classified document container.

I looked at hundreds of pages that day. All described the behavior of space interceptors and ICBMs. The pages were filled with equations that I recognized. I wondered if it had been worth the gauntlet of stress to see Newton's classical equations of motion—they'd been derived 300 years ago and were in any freshman's physics text. The equations were stamped TOP SECRET.

No-Fly

The Present

Lela Jones, Transportation Security Agency (TSA) employee at San Francisco International airport (SFO), turned away from the x-ray image of a suitcase. There was a disturbance inside the portal to the magnetometer machine. A tall man argued with the security officer. The officer looked at Lela with eyes that implored assistance.

Lela nodded and waved her arm at the tall man. "Sir," she said, "please return to the end of the line and have your boarding pass ready!"

The man stared at Lela with wild eyes. Suddenly he lunged across the X-ray machine belt ...

• • •

Three Months Earlier

Douglas L. Mathis, the Attorney General of the United States, smiled at Greta von Solange of *Wolf News*. He straightened his tie and pulled down the back of his suit jacket. "You can turn on the cameras now."

Von Solange smiled back. "Welcome to *Wolf News*, Mr. Attorney General."

"Please, Greta, call me Douglas."

"Yes, thank you, Mr. Attorney General." She turned to the camera. "Tonight we're pleased to have the Attorney General of the United States, the Honorable Douglas *L.* Mathis with us."

Mathis noticed von Solange stressed his middle initial. He only used his middle initial because he loathed his middle name—Leslie, a girl's name. He looked at his initials on the cuffs of his shirt and pulled down his jacket sleeves to cover the monogram. Mathis, a consummate politician, nodded pleasantly at Greta. Inside he seethed. But for the president's orders, he never would have agreed to appear on *Wolf.* As far as Mathis was concerned the network was a hotbed of conservative radicals.

"Thanks for inviting me, Greta. At times like these every free-thinking American needs to know how the government is watching out for them."

"These are trying times, indeed," agreed von Solange. She stared at the Talking Points script the attorney general's staff had prepared and laid it aside. "The Nigerian that tried to bring down Northwest Flight 253 on Christmas Day, 2009, is a terrorist and an enemy of our country—"

Mathis stiffened. What the hell? That wasn't on the script. He ground his teeth. "Now Greta, I think he was a criminal, and we'll deal with him in the time-honored traditions of our country. After all, he's no different than Sacco and Vanzetti were in the '20s—just another anarchist."

"He was a criminal, not a terrorist?" asked von Solange. "Is that what you believe?" She paused while Mathis struggled with the question. Then she said, "That's right—your administration doesn't use that word, does it? Sort of like the policy at *Reuters*, right? One man's terrorist is another man's freedom fighter?"

"No, that's not … turn off the cameras. Off the record!"

Von Solange sighed and turned to the cameraman. She made eye-contact and drew her hand across her throat. The cameraman nodded and turned off the camera and lights.

"Yes?"

The attorney general growled, "This is just more of that right-wing bullshit. Fair and balanced, my foot! Now, if you people want to have a polite conversation, let's start again—and stick to the script my office gave you."

• • •

Sam Carruthers sat in his favorite chair in the den of his home in White Plains. Sam was a large man—about six foot two, with a humorous smile and a mischievous personality. He had large eyebrows that framed dark intelligent eyes, cropped brown hair streaked with gray, and nicotine-stained fingers from years of smoking cigars. He lit a cigar and swirled a fine eighteen-year-old single malt Scotch whisky in a Waterford tumbler.

Sam, as a young electrical engineer graduate from MIT, had worked on national security computing problems. Before retirement, he'd worked for IBM in White Plains as a research director who specialized in artificial intelligence, knowledge-based systems and enhanced data mining techniques—a process which filtered Internet traffic and made informed guesses about people's interests. Sam had made a small fortune on his share of a few IBM patents. Google and Yahoo paid big bucks in royalties to IBM, and Sam received his portions twice a year.

He reached for his remote, turned on his television set, and tuned to *Wolf News*. Greta von Solange, in his opinion the most monumentally boring person on cable TV, was interviewing the attorney general. Funny, Sam thought, her vaporous trademark look was absent; she looked aggravated and her smile seemed strained.

"*So, Mr. Attorney General,*" she said, "*you think that you'll have no problem applying the criminal code to people who attack us?*"

"*No question, Greta. Anyone who attacks us on our soil is subject to the weight of the entire American justice system.*"

"*You don't think that it might be time to put some teeth back into the Patriot Act?*"

"*Absolutely not. We're a nation of laws, and we don't need to abandon the Bill of Rights. If we do that, we're no better than these criminals.*"

Sam rolled his eyes and shook his head in disgust. A "nation of laws" was a joke to him. He'd concluded long ago that Congress and the White House enforced laws selectively, often to maintain the ruling party in power, or politicians in office. And this guy, Mathis—he was a pompous ass and a naïve fool. More people died on 9/11 than at Pearl Harbor; the nation was at war, and this guy treated mass-murderers like common criminals.

The attorney general continued. "*When we abandon our fundamental principles we give up our freedoms. We can and should rely on our security measures.*"

"*How then,*" asked von Solange, "*did our security system fail with the Nigerian bomb— … ah, criminal?*"

"*The No-Fly List, along with the enhanced screening Selectee List, is absolutely foolproof,*" said Mathis. "*Unfortunately, the CIA let us down when they didn't pass on the information.*"

"*Do you mean the information that the State Department received from the Nigerian's father about his son's Islamic radicalization?*"

Mathis frowned. "*I understand the secretary said that the State Department complied with all inter-agency guidelines established after 9/11. But I can't get into that.*"

Von Solange nodded. "*The Talking Points memo that your staff forwarded to* Wolf News *stressed the value of the No-Fly List and its role in protecting Americans.*"

"*Yes, one thing is certain. The No-Fly List is an essential tool in our fight against these criminals.*"

"*I see. I believe a moment ago you said it was foolproof.*"

"*I'm confident that great care has been taken by our administration to ensure that only those people who deserve to be on the list are placed on it. We do everything possible to avoid false positives. There is a Redress Management System for those unfortunate few who were placed on the list in error by our predecessors.*"

"*Thank you so much, Mr. Attorney General, for your time on* Wolf News."

Von Solange smiled sweetly, but Sam thought it was a phony smile. "*We hope you can come back sometime—*"

Sam laughed and switched off his TV. The administration loved to blame all of its problems on the CIA, Bush II, global warming, Congress, the Republicans—just about anyone or anything except itself. So, the No-Fly List was an essential foolproof tool, eh? Sam had to think about that. Maybe a little research ... after all, he really had nothing to do since Edna passed and the kids moved to California. And besides, it might be fun.

• • •

Sam did not know how the government populated the No-Fly and Selectee Lists. So he turned to his computer. Internet browsing turned up the fact that the lists were the smaller components of a larger Terrorist Screening Center Database which contained about a half-million names. Apparently, the names in the database could come from anywhere; the standard was simple—any person who was known or reasonably suspected to be engaged in terrorism-related activity could be included. Any connection could snag someone. In some cases, no connection was necessary—for example, an innocent email address might be scooped up by a virus. Or, as in the case of the Nigerian, a parent, relative, neighbor, or friend might rat out someone. Of course, international communications with specific persons of interest, such as radical imams in Yemen, also triggered the attention of the authorities—although Sam believed political correctness made it a crapshoot whether the government did anything with the information.

Sam dragged an old blackboard out of a closet. He fetched an eraser and several hunks of white and yellow chalk from a drawer. It felt good to get back to work. At the top of the blackboard he wrote "Problem Statement" followed by "Put Mathis on the No-Fly List." Then he sketched out a "Plan of Attack."

Sam struggled as he inferred, based on years of experience and his knowledge of information technology, just what kind of items flagged the attentions of the Intelligence agencies. He knew they listened to damn near everything. He figured data collected by NSA, CIA, the Defense Intelligence Agency, and the FBI were fed into the National Counterterrorism Center in McLean, Virginia, buttressed by human intelligence reports—and ultimately stored at the TSA screening center. Perhaps the White House had its own set of agents, too, operating *a la* Nixon, and fingering political enemies.

Sam reasoned that NSA screened international telephone calls while the FBI watched for the purchase of weapons and bomb-making materials, such as ammonium nitrate and diesel fuel. He guessed the agencies passed on their data to the screening center which saved the data, correlated the disparate elements with a single individual, assigned a "weight" to each piece of information, and then collectively evaluated some index for each individual on the lists. The TSA, he thought with a smile, would use technical jargon like "risk coefficient."

Maintenance and update of the No-Fly List, he presumed, involved human interaction since it only contained 4,000 names. But that would be problematic for the Selectee List which contained 20,000 names. Between the Selectee List and the main database, Sam figured it would be an enormous effort to manage the data by hand. He computed that if two man-minutes were spent on each record per year, it would take eight man-years of effort just to examine the data once. Undoubtedly, data-mining algorithms were identifying names for the main database based on those risk coefficients.

Sam made a list of triggers that might place a name on the lists. Suspect email traffic—independent of the content—would lead to traffic analysis of the sender and recipients and serve as flags. Keywords and apparent code words would take more time to analyze automatically, but that could certainly be performed. The same analysis applied to voice traffic, and Sam believed NSA had the computational horsepower necessary to contribute to the database. Of course, the automated tracking of website browsing and activity at blogs was trivial. It generated a lot of data traffic for the agencies, but Sam suspected they could cope with the load.

Many key words weren't difficult to guess. He compiled a general list with words like bomb, airliner, jihad, virgins, gardens of paradise, al burak (Mohammed's horse), Mecca, prophet, ladder of light, al Qaeda, imam ....

In two hours Sam developed a list of 200 key words. After he heated a frozen three-cheese pizza for dinner, he returned to the blackboard and began to work on other threat indicators.

Sam planned a program using pre-paid cell phones. He'd simply call international numbers in places like Paris, Indonesia, Chechnya, and Palestine, and babble nonsense along with some of the key words. He planned to use the single word *tabernacle* with greater frequency as bait for the analysts and computer algorithms when they searched for common properties among the different threats.

A pristine laptop was necessary to fake an identity. The next morning Sam drove over to the White Plains Metro-North station and took the train to Grand Central Station. He descended to the subway and took the number 6 train to the City Hall/Brooklyn Bridge station. Sam walked over to J&R Electronics and purchased a Dell INSPIRON 15 notebook for $399, plus tax, in cash. Then he wandered the financial district and purchased multiple prepaid cell phones, also with cash. He picked up a cigar at his favorite tobacco shop on Warren Street and took the computer over to City Hall Park, to use the free wireless Internet hot-spot maintained by the city.

Sam shooed away two pigeons and plopped down on a bench in front of a large circular fountain. He lit the cigar and looked around. It was a lovely day and New York's finest were out in force. Sam could see some mounted policemen on the Broadway side of the park. A great day, he thought, to launch his project.

Sam intended to restrict himself to free Wi-Fi hot spots. Personal identification wasn't required, and deception was simple. He booted up his new machine and registered the operating system with Microsoft. He used Douglas L. Mathis as the user name with an address in Potomac, Maryland. He set up an Outlook Email account and established an email address for Douglas L. Mathis at gmail.com. He brought up his browser and surfed for radical Islamic websites; in the process, he collected contact email addresses for future use.

Sam rode the subway back to midtown. For the next stages in his plan, he purchased a handful of American Express and Visa gift cards at various establishments on Seventh Avenue and along Forty-Second Street. Then he wandered back to Grand Central Station, enjoyed the Oyster Bar on the mezzanine, and descended to the tracks for the return trip to White Plains.

As Sam sat on the train, he pondered his project time and cost estimate. His goal was to trigger TSA suspicions without spending too much money or being too obvious. The total project, he estimated, would cost about $10,000 and take three calendar months. He resolved to do it for less than $8,000.

A few days later, Sam drove to a bank in Tarrytown and used cash to purchase several $500 cashier's checks made out to Douglas L. Mathis. These would be endorsed to radical Muslim charities. He planned a series of purchases using the prepaid gift cards for ammunition, fertilizer and fuel, and reservations for suspicious airline itineraries. Sam programmed his laptop to randomly generate emails with code words selected from his list—with an increased frequency in the use of the word *tabernacle*.

For the next three months Sam had fun. He visited many municipal hot-spots, sent thousands of emails, browsed radical websites, ordered ammunition and fertilizer in Douglas L. Mathis' name with bogus shipping addresses, and sent donations to the charities. He booked multiple airline reservations in Mathis' name and occasionally fetched a few of the tickets at the airport, where he paid cash (wearing a disguise and using a phony New York State drivers license which he'd forged on his own computer system). For his *pièce de résistance*, Sam booked Douglas L. Mathis into a 747 pilot training school in Tempe, Arizona. Time flew.

• • •

The Present

The TSA Building on North Lynn Street in Roslyn, Virginia, received little maintenance. The building contents were so sensitive that cleaners were never allowed in the building. Trash and red burn-bags lined the walls and some stairwells. Dirty windows obscured the hallways. The elevators hissed, jerked, and groaned as they traveled from one grungy floor to another.

On the sixth floor, Jerry Allen, analyst, stared at a folder labeled "Top Secret Tabernacle." The contents made him nervous. Over the past three months, the volume of data in the file had doubled weekly. FLASH alert traffic from NSA and the FBI had poured in reporting suspicious emails, international telephone conversations, purchases of ammunition and bomb-making materials, and contributions to charities including Hamas and Hezbollah. The subject even had reserved a spot for pilot training. Several CIA agents in the Middle East and Bosnia had reported overhearing troubling conversations in cafés where the word *tabernacle* figured prominently. The problem was the data linked directly to one subject's name—Douglas L. Mathis. Jerry knew the attorney general had the same name. Jerry picked up the phone and called his supervisor, Joe Reacher.

"Joe, this is Jerry, over at the data center."

"Yeah, what's up? I'm in a big hurry. I got a date."

"Listen Joe, I'm getting a lot of red flags on a single individual—an American. I think I got to migrate him up to the No-Fly List."

"Is he on the Selectee List for advanced screening?"

"No … I ah … sort of have been sitting on this one. But there's a really disturbing code word that keeps popping up and—"

"So, put him on the No-Fly." Joe sounded impatient.

"Well, you see, there's this problem, His name is—"

"Look Jerry, if his risk coefficient is over 300 you know what to do. Say, what is his risk coefficient?"

"It's 1,300—I've never seen one so high. Shit, even Osama Bin Laden was only 1,250."

"Well then put him on the No-Fly."

"But Joe, his name is—"

"Fuck it, Jerry. Better safe than sorry. It's a no-brainer with that kind of risk coefficient. I got to go now. I'm meeting Dawn at Brunswick Bowl in Arlington."

"Okay, you got it. Give my best to Dawn."

Jerry cradled the phone, turned to his keyboard, and inserted Douglas L. Mathis into the No-Fly List.

• • •

The phone rang in the office of the TSA Emergency Operations Office. Al Fairbanks, the young duty officer, turned away from his on-line Sudoku game and picked up the handset. "TSA Emergency Ops. This is Fairbanks, Night Duty Officer."

"Fairbanks," shouted a voice, "this is Attorney General Douglas L. Mathis."

Fairbanks paused. Aw, Christ, someone was screwing with him. It was late and he didn't need this crap.

"Are you there, Fairbanks? This is—"

"Yes, sir, I heard. Please give me your field verification code."

"I don't need a field verification code, Fairbanks. I'm the attorney general!"

"Well, er … sir, I must have your code or—"

"Do you want to keep your job, Fairbanks?"

Fairbanks looked around, miserable. The place was deserted at 7:30 PM on the Fourth of July weekend. His supervisor, Melissa Beers, had gone to a wedding in Detroit—her sister had embraced Islam and was marrying a diplomat's son from Jordan. She'd called earlier saying she'd delayed her return—an issue with airport security. Melissa's boss, the director of Emergency Ops, was fishing in Oregon and everyone else had bolted for the fireworks display on the mall. But what the hell, Fairbanks figured, he'd play along—at least for a while. Maybe the guy really was the AG.

"Well, perhaps we can keep going," he said. "If it's unclassified, maybe … well, how can I help you?"

"Bring up the goddamn No-Fly List," roared the caller. "I've just been denied boarding in SFO; they said I'm on it."

Fairbanks blinked. The list was confidential, secret, damn, it was top secret—parts were sensitive compartmented intelligence codeword level, maybe above that. Fairbanks wasn't really sure. "Sir, that's classified information … I can't—"

"Don't give me that bull. How can it be classified if any redcap at an airport curb can pull it up?"

Fairbanks swallowed. "Sir, I'm obliged to tell you that there's a Redress Management System. If you've been misidentified, or believe you're on the No-

Fly List or Selectee List in error, you may apply to have that error corrected. Please submit—"

"Fairbanks, are you out of your mind? Just open the file and tell me if my name's in there."

"Well, er, okay, give me a minute." Fairbanks began to wonder if it was a joke or not. He opened up the No-Fly List on his desktop system and began to key in letters. "That's M-A-T-H-I-S-S right?"

"One *S*," yelled the caller.

"Got it. Yes, sorry, right, there is a Douglas L. Mathis in the file, address on Whites Ford Way in Potomac, Maryland. Is that … er … is that you, sir?"

"No." The caller paused. "That goddamned *L* … ah, well, yes, that's my address but that can't be. How'd I get on the list?"

"I can't tell you, sir." Fairbanks sweated and felt his stomach churn.

"What do you mean? Open up the record and give me the data."

"I can't do that."

"Well, then take me off the list."

Fairbanks' head began to burn with a migraine behind his right eye. He rubbed the eye and began to push his thumb into the eyeball. "I can't do that either, sir."

"Why not?"

"Well, for starters, even if you gave me your field verification code, I don't have the authority to change data elements in the files. And even if I did, the only way to remove a name is with a direct order from the attorney general."

"But I *am* the attorney general, you dimwit. Where's your director?"

"He's fishing on the Mackenzie River in Oregon, sir, for trout—cutthroat I believe."

"Call him. Now! I'll wait."

Fairbanks placed the call on hold and rang the emergency cell number for his director, Ray Elliott. After speaking for two minutes, he hung up and went back to the original call.

"Sir, are you still there?"

"Fairbanks, what'd he say?"

"He said that the rainbow are hitting but not too many cutthroat."

"Fairbanks!! I'm going to cut your balls off."

"Sorry, sir. I got distracted. I meant to say that he said he cannot give me classified information over an insecure line. Further, he reminded me that I must have your field verification code. Or, you can call him."

"Who's his deputy?"

"That would be Melissa Beers."

"Let me talk to her."

"Ah, well, that's a problem. We expected her back from Detroit this morning but there was a mix-up … er … some problem, at the airport."

"What's that?"

"It seems she was on the No-Fly List, too."

• • •

Sam Carruthers switched on his TV and tuned to *Wolf News*. On the screen, Greta von Solange beamed. Her more customary and sanctimonious mien had been replaced by something that looked akin to glee.

"*A* Wolf News *Alert!*" flashed across the TV screen. "*We have breaking news,*" said von Solange. "Wolf News *has learned that Attorney General Douglas L. Mathis was arrested by police at San Francisco International Airport. He was charged with assault with intent to commit great bodily harm on a TSA employee.*"

The camera zoomed in on a uniformed TSA employee sporting bandages on her throat, bruises on her face, and a large black eye. "*Lela Jones,*" continued von Solange, "*was treated by paramedics for several injuries and released. She said that the attorney general tried to strangle her when he leapt across an X-ray machine belt at SFO airport security. A White House spokesman said the president has been advised and believes it's a terrible misunderstanding. Republicans have called for a full and complete independent investigation. This is Greta von Solange,* Wolf News."

Junk Science

Jerome Maxwell Amundsen, chief executive officer of EcoFriendly Fuels (EFF), a company that produced ethanol, smoothed the jacket of his smartly tailored suit and smiled at the chairman of the House Subcommittee on Energy and Alternate Fuels. "I take it," said Amundsen, "that we have an agreement?"

The chairman, a Democratic congressman from Iowa, looked at the rest of the members of his subcommittee. It was a secret meeting, no staffers present, and the congressmen were dressed casually. Half the group was in the bag. Amundsen had offered each of them a half-million off the books, and the booze had flowed freely. The congressmen grinned and nodded their assent.

"It's a deal," said the chairman. "It may be the coldest winter in one hundred years, but we're concerned about global warming. Ethanol produced by EFF can provide the country with a source of renewable energy, a green solution to our nation's energy woes. Further, such energy contributes zero dollars in profits to our enemies in Venezuela and Iran. And, of course, there're your … ah … contributions."

Amundsen grinned inwardly. Who cared who got those profits if they weren't his? But damn right it was cold. Record snow fell in the Mid-Atlantic States, it was in the twenties in Florida where iguana dropped out of trees, aircraft dumped hay in Montana for the cattle and wildlife, and wolves roamed the suburbs of western towns in search of prey. Still, the cold meant nothing to the members of the subcommittee who were obsessed with global warming. And it meant nothing to Amundsen. One, ten, fifty cold years in a row—to him it simply was not possible to draw a general conclusion about warming—or cooling—based upon such limited data.

"Okay," said Amundsen, "the *contributions* will be wired tomorrow. I'm relying on you guys to extend the ethanol subsidies for another three years."

Amundsen walked over to the chairman and shook hands. Several of the congressmen wobbled to their feet and, after patting a few backs and some glad-handing, Amundsen departed. The meeting had convened in a cottage in the Florida Everglades Wildlife Management Area about twenty miles northwest of Hialeah. Amundsen had to return to his Gulfstream at the local airport. He climbed into his rental and began to drive south. An occasional snow flake fluttered down.

He turned on the heater, but it blew cold air. A chill went through him. He wore only his tropical Armani gray; he should've dressed in a heavy wool suit and brought his cashmere overcoat.

Still, he reflected, the meeting had been successful. The congressmen were like putty in his hands. Global warming was the rage; Al Gore had convinced the world that the oceans were going to boil. Even after the former VP apologized for his vote in favor of an ethanol tax credit—he'd said he'd done it for the farmers of Tennessee—the people still believed him. They'd given the former vice president a Nobel Prize and an Academy Award for junk science.

Amundsen checked his watch. His wife expected him in Omaha—damn, it was twenty below there—in three hours. His crew would be warming up the Gulfstream. He turned on his wipers as more snow fell and his headlights bounced off the glazed road. He slowed a bit; the radio had reported patches of black ice on the highways.

Yes sir, thought Amundsen, junk science was making him a billionaire. With the extension of the blender's tax credit, the fools would continue to pay him forty-five cents a gallon to produce ethanol—which actually contributed to greater national energy consumption. After processing and distilling the corn and transporting the alcohol to market, the net unit cost per BTU was higher than for gasoline. The net contribution to the carbon footprint was greater, too.

The subsidy, combined with a tariff of fifty-four cents a gallon imposed on imported ethanol, and the federal law that demanded an increase in the production of domestic ethanol each year, meant EFF had it made.

Who cared if the ethanol production sucked up forty percent of the nation's corn supply and generated giant algae blooms in the Gulf of Mexico? The politicians wanted global warming. It was a great populist cause, and the game was afoot. Gore had said the evidence was firm that the earth was heating up. It was statistically valid, said some scientists. The United Nations (UN) had agreed and cooked its books to support the desired conclusions.

Forget that the UN made a 315 year error in its forecast of when a Himalayan glacier would melt. Never mind that the former head of the UN's puppet climate research center at the University of East Anglia had said on *BBC* that the earth may have been warmer in medieval days. So what if Greenland once was warm enough to attract Viking settlements?

More snow drifted down. Amundsen turned on the defroster and rear window heater. The forced air began to lose its freezing bite. He increased the speed of the wipers as snow melted on the windshield. The wipers left long streaks that blurred his vision.

Good heavens, he thought—if you ignored forest fires, asteroid strikes, and volcanic eruptions, the earth had begun to warm up when the first caveman lit a fire. That was global warming, all right. But what about those pesky ice ages between then and now? How the heck, he mused, could the

UN's and Gore's data be statistically valid? The reliability of a statistical sample, or the confidence that one could place in the results, varied with the square root of the size of the sample. And the East Anglia guy had admitted that over the past fifteen years there'd been no "statistically significant" warming. How could the people understand? Amundsen laughed. Half the country was statistically illiterate—hell, maybe ninety percent. Most PhDs couldn't tell the difference between the average and the mean, let alone the median.

Almost one-third of the population of the U.S. couldn't balance its check books. Few people knew what a sample or a square root was. An entire conference at Copenhagen had been dedicated to global warming based on samples of 50 to 200 years of historical data. But there were known weather cycles that lasted 20,000, 40,000, and 100,000 years. There might be longer cycles not yet discovered. No one knew what had caused the dinosaurs to disappear. Lots of theories: an asteroid-induced ice age, blight in the food supply, overeating, a dinosaur pandemic; but no one really knew. Maybe, just maybe, it simply became too cold—or too hot. The longer cycles, which could increase the confidence in the analysis by ten to thirty times, had been dismissed for political reasons. Without consideration of those cycles, there was little basis to conclude anything. But that didn't matter to the politicians. It was just the latest version of the Big Lie. Still, warming up or not, the ethanol subsidies were a goldmine for EFF.

Amundsen gripped the wheel tighter. Damn, it was hard to see. Was that a deer on the road? Jesus, it was a huge cat. And black—it must be one of those endangered Florida panthers. Looking for food? Was it going to move? There was no shoulder here, just forest and swamp. He hit a patch of black ice. The car began to slide.

• • •

Amundsen groaned. He smelled gasoline. His mind wandered. The windshield was broken. Blood covered his forehead. His car had slid off the road, barreled through the tall Florida grass, and slammed into a tree. As he became more alert, he realized he should get out of the car; it might explode. His right arm hurt, and it took an effort before he disconnected his seat belt and opened the door. He limped out of the car. There was frost on all the ferns, sheets of ice that looked like glass on puddles, icicles on the trees. It was cold!

He reached into his pocket for his cell phone. No signal! Disoriented, he tried to backtrack through the weeds trampled by the car. A roar erupted behind him. The panther! Amundsen began to run—left, right, and left again.

He heard another roar and turned around expecting the cat to attack. Then he heard a large splash in the swamp, and the panther retreated into the bush. Amundsen didn't want to consider what kind of a threat would drive off a panther in the Everglades. He turned and began to run again. Amundsen tripped over the root of a cypress tree and banged his head on a rock. He felt himself slipping away. He tried to crawl but lost consciousness.

Several inches of snow accumulated before Amundsen opened his eyes. He lay in a puddle of water, but he was warm. Snow lay on a thin layer of ice that had formed around him on the surface of the puddle. Why wasn't he cold? It felt like he was sweating. He struggled out of his suit jacket and began to crawl. Amundsen wasn't sure in which direction to go. Ten minutes later, he found his suit jacket again; he'd returned to the same puddle. It was hotter, he thought, and he was tired. Amundsen closed his eyes … just a short nap.

• • •

Two weeks later, the press assembled in the Oval Office. A White House pressroom-pool camera was focused on the signature page of the new HR 1745 Alternate Energy Bill, which sat in the center of the president's desk. Half a dozen ball-point pens, emblazoned with the presidential seal, were lined up next to the document. Several members of the House Subcommittee on Energy and Alternate Fuels hovered behind the desk. A large American flag dwarfed the six other flags that stood behind the congressmen.

The president and the chairman of the subcommittee were huddled in the corner. The president, taller than the chairman, leaned forward and the two men whispered.

"You say the man froze to death? In Florida?" asked the president.

The chairman nodded, eyes darting left and right. Sweat gleamed on his forehead.

"Well, maybe we should name the bill after him."

"That sounds like a good idea, Mr. President. But I don't think you should report he froze to death."

"Why not? The people have a right to know, don't they? My campaign was dedicated to transparency."

"Mr. President, we're engaged in a massive rewrite of America's energy policy. If the people begin to doubt global warming, can you imagine what would happen to our fundraisers? I'm talking about the entire Democratic slate in the next election. Further, we certainly don't need any serious scientific scrutiny—we're already on shaky grounds."

The president nodded.

The chairman dropped his voice. "And, Mr. President, can I have a moment after the signing ceremony? With the increase in the demand for ethanol, we need to increase the production of corn. That means more subsidies."

"And that means more pork bellies, doesn't it?" asked the president.

"I hope you can support it. Iowa's the leading producer of hogs in the country."

The president grinned. "Perhaps I should short pork bellies futures."

Both men walked back to the desk. Everyone shook hands and the president sat, picked up a pen, and looked at the camera. The lights came on and the broadcast commenced.

"*Good evening, my fellow Americans. We're here tonight with the chairman and members of the House Subcommittee on Energy and Alternate Fuels.*" The president looked directly into the camera. "*As you know, we inherited a serious global warming problem from the previous administration. Nevertheless, after eight years of neglect, and despite serious resistance from the minority, I'm pleased to report that Congress has adopted legislation to expand our use of renewable energy and thereby moderate global warming. This will increase green job growth and reduce our reliance on foreign energy sources. It will make America more secure for future generations. Your children and grandchildren will look back on this historic moment with gratitude. I'm proud that the Sierra Club has hailed my administration's first year as the best year on the environment of any president since Teddy Roosevelt. This bill furthers our accomplishments.*"

The president signed the bill using the multiple pens and passed one to each of the members of the subcommittee. He smiled again at the camera. "*I have just signed the Jerome Maxwell Amundsen Memorial Alternate Energy Bill. I know I speak for the nation when I say we regret the untimely death of this man who inspired all of us to add ethanol to our arsenal of weapons against global warming. We need more Americans like him. Good night … and God bless the United States of America.*"

Patient Zero

The classified memos arrived on January 27, 2009, a week after the president's inauguration. The directors of the National Security Agency, Central Intelligence Agency, National Bureau of Standards, the National Aeronautics and Space Administration, and the Social Security Administration were directed to connect their massive computer systems to an Internet IP address for a Top Secret COSMIC application developed by the Council of Economic Advisors. The connections were to be maintained interrupt-free for seventy-two hours ...

• • •

February 18, 2009, Chicago

Bob's Kosher Vienna Red Hots sat on a small gravel lot at the corner of Division Street and Washtenaw Avenue, one block west of Humboldt Park. Bob's hotdogs were popular with high school students, the local neighborhood's residents, and the medical staff from St. Mary of Nazareth Hospital Center. Bob Rosen had purchased the business after he walked away from a life insurance practice which had collapsed during the economic downturn.

Maybe, thought Bob, Jeannie had been right when she called the hotdog business a loser. His wife, before she'd passed, called him "My Willy," after Willy Loman, the character in *Death of a Salesman*. Loman had been an outstanding salesman, but his kids considered him a bust just before he retired. And, in his day, Rosen had been a great salesman; he'd sold shoes, aluminum siding—*you'll be the model house in the neighborhood and you'll get a forty percent discount*—automobiles, driveway re-paving, real estate, cemetery plots, and finally, insurance. Unfortunately the red hots business was lousy. And, Bob was in hock to his bank, late on an installment payment for his equipment.

Bob, seventy, was tall, bald, and pudgy, turning to fat. He drove up to his hotdog stand and parked his 1966 Cadillac—a powder blue two-door hardtop with a cracked dashboard, broken antenna, and long tailfins. He crunched over to the front door in his old Air National Guard (ANG) boots. Bob wore faded jeans, a cheap gray sweater from Sears, and a black Bogner parka. The Bogner was his pride and joy; he'd bought it the previous spring from a thief on Division Street with the thirty-four bucks he owed the bank.

The hotdog stand was shaped like a railroad car with windows on one side. A large, vertical sign mounted on the roof, illuminated by floodlights, sported the word "BOB'S." The cooking area was a narrow rectangular section that faced a service window for walk-up traffic. Occasionally, customers drove over the gravel and parked in front of the window. A counter, chipped and stained with old cigarette burns, stood opposite the cooking area, with four bar stools for walk-in customers. Two old round Formica tables and four cheap wooden folding chairs served as the "dining room." A small countertop in the passageway which led to the rear offered condiments, napkins, and plastic flatware; next to it was a storage room with a large sliding door. At the end of the passageway was a common restroom on one side and a large, chipped sink and potato-peeling machine on the other.

When Bob unlocked the door a rat squeaked, scampered over his boots, and ran out of the stand. Damn, he thought, he should have whacked the rodent with the baseball bat he kept under the counter. Rats had plagued Bob's business since the homeless established an encampment in Humboldt Park, just off California Avenue. Bob had complained to the city's Public Health Department. But everyone in Chicago and the state of Illinois had their hands out. Since Bob refused to pay bribes, the rats remained in the stand. He shook his head in disgust and hung his Bogner on a coat hook by the entrance.

Bob switched on the outside lights and pulled some hotdogs out of the refrigerator. When he turned on the gas burners for the deep fryer, he noticed another rat floating belly-up in the cold French fry grease. Bob poked at the carcass with his tongs, and it rolled over. Its gray fur was covered with yellow, congealed oil.

Bob always tried to make an extra buck, and he wasn't about to replace the grease; he figured he'd just heat it more than usual. This behavior was consistent with a scam he ran from time to time. Sometimes Bob would drop a day-old hotdog onto the gravel outside the service window. When an especially drunk or obnoxious customer drove up to the window, Bob would pass over a bun with all the trimmings, but no hotdog. When the customer complained, Bob would lean out the window and point at the hotdog embedded in the dirt and gravel. "Must have dropped it, partner," he'd say. "Want another one? That'll be another three bucks." Sometimes he felt bad about the scam. If the driver's eyes filled with tears, Bob would feel some remorse and give him a hotdog. But, if the customer's eyes filled with rage, or he became louder and swore, Bob stiffed him and watched him drive off.

Bob grabbed the dead rat with the tongs and looked furtively out the window. He heard distant sirens. A Chicago Transit Authority bus thundered down Division Street. Bob wondered how to dispose of the dead rat. He was distracted when a black Ford drove onto his gravel lot. The car kicked up a cloud of dust that settled on Bob's Cadillac. A large man climbed out of the sedan. He wore a dark blue suit and brown cowboy boots. His hair was gray, cropped short like a Marine's. His jacket was open and Bob spotted a badge on the man's belt next to a large handgun. Bob dropped the rat back into the grease, wedged it on the bottom with the tongs, started the boiler, and turned up the gas.

He put on an apron and switched on the television set, a seventeen-inch old Sony mounted on an angle-iron bracket in the corner. The TV was tuned to a *WGN LiveNews* report. A Chicago alderman, the former managing partner of a prominent law firm on LaSalle Street, had been arrested for soliciting sex with a minor in a men's room in Terminal K at Chicago's O'Hare International Airport. Bob turned away from the TV, slid the service window open, turned on the space heater, and threw a half-dozen hotdogs into the boiler. He dropped some buns into the steamer as the man with the badge walked in.

Bob turned to greet the man. "Can I get you a hotdog? If you want fries, it'll take a while. I need to peel some potatoes." Bob knew he wouldn't have time to blanch the fries—cook them halfway and let them sit an hour or so. But, given the rat, that didn't seem to him like a big deal.

"Take your time," said the man. "Are you Bob?"

Bob hated the question. Everyone asked if he was Bob. Maybe, he mused, he should have called the place Willy's. Jeannie would have seen the joke in that. He shook his head in frustration. "I'll be back in a few minutes."

Bob went into the storage room, grabbed a twenty-five pound bag of Idaho potatoes, and dragged it over to his potato-peeling machine. It looked like a cross between a Franklin stove and clothes dryer. He pulled the handle on the cast-iron door. It squeaked open, exposing a hollow perforated cylinder with a rough inner surface. Bob ripped open the potato sack, threw in a handful of spuds, opened a water valve, and turned on the machine. The cylinder began to spin, abrading the skins off the potatoes. A few minutes later, Bob turned off the machine, closed the valve, and removed the potatoes. He placed a few, one-by-one, in a press, pulled a long handle that forced the skinned potatoes through a rectangular wire grid, and cut a bunch of standard-sized fries. He dropped the fries into a basket and brought it back to the cooking area.

The man with the badge was watching the *WGN LiveNews* broadcast. A reporter was interviewing a young airport cop who'd arrested the alderman. "*These charges will stick,*" said the cop.

"People never learn, do they, Bob?" asked the man.

"Learn what?" Bob retrieved his tongs and dropped the basket into the hot grease over the dead rat. It was beginning to smell like cooked meat inside the stand. Bob hoped it wasn't too noticeable and turned on a small fan.

"*He's guilty as hell*," said the cop on TV. "*He even apologized*."

The man pointed at the television set. "Americans, Bob—you're Bob, right? That's your Caddy out there. Americans are God-fearing people. They don't countenance abnormal behavior."

Bob was unsettled by the reference to his car. Why, he wondered, did this guy care whose car it was. "What? You mean the alderman? Shit, he's a politician. They're all abnormal. At least he ain't taking bribes." Bob checked the boiler. The dogs were hot. He pulled a bun out of the steamer. "How do you like your dog?"

"No hurry, Bob. You're Bob, correct?"

The man's persistence aggravated Bob. "Look, you want a dog or not?"

"Mustard, all the trimmings, hold the peppers. Say Bob, do you know how banks make money?"

"Banks make money by screwing the customer. That's why bankers always live in the big house at the top of the hill." Bob slipped a hotdog in the bun and smeared mustard over it. He reached for the tomatoes, onions, and relish. He wished the guy was outside the service window so he could stiff him on the hotdog.

"Not that kind of money, Bob. Banks make money loaning money. They give you a thousand, say, for that potato-peeling machine in the back; you buy it, and the seller deposits the thousand in his bank. That bank sets aside fifty bucks or so for its reserves, and then loans out the remaining nine-fifty to someone else, and they buy something—before you know it $10,000 have been created."

"That's interesting, but who gives a shit?"

"You should, Bob. Your potato-peeling machine represents a lot of money."

"So what?" Bob was unimpressed. He thought his machine was a piece of junk; he'd used a professional machine once in the Illinois ANG when he peeled 2,000 pounds of potatoes in one day. Bob thought that machine probably cost a hundred grand.

"I'm talking big bucks, Bob—about a trillion."

"Who are you anyway? What's with the badge?"

The man smiled and took out a cell phone. He pushed a speed-dial button, paused, and said, "Now!" He looked at Bob grimly. "I'm a federal marshal, Bob, and I have an arrest warrant with your name on it."

Bob figured the guy was jerking his chain, but his aggravation had morphed into anger. "You want fries with that dog? Usually they're an extra buck but, for you, today I got a special—no charge. Arrest warrant for what? I'm not an alderman and I don't do little boys."

Bob noticed the sirens again. They were louder.

"I'm not talking about little boys. The real question, Bob, is whether you're going to stand up for your country and take your medicine like a man."

Bob pulled the basket out of the grease and dropped the fries into a shallow tray under a heat lamp. The extra-crispy dead rat began to surface. Bob put more potatoes into the basket and dropped it back in the grease. The rat was re-submerged. Bob salted the cooked fries, put a handful on a sheet of wax paper in a plastic basket, added the hotdog, and pushed the basket towards the marshal. "That'll be three dollars." Bob turned up the speed on the fan.

"Don't I get a pickle?"

Bob grabbed a pair of pickle slices out of a tray, wrapped them in a sheet of wax paper, and pushed them across the counter.

"Thanks." The marshal took a bite of the sandwich. "That's good, Bob. Say, are you familiar with the term 'Patient Zero?'"

"I ain't good with arithmetic."

The marshal smiled. "It means the primary case in an epidemic, like the first person that caught AIDS from chimpanzees, and then spread it around."

Bob looked at the TV. The scene had shifted to City Hall and the alderman was being interviewed. "*I was in a hurry to catch a flight,*" he protested. "*That cop at O'Hare told me all I had to do was apologize to the kid. I didn't do anything. So I figured okay, I'd apologize and get out of there.*"

Bob pointed at the TV with his tongs. "You want an epidemic—get him."

"*It was entrapment,*" claimed the alderman.

"It's a tasty pickle, too, Bob. But I used AIDS as an example. Americans are peace-loving people, but when the public gets through with you, you'll wish you had AIDS."

"What the hell are you talking about?"

"Don't you want to know about my warrant, Bob?"

"Stick your warrant. I ain't done nothin'. I pay my taxes, and I stop for stop signs. I haven't been to a hooker in forty years."

"Yes, Bob, but we think you're a terrorist."

Red and blue lights splashed on the walls of the hotdog stand. The wails of sirens slipped away, and two Chicago Police Department blue-and-white squad cars jumped the curb and slammed onto the gravel. A large van with *WGN LiveNews* markings pulled up alongside the curb. It had a satellite dish and an antenna array on its roof. Doors slammed, and several policemen and a news team milled about.

"You think I'm a terrorist?" challenged Bob. "What are you, a comedian?"

"Those are real police, Bob. This is not funny."

"I'm beginning to think you're a hallucination."

"Who do you work for, Bob? Are you a Muslim? A sleeper agent? Don't lie. We have the evidence. You're our 'Patient Zero.'"

"I started an epidemic?" Bob didn't feel sick. He wondered if strokes began with hallucinations.

"Bob, the government has the goods. We've backtracked through all the transactions that led to the collapse of the American economy."

"Good for you."

"Yeah, well, you remember when you missed the payment on the loan for your potato-peeling machine? Last March?"

"Big fucking deal! Rome's burning, the assholes in Congress are pissing away trillions, and you're hassling me over a thirty-four dollar payment?"

"Bob, you took out a second mortgage for that loan from Ashland Savings and Loan. Ashland syndicated the loan and sold it to Harris Trust. Harris leveraged it with other real estate paper and sold it to Freddie Mac; then they bought credit default swaps from AIG— need I say more? You, Bob, it was your missed payment—it was collateralized by your first mortgage, and that was under water. It triggered a default at Ashland Savings and Loan which launched defaults up the line. The banks ran out of reserves, Bob—they'd loaned too much money to deadbeats like you. Even Société Générale in France and Deutsche Bank in Germany took a beating. And you started it. What'd you do with the money, Bob?"

Bob looked at his Bogner. The payment money had gone to the thief. No way was he giving up the parka. "You want the potato-peeling machine, take it."

"The public doesn't want your machine, Bob. It wants its money. Pay it back. It's that, or your neck."

Bob was speechless. The guy was a lunatic, but those *were* Chicago cops out there. Maybe he needed a lawyer. "Do I need a lawyer?"

"You could ask the alderman. I suspect he'll be out of work soon."

"Yeah, sure." On the other hand, Bob hoped, maybe the cops just wanted a hotdog. Jeannie had always said he was too paranoid.

"You've done terrible damage to America, Bob," said the marshal. "The public demands accountability. It's too bad for you, but you're the guy. You're the proverbial butterfly that flexed its wings in Hong Kong and started a hurricane in the Atlantic. It's time to come to Jesus."

"So what's the crime?" demanded Bob. "I missed a payment? There's no debtors' prison in America."

"It's bank fraud, Bob. You lied on your loan application—you overstated how many hotdogs you sold. Did you do it deliberately? Don't you care about the babies who can't get their daily milk?"

"This is all a joke, right? And you still owe me three bucks—make it four, the fries ain't free." Bob figured screw the smell, and turned off the fan.

Bob was startled when bright lights streamed into the hotdog stand. A *WGN LiveNews* reporter with a microphone and a cameraman had snuck up to the service window. Bob heard, "*This is Angie Baker reporting live …*" on the TV. He turned away from the lights and saw himself framed in the service window on the Sony.

"Huh?" Bob looked at the marshal and back at the TV. He saw the back of his head, the marshal smiling grimly, and his Bogner on the hook. A mirror on the wall, with the words *Diet Coke,* bounced the camera lights back into his eyes. He blinked.

On the screen, Angie Baker was excited. "*Federal agents at this moment are …*"

Something ran across Bob's foot. He looked down and saw another rat. He bent down and reached for his Louisville Slugger.

"*… effecting an arrest—gun!*" Angie shrieked. "*Oh, my God—he's reaching for a gun. A shotgun …*"

The marshal pulled his handgun out of his belt holster and fired three times. Bob dropped to the floor with three slugs in his chest, his white apron stained with blood. The marshal, weapon in hand, peeked around the counter. The news team's lights illuminated Bob's hands clutched around a baseball bat.

Two Chicago cops ran into the hotdog stand.

"Someone yelled 'gun,'" said the marshal, pointing at the bat.

"Yeah, we heard it too," said one cop. He bent down and felt for a pulse. He shook his head. "This guy's dead." The cop retrieved the baseball bat and pointed his thumb at Angie Baker. "It was that fool reporter—but it was a good shoot. Not to worry, she'll definitely cover her ass."

The marshal yelled, "Turn that camera off." When the lights faded, he faced Angie. "This was the guy, but I guess we'll never know who he worked for—al-Qaeda, even—this was too clever, triggering another depression. And you folks need to leave now. This is a crime scene."

As Angie dragged the cameraman away, she muttered, "Did you hear what that guy in the suit said? Al-Qaeda? Wow!"

The marshal slid the service window down. He grabbed Bob's Bogner off the hook by the door and draped it over Bob's head.

"Hey," said one of the cops, "let's grab a hotdog."

"Why not?" The marshal lifted the French fries basket. "With fries, too. Hey, what's this thing floating in the grease?"

• • •

Harvey Wachowski was at home in the Bridgeport section of Chicago—not too far, he used to brag, from where the old mayor Richard J. Daley had lived. Bridgeport was a solid white working-class neighborhood, Harvey's oasis in the predominantly black south side of Chicago. Harvey was home a lot these days; he'd been laid off from his job at Caterpillar Tractor—where he'd welded forks on forklifts. Harvey was depressed, wondering how he'd make his next mortgage payment. Louise—"Leesie"—was in the kitchen opening a can of Spam for dinner. Harvey reached for his beer and clicked his TV remote to a *WGN LiveNews* broadcast.

He recognized the reporter, Angie Baker. She looked startled when a live segment commenced after a Budweiser commercial. But she composed herself and smiled for the camera. "*Tom, yes … we're here, live, at Bob's Kosher Vienna Red Hots on Division Street. As I was saying before the break, Federal agents have dispatched the man responsible for the economic mess. Bob Rosen …*"

Harvey was outraged. He blurted, "Fucking Jew!"

Angie waved an arm for emphasis. "*… was shot in his hotdog stand when he reached for what agents thought was a shotgun. It turned out to be a baseball bat. Chicago police have called it a righteous shooting. We can attest to that ….*"

"Leesie," shouted Harvey, "they got the sum'bitch!"

"How's that, Harv?"

"They got the guy who cost me my job."

"Really?"

"Shhhh. There's more—"

"*… We can thank President Obama,*" continued Angie. "*The threat to the nation has been removed.* WGN LiveNews *has learned that last month the president ordered the secretary of the Treasury to find the person or persons that triggered the economic mess. The Council of Economic Advisors, with the assistance of unnamed federal agencies' computers, worked backwards through the avalanche of bank defaults. They identified Rosen as the man who launched it all when he defaulted on a loan from Ashland Savings and Loan. He's been identified as an al-Qaeda operative.*"

"Did you hear that, Leesie?" yelled Harvey. "The rat bastard was a Jew banker working with the camel jockeys. It was an international Jewish conspiracy."

"You want catsup with your Spam, Harv?"

"Mustard, Hon." Harvey swilled his beer and turned back to the TV.

Angie smiled at the camera. "*The public can rest easy again. And, you heard it here first! Only on* WGN LiveNews. *This is Angie Baker, reporting live, from Bob's Kosher Vienna Red Hots. Back to you, Tom.*"

Sanctuary City

Al Jackson, a criminal trial lawyer, stared at the woman across the small table. They sat at the Buena Vista, a popular bar and restaurant near Ghirardelli Square on the northern tip of San Francisco. Tippi Sohn, a paralegal and graduate from Colorado State, enjoyed her bacon and eggs—over easy. A streak of strawberry jelly left over from the rye bread—dry—on her chin caught Al's attention. Tippi ate with enthusiasm. Al knew she always ate after sex, and God knew she needed food. Al shifted uncomfortably with mixed feelings. On one hand, Al knew he shouldn't stick his pen in the company inkwell; on the other hand they called Tippi "Pike" at the office—after Pike's Peak near Denver, the mile-high city. Some of the guys in the office figured Tippi did a mile a month in bed. Al wasn't sure who was being exploited—the men or Tippi—but Jimmy Travis, one of the partners at Al's firm, Caruthers and Sturm in the Russ Building on Montgomery Street, had sworn Tippi ran him into the ground after she'd encouraged him to take three times the normal dose of male enhancement drugs.

Tippi was forty-two, long-legged, still slender, with a perky nose, flashy black eyes, and streaked blonde hair. Al, two years younger, wondered why she liked him. He was short, dumpy, and thick around the middle, with a big bald spot on top. He needed a pop of Jack and a dose of Viagra to keep it up. When he'd asked her why she found him attractive, she'd replied, "Don't worry, Honey. It's not attraction. I just need a few more laps."

Al shrugged off the thought and turned to his fried eggs and morning steak—medium. The food was good, but his thoughts focused on his poor batting average in criminal court. He looked up when Tippi flashed a *San Francisco Daily Reporter* headline at him. The headline read: "SF Rejects Federal Guidelines for Felonious Illegal Minors."

"Al, what do you think of this?" she said. "San Francisco has ratcheted up this Sanctuary City crap. The district attorney says she won't prosecute or deport any illegal under the age of sixteen. The city has set aside $22 million for half-way house treatment. I guess the fools believe they can rehabilitate and return them to society—to make a contribution. Ha!"

"Lemme see that." Al grabbed the newspaper and scanned the story. "The mayor," he said, "has directed the cops, hospitals, churches, and all medical practitioners to ignore federal and state law? That's nuts! They're required to notify only the San Francisco DA's office of any assaults, rapes, murders, and armed robberies committed by an illegal minor."

"Read on," laughed Tippi. "It gets more interesting."

Al nodded. "Damn," he said. "Those authorities that notify the Feds or state could have their badges or medical credentials lifted. They may also be subject to civil liabilities for failing to protect the rights of the illegal."

"What's next?" smirked Tippi. "Before you know it, we won't be able to kiss asses anymore—unless they're illegal."

Al laughed. "The freaks are in control of the city. We should use Sherman tanks to navigate around the drunks and panhandlers. But who knows what the Feds or the governor will do—probably zip. Screw it."

Al's cell phone rang.

"Al? It's Hymie. I got a case for you."

Hymie Macpherson was Al's boss and the gofer for Bill Carruthers, the senior managing partner at the firm. If Hymie was calling, thought Al, the firm probably wanted a loser since his monthly batting average was only .250 over at the criminal courthouse.

"Yeah? What's up?"

"Last night, in the bushes near the Marina Green, a girl got attacked. She was beaten, raped, and sodomized. Her name's Catherine Gollub. Recognize the name?"

Al did. The Gollubs, an old and socially prominent San Francisco family, owned about ten percent of the swank Pacific Heights neighborhood. Sy Gollub's grandfather had made a fortune selling cable cars to the city.

"How old is the girl?" asked Al.

"It might be a 'was,'" said Hymie. "She's almost seventeen, a cheerleader, and plays the leading attack position on the Hollyhook High lacrosse team. She was hemorrhaging when they took her to the county hospital and may not make it. Her father wanted to take her to a private hospital in Marin, but she's too weak to move. It's touch and go."

"So what do you want me for?"

"Bill Caruthers and Sy Gollub are poker buddies. They play in a friendly game each week, in the back room over at First Church of Christ on Washington Square. Gollub asked Carruthers what to do, and Bill promised we'd take care of it. He offered to make sure the rat that did it gets life—if the girl dies, burned."

Al frowned. The legal profession disapproved of those who lost a case deliberately. He needed time to think about the request. "That's some friendly game," he said. "Father Timothy told me Carruthers took Gollub for a hundred long last week. He feels a little guilty, eh?"

"Look Al, we got to do the right thing here. You know Carruthers will take care of you."

The right thing, my foot, thought Al. "You're really asking me to lose, aren't you?"

"God moves in mysterious ways, Al. Go see the creep. He's in county jail on rape and attempted murder."

"What's his name?"

"Pancho Villa."

"What? You're kidding. Is he legal?"

"Legal as can be. A minor, born and bred in Lodi in 1994. He has some, ah … adjustment problems."

"What a surprise."

"Listen Al, Bill Caruthers called Judge Mason over at Superior Court and asked him to assign the case to us on a *pro bono* basis. The judge knows Gollub through the St. Francis Yacht Club. He was, uh … agreeable … you might say. We needed to meet our quota anyway, so the Public Defender ain't in the case."

So the fix was in all the way up to the judge. "Ain't that convenient?" said Al. But maybe he could get out of the assignment. "Damn, Hymie, I got something going right now. It might be a few hours before I can get there."

"Cut the shit, Al. Tell Pike to get back to the office. Jimmy Travis was asking about her. Now, since Villa's a citizen, the DA will prosecute. Besides, Gollub pumped a few thou into her campaign fund last year and she owes him."

"All right, I'm on it. I'll file an appearance and see him in an hour."

"That's the spirit."

Al watched a Hyde and Powell cable car, carrying a flock of tourists, lurch its way up the hill. He scanned the *Daily Reporter* and found a small article about the attack on page A7, buried next to three Massage and Public Baths ads. The article had the newspaper's usual typos and copy-edit errors, but Al was able to decipher it:

ATTEMPTED MURDER AND RAPE NEAR MARINA GREENE

(San Francisco) Police arrested a minor, who's name was withheld, for assault, rape, and attemted murder yesterday. The incident took place in the bushes near the Marina Green kiosk. It's alleged the young man raped a teenage girl repeatedly. The victim was also brutally sodomnized and lost a great deal of blood. Assistant District Attorney (ADA) Henry Hu said he plans to try the assailant as an adult and will file first degree murder charges if the girl dies. Bail was set at $50,000.

Goddamnit, thought Al, if he lost this one his monthly batting average would drop to .200. Despite that, Caruthers would probably promote him. Then the rest of the lawyers in the firm would hate him. The only girl he'd get would be Pike—and she'd screw a picket fence if a snake were on it. Worse, no other firm would ever hire him for criminal law, his only true love. He had to mount some form of defense.

Al threw down the newspaper, told Pike to head back to the Russ Building, and grabbed the next cable car for Market Street. He'd have to walk to the jail, but it was a beautiful day in the city. If he was lucky, he wouldn't step in any shit, and no bum would spit in his ear.

• • •

A deputy escorted a shackled Pancho Villa into the consultation room. Pancho had a dark complexion, filthy fingernails, torn tennis shoes, and a bump on his head. His pants sagged at his hips; a black T-shirt sported the picture of a snarling tiger. Blood stains spotted his pants and shirt. Pancho, skinny, was five foot six and had a shit-eating grin on his face. Tats ran up and down his arm; the most prominent one said "Mom" and had an arrow through a drawing of a heart. One front tooth was missing.

The guard removed the shackles and departed.

"Yo, you my lawyer?" said Pancho. He farted.

"That's me, Al Jackson. You get the cream of the crop." Al waved his hand in the air to relieve the stench.

"Bullshit, man. The cops in here told me you're the worst lawyer in Frisco. Where's the Public Defender?"

"Listen, asshole, the judge assigned my firm. We're doing this *pro-bono*—"

"Pro-boner? What's that, you ram it up my ass?"

Pancho's smile irritated Al.

"What were you doing there?"

Pancho grinned some more. "There's always an unlocked car in that lot. I was, you know, looking—"

"Tell me what happened."

"There was a bunch of girls. They were playing some game with sticks. Then I guess she hurt her ankle or something. The rest of her team went running—you know, to the Golden Gate Bridge—and she sat down, on that little beach. She was dressed in those sexy shorts that screamed 'screw me.' As I got close to her, she stood and swung her booty around—a nice tight little ass. What could I do? I didn't want to do it but hey, we're talking hot snatty-poo here. She asked for it."

Al covered his eyes and dropped his head. The kid was nuts—an aggressive, violent, and vicious predator. Not a shred of remorse. No way would a jury find the animal innocent. Hell, Al wouldn't even have to try hard to satisfy Caruthers.

"Do you realize that you're in deep doo?" said Al. "That girl with the booty you attacked—make that the rich white girl with the powerful daddy you attacked—was viciously assaulted. She may die. The city will want your head."

"My head?" asked Pancho. "What, where you from? They don't prosecute anyone in this city for nothin'. The judge can slap my wrist, and I'll do a year in juvie with my eyes closed."

Al looked at Pancho with disgust. "They don't prosecute illegal minors in this city, you moron. You're an American and you picked the wrong target. Now, tell me about yourself. I need some ammo if we're going to have a chance."

Pancho yawned and began his tale: He was fifteen, born in a trailer. His father had been an illegal migrant worker who'd died in a van accident on California Highway 99 with thirteen other men. Pancho's mother was from South Carolina, a cotton picker, who'd eventually become a prostitute. The kid had dropped out of school in fifth grade. He had a history of petty crime, car theft, and arson. He came to San Francisco a year ago to live with his uncle, Hernandez Villa, a naturalized citizen in the Hunters Point district. The uncle owned a small bungalow in an alley off Cochrane Street.

"Have you ever been arrested in San Francisco?"

"Is a duck's ass water-tight?" Pancho grinned and picked his nose. "B-and-E. I got out of Glenwood Juvenile Detention Center last week after twelve days of a three month stint. Some judge said overcrowding—so they released us nonviolent ones early." Pancho looked at the snot on his finger and smeared it on the table.

"This one's serious, Pancho," warned Al who shook his head in disgust. "They may prosecute you as an adult. And state prison ain't juvie or county jail. They'll eat you for breakfast, spit you out at lunch, and ream you at dinner."

"You're my lawyer. It was self-defense. The bitch swung her stick—hey, what kind of stick was that?"

"Lacrosse."

"Lacrosse—whatever. The bitch swung that stick at me. That's how I got this bump." He pointed at his head.

"So you dragged her into the bushes, beat the shit out of her, raped her, and then rolled her over and sodomized her?"

"Hey, man, I wasn't sure she was down. I'm just a little guy."

"I don't know," said Al, "if I can beat this one. The people want justice."

"Come on, man," said Pancho. "No one wants to prosecute a poor kid like me—Latino, underprivileged, no education … hey, my momma picked cotton. That ought to work. Just bleed a little in front of the judge."

Al shook his head, rose, and banged on the door. The guard returned and re-shackled Pancho. Al watched through barred windows as Pancho flipped the bird at his escort.

• • •

Dinner that night was at Vanessi's, an Italian restaurant which had moved from North Beach to Russian Hill, but neglected to take along its quality. Dan Black, Al Jackson's best friend from college days, attacked his veal piccata.

"They want me to lose this case," complained Al as he twirled linguine on his fork. "The defendant's a monster that should be beheaded in a public ceremony. But even he's entitled to a defense, I suppose. I never tried to lose a case before."

"Do they actually prosecute minors in this town?" asked Black. He worked in the U.S. Consulate in Frankfurt and was back for his first visit home in three years."

"Are you kidding? They either give the perp money—especially if the dumb shit attacks a tiger in the zoo; or, if he's illegal, they send him into their 'Back on Track' program for rehabilitation. They haven't done anything serious against illegal aliens in this town since '89, when they passed the City of Refuge Act."

"I heard the DA spends all her time campaigning. Does she ever prosecute a murder?"

"Maybe if a dog does it and the victim's gay. Usually, she pleads everything down to avoid a trial. But, in this case, they're after the kid. The vic's daddy has big bucks and the townsfolk want justice; it'll be like a scene in *Frankenstein* with torches and pitchforks."

Al's cell phone vibrated in his pocket. He grabbed it and looked at the calling number. "Shit," he mumbled.

"What'ya want, Hymie?"

"The girl died," said Hymie. "Turns out she was at the top of her class, a 4.0 GPA, scored 1485 on her SATs, and was in model training. And, oh yeah, the girl was gay. Gollub wants revenge so your work's cut out. Caruthers is counting on you."

"Damn, the poor kid died," said Al as Hymie hung up. "It's murder now. That DA might actually decide to prosecute—if she's got the time and doesn't want the *Dykes on Bikes* riding their Harleys into her office."

"Too bad he's not an illegal," pondered Black. "You say the city shields illegal minors?"

"The City Council and the mayor won't even let them be deported."

"Well," said Black, "that would solve your problem."

Al Jackson looked up. Something clicked in his brain. *Illegal.* The word had a nice sound. Maybe there was something to that. If you were an illegal in this town, you could get hammered on rotgut, drive a car into a crowd of school children, kill a couple, maim a few, and there'd be a demonstration against police brutality in front of City Hall. Al ordered a double Scotch. "That's a thought, Dan. I got to do some homework."

"Good luck."

• • •

Al checked the statutes and spent the night arguing with his conscience: Pancho was a killer; Pancho deserved a defense; Pancho was a minor; Caruthers and Gollub wanted the kid dead; Al had taken an oath; Al would be promoted; the judge was in on it. On and on it went until Al drifted into a restless sleep at 3:00 AM. After three hours' sleep and a quart of black coffee, Al visited Pancho's uncle in the Hunters Point district. The old man ran a hotdog push cart near Moscone Center and kept a neat home.

"He's a good boy," said Uncle Hernandez. "He helps push the cart every day before he meets his friends. Then he helps me push it home after work."

"I'm glad to hear he's got values," said Al. "I have to defend him, and I'll be sure to bring up those qualities. Tell me, Hernandez, can you post bail for him?"

"I could put up the house. It's not worth much, but—"

"That'll do," said Al. "It's got to be worth at least fifty K even in this rotten market. You post the bond this morning, before they bump it up. I have an idea."

• • •

Two days later, Al Jackson filed a motion to dismiss the murder and rape charges against Pancho Villa. Judge Mason, after he read the motion, called ADA Henry Hu and Al into his chambers.

"What's this bullshit?" asked the judge. "I expected a defense, not this." He waved a two-page motion in front of Al's nose.

"A motion?" asked Hu. "I haven't been served a copy yet."

Al handed a copy of his motion to Hu.

"Jackson," said the judge, "just moved to dismiss the charges on the grounds the kid's an illegal."

"Illegal my foot," said Hu. "The creep was born in Lodi. It may be in a different country than San Francisco—hell, everywhere's a different country—but it's still the good old U-S-A!"

"What do you care, Henry?" asked Al. "Your boss should be happy—trials are real work."

"What's the law?" demanded Hu.

"Well, there's this pesky little statute called the Immigration and Nationality Act, USC 1481. It seems that Section 349 provides for the renunciation of American citizenship."

"He renounced his citizenship? How'd he do that? He doesn't have a passport, and that can only be done in a foreign country in front of an U.S. official."

"Bingo!" said Al. "I marched this kid up the hill to the German Consulate on Jackson Street. He renounced his citizenship in front of Dan Black, a U.S. State Department official from our consulate in Germany. We were on foreign soil when he performed the act. The little prick took an oath and signed it in Black's presence. Pancho is now a stateless minor. Given the mayor's orders, you, Judge, must dismiss and refer the boy to the 'Back on Track' program for job training—even if it's illegal to get a job. You wouldn't want any demonstrations in front of City Hall, would you?"

"What do I tell Sy Gollub?" asked Judge Mason.

"Tell him the kid promised to stop riding cable cars for free."

• • •

Al walked out of Superior Court onto Bryant Street. He lit a cigar in celebration. His batting average was .400 and his conscience was clear. After lunch, Al intended to follow the court order and deliver Pancho to the Harvey Milk Memorial Halfway House. As Al stepped off the curb, his foot plunged into dog poop. He was wiping his shoe on the edge of the curb when his cell-phone rang.

"What's up, Hymie."

"I got good news and bad news. Pike's looking for you. That's the good news. The bad news is the *Dykes on Bikes* are looking for you, too. And, oh yeah, you're fired."

Al looked down Bryant Street. A pack of motorcycles roared towards him.

The *Miracle* of Alvito

June 2, 1944

It rained the day of the funeral. The Italians called it a *diluvio.* Water pooled in the church graveyard and streamed into Piazza Marconi, yet the entire population of Alvito turned out to honor the dead man. The people listened reverently to the young priest who delivered the eulogy. They watched the gravediggers fill in the grave with rocky soil. They watched as rain turned clumps of dirt into red mud. They watched as the dead man's friend and the German officer saluted at the edge of the grave. The townspeople were wet, hungry, sick, and worn out from war, but they remained as the deluge continued. They'd witnessed a *Miracle* and they prayed for the dead man's salvation.

• • •

May 8, 1944, 1:30 PM

Surrounded by ridges and large mountains to the east, Alvito was a small town in the Valle di Comino at the edge of the National Park of Abruzzo. With roots to the Roman Empire and Dictator Sulla, the town had been established circa AD 1000. Alvito was one hundred miles southeast of Rome in the province of Frosinone—fifteen miles north of Cassino, the closest large city. Its population was small, typical of Italian mountain villages. Its name could be traced to the Latin *Olivetum* (olive-yard).

The battle for Cassino raged. After Mussolini was sacked and the Italian government fled south, the Germans had occupied northern Italy, and the Americans and British had landed on both sides of the southern Italian Peninsula. German Field Marshall Kesselring then deployed *XIV Panzer Korps* to stop the allies at Cassino. German forces also occupied Alvito, astride a secondary, but strategic, crossroads on the supply route to the German forces.

Father Martini, twenty-six, was the town priest. He was a small man—five foot six. The priest had a ruddy complexion and an intense personality. He'd recently taken over church duties after Father Antonio D'Auria passed away. With his new responsibilities, Father Martini had taken it upon himself to protect Alvito from the occupiers. Although some townsfolk thought it was collaboration to do so, he'd cultivated a relationship with the German garrison commander, *Herr Oberst* Hermann Küchler. The priest was surprised he actually liked the colonel, a thirty-five year-old Bavarian. Perhaps, Martini thought, it was due to the *Oberst*'s education in philosophy. Küchler was a cultured and refined man who seemed to hold the Nazis in contempt, although he rarely said anything explicit. The two men were on a first name basis when others weren't within hearing distance.

As he sat in the sunlight with his new friend, Father Martini told himself collaboration wasn't bad if it saved lives, and besides, the Pope was a master at getting along with the Nazis. And Pope Pius XII's real name was Eugenio Pacelli—another Eugenio like him, so how bad could it be? Still, the priest's family was mixed on the question of collaboration. Martini's older brother, Roberto, thirty-six, who owned *La Farmacia*, urged him to cooperate with the Germans: "We must save the town." His sister, Isabella, sixteen, was critical and vitriolic: "How can you talk to these monsters?" She was a hot-headed Italian beauty, and the priest hoped she wouldn't cause trouble. His father Antonio, the old mayor, equivocated, worried about how the partisans might react. Nevertheless, Father Martini was resolved to find an honorable way to deal with the occupation.

Martini lunched with Küchler in the Piazza Marconi when *Korporal* Wandt, one of Küchler's men, rushed into the piazza and spun the hand-cranked siren on Küchler's command vehicle.

"Here they come again," said Küchler. "Perhaps it's us this time."

"*Herr Oberst*," said the priest, "they're bombing because your forces are here. You're an educated man. You've studied philosophy. Why can't you just put up a white flag?"

"Are you mad, Father? General von Senger would shoot us all, and, if he missed, my knowledge of the philosophers wouldn't protect us from the *Führer*'s wrath. The *Gustaf Line* protects the *Adolph Hitler Line* to the west. If it fell, can you imagine the storm that Berlin would unleash? The allies would take Rome. Surrender is out of the question."

The priest shook his head sadly. Despite the fear that the *Oberst* would take his remarks poorly, he boldly asserted, "*Herr Oberst,* you know the war is lost. The Americans have landed at Anzio; the British have taken Ortona. They'll cross the mountains soon. Your cause is hopeless."

Küchler smiled. "Of course, Father. It's been futile since those fools in Berlin decided to invade Russia. But I'm not suicidal. We're talking about survival. We have to bear up and, please, try to keep your people and the partisans calm. I'm doing my best to avoid reprisals, but if the battle over Cassino intensifies, we may get visits from the SS."

The priest frowned. "We need to think of something. If the bombs come any closer the town will be destroyed."

"I'm surprised we haven't been hit already. Headquarters reports that with the exception of Alvito, the entire province of Frosinone has been bombed."

"I'll pray tonight to San Valerio, our patron saint, for both of us."

"If I recall, Father, he was a Roman soldier."

Father Martini nodded and sipped an espresso fortified with rye and chicory root. "He was canonized for making people feel worthy and healthy. He represented the good that soldiers can bring instead of the evil of war. His bones were transferred to Alvito from Rome in AD 1656 to protect the people from plague. We hope they will protect us from the bombs."

"That would be nice, Father, but for the moment we'd best head for the shelters. It would be wonderful if your saint would end this crazy war—but don't tell anyone I said that."

Both men headed for the shelters, and the bombs narrowly missed Alvito, falling south towards the bridge over the Mollo River. Father Martini wondered what the real target was; every day the bombs marched closer to Alvito. Perhaps today the bridge was the target. The Mollo was a tributary of the Melfa which flowed into the Liri River. The Liri River Valley dominated the approaches to Cassino from the north. In the event of a breakthrough at Cassino, the valley could serve as an invasion route for allied forces headed for Rome. Martini knew that Küchler feared the Allies would attack the bridge. The *Oberst* had set up an anti-aircraft gun battery on its approaches. Father Martini hoped the problem wasn't complicated by partisans—or the SS. Pray those barbarians never came to Alvito.

• • •

May 9, 1944, 3:30 AM

A U.S. Army Air Corp C46 transport, on a northern heading and painted black for night runs, flew over the Liri River. Large peaks loomed in the east. The countryside was jagged with small mountains and ridges which separated tiny valleys. At three thousand feet, the wind shredded the cloud cover, and the light from a full moon glinted off the surface of countless lakes, rivers, and streams. The transport's hatch was open and the pilot had turned on a red lamp. The aircraft would be over the drop zone in one minute. Standing near the door next to the jumpmaster were Captain Carl Rugby and his squad of four U.S. Army Rangers. Rugby, twenty-six, was a short, wiry man raised in a rough neighborhood in south Philadelphia and who'd studied cartography at the University of Pennsylvania. He felt the wind as it whipped past his face.

"Okay," yelled Rugby, "Jameson with the BAR goes first, then Allen with the explosives, then Weiss with the radio, then you, Michalak, with the spare radio; then me with the extra weapons. Clear?"

"Bullshit, Captain," shouted PFC Allen, with a nervous shudder. "I hate explosives ... *beep* ... and I especially hate jumping." Allen had seen considerable combat and he'd developed a nervous twitch which manifested itself as an accompanying beep. It sounded like a loud hiccup.

"Yes, Private," said Rugby. "Thanks for volunteering. Any other comments? And don't whisper!"

"Yes sir, Captain," said Staff Sergeant Ray Michalak, a tall twenty-two-year old with a dark complexion and wavy brown hair. "Thank God I'm not jumping with the explosives. I got to carry a radio."

"Screw you, Ray!" shouted Allen. That earned him a big smile from Michalak.

"Quiet down, Allen!" commanded Rugby. "Pay attention; we need the explosives. Jameson, you keep that BAR ready to cover the drop zone. And you're right, Michalak; if we can't blow the bridge on the Mollo, we need the radios to send traffic reports. You and Weiss better not mess up. Now get ready!"

The pilot triggered a green lamp. The jumpmaster shouted "Go" and Jameson, Allen, and Weiss jumped in sequence. Michalak was almost out the hatch when a twin-engine Messerschmitt 110 *Zerstörer* interceptor, one of the few serviceable German night fighters in the theatre, attacked directly out of the moon. Armed with two 20 mm cannon and four 7.92 mm machine guns, it pounced on the C46. Cannon shells struck the rear of the cabin. The shells left gaping holes in the fuselage and just missed the two Rangers and the jumpmaster. One shell damaged the rudder. *Luftwaffe* combat doctrine dictated that pilots finish off a transport before pursuing other targets. But the three parachutists were too tempting. The Messerschmitt came about to attack them with its machine guns. Exploiting the opportunity, the C46 pilot pulled the yoke back, threw the throttles forward, struggled to control his yaw, and raced for safety in the clouds. Just before the transport entered the cloud cover, Rugby and Michalak saw their men raked by machine gun fire and the demolitions explode.

"Tough luck, Captain," yelled the jumpmaster. "We're miles north of the drop zone, and you've lost half your squad. We can't outwait that fighter. With this damage, we got to get home. You still want to jump?"

"We go—now!" barked Rugby. Michalak jumped, followed by the captain.

As he drifted down, Rugby watched Michalak below him and thought back to the meeting which had resulted in the loss of his three men. It had been the previous week, in Naples, with a Fifth Army G2 major.

"Captain," the major had said, "Fifth Army has a tough one for you. We want you and your Rangers to blow the Mollo River Bridge south of Alvito, and then report on German reinforcements in the Liri River Valley."

"If I read the map correctly, that's a secondary supply route to Cassino."

The major had nodded. "We're routinely bombing the main road south from Rome, Highway 7—the old Appian Way—and Highway 6, the alternate route, is unusable. It's been flooded by German engineers to protect the northwest approaches to Cassino. The Germans are occupying the high ground at the old Benedictine abbey—it's the anchor of their *Gustaf* defense line. We need to take that mountain. Get the bridge and we can choke off their supplies."

"It looks like the abbey dominates all the valleys north, including the Liri. I thought we bombed it to rubble."

"We did, and we're getting a lot of flak in the press for that. The abbey was built in the sixth century. But the Fourth Indian Division demanded the structure be bombed after taking heavy casualties. The Indian commanders thought German artillery spotters were up there. No one knows for certain if the observers were there, but German paratroops occupied the ruins after the bombing."

Rugby had shaken his head. "But I'd heard that Kesselring ordered the site to remain unoccupied and he'd informed the Allies."

"General Clark wasn't convinced the abbey was occupied. He demanded a direct order to authorize the bombing from the theatre commander—British General Alexander—and he got it."

"So the abbey was destroyed, and the Germans ended up on the high ground anyway?"

The G2 major had nodded and pointed back at the map. "The place is criss-crossed with rivers and streams. With the spring rains, the lack of that bridge should really mess up German reinforcements to Cassino. I can't say when, but there's going to be another major assault."

"How many assaults will that make, Major?"

"Four."

"Jesus, what are the casualties?"

"Intel figures the Krauts have suffered fifteen thousand. We've taken over forty thousand. That includes us, the Indians, Brits, New Zealanders, and others."

"Hopefully we won't add to the total." Rugby had paused, eyeing the major who seemed to be casual about such horrendous losses. When he'd seen nothing in the major's eyes, he'd added, "Okay, understood. I've got good men. We'll do our best. The *Gustav Line* and Cassino are the keys to Rome, and maybe Italy."

"Don't forget Kesselring has another set of fortifications about twenty miles west of your drop zone, called the *Adolph Hitler Line.* But you're right, Captain. Cassino's all about Rome. Good hunting and good luck."

In the moonlight, Rugby and Michalak were still about thirty feet in the air when a strong gust of wind snarled Michalak in his parachute shrouds. His chute began to collapse, and he struck the ground hard with his ankle at an awkward angle. Rugby was right behind him on the ground.

A crest of hills lay between the American soldiers and the Mollo River. To the north, they saw the ruins of a small castle. The moon cast long shadows in their direction. A road on their right meandered east, toward San Mario del Campo and the Appennino Mountains. The area seemed deserted.

"Shit, Captain!" said Michalak. He clutched his ankle in pain. "Those guys were my buddies."

"Yeah, I know." Rugby grieved over his losses. Allen was a smartass, but he knew his demolitions. Jameson was a rock, and Weiss was a musician with Morse code; they were all damn good men. Three more dead, fumed Rugby, for that G2 major. The good news, if there was any, was that Michalak could tap a key, too.

Rugby shook his head clear and studied the ruins. He remembered the *Castello* from his briefing. It had been constructed at the end of the eleventh century and rebuilt after a major earthquake in AD 1349. The Borgias had lived there. It was pretty far away, and he figured he first should check the town for a hideout.

Rugby turned to Michalak. "I'm going to miss all of them. But now we got to think about us. I guess we can forget about the bridge. What about your ankle? Is it broken?"

"It sure feels broke—but at least it ain't bleeding. I might be able to hobble if we splint it. It hurts like a bitch, though. What're we gonna do?"

"I don't know," said the captain. "Maybe the town or the *Castello,* if we can get you there. Meanwhile, we got to get under cover before daylight. That German pilot's going to report a drop was underway."

"If you help me crawl into the bush, I'll contact headquarters while you come up with some ideas."

"Okay." Rugby applied a sloppy splint to the sergeant's ankle with a stick and some parachute shrouds. He buried the rest of the parachutes.

Rugby dragged Michalak into a thick clump of bushes, stashed the extra weapons, and helped him set up the radio.

"Use the battery and remember—no more than one minute on the air," said Rugby.

Michalak nodded. "It really hurts, Captain. Can I have some morphine?"

"I've only got two ampoules in my kit. You want one now?"

"How about you give me one, and I'll inject it after I transmit; it could knock me out for some time."

Rugby handed Michalak an ampoule.

Michalak nodded gratefully. "Hey, Cap, how about getting me a beer while you're out there?"

"Listen up, Ray! One minute. We don't need them triangulating us with direction-finding (DF) equipment. I'll check out the road. If we can find a place to hole up, we'll see what we can do about the ankle. Too bad Weiss had the first aid kit, and we're going to run out of morphine."

"Okay." Michalak paused and tried to get comfortable as the captain checked his weapon.

"You speak the local lingo?" asked Michalak.

"No Italian, but I speak some German. My grandparents were immigrants from Germany and I'm pretty good."

"Shit, Captain, we sure don't want you speaking German to anyone."

"Let Fifth Army know what happened."

Ninety minutes later, as dawn broke, Rugby returned. He shook Michalak awake. "The whole town's occupied by the Germans. We better spend the day in the bushes. Did you make contact?"

"Yeah, I reported our casualties and that the best we can do is monitor traffic—if the Krauts don't get us. But the battery crapped out at the end. We'll need to use the crank."

"Okay, it was sooner or later. Relax now. We'll figure out something. I can give you another shot in the afternoon."

The men spent the next twelve hours in the dense underbrush. Every few hours a German patrol passed their hiding place.

• • •

May 9, 1944, 6:00 PM

Isabella Martini placed a quarter wheel of cheese, a few bottles of the regional wines, and a small assortment of meats in the church's cart. It was a cool evening, and she'd draped a shawl over her shoulders. She and her brother, Father Martini, were late for their weekly supply trip to the Franciscan *Convento di San Nicola*, located on the road toward San Mario del Campo.

As they hitched the church's horse to the cart, *Herr Oberst* Hermann Küchler appeared. He said, "Eugenio, you're a little late to be visiting the *Convento*."

"I had to give the sacrament to old Baglio, the butcher. He's quite ill. His son was adamant I come this evening."

"Father, if I were a believer, I would insist upon you for my last rites."

"One would think a Bavarian would be a religious man. Would you like to come with us tonight? You can drive." The priest smiled with mischief in his eyes. "I believe our horse speaks German."

Küchler laughed and looked at Isabella, whose nostrils flared. She'd made it clear to the whole town what she thought of the Germans. They were all the same, barbarians—even this one—who was educated in philosophy. She knew how Küchler appraised her and she didn't want to encourage him. She flashed her eyes at her brother and looked away.

"No, Eugenio," said Küchler, with a disappointed look. "Go with your God, and please don't get in trouble. You're the only person I can speak with south of the Alps. *Schöne Reise*, Isabella."

"*Arrivederla*, Hermann," said the priest.

Isabella nodded and said nothing.

Twenty minutes later on Via Colle Civita, Isabella and the priest were startled by a soldier who barred their way, rifle in hand. His face was blackened and he wore an American flag patch on his shoulder.

"*Chi è?*" asked the priest. "*Che vuole?*"

"Excuse me, Father," said the soldier. "Do you speak English? I'm sorry to interrupt your journey, but there's a war on, you know."

"You're American? What do you want?" Martini spoke in stilted English.

"Captain Carl Rugby, U.S. Army Rangers. I need some help. I have an injured man with me. It's his ankle. I've exhausted my supply of morphine, and he's in pain."

"Are the Americans here? I thought they were fighting south of Cassino."

"They still are, Father."

"Captain, do you know the Germans are everywhere around here? When will the rest of your forces arrive?"

"I've seen the Germans. I don't know when we'll be relieved, but I urgently need to move my man and find a place to get under cover before dawn. Can you help?"

"Of course. But I need to deliver these supplies to the *Convento*—"

"I'll stay," volunteered Isabella in English. "My name is Isabella. Perhaps I can help." She smiled at the American captain.

Father Martini said, "All right. She's my sister, Captain. I will hold you responsible for her care. When I return it will be after dark. We will hide you and your man in the church basement."

"Thanks, Father. I guess I can trust you to return, seeing as how you're leaving Isabella behind."

Father Martini drove off and Rugby escorted Isabella off the road. They found Michalak pale, feverish, and semi-conscious.

"He looks like he's in shock," said Isabella. "We need to keep him warm and elevate his legs—even the one with the splint." She took off her shawl and draped it over the sergeant.

Some moments later, Michalak opened his eyes. He saw a beautiful young woman with large hazel eyes, long black hair, and a willowy figure. He blinked several times.

"Captain, I asked for a beer, and you brought me an angel."

Isabella smiled and began to flush.

Michalak tried to sit up.

"Take it easy, Sergeant," said Rugby.

"Now, Sergeant, please lay back," said Isabella as she examined his injured leg. "You have a broken ankle. We will need to re-splint it later, and that will be very *doloroso*, uh … painful. I recommend you rest now."

"Are you a nurse? What's your name?" asked Michalak.

"I've had some training at the *Convento*. That is where I learned my English." Isabella was unsure whether she should give her name to the handsome soldier.

"Her name is Isabella," said Rugby. "His name is Ray."

Michalak settled back and smiled, his head cradled in Isabella's lap. Her heart skipped a beat. She wondered if it were apparent she was flustered.

As they waited for Father Martini to return, Isabella thought of her brother, the priest. This was the first time she'd been proud of him since the Germans had arrived. He would have to deceive them now; she wondered how he'd deal with that.

• • •

May 9, 1944, 10:30 PM

Under cover of darkness, Rugby and Michalak were spirited into the basement of the church, *La Parrocchiale di San Simeone*. It had been built in AD 1700 to house the patron saint San Valerio's bones. Rugby thought it was an impressive baroque structure, and the priest told him the ceiling was gold-trimmed. Rugby asked the priest why the Nazis hadn't looted the ceiling.

"Captain, Italy was an ally of Germany for several years. Fortunately, the local German commander is a civilized man. I hope he doesn't learn we're hiding you here. He would have to do something about that."

"Look, Father," said Rugby, "we'll need to use a radio from time to time. I hope they leave us alone, too."

"I will pray for that," said Isabella.

They laid the sergeant on a long table in the basement, and Isabella began to reset the splint on his ankle. He was in serious pain but didn't utter a sound. Rugby could tell from Michalak's silence that Isabella had captured the sergeant's heart. She seemed unsettled and the captain sensed an attraction for Michalak; he hoped it wouldn't be a problem for the priest. Rugby intended to tell Michalak later to cool it.

As the Martinis were leaving, the priest said to Michalak, "Isabella will ask Roberto, my brother in *La Farmacia,* for something for your pain tomorrow. Supplies are almost exhausted but perhaps he can prepare something for you."

"That would help a lot, Father. Thank you, Isabella," said Michalak.

Isabella gave Michalak a wide smile, and Rugby thought the girl looked thrilled at the chance to return. She seemed to float up the basement steps.

• • •

May 10, 1944, 6:00 AM

The next morning Rugby climbed the bell tower and strung an antenna. He logged military traffic. Later, as Rugby cranked the hand-powered generator, Michalak keyed an encrypted dispatch which included their location.

Fifth Army Headquarters was dismayed to learn American Rangers were hidden in the church of a town targeted for a massive bombing campaign. The report of the soldiers' location went up the chain of command to Lieutenant General Mark Clark. The general already was uneasy about the negative publicity and international criticism he'd received from the bombing of the old Benedictine abbey. Furthermore, Clark considered bombing friendly forces repugnant. He stayed the targeting of Alvito until he checked with his theatre commander.

Although food was in short supply in Alvito, Isabella brought a bewildering array of provisions to the soldiers. Michalak's ankle was in poor condition, but he managed to hobble with a crutch. As the days passed, he and Isabella spent increasing amounts of time together, usually in the shadows of the basement where large casks of wine made from spicy local grapes, known as *Cesanese*, were stored.

The Rangers continued to report to Fifth Army. For two weeks, they broadcast at random times and intervals, changed frequencies routinely, and minimized their transmission times.

• • •

May 24, 1944, 9:00 AM

Over the past week, an SS DF station in Rome, searching for OSS transmissions, had detected several broadcasts on known enemy frequencies. Additional bearings taken from Florence triangulated a transmitter in the vicinity of Alvito. After a series of discussions among the intelligence officer of *XIV Panzer Korps*, Field Marshall Kesselring's staff, the Gestapo, and the SS Command in Italy, *Herr Oberst* Hermann Küchler received a call on his field telephone from an SS officer.

"*Oberst* Küchler? SS *Obergruppenführer* Lohse, in Rome. What's going on in Alvito?"

"What do you mean?" asked Küchler. "The road is open, and supplies are flowing to the front. If there's a problem, it's not here. In fact, I'm surprised they haven't bombed us yet."

"Yes, General von Senger noticed that, too." Ominously, Lohse added, "So did Kesselring."

"It's luck, I guess," said Küchler. "I still expect them to bomb us—and soon! The Allies took Monte Cassino. I understand they broke out of the Anzio beachhead yesterday."

"*Richtig*," said Lohse. "They're also mounting an air assault on the *Adolph Hitler Line*, which *der Führer* has renamed the *Dora Line*."

Küchler snorted at the hypocrisy. "But that could destroy our right flank. I could be under attack from three directions!"

"Yes, but retreat would be ill-advised. You know what happens to deserters. SS detachments are roaming behind the lines in search of any cowards. Your job is to stand and die for *der Vaterland*."

Küchler rolled his eyes and waited.

"However," said Lohse after an awkward silence, "that's not the reason I called. We've noticed enemy radio traffic coming from your vicinity. What do you know about that?"

"*Nichts*. I'll have to look into it."

"Precisely. And to help you along, I've sent you a mobile DF team. SS *Sturmbannführer* Nassler will be there soon. A good man. You can thank me later, perhaps. Now do your job. I suggest you start burning your files."

• • •

May 24, 1944, 2:00 PM

Father Martini shared a spartan meal with Küchler. Bread, wine and a small cheese were all the café could offer. The townspeople hoarded the other foodstuffs.

The *Oberst* had been silent for some time, and Father Martini sensed he was tense.

"Eugenio, has anything unusual been happening in town? Have you seen any strangers?"

"What do you mean? I've noticed that the siren has been silent, of course, but nothing else." Father Martini thought his lie might be a sin. He felt guilty for betraying his friend, but Alvito was more important. And besides, his sister was in love with the young sergeant.

"Listen carefully, Father," said Küchler. "The SS are coming to town. They're curious about some radio traffic. If you know anything, for both our sakes, you must tell me now. They could exterminate every person in town! They've done this sort of thing before."

Father Martini, troubled, looked away. But he knew that Küchler's suspicions were aroused.

"Father, please, if anyone in this town is working for the Allies, I need to know." Küchler stared directly into Father Martini's eyes.

"No, I know nothing." The priest averted his eyes and focused them on the old church. "Hopefully, San Valerio will give you an excuse to surrender soon. There are rumors the Allies are almost here."

"The SS are not keen on surrender. Be very careful. If you're lying to me, we're both in trouble."

"Enjoy your lunch, Hermann. I pray for our deliverance."

Küchler shook his head, threw some coins on the table, and stormed away.

• • •

May 24, 1944, 3:30 PM

After the meal, Father Martini went directly to the church basement. Though torn between his concern for the town and the betrayal and stigma of spying, he resolved to warn Captain Rugby about the SS. Maybe the Americans would stop broadcasting. "Captain," he said, "I just spoke with the *Oberst.* Although I don't like to spy for either side, I must tell you the SS are coming. They know about your radio."

"Damn," said Rugby. "They picked up our general location. The best I can do is stop broadcasting today, but I'll need to get back on the air tomorrow. The battle is in its final throes; our messages might save lives."

"Where are the Allies now?"

"They're close; they could be here in an hour or a week. Who knows? Ask San Valerio."

"It would be a tragedy if anyone dies with liberation so near. I'm sure the saint will protect all of us, including the *Oberst.*"

"I hope you're right, Father."

• • •

May 24, 1944, 8:00 PM

Küchler was unsettled the rest of the day. He was in his office when *Korporal* Wandt saw Isabella Martini carry a basket of vegetables, wine, and a small chunk of Mortadella sausage into the church. When she departed a few minutes later with an empty basket, Wandt reported to Küchler.

"She took food into the church and left it there?"

"*Jawohl, Herr Oberst.*"

"*Gott verdampft.* They're feeding someone in there and hiding it from me. I'm going to deal with that priest now!"

Thirty minutes later, Küchler found Father Martini in his church by the communion-rail. He confronted the priest and demanded to know who the food was for. "Don't tell me that food was for you, Father. I've had enough of your lies. I thought we were friends."

"Hermann, we are friends."

"It's *Herr Oberst,* Father. What's going on in the church?"

"I was praying to San Valerio that it would all be resolved by the arrival of the Allies."

"I demand that you explain yourself."

"Please. No fighting. I'll make an introduction, if you agree to come alone—and unarmed."

"Alone? Unarmed? You want me to trust you now?" Küchler shook his head in disgust.

"I beg you," said the priest. "I give you my word, in the name of the Holy Virgin, that it will be safe."

To Küchler, Father Martini seemed quite distraught—and those pledges to the Virgin were usually sincere. Frustrated and angry, Küchler wondered what to do. Should he assemble a raiding party? Go in without backup? Fortunately, *Korporal* Wandt knew his objective. If he didn't return, Wandt would organize a search party. The *Oberst* stared at the priest for some time. Finally, Küchler decided to meet him halfway.

"Okay, Father, I'm willing to come alone—but armed." Küchler pulled his Walther P-38 sidearm out of the holster. "Let's go—you first."

Father Martini led the way down the steps to the basement. When Küchler reached the bottom step, he saw an American officer. Küchler pointed his weapon at the man, and the American raised his hands.

"*Was ist los? Einer Amerikaner*?"

"*Jawohl, Herr Oberst*, Captain Carl Rugby, U.S. Army Rangers."

"*Sie sprechen Deutsch*?"

"*Ja, aber möchte Ich lieber Englisch*," answered Rugby.

"Okay, *Englisch geht.* What are you doing here? Do you have a radio?" Küchler was nervous and wanted answers.

"C'mon, *Herr Oberst*, that's a full colonel in the *Wehrmacht*, right? I can salute you, but I can't tell you what I'm doing." Rugby snapped to attention and saluted Küchler.

"Very well, you're under arrest."

"Please *Herr Oberst*, don't do this," pleaded the priest

Küchler returned the captain's salute. "Father," he said, "I cannot have enemy agents in my town. At least he's still in uniform, although I doubt that will make much difference to the SS. I'm afraid I have no choice. Captain, you're my prisoner."

"I don't think so," said Michalak, who hopped into the light from behind some wine casks. He was armed with a rifle pointed at Küchler. Isabella, who'd returned earlier with a small container of olive oil and a half-loaf of bread, followed Michalak with a terrified look on her face.

Küchler looked at the priest with disappointment. "So, Father, there are more than one, eh? What else haven't you told me?"

"I guess we have a Mexican standoff here," suggested Rugby, with his hands still raised.

"I don't know what that means," said Küchler. "But I have a company of men who know where I am."

"Uh-huh," said Michalak. "Tell me *Oberst*, sir, have you noticed Alvito hasn't been bombed? Can you figure out why? Well, maybe it's because of us. If we don't keep reporting in, you can kiss your ass goodbye. Maybe you want to chew on that?"

Küchler thought about it for a moment. His hopes for survival receded as he considered his position—squeezed between the SS and the American Rangers. He was at a disadvantage and likely would die in the firefight. His troops undoubtedly would kill the Americans and the priest and his sister, but that was little consolation. And when the SS troops arrived, they might slaughter the rest of the people in town. Even if he survived a shootout, the bombings might devastate Alvito. He needed time to think. He lowered his weapon slowly, followed by Michalak.

"*Herr Oberst,*" implored the priest, "please don't do anything that will endanger the town."

"Father, these Americans are endangering your town. What were you thinking when you allowed them to hide in your church?"

Rugby said, "*Herr Oberst,* don't blame the priest. Sanctuary is a tradition in the Church. But why do we have to fight? *Vielleicht Man soll die schlafenden Löwen nicht wecken.* May I propose a truce?"

"I don't know," replied Küchler. "I could kill you but yes, it would be prudent to let sleeping dogs lie. We can suspend hostilities—for now." He holstered his pistol and Michalak propped his rifle against a wine cask.

"*Herr Oberst,*" said Rugby as he lowered his arms, "we need to talk about the military situation. What's your name?"

Father Martini introduced Küchler. The *Oberst* nodded and suggested that he and the captain sit at the table. Michalak hovered near his rifle.

"The military situation?" asked Küchler. "Men are dying like flies on both sides. Why should it be different for us?"

"Look, Küchler, the most dangerous time in war is at the beginning and end of combat operations. We both know the battle for Rome is almost over. If you play your cards right, you and your men can survive."

"Captain, I'm listening, but I must admit that survival seems remote."

"Do you play chess?" said Rugby. "Perhaps the good Father could find us a set, and Isabella might fetch us some wine?"

Father Martini rushed upstairs and returned with a chess set. Isabella poured some wine. Küchler noticed she smiled at him for the first time; perhaps she was having second thoughts about him.

"I should tell you, *Herr Oberst,*" commented Rugby wryly, "that I was chess champion in my Boy Scout troop." He played white and opened the game with the queen's pawn.

"Really, Captain? I was champion of the *Bayrisches Schachjugend*, the Bavarian Youth Chess Club." Küchler smiled at Rugby's aggressive opening and, on his second move, accepted Rugby's queen's gambit.

After several more moves, Rugby moved his queen onto the board.

"Captain," Küchler advised, "it's dangerous to place an unprotected queen in contested territory."

"Dangerous? But that's what Rangers do."

Küchler smiled and advanced a bishop. "So what are we going to do, Captain? The SS will kill us both if I don't close you down."

"I can understand that. Still, I'm sure you don't want to be bombed, and your war will be over any day now." Rugby countered with a knight.

"True. When will your forces arrive?" Küchler took a pawn.

"Unless you wish to die fighting, or become POWs, you and your men should leave now. We've been told German defenses are collapsing—even the *Adolph Hitler Line* is crumbling."

"Ha! It's the *Dora Line* now. Our propaganda minister, Goebbels, is earning his keep." Küchler snapped up another pawn.

"We have propaganda, too," said Rugby. "In any event, I expect relief within hours, or a day or so. Of course, the timing also depends on your people. You mentioned the SS. Are they coming here? When? How many?"

"Enough to find your radio, arrest me for treason, and murder everyone in town."

"You could surrender the town to me." Rugby frowned at his board position.

Küchler placed his queen next to Rugby's king. "I don't think so, but let me think about my options tonight. I must consider my men. Meanwhile, checkmate!" He nodded to the priest, Isabella and Michalak. "Good night, Father. *Signorina*. You too, Sergeant. Thank you for not shooting me."

"Are you coming back with your men, *Herr Oberst*?" asked Michalak.

"Sergeant, Sun Tzu said 'All warfare is based on deception.' If I say no, will you believe me?"

"I will," declared Rugby.

"Thank you Captain. For the moment I shall honor our cease-fire."

As Küchler walked back to Town Hall, he decided not to bring *Korporal* Wandt into his confidence about the Americans—at least not until he decided what to do about his troops. The *Korporal* was loyal to his commander but, with the imminent arrival of the SS, that information would be dangerous. It might place Wandt in a compromised position. Instead, Küchler told Wandt the townsfolk were stockpiling food in the event of prolonged combat upon the arrival of the Allies.

• • •

May 25, 1944, 10:00 AM

Küchler had spent a restless night when *Sturmbannführer* Jens Nassler's staff car, followed by his DF van, rolled into Alvito. Nassler was a former *Hitlerjugend* member and Nazi party loyalist. His specialty was hunting partisans and OSS agents. With the van, and a detector on his staff car, his team could locate a transmitter in under an hour. With two bearings, and a known distance between the two detectors, it was a simple calculation to fix the location of the target. Nassler's orders were to close down any hostile transmitters.

The *Sturmbannführer* strode into Küchler's headquarters in Town Hall and demanded an immediate audience with the *Oberst*. Küchler, who'd dreaded the meeting, invited Nassler into his office.

"Welcome, *Sturmbannführer*. Congratulations. You've beaten the Allies to Alvito."

Nassler saluted, apparently oblivious to the sarcasm. "The Allies will never breach our lines. I'm confident in *der Führer*. I look forward to serving him by tracking and destroying the enemy radio."

"Good for you, Nassler," said Küchler. "Is there anything you need from me to start work?"

"I need to consult with your men who control the electricity; we may need to switch power off, block by block, as we search for the enemy's radio."

"Of course. But Alvito is a small town; I'm not certain there is more than one transformer. In fact, there aren't too many blocks. Nevertheless, *Korporal* Wandt will make the necessary introductions."

"Thank you, *Herr Oberst. Sieg Heil!*"

In response, Küchler made a half-hearted Nazi arm gesture. Nassler turned on his heels and departed.

That afternoon Nassler sent the DF van east and climbed into his vehicle. When he turned on his detector and tuned it to an enemy frequency, he picked up a brief signal. However, by the time the van was prepared to track, the transmitter had ceased broadcasting.

• • •

May 25, 1944, 3:00 PM

Küchler, supervising the destruction of his company's records, heard the sound of mortar and small arms fire. Allied forces were skirmishing within sight of Alvito. He retrieved his field glasses and headed for the bell tower. When he climbed the steps, he discovered Captain Rugby watching the battle through his glasses.

"So, Captain," conceded Küchler, "it's a matter of hours, is it?"

"Yes, *Herr Oberst*. I see the SS are here, too. You didn't tell them about us?"

"No. My war is over. The SS officer is a fanatic named Nassler. The fool thinks the Allies have lost the war."

"Are you certain you don't want to surrender?" asked Rugby. "How about your men?"

"I've decided to release them. They are free to choose their own fate—retreat if possible, surrender, or fight. I suspect most will wish to withdraw to fight again. After all, these are *Wehrmacht* soldiers. Sadly, retreat is perilous with the SS slaughtering any troops they find without orders. Some of the men, undoubtedly, will choose surrender."

"All right, *Herr Oberst*. Those who surrender will be treated honorably by me. And what will you do?"

"I think tonight I shall consider my options—surrender; death by hanging; death by firing squad; or a painful death. Perhaps I'll cheat the hangman and take cyanide. I can probably get some from that SS idiot."

Rugby smiled at Küchler's cynicism. "Please don't do anything rash," he counseled. "We still can survive this madness. *Alles ist noch möglich.*"

"Still possible?" said Küchler. "Perhaps. But you must be careful, Captain. If Nassler finds you, he'll kill you in a heartbeat. He already has a single DF bearing on you. In fact, I still should kill you. However, I fail to see what that would accomplish and your sergeant is probably covering the stairs. Our truce continues. *Tschuss.*"

• • •

May 26, 1944, 10:00 AM

As battle raged on the outskirts of town, Nassler's men triangulated Rugby's transmitter in the church. Nassler rushed into Küchler's office to demand he organize an *Aktion,* including reprisals. But he found only *Korporal* Wandt.

"I think you'll find him at the church," said Wandt. "He's with the priest. They're discussing what happens when the Allies arrive. We've received no further orders, and some of the men have left."

"Some of your men have deserted? You *Wehrmacht* men are cowards!"

"They retreat so that they may return to battle," said Wandt, giving Nassler a hostile look. "And I'm still here. Someone must protect the *Oberst.*"

"No one can protect him from me, if he's planning to surrender!"

When Nassler arrived at the church, he placed his driver and two other storm troopers from the van inside the entrance.

Nassler wandered the first floor. He observed the ceiling trimmed with gold and fumed that it hadn't been sent to Germany. He became angrier when he saw valuable art, including a crucifixion in the sacristy by Cavalier d'Arpino, and a wooden statue of *La Madonna di Loreto* sculpted by Giovanni Stolz. Determined to find both the transmitter and Küchler, he eventually discovered the steps to the basement. As Nassler descended, he heard people speaking and recognized Küchler's voice. He cocked his *Schmeisser* MP40 machine pistol and charged down the steps.

At the bottom he was startled to discover a priest, Küchler, and an American officer seated around a table. Confronting them, Nassler shouted, "Küchler, you're a traitor. I'm going to kill you!"

"Go ahead, Nassler. I'm all yours." Küchler stood and turned to block Nassler's fire and protect the priest.

Father Martini said, "Wait—" but he was interrupted by Michalak who lunged out of the shadows, firing at the same time. His bullets riddled Nassler, but Nassler's MP40 fired several stray rounds that flashed around the basement, striking wine casks. One round ricocheted off the stone walls and struck Rugby in the chest. He fell bleeding at Küchler's feet.

For a few moments, everyone froze in position; the cellar filled with the smell of cordite and smoke from the weapons. Shaken, Küchler looked down at Rugby. Wine from a ruptured cask spread on the stone floor, mixing with Rugby's blood. Isabella gasped and ran to Rugby who was beyond help. Kneeling in Rugby's blood and the wine, she cradled the captain's head in her lap.

At that instant, gunfire erupted in the church. Father Martini crept up the steps and peeked around the door well. The bodies of three storm troopers were sprawled on the floor. A platoon of British soldiers was spreading throughout the church. The priest raised his hands and shouted, "Over here! *Benvenuto a Alvito.* God knows we need you."

Several soldiers dashed over and patted the priest down while a British non-commissioned officer strode up. "Father," he said, "I'm Colour Sergeant William Lawrence, British XIII Corps Combat Assault Team. The Germans are in full flight. My orders are to secure the church and determine the status of two American soldiers who are hiding here."

"I'm afraid the American captain just died. His sergeant is alive, down in the basement. He's injured, but he'll be fine."

As Lawrence turned to go down the steps, Father Martini called, "Wait, Sergeant. There's a German *Oberst* down there, too, and a dead SS Officer. My sister is also there. Please hold your fire. I'm sure the *Oberst* is peaceful."

"Okay, Father," said Lawrence. "Let's both go. Since you're so certain, you can go first."

Following the priest down the steps with his weapon at the ready, Lawrence smelled the cordite in the air. He stopped when he saw the dead SS officer at the bottom of the steps and an American sergeant armed with a rifle.

"Who are you, mate?"

"Sergeant Ray Michalak, U.S. Army Rangers."

Lawrence continued to the bottom of the steps where he found a dead SS officer. An *Oberst* sat at the table. A young woman, her dress drenched in blood and wine, was on the floor holding a dead U.S. Army captain. The priest went directly to the girl. Lawrence stepped over the dead SS officer.

Lawrence pointed at Küchler. "Sergeant Michalak, who's the German?"

"Excuse me," said Küchler. "I'm *Oberst* Hermann Küchler, *XIV Panzer Korps*, the local garrison commander."

"Thank you, *Oberst*. And who is the dead SS officer?"

"That was *SS Sturmbanführer* Nassler," said Küchler. "He brought a direction-finding team to Alvito."

"What about your men, *Oberst*?"

"I have a company of soldiers. However, I've released them from their duties; I suspect many have melted away."

"Yes, *Oberst,* but not all of them. We've taken quite a few prisoners—and that includes you."

"Perhaps not," countered Küchler. "I've already surrendered to Sergeant Michalak."

"That's right," echoed Michalak. "He's my prisoner."

"And the girl? Is that your sister, Father?"

"This is Isabella," said Father Martini.

"Sergeant," said Lawrence, "this *Oberst* may have important information, and he speaks English. He's quite a valuable catch. I need to deliver him to an Intelligence officer."

"No!" demanded Isabella. "He stays here; he's a prisoner of the Americans. I will not have him lost in the confusion of battle. Along with this poor American captain and Sergeant Michalak, he saved the town."

Küchler smiled at the firmness in her voice, her new regard for him, and her innocence about the realities of war.

"Can't your Intelligence officer come here to interrogate him?" added Father Martini. "Please, let him stay here until the front lines stabilize."

"Well, it's rather irregular, but I'll refer the issue to my lieutenant. I do think, though, that it might be a rather jolly idea, Sergeant Michalak, to relieve your prisoner of his weapon."

Küchler grinned ruefully, retrieved his Walther pistol, and handed it butt first to Michalak.

Lawrence saluted the *Oberst*. "Thank you, sir, for surrendering your weapon. And Sergeant, I will send you a medical corpsman to look after that ankle."

"Can you arrange to remove the dead SS officer?" asked the priest.

"Of course. We'll also collect the captain's body."

"No thank you," said Father Martini. "Captain Rugby should stay here. I will give him the last rites. We'll take care of the arrangements."

"All right Father, I'll notify Fifth Army, and Sergeant Michalak should take one of the captain's dog tags."

• • •

August 14, 1969, 10:30 AM

Father Eugenio Martini hummed with excitement. For hundreds of years, August 14th had been the date dedicated to the town of Alvito's patron saint, San Valerio. For the last twenty-five years, the citizens of Alvito had celebrated the *Miracle* on the same day. As a bonus, the town commemorated the twenty-fifth anniversary, albeit a few months late, of its liberation from German occupation—May 26, 1944.

Father Martini's hair had thinned and turned gray, and his waistline had expanded over the years. He was in Landini's Dry Cleaners shop inspecting the annual cleaning of the World War II relics. The American Rangers' uniforms were symbolic evidence of the *Miracle.* They normally had a place of honor in *La Chiesa del Miracolo* (The Church of the Miracle), formerly *La Parrocchiale di San Simeone.* Since the end of the war the relics were displayed in a pageant that honored San Valerio. The parade began with a procession that left the church, crossed Piazza Marconi, marched up Corso Silvio Castrucci, and then turned and proceeded up the hill to the *Castello.* The castle was decked out with decorations. Rows of tables, enormous casks of wine, kegs of beer, and a panoply of food awaited hundreds of visitors.

"Father," said Landini, "are the uniforms to your liking?"

"Yes, thank you. Please mount them on these poles. They'll follow our statue of *La Madonna di Loreto* in the procession."

"There's talk in town that we'll have some important visitors," said Baglio. "Is that true, Father?" Baglio, who owned the butcher shop next door to Landini's, had been pressed into service to help mount the uniforms.

"I'm expecting *Herr Oberst* Küchler—well, I guess he's not a colonel anymore—and my sister and her husband."

"So the American is coming too?" asked Landini. "That will be nice, Father—a very special celebration."

"And a wonderful reminder of our *Miracle* and the grace of San Valerio. That is why the uniforms must be perfect."

"But, Father," worried Landini, "you know I can't do anything about the blood and wine stains on one of the soldier's uniforms."

"Of course," said the priest. "Don't worry yourself. It was God's will and the people will understand."

• • •

A tall, distinguished looking man in his early sixties, dressed formally in a well-tailored blue suit and tie, stood next to the old café in Piazza Marconi. *Herr Professor* Herman Küchler waited patiently for the procession to begin.

The band assembled, and the piazza was crowded with residents and visitors. With a beat of drums, the procession began at the church, led by Father Martini and his brother Roberto, the mayor. The statue of the Madonna, a priceless carving, was next followed by the American Ranger's uniforms, the band, town notables and sisters from the *Convento*, the choir, provincial and national flag-bearers, and others, including a few of the town's mangy dogs. Following the time-beaten path, the Martinis led the procession into Piazza Marconi.

Halfway across the piazza, with the crowd cheering, the German professor waved at the priest. Father Martini saw the gesture, grinned, and whispered in his brother's ear. The priest broke out of the procession—which halted and milled about in confusion.

"*Herr* Küchler," greeted the Father. "*Benvenuto*. It's so good to see you again."

"Father, you old devil, it's a special treat for me too. And please, call me Hermann. Will the others be here?"

"Yes, of course, Hermann. They said they were coming after I told them you would be here. I'm expecting Isabella and Ray."

"Is your sister still as beautiful as ever?" asked Küchler.

"See for yourself. There they are. We'll talk at the festival. I must continue the procession."

The priest returned to his position, and the band burst into a cacophony of noise. The procession, in disarray, re-formed in a different order and resumed its march.

Küchler turned and smiled a welcome to a handsome couple that wove their way through the crowd. The woman, about forty, was ravishing; and the man, tall and tanned, walked with a limp.

"*Herr Oberst*," murmured the woman. She wrapped her arms around Küchler.

"*Gruss Gott*," he said, embarrassed. "Isabella, my God, you have become more beautiful with age. And, please, I'm not an *Oberst* anymore."

So, Hermann, *wie geht's*?" jested Isabella's husband, Ray Michalak. "You look good. How's your chess game?"

Hermann Küchler smiled again. "You look good as well."

The three friends sat down at the café on the edge of Piazza Marconi. Isabella ordered a carafe of water. The men ordered beer.

"They're calling it a *Miracle*—the fact that Alvito was never bombed," said Küchler.

"I think it was a *Miracle*," said Isabella. "During the battle for Cassino, it felt as though the bombs were about to rain down upon us. With you and your troops stationed in town, we were convinced that we were a target. And then Ray and Captain Rugby arrived."

Küchler nodded. "My superiors also wondered why we were never bombed. That's why they sent that lunatic, Nassler, to look for Ray's radio."

Isabella smiled. "The townspeople believe they were saved by the two soldiers who hid in the church. They were soldiers like San Valerio. The people believe the saint sent the Americans."

Küchler looked up at the old church bell tower where Rubgy's antenna had been strung. "I don't know about the saint, but I owe them my life."

"Hermann," said Michalak, "what happened to you after the war?"

"I was interrogated in Alvito by the British. After Rome was liberated, I was sent to the Modena Allied POW camp. I was released in late 1945 and returned to Bavaria. I live in Ulm now."

"Was it difficult in the POW camp?"

"I was grateful to be alive. And you? Couldn't they fix that ankle?"

"It was beat up pretty good," said Michalak. "But after we buried the captain, the Brits got me to an American hospital ship in the Port of Naples, the *USS Ernest Hands.* They had to re-break the ankle, and then put on a cast. They jerked around with it several times. It finally healed, but I've always had a limp. I got back to the states in the spring of 1945. In 1946, I came back to Alvito and married Isabella."

"What say we take a walk?" said Küchler. "We can stop at the cemetery, visit Captain Rugby, and then join Isabella's brothers at the festival. I believe the mayor has a gift for me—a ceremonial key to the town. Not bad for an occupier, eh?"

The Strike

February 22, 1988

The trip to Europe was productive. I'd visited clients in Berlin and in and around Paris. Even though the Middle East was in an uproar, with civil war in Lebanon, Israeli attacks on refugee camps, and Palestinian hijackings, I felt I was far enough away from the battles and bombings. Europe was quiet. The Baader-Meinhof terrorists in Germany were dead or in prison; only the Red Brigade in Italy was still active.

Business was good, but I needed to get home, not only to greet important clients from Japan but also to meet my wife's expectations after a long trip. At the moment, I was ensconced in the fabulous George V Hotel near the Avenue des Champs-Élysées. I liked the hotel; it offered a Michelin-starred restaurant, a great bar, and a generous peanut policy. Still, I looked forward to my return to San Francisco via New York. The carrier was Pan Am, my favorite airline. I'd logged perhaps a million miles on it. I expected an easy upgrade from Business to First Class and Pan Am knew how to do First Class.

After my early morning shower, I looked out the window at the traffic on Avenue George V. The heavy fog was unusual for Paris but worse, Orly Airport sat in a depression. It often suffered weather-related delays. I decided to call Pan Am and check the flight information before I left the hotel.

"Hello, this is Pan Am. I'm Christie," said the clerk. "How may I help you."

"Hi, Christie. I'm on Pan Am 49 today, Orly to JFK, with a connection to SFO. I'm checking if the flight's on time."

"We show it departing on time. The aircraft's inbound now from Chicago. Your departure's scheduled for 12:01 PM. There should be no problems."

"There's fog in Paris this morning," I said. "How's the weather at Orly?"

"We're showing clear and sunny."

I ordered a room service breakfast and turned on the TV. Things were nasty in Lebanon. Vicious battles raged daily. A bomb had been discovered on a plane waiting to take the current president of Lebanon to Yemen.

That was scary stuff for any American, especially one about to fly. I was grateful I was nowhere near the Middle East. Thank God, I thought, I'm headed west, not east.

I enjoyed my breakfast, packed, and checked out. Not keen on traffic delays, I caught an early taxi for the airport. We headed for Pont D'Alma, east along the river to the Périphérique, and northeast.

The skies cleared for a while, but then the fog returned. A few miles from

Orly, it thickened and enveloped traffic. Visibility was fifty feet when I arrived at my terminal.

I sat in the taxi and debated the dilemma of whether I should go, or delay the trip and return to Paris. They'd said the plane was inbound. Maybe it was on the ground already. Even with the fog we might depart. Take-offs were easier than landings in crummy weather. Maybe it would improve—the weather forecast for the airport was clear and sunny. If I went back to Paris, I'd be late for my meetings in California. My wife would be upset. On the other hand, there likely would be delays at Orly, perhaps interminable. I hated to wait at airports. There could be worse things than another day in Paris at the George V. But, with the taxi driver banging on the trunk lid to get my attention, I made a snap decision to risk the delay and climbed out of the vehicle.

I joined the line at the Business Class check-in counter. Some departures had been cancelled. But the aircraft inbound for my flight still was en route. The weather was expected to improve shortly. I waited impatiently, kicking my luggage forward as the passenger queue shrank at glacial speeds.

Twenty minutes later, Pan Am announced that due to inclement weather the inbound flight would overfly Paris and land in Rome. Once the weather improved the airplane would return to board the passengers for JFK. The estimated time of departure was unchanged.

Uh-oh, that information was ominous. I began to doubt my decision not to return to Paris. But I saw little advantage in changing the plan. I checked-in, received an upgrade to First Class, pocketed my boarding pass and luggage tags, and watched my bags disappear on the conveyor belt. I passed through security and went to the Premium Class lounge.

People scattered around the lounge scowled. Arrivals had stopped. The flight departures board showed increasingly long delays.

Time crawled. The fog began to lift. The clock inched past 10:30 AM. At 11:00 AM I looked out the window and was encouraged. The skies were clear. An announcement informed the passengers that the aircraft assigned to the JFK flight had left Rome and was expected in Paris at noon. There would be a one-hour delay in our departure. I began to relax—with a three-hour layover at JFK, I could lose an hour and still make my connection to SFO.

Precisely at noon, the lounge attendant announced that Pan Am's mechanics, pilots, and flight attendants had walked off their jobs. The airline was on strike worldwide! My flight was cancelled. The flight from Rome would continue to New York and overfly Paris yet once more. The only Pan Am flights the rest of the day were those already in the air. The attendant said that there would be further announcements for the marooned passengers. I considered returning to Paris but, alas, my luggage was checked, swallowed up in the bowels of Orly. I was committed.

The hours went by slowly. The TV was filled with reports about the unrest in Beirut. To get my mind off the delay I devoured a paperback, read every newspaper in the lounge, visited the cafés in the airport, and generally stewed—as did all the other passengers for eight more hours.

Finally, at 8:00 PM an announcement declared that an aircraft bound for New York had been diverted to Orly to fetch Pan Am's JFK passengers. We were told to proceed immediately to Gate 11 for a new round of check-ins and boarding passes.

I'd accepted the fact that I'd missed my connection and that I'd be stuck in New York one night. I assumed my upgrade was toast and now I worried whether I'd get a Business Class seat. Still, I was anxious to get out of the airport, so I hurried to the gate.

Parked on the tarmac was a large Boeing 747. My expectations soared. My upgrade might still be good. And then I saw the markings: *Royal Jordanian Airlines!* The display above the check-in counter stated the flight had originated in Beirut. The door opened, and about one hundred passengers from Lebanon deplaned. The gate agent announced that the aircraft would be re-catered with western meals. Still, many of the travelers were dressed in Arab garb. They all looked happy to be out of the Middle East. Sadly, the elation I'd felt, based upon an imminent departure, faded as I realized I had to share an airplane with them. I was more than uneasy. The rest of my fellow travelers didn't look happy, either. I wished I'd stayed in Paris.

The aircraft had two classes, Business Class and Economy. I was seated in 2A on the upper level. The cabin was configured equivalent to First Class, with two seats on each side of the aisle. The Purser offered me a drink, and I began to relax, shrugging off the idea of all those Arabs downstairs, and in seats behind me. Out-of-sight, they were out-of-mind. My paranoia eased. Then, just before the attendants closed the doors, three large men entered the cabin dragging a skinny acne-scarred Caucasian with a nasty sneer on his face. He was handcuffed, dirty, and smelled like a toilet. The men took all the seats in row 1.

"Hey!" said the passenger in 2B. "I know that face. I saw it in the paper yesterday. He's Italian, Red Brigade—they're extraditing him to the U.S. for killing Americans in a bombing. I hope those guards are armed."

So there I was—a day late surrounded by guns and Arabs and seated behind an Italian bomber. All because of a Pan Am strike. I resolved in the future to fly the friendly skies of United.

Chu

April 4, 1943, Tokyo

Admiral Isoroku Yamamoto, fifty-six, talented calligrapher, architect of the raid on Pearl Harbor, and commander of the Combined Fleet, stared at his orders. Emperor Hirohito had requested Yamamoto visit Japanese units in New Guinea to strengthen troop morale. The fighting spirit of the Japanese had fallen after recent battles: the 1942 Doolittle raid on Tokyo punctured Japan's sense of invincibility; the Battle of Midway cost Japan four aircraft carriers—negating its only advantage in naval vessels; and the Battle of the Coral Sea, while technically a draw, was the first time Japan failed to win a battle of capitol ships. Yamamoto had feared that Japan awakened a "sleeping giant" at Pearl Harbor and now the chance for a quick, decisive blow and an early American capitulation had been frittered away at Midway. Yamamoto, a small, wiry man who'd lost two fingers at the Battle of Tsushima, had studied at Harvard and worked in the west. He knew the landings in Guadalcanal were the beginning of an inexorable, island-hopping strategy to attack Japan with superior force and matériel. The war was lost.

Vice Admiral Jinichi Kusaka, his aide, was glum. "Admiral Yamamoto," he said, "I don't think you should go. Our communications security may be breached. Front-line units have broadcast your itinerary in low-level codes, and the field units are re-broadcasting it in the clear. We haven't had time to distribute new high-level codes."

Yamamoto nodded. "You're right, Kusaka-san. The repeated destruction of our resupply efforts to Guadalcanal suggest our field codes are compromised. But this is not surprising; I read all their diplomatic messages when the capital ship ratios with the Americans and British were negotiated in 1930." Yamamoto smiled. He remembered that the conference had not addressed carriers—in his opinion the real strategic weapon in the Pacific. Too bad, he mused, about Midway.

"Then why go?" asked Kusaka.

Yamamoto knew he'd be deceiving the troops, encouraging them to fight the Americans, to each kill at least ten soldiers before they died an honorable death. Yet one more time he'd be obliged by his *chu*—duty to country and the emperor—to spur false hopes of victory. Yamamoto had been a reluctant planner of the attack on Hawaii and regretted the "mindless rejoicing" at home afterwards. But every Japanese had *chu*. They were born with it, and only death could unburden them. And there were other binding commitments: *ko*—to family; and *giri*—to friends, co-workers, the team, the army unit. These duties were drummed into Japanese children and touched every personal and work relationship as they aged. The Japanese spent their entire lives under these yokes.

"*Chu*," answered Yamamoto. "Many soldiers have died an honorable death under my command; how can I not face the same conditions I ask of my men?"

Kusaka frowned. "What can you tell the men that would justify the risk?"

"I will remind them of their *chu* and *giri*, that the Americans are weak and pampered, and that western culture is corrupt. I'll remind them that Japan launched the Greater East Asia Co-Prosperity Sphere to bring Japanese culture and the spirit of *chu* and *giri* to the people of Asia."

Yamamoto didn't tell Kusaka that he knew it was a fool's mission and that should the worst happen—if he had to die—there would never be a better time. He would satisfy his *chu* and join the spirits of all the dead soldiers. "Not to worry, Kusaka-san. My flight will likely be out of range of any Allied aircraft."

Yamamoto flew to Rabaul. When he deplaned, Yamamoto passed several scrolls with his disfigured hand to an aide. "I'm happy to serve the Emperor. Please deliver these scrolls to him should I fail to return."

• • •

April 13, 1943, Washington D.C.

Frank Knox, Secretary of the Navy, walked into the president's office. Franklin Delano Roosevelt wheeled his chair to the desk. "What's up, Frank?"

Knox smiled. "Yamamoto's flying to Bougainville in five days to cheer up the troops. I spoke with the chiefs and they recommend we jump him—but it's a long flight and risky. It's your call, Mr. President."

"How'd you find out? Purple?" (Purple was the codeword for the high-level military and diplomatic Japanese codes broken by the Americans before the war.)

Knox nodded. "They're also broadcasting his schedule to their units in low-level codes. We even had one in the clear. The signals were picked up in Alaska and Hawaii."

"Then they must know we know. What about Purple? Do we think they know we've broken their codes?"

"I doubt if it's a trap. Either they think the admiral's out-of-range of our fighters—or he doesn't care."

"Okay, get him!" Roosevelt agreed to send a flight of seventeen P-38

Lightning fighters, equipped with extra fuel tanks, to intercept Yamamoto. The round trip distance from Guadalcanal, their home base, to Bougainville was 860 miles.

• • •

April 18, 1943, Solomon Islands

The roar of the twin engines on the Mitsubishi Betty bomber bounced off the thick, double-canopy jungle. Birds fluttered. Shadows from an escort fleet of Zeros flitted across the trees. Admiral Yamamoto wore green fatigues, but his ceremonial sword lay on the bench seat. The admiral sipped green tea as his aircraft flew at 5,000 feet. He was startled when the bomber suddenly rolled and dove. Four Lightnings strafed his plane while other fighters engaged the Zeros. Yamamoto died gloriously in combat when the Betty crashed and burned.

Japan promoted Yamamoto to a Marshall and Fleet Admiral, awarded him the Order of the Chrysanthemum, and gave him a state funeral. On one of Yamamoto's scrolls was a Meiji poem, written in his hand:

"So many are dead.
I cannot face the Emperor.
No words for the families.
But I will drive deep
Into the enemy camp.
Wait, young dead soldiers,
I will fight farewell
And follow you soon."

Part III

General Fiction

A Sure Thing

Rick Martin's Moonlight Café and Bar on McNamara Road was the place to party in Anderson County, Texas. Good drinks, the best barbecue south of Galveston, stunning women, a rocking band, and generous slot machines, made for large and happy crowds. The daily Greyhound from New Orleans to Corpus Christi took a dinner break at Rick's. The big gravel parking lot also accommodated eighteen-wheelers. Rick's quarter slot machines, the only one-armed bandits in the county, hummed all evening.

Each machine took in about thirty dollars an hour and returned twenty-five to the customers—yielding a profit of five dollars. With ten slots operating six hours nightly Rick made three hundred a night on his machines.

But Rick had problems. The Christian Women against Gambling (CWAG), led by a local religious zealot, Sister Bertha Williamson, had demonstrated in front of the Moonlight Café and Bar. CWAG also had petitioned the county supervisors for a hearing to air its grievances. Rick knew there was a meeting scheduled, but he hated politics and couldn't be bothered. He was confident things would stay the same. After all, the Moonlight Café and Bar in Quail Vale, just south of the Anderson County seat, had been in Rick's family for three generations.

His grandfather had left it to his dad, and Rick had assumed responsibility for the business the previous year. Rick was forty-five, thin, six feet tall, and had some gray in his hair. Despite a mild limp from being thrown by a horse, he ran three miles and worked out daily with weights. He rode his favorite palomino weekly. There were plenty of women, but Rick's true loves were the slots and the math that drove them.

Rick had attended the University of Nevada and studied applied math. After graduation he'd worked as an engineer at Gally Slot Machine Manufacturing Company. Rick could fine-tune a slot machine to return any percentage—subject only to the laws of statistics and large numbers. Yet few customers complained; his slots returned approximately eighty-four percent. The house took only sixteen percent.

The law left Rick alone. Slots were legal in Anderson County. He ran a clean shop; prostitution was discouraged; bar fights were squashed; the toilets were clean; the liquor license was legit; and the kitchen always received a stamp of approval from the food inspectors. Further, Rick's Moonlight Café and Bar sat on unincorporated land; the only law came from Sheriff Kepler. He was a good natured man whose favorite arrests were DUI and speeding—he'd convinced the county supervisors to set the speed limit on McNamara

Road to fifty-three miles per hour. Half the speedometers in the county were broken and, on busy nights, the sheriff stashed his arrests in Rick's storm cellar. After he assembled a large enough group to fill a wagon, he would ship it to the county jail in Quail Vale.

• • •

One morning in June, Rick jogged up McNamara Road into Quail Vale. When he stopped for a cup of coffee in the Quail Run Coffee Shop, he noticed a shocking headline on the *Anderson County Gazette*. He grabbed a copy and, over coffee, read:

SUPES SLUG SLOTS

(Quail Vale) Emotions ran high last night in a meeting of the Anderson County board of supervisors. An unlikely coalition of the Christian Women against Gambling (CWAG), headed by local activist Sister Bertha Williamson, and the Association of Choctaw, Chippewa, and Apache Chiefs (CCAC), demanded the supervisors outlaw gambling in the county. Sister Bertha spoke on the evils of gambling and the impact it had on the poor and homeless. She said, "These people risk it all on Rick Martin's one-armed bandits. Their children are left helpless and thrown on the county's welfare system, which can ill afford it."

Chief Running Red Hawk, from Deer Prairie, a large Choctaw Indian reservation near Corpus Christi, represented the CCAC. He said that small-scale casinos presented insurmountable political problems to the Indian nations, which wished to renegotiate their treaties with the United States. Such revisions, claimed the chief, would permit large-scale casinos on tribal lands. In response to questions posed by Sister Bertha's followers, the chief said the poor would be discouraged from entering CCAC Indian casinos. He promised a "Means Test" to protect them.

County Supervisor Bob Jenkins asked if anyone

> wished to speak against the motion to outlaw slot machines. He noted that Rick Martin had been invited to the meeting but failed to respond. Several supervisors spoke against the motion Nevertheless, after heated debate, the supervisors voted three to two with four abstentions to outlaw slot machines effective August 1.
>
> There was loud applause from a crowd of CWAG women. The women held hands, and sang "We Shall Overcome." Sister Bertha addressed her followers saying, "Next, we go after the firewater ..."

Oh, my God, thought Rick. Loss of the slots would cost him a hundred grand a year. And they were going after the booze next? The threat elicited panic. He gulped down his coffee and ran over to the county jail. Sheriff Kepler was hanging a wanted poster on the bulletin board when Rick barged through the door.

"Sheriff, what can I do about this new law against slots?"

"Rick, I wondered why you weren't at the meeting. CWAG had the audience wired, but most people in the county like you. I'm sure the supervisors would have rejected the law if you'd argued against it."

"Well," said Rick, "I'm gonna fight it anyway. My dad's lawyer's up in Galveston, and I'm going there today."

Sheriff Kepler frowned. "Rick, the machines will be illegal in August. You better get rid of them. I'm sworn to uphold the law; I don't want to have to arrest you."

Rick felt his bile rise. "Sheriff, you do what you got to do. Meanwhile, you better find a new place to stow your drunks. As of now, my storm cellar's off-limits."

"Sorry you feel that way, Rick."

• • •

Rick's visit to the lawyer proved fruitless.

"We can appeal it," said the lawyer. "But we'll lose. I recommend you save the legal fees and forfeit the machines. Meanwhile, you should pay more attention to those notices of hearings in the future. You sure don't want the county going dry on you."

• • •

July came and went and Rick dithered. Each slot generated thirty to fifty dollars a night. Business was so good he considered installing more machines. Salesmen from Gally encouraged him to fight the new ordinance.

Unable to make a decision, Rick kept his machines. It was difficult to abandon an income stream of $500 a night. But Rick sensed it wouldn't last forever.

Sheriff Kepler arrived on August 8 in a convoy of two cruisers and a large U-Haul truck. He served a warrant on Rick, ordered his deputies to confiscate the machines, and told Rick to present himself in the courthouse the next morning—to be booked on a charge of illegal gambling. Half an hour later, the Moonlight Café and Bar was deserted, and the band departed.

The next day Rick was booked, fingerprinted, and released on his own recognizance. He returned to his café and sat at one of his tables. Rick was pondering his future when Jesse James Johnson, a horse trainer and old cowboy, joined him with a beer.

"What'ya gonna do, Rick?"

"Beats the shit out of me, Jesse. I need to replace $100,000 a year in income or I'm out of business."

"Well, I don't have any business ideas, but I got a hot tip. *Incitatus,* in the third at Belmont on the twelfth of August, is a sure thing."

"A sure thing? How is that possible?" Rick looked at the empty wall where his slot machines once stood; now *they,* he thought ruefully, had been a sure thing.

Jesse grinned. "There ain't no one that knows horseflesh better than me, and I'm telling you, it's a sure thing. And, when there's no risk, it ain't gambling."

At that moment something clicked in Rick's brain and he had an epiphany—if it was a sure thing, if there was no risk, it wasn't gambling! He grabbed the phone and called the chief engineer at Gally.

"Let me ask a question," Rick said. "Is it possible …?"

• • •

Six weeks later, Rick's Moonlight Café and Bar was crowded. A bank of new slots filled the space vacated by the old machines. The band played, people danced, beer flowed, and quarters dropped into the slots which still returned eighty-four percent—just under slightly different conditions than usual.

At 10:00 PM the sheriff pulled up in his cruiser alone. He went into the café and asked Rick to follow him out to the parking lot.

Gray dust clouds floated in the air, illuminated by the mercury vapor lights, and stirred up by the sheriff who kicked repeatedly at the gravel with the tips of his boots. The two men leaned against the side of the cruiser.

"Rick, what's this bullshit? Those slots are illegal."

"Sheriff," Rick said with confidence, "these machines may look like traditional slots, but they're not illegal. They're nothing but mechanical games, like pinball machines. There's no risk and you know exactly what'll happen before you put in a quarter."

The sheriff seemed bewildered. "What do you mean?"

"C'mon, I'll show you."

They went back into the café and walked up to one of the new machines. It looked like a standard slot machine; it had three wheels and an arm on the right side capped with a large red ball.

"Look at this machine," said Rick. "The wheels at the pay-line show cherry-apple-watermelon, right?"

"Er, … yes."

"Well, according to the pay-table on the front, the cherry is a winner. That means the machine will pay you two quarters if you put in one quarter. It's determined in advance. Try it."

The sheriff put a quarter in the slot, pulled the arm down, and received two quarters in return. The wheels at the pay-line now displayed bar-bar-lemon.

Rick smiled. "This time the pay-table says you'll get back nothing. That's also completely determined in advance. There's no uncertainty, so it can't be gambling. Try it."

The sheriff dutifully put in one of the two quarters and the machine gobbled it up, yielded nothing, and the wheels moved into new positions.

"Well, what about the next roll?" asked the sheriff.

"What about it? Don't they call that speculation in the law? No one says you got to speculate."

"But Rick, they're gambling! They're just betting they'll get a winner on the next roll."

"So let's see," said Rick. "The wheels say there's no payout, but somebody puts money in the machine anyway. You say that's illegal? Since when is it illegal to be stupid?"

"But what about the poor people? What if they're down to their last quarter?"

Rick smiled. "Now that would be really dumb, wouldn't it? To put your last quarter in the machine when you know without doubt it's a loser?" Rick figured that's what happened with this machine—some fool had dropped his last quarter in the slot.

"I can't deal with this logic," said Kepler. "I got to report this to the supervisors. This is way above my pay grade."

"You do that, Sheriff. Have a nice evening."

• • •

After the sheriff reported, the county supervisors consulted with District Attorney Alex Lohse. He noted Rick's argument was interesting but the local county court would reject it. "The problem," he said, "will come if and when Rick appeals it to a higher court, where there might be thinking creatures."

The supervisors decided to ask Judge Barney Green for a warrant to confiscate the new machines. Sheriff Kepler was ordered to grab them. At a hearing to determine the status of the new slots, Judge Green ruled they were gaming devices. Rick, after consulting with a legal scholar at the University of Texas, decided to bring a case in federal court on constitutional grounds.

• • •

Several months later, a troupe of lawyers from the American Civil Liberties Union marched into the U.S. District Court for Southern Texas in Galveston. The ACLU represented Rick; the county was represented by Alex Lohse. The case was called by Judge William Kennedy.

"I understand this case is being argued on constitutional grounds. Is that correct?" asked the judge.

"Yes, Your Honor," said the lead ACLU lawyer. "We believe that the definition of gambling is so explicit, and, in contradistinction, the law so vague regarding enforcement, as to render it unconstitutional in this case."

"Well, what is the definition of gambling?" asked Judge Kennedy.

The lawyer said, "If I may, Your Honor, we've assembled definitions of gambling from several sources. Gambling is: (1) the act of playing for stakes in the hopes of winning; (2) to bet on an act or undertaking of uncertain outcome; (3) to play a game of chance for stakes; (4) any matter or thing involving risk or uncertainty; and (5) a person must have something at risk to be considered gambling."

"Your Honor," continued the lawyer, "this is only the tip of the iceberg. Every definition requires unpredictability, risk, chance, and uncertainty."

"All right, thank you. And why does that not apply in this case?"

"Your Honor, our client, Rick Martin, did not operate games of chance. In every instance, in every play, the player knew precisely, and in advance, what would happen. May we demonstrate?"

With the judge's permission, one of Rick's new slot machines was wheeled into the courtroom. The ACLU attorney pulled the arm ten times. The machine swallowed ten quarters and spat out a total of seven quarters.

Rick's attorney said, "Your Honor, I hope you noted that at every step we knew precisely what would happen, in advance. It might have been dumb to insert those quarters, but it was not gambling by any definition."

"Thank you. Mr. Lohse, what say the county?"

District Attorney Lohse rose. "Judge, the county submits that the devices owned by Mr. Martin are gambling machines in that the players assume risk by really betting on the next roll of the machine."

At that, the ACLU lawyer leapt up. "Objection! What is this 'next roll' stuff? That's speculation—pure and simple. At no time in the act of using the machine is there uncertainty. How do we know the player thinks that he wants to know what the next roll will be? What if he just likes to watch wheels spin and lights flash, like people who play a pinball machine? How can we get inside the head of the player? The only thing that's certain," he concluded, "is the predetermined result on our client's machine."

Judge Kennedy pondered the argument for a while. "Objection noted. I'll take the case under advisement. Briefs in two weeks," he ordered. "Replies, if any, in two more."

• • •

Six months after the trial, Judge Kennedy ruled that Rick's new slots were not gaming devices. Rick's patent application, filed after his epiphany, was approved. Most casinos in the country based their slot machines on Rick's patent. Even the Indian tribes were happy. They planned to substitute their existing slots with Rick's non-gambling machines. That would enable them to ignore the restrictions placed on them by the State Gaming Commissions and dramatically increase the number of machines in their casinos. Rick was a wealthy man.

Tiger!

Air Pacific flight 687 left Honolulu at midnight. The tour group of divers scattered around the rear of the Boeing 737's cabin slept as the aircraft droned on towards Fiji. Sprawled in an aisle seat, Don Leatherman snored with his mouth open. The passengers around him had stuffed plugs in their ears and drunk themselves to sleep.

Don was stocky with the body of a weightlifter. His arms were enormous, shaped by lifting thousands of tanks of compressed air in his dive shop on Maui. Don's Dive Shop was the preferred diving establishment for the locals in Kihei, as well as knowledgeable divers from the mainland. The shop wasn't as elegant or as busy as the Maui Dive Shop franchises, but Don's Dive Shop was known for its friendly environment, impeccable attention to detail, and excellent diving instructors. Attesting to that popularity were nineteen divers on board who'd subscribed to Don's annual trip to Beqa Island. One of them, a new Open Water certified diver, Bill Casey, twenty-nine, rolled over and poked Don in the ribs with an elbow. Don awoke with a grunt.

"Yo, what's up?"

"Sorry, Don. Accident."

"No problem. Tell me, Bill. Are you going to the shark feed?"

"Gee, I don't know. That's scary stuff."

"Aw, come on," said Don. "I've been doing this for years. The shark feeds are tame as hell. The sharks are well fed, and there's a bunch of Fiji guys that act as handlers—you know, in case one of the fish gets nosey."

"It's optional, ain't it? And it costs an extra hundred dollars?"

"Yeah, but it's worth it! There'll be a herd of sharks. They're six-to-ten feet if they're an inch."

Casey flinched. "Jesus! And they're tame?"

Don smiled. "Let's not take the Lord's name in vain, Bill. *Tame* might be a stretch."

"Well, how's it work? Do we just jump in the water and watch them eat? What do they eat?"

Don studied Casey. This was his first trip with Don's Dive Shop. Only five dives were required to reach Casey's level of certification; most such divers were not very skilled. They had buoyancy management problems and few specialties, such as "Navigation" or "Deep." And they consumed vast quantities of air which limited their time in the water. Maybe he shouldn't take Casey to the shark feed. Still, it was another hundred bucks.

"It's really pretty safe, Bill," said Don. "The Fijians do this once a week.

They get several boats of divers together from the different resorts on the shores of Beqa Lagoon, and everyone dives to fifty feet."

"Fifty?" asked Casey. "That seems deep to me. I only feel safe at thirty-five feet. At that depth, I know I can make it to the surface without breathing—you know, just exhaling."

"Bill, no one's going to run out of air. There are twenty of us, which means there are forty air supply regulators plus the Fiji guys and the other boats' divers. The boats' crews drop extra tanks on ropes fifteen feet down with extra regulators. You can hang off of them, if necessary, and perform your safety stop on their air. And it's not like we're going real deep. You just need a five minute stop—and even that's overkill given our dive profile. In the worst case, you could stay down a long time."

"So, what happens next?"

"The Fijians have constructed a small wall out of rocks and coral on the ocean floor. We line up behind it. With all the divers putting up bubbles, we create a seemingly impenetrable wall—no shark's going to come through it. Then some Fiji guys stand in front of the wall, and some station themselves behind the divers. They're the handlers, with long poles or spears to discourage any accidental interest. Another guy feeds the sharks. These are bull sharks, pretty non-threatening, too." Don decided Casey didn't need to know bull sharks were an aggressive and mean species, or that they'd been known to cruise up the Ganges River feeding on Hindus' corpses.

"Some guy feeds the sharks? How?" asked Casey.

"He digs fish parts out of a portable dumpster, like a yard recycling bin—they call it a chum bucket—and throws the food into the sharks' mouths as they swim by."

"Do these guys have all of their hands? That sounds really stupid."

"Well," said Don, "I agree you got to be careful, but diving is supposed to be exciting. And besides, it's the pros who take the risk. Bring your underwater camera. You'll be so busy taking pictures; it'll be over in no time."

"And what keeps the sharks from fighting over the food? They line up?"

"That's right, Bill, it's almost like a circus act. They swim in a circle, head-to-tail like a daisy chain—similar to elephants walking. The sharks take turns, too. They peel out of the circle and make a pass at the food. Then they get back in the circle."

"Uh-huh. Six-to-ten feet sharks? Over my dead body." Casey looked at Don like he was out of his mind, pulled the blanket over his head, and rolled over.

"Don't be a wuss, Bill; girls will be there." Don smiled, closed his eyes, and was snoring again in two minutes.

• • •

Fourteen hours later, the divers were ensconced in the Lawaki Beach House on Beqa Island. The island was situated in a large lagoon five miles south of Navua, the capital city. The waters in the trench between the main island of Viti Levu and Beqa Island were 800 feet deep. A reef encircled the island, and a barrier reef protected the larger lagoon. Hundreds of species of coral radiated vibrant colors, and the reefs teemed with over a thousand varieties of tropical fish and other sea creatures. Diving conditions were excellent—tremendous visibility and warm waters.

Upon arrival, the divers had checked out their gear, enjoyed a welcoming lunch, and were assigned to their own private bungalows or shared condominiums along the ocean. Casey paid a premium for a private room. He received a small bungalow with a private splash pool located on the beach.

The bungalow had a thatched roof, king-sized bed, sitting area, a powerful air conditioner, and a small lanai. Casey unpacked, locked his wallet and passport in a handy wall safe, and went to the lodge.

He stocked up on ice and returned to his bungalow. He was relaxing in a hammock tied to palm trees when two women from a nearby condominium strolled up with a bottle of vodka and three glasses. The women had sat two rows behind Casey on the flight to Fiji and attracted his attention. He'd kidded with them on the boat ride to Beqa Island.

"Got any ice?" asked Celia, a fine looking woman. She was thirty-five, five foot four, and had a trim athletic figure. Celia had over three hundred dives in her logbook. Her girlfriend, Jennifer, was a little younger, but Bill thought Jennifer was prettier. Jennifer had long dishwater-blonde hair, large brown eyes and dimples, and a sensuous mouth flanked by high cheek bones. She was a certified master scuba diver with a rescue diver specialty.

"Sure," answered Casey. "I already got an ice bucket from the lodge."

Ice tinkled and drinks were poured.

Casey's mind began to speculate. Here were two attractive women, thousands of miles from home, and the trip would last ten days. Maybe he'd get laid—if the girls weren't gay. Maybe he would anyway. Maybe he could fulfill a dream—a *ménage á trois.*

"Bill," said Jennifer, "Celia and I wonder if you're going on the shark feed dive. We want to go, and we'd like to have a strong dive buddy to hold onto if there's a problem. You look pretty strong."

"Right," added Celia. "Don told us it's fairly safe. But we thought, you know, a group of three would offer more safety in numbers."

"I'll certainly consider it." Casey smiled to himself. It was interesting how something unthinkable suddenly became thinkable.

The women smiled sweetly, removed their bikini tops, and jumped into the plunge pool. Casey joined them for a giggling, splashing, and vodka-accelerated riot of fun.

After several days of dives in the lagoon, the three became quite close. Casey slept one night with Celia. He hoped things would develop with Jennifer too—especially at the party after the shark feed. It was scheduled for later in the week. Casey still hadn't decided whether he'd go to the shark feed. But he suspected real men weren't afraid of fish, and Jennifer, he thought, liked real men.

• • •

The day before the shark feed, the divers took a walk around the island. It had been formed several million years ago during a volcanic eruption. Beqa was tropical, with lush palm trees, ferns, banana plants, and two small villages at opposite ends of the island. The natives were friendly, spoke English, and, in rites of passage and to entertain tourists, walked barefoot on stones heated in an open fire. Their children had entertained the divers each night with songs. A local drink called Kava—a mild intoxicant—was served to the divers after dinner. During the ceremony that evening, and a little high on the Kava, Casey was selected by the diving group as the *Ratu*, their tribal chief.

Don smiled. "That means, *Ratu* that you lead the divers down to the shark feed tomorrow."

Casey turned pale. "But I haven't decided to go." He looked to Celia for support.

"Oh, *Ratu*, Jennifer and I thought you'd be our dive buddy." Then Celia leaned over and whispered in his ear, "And we have a special treat planned for you afterwards."

Casey's mind raced. Fear fought with lust—and lost. Maybe that treat was both of them. "Er … ah, okay, I suppose it's safe. Right. I'll do it."

The next morning, Casey elected to skip the early dive and remain on land to steel himself for the shark feed. The lodge had a satellite Internet connection, and he browsed the net while he studied the characteristics of the island and the lagoon. He learned that many animals, from fruit bats to mongoose to lizards, populated the island. The sea life included dolphins, turtles, and shellfish. The divers already had seen some neat octopuses. Casey was tempted to sign up for an additional night dive which offered a different array of sea life than a day dive.

Before he logged off, Casey decided to look up "bull shark" on *Wikipedia*. Their size was consistent with Don's remarks:

> "*Bull sharks are large and stout. Males can reach up to 7 feet in length and weigh 200 pounds. Females can be much larger: up to 11 feet and weigh 700 pounds. Bull sharks are wider than other sharks of comparable length, and are grey on top and white below. The diet of a Bull shark includes fish, other sharks, rays, dolphins, turtles, and even terrestrial mammals.* Relatively calm Bull sharks can suddenly become violent."

What the hell, thought Casey. Don hadn't mentioned violence. He began to wonder if the treat Celia had promised him was worth the risk. Those goddamn fish were terrifying. He did more searches. He learned that bull sharks were in the same category as the tiger and great white sharks; they were the most aggressive species of sharks in the ocean. Further, they were territorial, and the divers were going into their territory. Damn!

Casey returned to his bungalow and found Jennifer waiting for him. "Jennifer," he mumbled, "maybe we ought to rethink this shark feed thing."

"Bill, I don't want to talk about sharks. Let's take a swim and skip lunch. Celia tells me you're a great lover."

Casey's thinking apparatus suddenly shifted to a different part of his body. All thoughts of sharks disappeared, and two hot intermingled bodies sank into the plunge pool.

• • •

That afternoon the divers boarded a dive boat and headed north to the shark feed location. As one of the crew tied the boat off to a buoy, they noticed three other craft headed for their position.

"Everyone in the water," barked Don. "We want to be first group at the right end of the wall. That's where the sharks pass, after they grab their food."

The gang slapped on their gear, cranked open their air tanks, and jumped en masse into the water. Don carried a large underwater video camera. A reluctant *Ratu*, Bill Casey led the descent. On the sea floor, the divers lined up behind a short wall. Jennifer, Celia, and Casey anchored the right end of the line. Soon the waters filled with divers from the other boats—all assembled in linear fashion to the gang's left. Casey admitted to himself that the divers' air bubbles looked like an impenetrable wall.

In front of Casey, and about twenty feet to his right, he saw a half-dozen bull sharks. They swam head-to-tail in a tight circle. A Fiji diver was center-right in front of the wall—perhaps fifteen feet—with a chum bucket. He held up small fish parts. A huge sphere-shaped cluster of fish hovered over his head; they dived at the parts, nibbling. Four handlers with long poles and a few spears lined up behind the divers, and two handlers stood in front of the ends of the wall.

Every minute or so, a bull shark peeled out of formation and swept toward the chum bucket. It was rewarded with a large fish head or carcass, perhaps a tuna, which the shark snatched with enormous teeth. Then it cruised along the front of the wall, passed within several feet of Casey and the women, and returned to the waiting circle. It was awesome and Casey laughed into his regulator. The other divers were engaged in a photo-taking frenzy while the fish and sharks were in a feeding frenzy. So much food was delivered to the sharks that the smaller fish in the sphere weren't threatened.

Don swam over to Casey and made a diver's "Okay?" sign with his thumb and forefinger. Casey responded positively. It was all working out and he had high expectations for a real treat back on land. Don pointed at his eyes and then himself, indicating that Casey and the girls should watch him. Don swam forward past the wall and planted himself below the swirling sharks. Don turned on his camera and lights and began to film. Just then the ball of fish disintegrated—fish scattered in all directions. Then the bull sharks peeled off and left the area. All the divers looked around. They wondered what had spooked the sea life. And then they saw it. A twelve foot tiger shark had stumbled on the feed. Panic ensued. Casey and the girls looked over their shoulders and discovered the handlers had abandoned their posts. The guy at the chum bucket scurried back to the wall. The handlers in front dropped their spears and joined the divers behind the wall. Everyone looked at Don out there alone with only his camera. The tiger looked at Don, too.

Tigers were solitary hunters. They usually searched for prey at night. The name was derived from the dark stripes that run down a tiger's body. This shark was an adolescent since its stripes were pronounced; they tended to fade as tigers aged. Tigers were dangerous predators—they ate anything, even metal and old tires.

Casey watched Don flatten himself on the bottom. Don held the camera in front and above him. The tiger made a beeline for him and swooped down. Casey wanted to bolt for the boat, but Celia, a more experienced diver, held onto him. She signaled that the group should stay together. Casey nodded. He remembered his research. Tigers, like lions hunting zebras, preferred stragglers or tried to cut an animal out of a herd. As long as the herd remained together, it was relatively safe. But Don was on his own.

Casey began to worry about his air. It was in short supply. The divers had been at a depth of fifty feet for over fifty minutes. A decompression stop at fifteen feet for five minutes was the prescribed safety measure. Even if the tiger let them race for the surface, they might get the bends. And, with the shark in the area, no single diver could use the air tanks that hung below the boats.

Further, Casey was cold. Don, guessed Casey, was probably sweating. The tiger came right at Don, and he couldn't move. As the tiger dropped, Casey saw Don ram his camera up. The shark ground its body down on top of Don. Casey gasped, as Don's entire body disappeared beneath the tiger. Casey wondered if Don would survive the attack. Would anyone get back to the boats with the predator in the water?

During his research, Casey had learned that only the great white sharks were responsible for more human deaths than tigers. The great whites might be larger, but he figured this shark weighed about 750 pounds. He was ready to abandon hope for Don when the tiger abruptly called off the attack. As it swam away, Don scrambled halfway back to the wall. Then the fish executed a 180 degree turn and returned. It was fast! Tigers could move twenty miles per hour, faster in a burst. The shark passed through the impenetrable wall of rising bubbles, twisted its bright yellow underbelly, and terrified every diver behind the wall. Playing coy, it retreated. Then it turned and charged again on Don, who'd managed to slither back to the front of the wall. With his back to the wall and his legs and rump on the ocean floor, Don took the full brunt of the charge. Once more he jammed the camera into the bottom of the shark's jaws. Frustrated, unable to open its mouth, the tiger twisted and ground down, but could make no headway.

As the tiger pulled away again, some of the Fiji handlers herded a bunch of divers up to the decompression tanks. Keeping a reef to their back and hanging on each other's arms to maintain a compact ball, those who needed air took five minutes while the tiger circled endlessly. When the shark made another exit pass, the divers scampered up to their boats, and another bunch of divers wormed their way up to the tanks. Bill Casey reached the extra air tanks with a few minutes of reserve air left in his tank. The women, who used less air, had about ten minutes.

That night, in addition to some long hot showers, there were a lot of wet suits thrown in the lodge's washing machines—with extra detergent. Still, divers were a hearty bunch, and by the time the banquet was over the tiger had grown another three feet. Later, dancing with Celia and Jennifer, Bill felt a rush of adrenaline explode in his system. By the time the women got him to his room, he was only semi-conscious. Bill never got his *ménage á trois.*

• • •

One year later, Don's Dive Shop organized another trip to Fiji. En route, Bill Casey, now an experienced diver with fifty dives, sat next to Stan, a new diver from Maui.

"Stan," he said, "are you coming to the shark feed on this trip?"

"Shark feed?" asked Stan. "No one told me about a shark feed. Is it included in the price?"

"It's just an extra hundred bucks," urged Casey. "But it's worth every penny."

"Ain't it dangerous?"

"Not at all," said Celia, who sat behind Casey.

"It's a kick," said Jennifer, who was seated next to Celia.

Casey looked at Stan and smiled.

The Piano Police

Davey Grant, seven, was small for his age and scared of everything: his shadow, dogs, bullies, smelly things like cooked cauliflower, and, especially, his piano teacher. Baron Szily was Hungarian, a descendant of a minor branch of a noble family in the days of the Hapsburgs. The baron wore an eye patch and had a wooden foot.

Szily spoke with a strange accent and never smiled. He wore a cape just like that Dracula guy who had scared Davey in *Abbot and Costello Meet Frankenstein*, the scariest DVD that Davey ever saw. The baron even clumped around like Frankenstein.

The boy had taken piano lessons since he was four. He'd progressed rapidly. Despite his skill he disliked counting out loud as he played his music. As might be expected, his reticence to count became a larger problem as the music increased in complexity. His previous teacher had been relaxed and encouraging, but this new teacher was more demanding.

Davey struggled with his fingering while the Baron said, "David, you must count! One and two and three and one and—"

Davey slammed his hands on the keyboard and struck a discordant note which reverberated throughout the room. He looked at his teacher with fear, anger, and frustration. "I hate to count. Hate it. It's so hard, it sounds stupid, and all my friends laugh at me when they hear I have to count out loud."

Szily, who'd studied under someone who'd studied under the famous Czerny, shook his head. These Americans, he thought, spoiled by their wealth and privilege. How could they understand the demands that music—fine music—placed on them? The baron rolled his one eye, snorted in disgust, and tried once more. "Counting, David, is absolutely necessary to play the music properly. Someday you might count in your head, but for now you must say it out loud. If you don't count, the Piano Police will get angry. Do you see my foot? That's what happens when the Piano Police get angry."

Davey looked at the baron's right foot. It was a big hunk of carved red wood, which the baron lifted and slammed down with a loud thunk on every other step. Davey could see himself running to first base with a wooden foot and all the kids laughing at him. He gulped with tears in his eyes. "I'll try. Please don't call the Piano Police." Deep down, Davey wondered if he could reach the pedals with a wooden foot.

"Yes, David," said the baron. "You must try. At your recital this weekend, I will expect to hear you counting every beat of the music. Beethoven's 'Für Elise' is a beautiful piece when it is properly timed. Now, be sure to practice for another hour while you count. I will see you Saturday." The baron stood, draped his cape over his shoulders, and stormed out of the room with a series of thumps.

Davey grit his teeth and turned back to his music. Those Piano Police meant he had to count—he liked his right foot. Crestfallen, he practiced his A-Minor scale and counted every note as he ran his fingers up and down the keys. Then he doubled the speed and counted twice as fast as he went up and down two octaves. Then, he tripled the pace and the octaves, and the numbers poured out of his mouth. It sounded awful.

• • •

Davey's father stopped Baron Szily as the teacher limped and banged his way down the hallway of the Lafayette Music School.

"So how's he doing?" Mr. Grant didn't like Szily, but he knew the baron was a great pianist.

"He's doing just fine, but he must have more discipline."

"But, Baron, he's only seven. He can't even reach the pedals."

"Music demands perfection," retorted the baron.

Despite his distaste for the man's personality, Grant knew that Szily had been shot and wounded by an explosion when he escaped Hungary during the 1956 Revolution. Grant wondered if that had turned Szily into a demanding teacher or whether the man always had been obsessed with perfection—which Grant knew was groomed and reinforced in classical musicians. After all, the man was a disciple of Czerny.

"I know he's afraid of you, Baron. I'm not sure that fear is the best way to motivate the boy."

The baron stopped and turned to face Grant. He poked his finger in Grant's chest. "The boy has nothing to fear. I merely stressed the need to count the notes. But he is just, I suspect, another provincial American. You should dampen your expectations."

"Baron, you're a great pianist, and I want the best for Davey. But you need to relax sometimes."

• • •

That Saturday, the Lafayette Music School's students and parents assembled for the recital of Baron Szily's students. The recital began, and Davey waited his turn.

At just that time, Bill Collins and Joe Franklin, two good ole boys from the Klan, were driving Bill's '79 Chevy pick-up truck down a county dirt road on the outskirts of Lafayette. Bill's .22 rifle obscured the view in the rear window, but Joe could see Thor, Bill's German shepherd, standing in the bed of the truck. The dog drooled, with his tongue hanging out. Bill's truck raised large clouds of yellow dust and left tracks that looked like a huge python had slithered down the road.

Joe looked nervous. He held his head while sweat stains spread across his T-shirt.

"Who cares if you owe Dutch that money?" asked Bill, who was half-snockered on cheap whiskey and driving erratically. "He's a wus and it's only a grand—what's the big deal?"

"He may be a pushover," said Joe, "but he's got tough friends. Jose, that spic buddy of his, can bench press 300 pounds. He'll be in my face if I don't settle with Dutch."

"So what you gonna do?" Bill was anxious. Joe was a wild guy. He did stupid and unpredictable things. Bill swallowed some more whiskey and handed the bottle to Joe.

"I don't know. Let's see if we can solve the problem at that 7-Eleven in Lafayette."

"Are you sure? They got tough cops in Lafayette, and the sheriff's one mean S-O-B, too."

Joe smiled and reached into the glove compartment for Bill's Colt .380 semi-automatic pistol. It was a small handgun holding five rounds in the magazine and one in the pipe. "Don't worry. We'll be in and out in no time. Turn left and head over there."

• • •

Twenty minutes later, Bill and Joe sped away with a grand total of $183.

Just as the strip mall which housed the 7-Eleven vanished in Bill's rear view mirror, a beautician in the shop next to the 7-Eleven called the sheriff. She reported that she'd heard a shot, and seen two men run past her window. They'd jumped into a truck with a snarling dog and a bumper sticker that said "Help Stamp Out Bumper Stickers."

In the truck, Bill shook. "Damn it, Joe, did you have to shoot the clerk? That's all the money he had in the cash drawer."

"I didn't like his attitude," growled Joe. "Look, I got to get more money. Head for the currency exchange in Lebanon."

"Why don't we just get drunk instead? We're in deep shit now. This is serious stuff."

"Look, Bill, I'm sorry. It's that goddamn Dutch. I got to get more money. What else could I do?" Joe waved the .380 in the air.

"Jesus, Joe, be careful. It's loaded." Bill wondered if Joe was crazy, or drunk, or maybe both.

Just then a siren whooped. Bill looked in his rear view mirror and saw a sheriff's cruiser barreling down on them. In the distance, he could see another cruiser with flashing lights. Thor howled like a coyote, and the two men looked at each other.

"Goddamn it, Joe. What are we gonna do?"

"Let's ditch the truck and hide out in that school over there."

• • •

The audience applauded as Davey Grant walked onto the stage with his sheet music. There were suppressed giggles in the crowd as he sat at the piano with his feet dangling above the pedals. A proud Mr. Grant sat in the front row, while Baron Szily sat, with his usual frown, in the last row on the aisle.

Davey opened his sheet music and prepared to play. The crowd hushed and he began. He hoped that the music would drown out the sound of his counting. He played well, but as he came to the end of the second page, he fumbled the sheet music. This caused him to stop counting so that no one would hear him. Baron Szily jumped out of his seat and stormed down the aisle shouting, "Count! I told you to count." Davey heard thump, thump, thump! He froze in fear, picturing Dracula and Frankenstein in the old movie.

Just then, two men with a gun and a large snarling dog burst into the auditorium, followed by three armed deputies. Davey saw the dog and the police and became hysterical. His right leg jerked as he hyperventilated and fell off the piano bench. As he lay on the floor, Davey's eye's filled with the vision of three policemen coming for his right foot.

Bedlam erupted as people stormed the exits blocking the progress of the deputies. Davey heard the shouts and passed out.

The baron turned and was confronted by a man with a gun.

"Get out of the way, you stupid cripple," hissed the gunman.

Baron Szily saw the police fighting their way through the crowd. He stiffened. "That's my student up there. There is no way I will let you pass. I saw enough scum like you in Communist Hungary. Get—"

The gunman shot the baron in the stomach. He fired again and the shot went wild, striking Davey in the right foot.

The baron, as he fell, wrapped his arms around the gunman's legs and dragged him down. Two deputies swarmed over them. Mr. Grant sprang up and raced for the stage. By the time he got to Davey, who was still unconscious, the gunman's accomplice had surrendered to the other deputy. The dog was restrained a few moments later. Paramedics arrived in ten minutes and attended to Davey and the baron.

• • •

Three days later, Davey was released from the hospital. His right foot was in a cast. Davey was pale and dopey. In the hospital, he'd asked repeatedly if his foot was still inside the cast.

As his father wheeled him to the front of the hospital, Davey asked again, "Dad, do I still have my foot?"

"Of course, Davey. I don't understand why you wouldn't let that pretty nurse write her name on your cast."

"Are you sure?"

"Why would you even think that?"

Davey nodded and decided to believe his father. Still, those Piano Police *had* come.

"What happened to my teacher, Dad?"

"The baron? He'll be in the hospital for some time, Davey. You know, he may have saved your life. He was shot, but he still helped the police catch the man with the gun."

"Dad, I don't want to play the piano anymore."

"But, Davey, I can get you a different teacher."

"It's not the teacher. I don't like to count. The baron told me the Piano Police would come for me if I didn't count. And they did."

Davey's father grimaced. The baron had terrorized the boy! Mr. Grant grabbed Davey's hand to reassure him. "It's okay, Davey," he said, both loathing, and loving, the man who had stopped the gunman. "The Piano Police will never come again."

Data

The voters of the state of California approved an amendment to the property tax code adopted in Proposition Thirteen. The revised code provided for the taxation of data bases on commercial computer systems. Software applications and other computer programs were exempted from the new tax.

The county of Santa Clara leapt at the opportunity to increase its tax base. The data base of IGF Credit DB Systems, Inc., a company that monitored the credit data of fifteen million Americans, was assessed a value of $100 million by the county's tax assessment board. Based on the new rates, it yielded an annual property tax of $3 million. IGF appealed the assessment on the grounds that the law was unconstitutionally vague, and offered no guidance to the public as to how to enforce it. Despite its appeal, IGF was obliged to pay the tax in advance. The appeal was underway in the California State Court of Tax Appeals.

• • •

In the matter of the IGF Credit DB Systems v
County of Santa Clara Tax Assessor: Case number A-2006-0001-33.

Presiding:
Judge Henry B. Winston, Senior Appellate Judge

For the County of Santa Clara:
Mr. Stanley Braidman

For IGF Credit:
Ms. Susan Lohse, Carruthers and Schwartz

• • •

The county had presented its case, and the judge asked IGF to present its arguments …

Ms. Lohse: We'd like to call an expert witness on software, Your Honor.

Judge Winston: What will this expert testify to, Ms. Lohse?

Ms. Lohse: Your Honor, the tax bill provides for a tax on data and not on computer programs. We shall show that data and programs are indistinguishable—that programs are data, and that data are programs. We have a distinguished expert to attest to these facts. After the expert's testimony, I'm confident the court will find for the appellant and order the refund of the $3 million.

Mr. Braidman: Your Honor, relevance? I object. This is absurd. Everyone knows that data are different from programs.

Judge Winston: Well, let's hear the expert's credentials. Personally I don't know what a program is. Perhaps this is relevant. Motion denied. Go ahead, Ms. Lohse, introduce your expert.

Ms. Lohse: I call Dr. Peter K. Lemming.

• • •

Peter Lemming took the stand. He was a diminutive man, about fifty-five, with graying hair and a large nose. He looked confidently at Ms. Lohse, straightened his tie, and cleared his throat in a professorial manner.

• • •

Ms. Lohse: So, Dr. Lemming, would you please state your credentials in computers and software?

Dr. Lemming: I have a doctorate in computer science from the University of Washington. I did a postdoc at Georgetown, and I'm vice president and director of computing research at Menlo Defense Research Institute, where I manage 175 people, many with PhDs. I've published professionally in refereed journals, of course. I started programming in 1968, which makes me a pioneer in computing. I've received the Distinguished Service Award from the Association for

Software Systems (ASS). Most recently, I was invited to speak on the Internet to the Boy Scouts of America.

Ms. Lohse: Are those sufficient credentials, Your Honor, to satisfy the court and qualify Dr. Lemming as an expert in this matter?

Judge Winston: It seems adequate to me, although I thought the modern day of computing began in World War II, which would make him a second or third generation pioneer. Mr. Braidman?

Mr. Braidman: I'd call him something else, Your Honor. But I have no questions at the moment. I'll wait for cross.

Judge Winston: All right, Ms. Lohse. Dr. Lemming is accepted as an expert in software.

Ms. Lohse: Thank you, Your Honor. Now, Dr. Lemming, can you explain what software is?

Dr. Lemming: Certainly. Software is what turns a general purpose computer into a special purpose problem-solving machine. It tells the machine what to do.

Ms. Lohse: Well, aren't computers smarter than us? Don't they know what to do?

Dr. Lemming: No, actually they're intellectual morons, incapable of original thought. They need to be told precisely what to do.

Ms Lohse: I see. Now, what is a program?

Dr. Lemming: A program is a precise list of instructions which tell the machine what to do.

Ms. Lohse: Could you give the court an example?

Dr. Lemming: Sure, like *store* or *multiply.*

Ms. Lohse: Surely computers can do more than that, Dr. Lemming. True?

Dr. Lemming: Well, I was being simplistic. Actually, at the most basic level, they can only add, shift, test for one or zero, and read or write.

Ms. Lohse: So how do computers do all that fancy stuff?

Dr. Lemming: They string together all those adds, shifts, and so forth into long—very long—programs.

Ms. Lohse: Okay, so what're data to a computer?

Dr. Lemming: Data are things programs work with to get answers.

Ms. Lohse: Suppose I want to write a program. What do I do first?

Dr. Lemming: You write your program and submit it as data to another program, which turns it into a machine language program—something the machine can understand in bits and bytes. We call that an object program.

Judge Winston: Wait a minute, Ms. Lohse. Sorry to interrupt. Dr. Lemming, if I may ask, that second program you mentioned? It treats the first program as data? How can that be? And it produces a third program?

Dr. Lemming: Well, you see, sometimes programs are data, and sometimes data are programs. We have other programs called operating systems that manage all this for us. Programs are data to operating systems.

Ms. Lohse: You see, Your Honor. *Res ipsa loquitor*; it speaks for itself. It's all the same. Programs are data.

Judge Winston: I didn't hear it speak, Ms. Lohse. Maybe they're the same, but I can't keep up with all these programs. I need some clarification. Now, Dr. Lemming, I believe you said operating systems are programs. How do they become programs? Do they start as data, and then grow into programs?

Dr. Lemming: Your Honor, I know it's confusing, sometimes even to me. And I'm a former president of the Association of Software Systems. The answer is those operating systems are data to other programs in one, or another, operating system.

Judge Winston: And can you mix data and programs together? How do you know which is which?

Dr. Lemming: Yes, even though we think of them as different, they're mixed together quite frequently. Dr. von Neumann would say that programs and data differ only by the manner in which they're interpreted at the time that the central processor looks at them.

Judge Winston: What's a central processor?

Dr. Lemming: That's the computer's brain, Your Honor.

Judge Winston: Thank you. Ms. Lohse? Are you finished? At this point in the proceedings, I think it would be useful to let Mr. Braidman ask some questions. I will allow you to continue your inquiry later, if necessary. We can always cut and paste the transcript during adjudication. Mr. Braidman? The county looks like it's in a big hole now. How can it tax one and not the other?

Mr. Braidman: Your Honor, I can't keep up with all this tautology. However, before the county concedes, we have a long way to go. First, I'd like to review the expert's credentials.

Ms. Lohse: Objection. The court has already accepted this witness as an expert.

Judge Winston: Mr. Braidman?

Mr. Braidman: Yes, Your Honor. It is unusual to reopen that issue—but the witness has opened the door with his own words.

Judge Winston: I suppose he's used some strange words. The motion is denied. But let's keep it handy. All right, Mr. Braidman, please proceed.

Mr. Braidman: Thank you. Now, Dr. Lemming, I believe you said you're the vice president and director of computing research at Menlo Defense Research Institute. Is that correct?

Dr. Lemming: Yes. I manage all research in computing.

Mr. Braidman: And are you being paid for today's testimony?

Dr. Lemming: Carruthers and Schwartz pays MDRI directly for my time. I only receive my normal salary, and a small stipend—an honorarium to compensate for my time under oath.

Mr. Braidman: You mean you get a bonus for telling the truth?

Dr. Lemming: Please, sir. I always tell the truth.

Mr. Braidman: Uh-huh. That's very comforting. Well, let's go back to your research. What subjects do you study?

Dr. Lemming: We do research in theoretical computer science, robotics, artificial intelligence, and telecommunications.

Mr. Braidman: Did you say artificial intelligence?

Dr. Lemming: Yes, I did, and we are very proud of our new AI laboratory.

Mr. Braidman: I see. Well, I won't ask where you got the funding for that laboratory. And what is AI?

Ms. Lohse: Your Honor! This is outrageous. Where does Mr. Braidman think they got the funding?

Judge Winston: Relax, Ms. Lohse. I don't care where they got the money, and I'm the only one that counts. Mr. Court Reporter, please repeat Mr. Braidman's question.

Court Reporter: And what is AI?

Dr. Lemming: We teach machines how to think. You know, things like recognize natural language and act like experts in certain fields.

Mr. Braidman: You teach the computer's brain, the central processor you mentioned earlier? Is that what you mean?

Dr. Lemming: Well, sort of. We give the machine a program which shows it how to think. And we give it data to assist the program.

Mr. Braidman: But Dr. Lemming, didn't you say that computers can't think for themselves. That they're intellectual morons? Which is it, Dr. Lemming? You can't have it both ways. Can the machine think without that data you have to give it?

Dr. Lemming: I object, Your Honor. He's twisted my words.

Judge Winston: You can't object, Dr. Lemming, you're the witness. Ms. Lohse, I was inclined to rule in your favor, but this witness is clearly unreliable. First he said that machines can't think. Then he said programs and data are the same. Then he said machines can think, but they need data which is different from the thinker part. In the presence of doubt I must rule for the county.

Mr. Braidman: Thank you, Your Honor. I move for an immediate dismissal of the appeal, letting the tax assessment and payment stand.

Judge Winston: So ordered! Court adjourned.

The Rolex

A tall, elegant woman walked south along Sixth Avenue. At the corner of Fifty-Eighth Street, Anna Kramer, forty-six, pressed the call-button and was buzzed into Rochester Jewelers.

"Is it ready?" she asked Barry Rochester, the proprietor.

"It is, Mrs. Kramer. We had to remove considerable sediment, but it polished right up. We also replaced the crystal. It looks brand new." He handed her a long, blue wristwatch box.

"And the appraisal?"

"We put a value of $38,000 on it."

Anna nodded. She opened the wristwatch case and admired the timepiece. Stunning, she thought. She closed the case, and Rochester put it in a small shopping bag that looked like a Godiva Chocolate bag. Anna paid her bill and departed.

Anna walked north to Central Park South and entered the lobby of the Ritz-Carlton Hotel. She strolled through a comfortable sitting room off the southeast corner of the lobby and went into the bar. It had a long, marble counter, stately columns, and comfortable stools.

Norman Baker, the popular bartender, smiled a welcome. Anna knew that Norman liked her. He always lit up when she ordered a neat Oban single malt Scotch whisky. It usually took her two hours to nurse the drink, along with coffee and a Perrier, but Norman didn't seem to care. He was friendly and always had time for small talk.

"Where's Mister Kramer?"

Anna smiled. Norman remembered all his customer's names.

"He's inbound from Maui, returning from another diving trip. Actually, he's two hours late. He's flying on United." Anna smiled to herself. George hated United Airlines. He referred to it as the "Largest Unscheduled Airline in the World."

"Maybe he'll bring you a present." Norman poured a generous measure of Oban.

Anna laughed. "Oh, he can't beat this one."

She opened her little shopping bag and pulled out the long, blue case. As she opened it on the bar, she noticed a handsome woman, in her thirties, on the neighboring stool. The woman was impeccably dressed in Armani. She had a martini in front of her and had turned at Anna's remark. Anna smiled at the woman and removed her eighteen-karat gold Rolex Oyster Perpetual Lady Datejust wristwatch from the case. The watch had a deep blue face and an eighteen-karat gold Jubilee band. Diamonds sparkled at the four corners of the face and encrusted the bezel.

Norman said, "Wow! That's got to cost a small fortune."

"You can't imagine," beamed Anna.

"What a beautiful watch," said the woman in Armani. "May I look at it?" She smiled at Anna.

Given the value of the timepiece, Anna looked to Norman for reassurance.

He smiled and nodded, and Anna handed her the Rolex.

The woman examined the watch. The diamonds on the face seemed to glow in the soft overhead lights of the bar.

"It's got an inscription on the back," said, the woman. "'*To Lisa, All My Love. George.*' You're very lucky, Lisa." She handed the watch back to Anna.

"Oh. My husband's name is George, but I'm Anna, not Lisa. He found it on a diving trip." Anna paused. "It *is* beautiful, but it has a sordid tale."

"What do you mean?" asked the woman.

"Sounds interesting," said Norman as he poured a cup of coffee.

Anna smiled and placed the watch on her left wrist. She sipped her Oban and stirred a cocktail swizzle stick in her coffee. She thought back to the day George had found the watch. "We were on Maui and George was diving …"

• • •

Anna had parked the couple's Avis rental and stood at the Kihei Boat Ramp when the dive boat returned from Molokini, the underwater volcano cone popular with snorkelers and divers. George flashed a big smile when he disembarked and lugged his gear down a small wooden pier.

"It was a great drift dive," he said. "We followed the outer wall for about a mile, in a strong current. I have to admit I was worried about the boat; if they had lost our bubble trail and failed to pick us up, there was nothing south of us except Antarctica."

"Did you see any rays?" Anna knew that George loved mantas.

"We saw an enormous stingray, very unusual for Maui waters, but the interesting thing was I followed an eel along the wall. When it went into a hole in the coral … well, wait until you see what I found."

George looked furtively over his shoulder and saw the other divers walking to their cars. The boat crew was busy as it winched the boat onto a trailer. George reached into his dive jacket and pulled out a gold watch. Sediment covered most of it along with minute traces of coral. But the watch was clearly an expensive piece. "I bumped the coral with my underwater light by accident, and I saw a shiny glint. I dug it out with my knife."

George placed the object in Anna's hands. "It's heavy—must be eighteen-karat."

She hefted it. Some diamonds sparkled. Anna gasped. "My God, you found this? It looks like a Rolex."

George smiled. "I rubbed off the stuff on the back. It's inscribed, too. Got two names on it—'Lisa' and 'George.' Maybe I can find out something about it. I'll look on the Internet tonight."

That evening, George powered up his laptop and used Google to search for "Lisa and George." He found a *Maui News* article dated October 5, 1999. The article reported that Lisa and George Siegel, newlyweds, had been sailing around the world on their honeymoon trip. They'd moored their sailboat to a buoy off Molokini. The next day, the boat had been found drifting in waters south of the island of Molokai. Siegel had been beaten to death, the cabin drenched in blood. Lisa Siegel was missing. The yacht's safe was open, and empty.

George read from the article:

> … Fishermen on neighboring boats had observed a small speedboat approach the sailboat at dusk. Two men who boarded the boat were welcomed by a woman.
> The Maui County medical examiner has ruled it was murder. Siegel had unconfirmed ties to the Los Angeles mob and rumors swirl that over $2 million in drug monies were looted from the yacht's safe. An air search and rescue mission failed to turn up the body of the woman.

"Maybe," said George, after he finished the article, "we should just keep the damn thing. If we return it we might wake sleeping dragons."

• • •

"So," asked Norman, "did they ever find the woman's body?"

Anna shook her head. "Another article a few months later said that DNA tests, on the couple's parents, confirmed the blood was both George's and Lisa's. The ME ruled it a double homicide."

The woman sipped her martini. "Did you ever report it?"

Anna shook her head. "It just seemed stupid and dangerous. I mean, ten years had passed."

The woman said, "Well, it's a lovely piece and it looks grand on your wrist."

"Let me refresh that martini," said Norman.

Both women smiled at the bartender.

As Norman turned to mix the drink, two men in dark gray Armani suits strolled into the bar.

"Lisa," called one of them. "Are you ready?"

The woman next to Anna nodded. "That's me. I need to go. Wear the watch well."

She pushed a $50 bill towards Norman and grabbed her bag. As Lisa rose, she extended a hand. Anna shook Lisa's hand, and stared at an ugly scar on her right wrist.

Lisa noticed Anna's curiosity. "It's okay. I'm often asked about it. I cut myself and didn't have a chance to get stitches right away. It left an unsightly scar."

Anna nodded. "I'm sorry."

Lisa shrugged. "These things happen sometimes."

Then she bent down and whispered in Anna's ear, "If I were you, I'd ask the jeweler to adjust the watch. I'll bet it loses three minutes a week."

Anna and Norman watched Lisa greet the two men. It was warm in the bar, but Anna shivered. She asked Norman for another Oban.

Big Numbers Are Larger Than Small Numbers

"God is an Integer"
—The Pythagoreans

Professor Karl Menger walked out of the Federal Express office on El Camino Real in Mountain View, California. A Black BMW 330i, racing a red 1961 Porsche 356, caught his attention. The professor gasped as the BMW struck a little boy on a bicycle. As the vehicles sped away, he recognized some digits on the license plate of the BMW. Menger reached into his jacket, grabbed his cell phone, and dialed 9-1-1. A few moments later, the scene was engulfed in Mountain View police cars. An ambulance crew tended to the little boy.

"So, your name is Karl Menger?" asked a policeman. "You're a professor at Stanford. Is that correct?"

"Yes, Officer. I saw the whole thing. *Es war schrechlich.* Excuse me, it was terrible. The poor little boy—"

"The paramedics say the boy has life-threatening wounds. On the 9-1-1 call, you said you saw some of the numbers on the license plate of the car that struck him. Is that correct?"

"Yes, *der Schwein.* It was a California license plate, and I saw the numbers 2-7-1-8. There were some other numbers, before and after, but I don't remember them."

"Well, thank you, Professor. Someone from the district attorney's office will be in touch."

• • •

A few weeks later, the boy remained in critical condition. By tracing the digits on the BMW's license plate, the police had identified a suspect. They arrested Mr. John Baptista, a wealthy businessman of Portuguese descent from Macao, who resided in Los Altos, California, for hit and run and assault with a deadly weapon. Mr. Baptista posted a huge bond, and trial was set for December 15.

• • •

Judge Shirley Juarez called the court to order. Representing the people was Assistant District Attorney Jack Webster; defense counsel was Ms. Susan

Lohse, Esq. from the firm of Schwartz and Carruthers. The prosecution began its case and introduced considerable evidence, including photographs of the license plate on Mr. Baptista's BMW and a smashed right front headlight. Mr. Webster called Professor Menger as a witness for the people.

Professor Menger was sworn in, although there was some confusion in the courtroom over his reluctance to swear on a Bible. This was due, in part, to his penchant for speaking German. In the trial transcript the translator explained that the professor, when asked to swear on the Bible, engaged in an internal but audible debate with himself in German, as to whether God was an integer or simply any kind of number.

Judge Juarez, not an expert on the distinction between integers and other numbers, nor, for that matter, an expert on anything involving numbers, instructed Professor Menger to concentrate on the issues—and to speak in English. She concluded, "Now, Professor Menger, let me explain something. As you can see, we do not have a jury. That's because this is a bench trial. I am the sole arbitrator. In simplistic terms, I'm the finder of fact. I'll be the one that determines whether Mr. Baptista is innocent or guilty."

• • •

[Court Reporter's Note: Partial Trial Transcript Follows]

Judge Juarez: Do you understand?

Professor Menger: Yes, Your Honor.

Judge Juarez: Okay Mr. Webster, you may continue.

Mr. Webster: Good morning, Professor. You're a mathematician?

Professor Menger: That's correct. I hold a PhD in mathematics from the University of Heidelberg. I am professor of mathematics at Stanford University.

Mr. Webster: Did you see an automobile accident at 12:30 PM on the eleventh of October on El Camino Real in Mountain View, California?

Professor Menger: I saw a black BMW 330i run down a little boy on a bicycle.

Mr. Webster: How did you know it was a BMW?

Professor Menger: I am German.

Mr. Webster: Thank you. Now, according to the police report, which is People's Exhibit number twelve, you said the car that hit the little boy had a California license plate, and that the first five digits were 9-2-7-1-8. Is that correct?

Professor Menger: No. I told the police that I saw the digits 2-7-1-8. I believe they followed the first digit. I do not remember the first digit. I don't know where the nine in the report came from.

Mr. Webster: Now, Professor Menger, why is it that you noticed the next four digits?

Professor Menger: That's quite easy to explain, you see; they are the first four digits of a famous transcendental irrational number, known as *e*, the base of natural logarithms. *Ich habe, entschuldigung* … [Translator's note: *lit.* I have, excuse me …] I have used it often as a combination for hotel safes.

• • •

Professor Menger thought fondly back to his days at the University of Heidelberg. In those days, many Germans with a safe chose Adolf Hitler's birthday as their combination: April 20, 1889—for example, 2-0-4-8-9. But not the professor; he chose an irrational number.

Mr. Webster interrupted the professor's reverie.

• • •

[Court Reporter's Note: Partial Trial Transcript Follows]

Mr. Webster: And what, sir, is an irrational number? Could you explain it to the judge? What did you call it? *e?*

Professor Menger: Yes. *e* is an irrational number whose digits never repeat and continue forever.

Ms. Lohse: I need a clarification, Your Honor. Is the professor telling us that the number goes on forever?

Judge Juarez: I think that's what he said. Excuse me, Professor. Did you say forever?

Professor Menger: Yes, Your Honor, it is infinitely long. The first 8 digits are 2-7-1-8-2-8-1-8. I am afraid I cannot memorize the rest. That would be impossible.

Judge Juarez: Well, Ms. Lohse, that's his answer. Mr. Webster, you may continue.

Mr. Webster: Thank you, Your Honor. And thank you, Professor. The people have no further questions for this witness.

Judge Juarez: Your witness, Ms. Lohse.

Ms. Lohse: Good morning, Professor. Any chance you saw the rest of the number?

Professor Menger: I don't understand. Do you mean the rest of *e*? That's not possible.

Ms. Lohse: Well, I thought you said that you saw eeeh on the plate. Didn't you?

Mr. Webster: Your Honor? Really! The defense should pay attention to the answers. If the court reporter checks the record, he will tell the court that the eminent professor said he only saw the first four digits of *e*.

Judge Juarez: Please, Mr. Webster, let's let the court reporter stick his own transcript in his mouth. Ms. Lohse, you may continue.

Ms. Lohse: I'm very sorry I was confused, Your Honor. Yes, I understand now that he saw the first four digits of eeeh.

Professor, I meant to ask you if you saw any numbers after the first four digits on the license plate.

Professor Menger: I am not a lawyer and please, Your Honor, don't get mad at me. But may I correct the question? I think Ms. Lohse wants to know if I saw any digits on the license plate *after* the first four digits of *e*, which were the second to the fifth digits on the license plate. *Nicht wahr,* [Translator's note: *lit*. Not True? *id*. Is that right?] Ms. Lohse?

Ms. Lohse: Professor Menger, you give the answers, and in English, if you please. We get to ask the questions. That's how American jurisprudence works. Now please answer your own question.

Professor Menger: No. I don't remember any more digits.

Ms. Lohse: Professor, I need to get a better understanding of this, what did you call it—irrational number? This is very important. A little boy is in critical condition due to a terrible accident. It's hard for me to understand how something irrational can be used to convict my client. Could you give the court another example of such an irrational number?

• • •

The professor found the question curious. He studied the court. The judge looked bewildered; the bailiff had glazed eyes. There were more irrational numbers than rational numbers, but Menger suspected that this audience might have problems understanding the concept. He decided to keep it simple. A circle, he reasoned, was a pretty simple shape.

• • •

[Court Reporter's Note: Partial Trial Transcript Follows]

Professor Menger: Well, there's *pi*. You would know it as the ratio of a circle's circumference to its diameter.

Ms. Lohse. Are you telling the court that this number, pie as you called it, also goes on forever? For a circle that any third grader could draw with a compass and a pencil?

Professor Menger: Yes, it would go on forever. It's an irrational number.

Ms. Lohse: Let's stay with this pie thing. Now if I draw a circle that's half the size, or for that matter, twice the size of the first circle, would I get the same pie?

Professor Menger: *Vorsicht!* [Translator's note: *lit.* (1) Caution! (2) Danger!] You are straying into dangerous territory, Ms. Lohse. You're about to introduce another irrational number called the square root of two. Further, a doubled—or halved—circle cannot be constructed using a pencil and a compass. That's called "squaring the circle" and it is not possible. Even the ancient Greeks knew this, although it was not proven until 1882. *Man soll den schlafenden Löwen nicht wecken.* [Translator's note: *id.* Let sleeping dogs lie.]

Ms. Lohse: Not possible? I suppose you'll tell us that the square root of two goes on forever, too. Does it?

Professor Menger: Yes, it goes on forever.

Ms. Lohse: And what about those other circles? Are all their pies the same, and do they go on forever?

Professor Menger: Well, *pi* is the same for all circles, but I misspoke. Actually, it goes on forever and forever.

Ms. Lohse: Don't you mean just forever?

Professor Menger: I meant one forever for the square root of two. But I mean forever and forever for *pi*. You see, there are some forevers that are longer than other forevers. You might want to study Cantor; he showed there is a whole class of forevers which he called infinities.

• • •

Ms. Lohse was secretly thrilled. The professor had fallen into a trap. She could not believe how lucky she'd been when Professor Menger had inadvertently picked *pi* as an example of another so-called irrational number. Still, she wasn't ready to spring her trap, so she continued her ruse with pie.

• • •

[Court Reporter's Note: Partial Trial Transcript Follows]

Ms. Lohse: Well, we're going to see about that forever and forever thing for pie. But, for now, let's see if I can understand this infinity thing with a simple case. Suppose I start multiplying one times one times one, and so forth, an infinite number of times. Doesn't that always result in one?

Professor Menger: Yes, you will end up at one, unless, of course, you make a mistake in the multiplication. But it will take you forever to get to one.

Ms. Lohse: But isn't one a rational number?

Professor Menger: Yes.

Ms. Lohse: Your Honor, how can it take forever to get to one? This is not rational.

Judge Juarez: Well, he did say that some things are irrational. However, I must admit that I am puzzled.

Ms. Lohse: This is absurd, Your Honor. Professor, let's go back to this infinity thing. You say it would also take forever to list all of the digits of an infinite number? Correct?

Professor Menger: Yes, it would take one forever.

Ms. Lohse: I'm confused, Professor. Did you say 'one forever?' But the digits are not all ones, are they?

Professor Menger: Good heavens, no.

Ms. Lohse: Well, bear with me a little. How do you know when you've accounted for all the digits in an infinite number?

Professor Menger: That's quite simple. We line the digits up with the integers, for example, one, two, three, and so forth. Or, if you prefer, we could use the even or odd integers, or the squares.

Ms. Lohse: And what about pie? If we lined the digits up with the integers, would it also take forever?

Professor Menger: I believe I said it would take two forevers for *pi*.

Judge Juarez: Excuse me, Ms. Lohse. I have a question for the witness. Professor Menger, what if I use one of your suggestions, such as the squares of the integers, like one, four, nine, and so forth? Wouldn't that get me there sooner?

Professor Menger: I am sad to say, Your Honor, that it still would take two forevers to list all the digits in *pi*. One can place the digits of that pesky square root of two in a one-to-one correspondence with the integers, or just the even or odd integers, or even their squares, as you inquired. But the use of the squares would still take forever. And it would take two of those forevers for *pi*.

• • •

Her trap sprung, Ms. Lohse went for the jugular! The professor had clearly committed himself to the preposterous notion that *pi* went on forever and forever. Grabbing tables of the digits of *e* and *pi* and waving them in the air, Ms. Lohse returned to the circus.

• • •

[Court Reporter's Note: Partial Trial Transcript Follows]

Ms Lohse: Well, Professor, I'm afraid I've got you. I don't see how the court can rely on your testimony. Your Honor, I can prove that *pi* does not go on forever. I have precedent. The general assembly of the state of Indiana, in 1897, passed a bill unanimously—in point of fact 67-to-0—that declared *pi* was a constant 3.2. That doesn't sound to me like a number that goes on forever. It's true that the Indiana state senate has yet to ratify the pending bill, so it's not Black Letter Law, but it demonstrates legislative intent. They even publish tables of these numbers.

Professor Menger: *Gott im Himmel.* [Translator's note: *lit.* God in Heaven. *id.* My God!] You don't understand. As I have already explained these numbers are infinitely long. One needs an infinite series to define them. And if I might add, the general assembly of the state of Indiana is populated by *arselochen*! [Translator's note: Expletive not translated.]

Judge Juarez: Professor Menger, please watch your language. I don't know what it meant, but it sounded crude. These are solemn proceedings. I must admonish you to answer only the question that you're asked. Mr. Webster, it looks to me like your witness is imploding.

Mr. Webster: Perhaps not, Your Honor. I think Ms. Lohse is wrong. There's got to be some reason the senate of the state of Indiana has not ratified that bill in over one hundred years. I would like to ask the court to line up the digits of *pi* with the integers. Perhaps we could work right through lunch to settle this 3.2 thing once and for all. My case rests on showing that Professor Menger recognized some of the digits of *e* on Mr. Baptista's license plate; his credibility is paramount.

Judge Juarez: All right, Mr. Webster. Perhaps that will clarify things. Ms. Lohse, considering that this is a felonious assault charge, I'm willing to grant the prosecution some leeway. However, I think we can accelerate the process. With everyone's agreement, perhaps we could use the squares of the integers.

Mr. Webster: Yes, Your Honor. I am very interested in seeing what happens when we get to 3.2. By all means let's get there faster.

Judge Juarez: Good. Clearly, big numbers are larger than small numbers, and I'm getting hungry. Let's see, if the court reporter can start lining up the digits of *pi*—I think we line up one squared or one, with three; two squared or four, with one; three squared or nine, with four; four squared or sixteen, with one … did I get that right, Professor?

Professor Menger: Pi does start with 3 point 1-4-1, but I am sorry, Your Honor. This process will take more than our lifetimes to complete. You can try to line up the digits of *pi* with the squares of the integers, but it will not get you to *pi* any sooner. And I can assure you we will never, ever, get to 3.2.

Ms. Lohse: Well, it can't take long to further discredit the people's witness, Your Honor. With your permission, let's ask the reporter to start at the one-millionth digit of *pi*. It shouldn't take too long that way.

Judge Juarez: All right, lunch can wait. Professor, please remain in your seat. You have not been dismissed. The court reporter will start with the one-millionth digit of *pi* and the square of one million and keep lining them up.

Dr. Menger: Your Honor, this is *verruckt*. [Translator's note: *lit.* crazy.] We will be here forever. *Sie sollen alles 'rausgeschmissen werden. Der Taten finden, mein Füss*! [Translator's note: *id.* You should all get the axe! *lit.* Find the facts, my foot!]

Judge Juarez: Well, Professor, we all know you think forever is really forever, although some of your forevers might be longer than others. But, for the purposes of judicial efficiency, let's start even higher, say, at the one-billionth digit. Go on, Mr. Reporter. We haven't got all day.

• • •

The Superior Court of the county of Santa Clara is still in session.

Ben and Greta

Late one February afternoon, Greta von Hohenzollern-Becker sat at the bar in the Aspen Lodge. A fire roared in the corner fireplace, and the strong aroma of burning wood flavored the air. Greta was in her sixties, but still had a fashion runway figure. Like many wealthy women who'd been raised in Europe, she was well-dressed. She wore beige, form-fitting ski pants, black après-ski boots, and a red Sonia Rykiel cashmere sweater, capped by an Hermès scarf that sported a hunt scene in India.

Greta looked out the window as she sipped on her second double extra-dry Absolut vodka martini, ruminating on the lack of excitement in her life. An advanced, double-black-diamond ski run filled her field of view. Despite the flicker from the flames that bounced off the inside of the large windows, she saw some lunatic racing downhill at about forty miles per hour without poles. She watched him catch an edge, cross his skis, and take a monumental fall. Five minutes later, the Ski Patrol pulled him out of the snow and escorted him to the foot of the mountain. She watched as he shrugged off any assistance and stumbled towards the entrance to the lodge. Given the seriousness of the fall, and his quick recovery, Greta thought the man must be in excellent condition—and a little crazy, too.

A few moments, later the fool sat down next to her. He seemed oblivious to the snow trapped in his hair and jammed down his collar. As the snow melted, a pool of water collected on the floor below his stool.

Greta smiled at him. "That's quite a fall you took."

"Good thing I was stoned," he quipped. "I might have been hurt." He smiled playfully, grabbed a few bar napkins to blow his nose, and waved for the bartender.

"Well, I'm trying to get stoned myself. My husband's in Bermuda playing golf, and I'm bored silly." My goodness, Greta wondered, did she really say that? She looked at him; he was shorter than she and a little older. He looked kind of cute.

He smiled. "What's your name?"

"Greta. Greta von Hohenzollern-Becker."

"Where are you from? The name, it sounds German."

"I was born in Rasternburg, in eastern Prussia. But I live in San Francisco now."

"Greta, I'm Ben. Ben Schneider, from Chicago. Do you know how to play Nim?"

"I don't believe so."

Ben described the game, in which several rows of increasing numbers of coins, from two to five, are aligned. Then players remove any number of coins, from any single row, on each move.

"The last one to remove a coin is the loser," he said. "I never lose."

Greta was curious. "How can that be? What if I go first?"

"Let's play. You can go first, or second. If you lose, I'll buy you a drink."

"What if I win?"

Ben grinned. "How about I buy you a drink?"

They called the bartender over and asked for a stack of quarters.

• • •

The next morning Greta's head pounded. She looked out through dry, bloodshot eyes. The bed was a mess and her clothes were sprawled on a chair. A half-full martini glass was on the dresser, and an empty beer bottle lay on the floor. Greta vaguely remembered falling off her stool the previous evening. She had a picture in her mind of returning to her room with Ben's assistance. She rolled over in bed and was startled when Ben came out of the bathroom.

He was dressed and sported a big grin. "Greta, you were wonderful. You're very exciting. Thank you for this special gift."

"Oh, my God," she exclaimed. "What am I going to tell my husband? I've never done anything like this before."

"Greta, don't worry about it. You think he's playing golf twenty-four hours a day? I got to go, or we'd do it again. Take care."

After Ben left, Greta lay in bed. She stretched languidly. She smiled and thought about the evening. She'd had sex for the first time in fifteen years. She wasn't sure, but she thought she'd complained about her husband. He deserved it, she decided—a little revenge. It was about time the goose got even with the gander. Despite her hangover, she felt strangely fulfilled. She wished Ben had stayed. He was exciting. Greta eyed the unfinished martini.

• • •

Ben flew back to Chicago. A few days later, he met his buddies for their monthly poker game in Sandburg Village, located near the Gold Coast of Chicago.

"I took an unbelievable tumble," Ben said with a laugh. "I broke a ski and binding on a double-black-diamond run. Damn near broke my neck. The Ski Patrol had to bring me down the mountain. Then I met this drunken woman—sort of attractive, too—in the bar. Her name was Greta von Hohen-something. She reminded me of Greta von Solange from cable TV. You guys know I can't stand TV commentators, so I bought her another drink, you know, for fun—to see if I could liquor her up."

Alan, Ben's racquetball partner who sold life insurance, listened with a mischievous smile. "So? I thought you can't get it up since you had your prostate removed."

"I can't," said Ben with a smile. "Neither can you, asshole. You ain't got one either. But we got hammered. She was a real talker. Her husband was in Bermuda, and it sounded like he was with his latest squeeze. I think she was looking for a little payback. But I liked her."

"So what happened?" asked Barry, the best poker player in the bunch, as he counted his chips.

"I introduced her to the game of Nim. We played for drinks. About an hour later, she fell off her stool. I helped her to her room, and ended up spending the night. The next morning I faked it, told her she'd been a great lay for an old babe, and left her smiling."

Barry was curious. "She actually thought you guys had balled?"

"I guess so. She was really loaded."

Alan grinned. "Did you get her phone number?"

"Why? You want to sell her husband some insurance?"

"I figure if we can get her between us, we could maybe each get by with a half a hard-on."

The men roared, but Ben frowned. He'd thought often about Greta, and he wondered how she was doing. He fingered a note with her phone number and reached for his cell phone.

• • •

Greta had returned to San Francisco and called her husband in Bermuda. She told him the marriage was over—he could move in with that bimbo he was screwing down there. California was a community property state, and Greta intended to keep the apartment in Pacific Heights, the Merrill Lynch cash management account, the vineyards in Napa, and the Mercedes. He could have everything else.

"But what happened?" asked her husband.

"Sex happened, you ninny. I realized what I've been missing. But no, not you, you've been chasing every skirt in town. What? You thought I didn't know? I have a lover now, and I'm going to have some fun. You tell the children. Good-bye."

The phone rang. Greta smiled when Caller ID indicated the area code in Chicago.

"Greta? It's Ben. How're you doing?"

"I'm so glad you called. I'd like to see you again."

"I'd like to see you, too. But … I have a confession. I have to tell you that we really didn't make love. I can't even do it; I've had surgery, and it doesn't work anymore."

"Ben, I don't care. Bring the quarters. I've got the Absolut. I've dumped my husband. When can we meet?"

"But, Greta, there was no sex. Do you understand that?"

"Ben, I need excitement, and you're an exciting man. I can pretend, too."

Identity

Chester P. Hurley, the loan officer and manager of the Chase Manhattan Bank branch located on the northwest corner of Madison Avenue at Sixty-Ninth Street, shrugged nonchalantly.

"Another check to jamaicaprocessing.com?" he asked. "How much this time?"

His assistant, Kathryn, studied the check. "It's $68,000—the amounts have been increasing over the last few months."

Hurley nodded. "Well, it's no big deal. Alex Spinoza's a high-end client, and it's all covered by his line of credit—and that's guaranteed by his home. Why do you keep bringing the checks to me?"

"I'm just trying to follow the rules; all overdrafts require your approval."

"Okay. The previous checks have been covered. I'm sure this one's not different." Hurley initialed the check, and smiled at Kathryn. She was twenty-two, a recent graduate of Hunter College, with legs that went to the moon. Boy, he thought, if he only had Spinoza's money, he'd bag her in no time.

As Kathryn left his corner office, which was nestled up to the window on Madison Avenue, Hurley reflected on his meeting with Spinoza.

"That's right, Mr. Spinoza," he'd said with a smile. "We can let you have a line-of-credit on your Westchester home—right now the bank can go $7 million on your home equity of $9.5 million. I might get more, too—if you're willing to disclose your tax returns."

Alex Spinoza, a heavyset man with a dark complexion, thinning hair, and freckled hands, smiled. "That's nice, Mr. Hurley. But I don't really need the money now. I just want to establish a slush fund, you know, for cash flow in case some options present themselves."

"I know. You said that in the application. But don't worry; we don't start charging until you actually draw down the line, and the rate's one point below prime."

Hurley had wondered if Spinoza really didn't need the money, but the bank officers had approved the line. Who was he to second-guess the loan? Still, he thought, Spinoza had a sleazy look. But that was the banking business; you had to deal with all kinds of assholes. Turning in his chair, Hurley looked out the window. He was rewarded by the sight of Kathryn hurrying down Madison Avenue. The wind pressed her dress against those magnificent legs, highlighting them. All thoughts of Alex Spinoza disappeared.

• • •

At the same time the wind gave Hurley a treat, computers in a huge datacenter in Norman, Oklahoma—a centralized credit card bureau—processed three $35,000 charges to Visa, MasterCard, and Discover Card. All the charges were from a company identified as jamaicaprocessing.com, headquartered on the Isle of Man in the English Channel. The company ran Internet servers. It was a blind cut-out established by PokerPlayerOnLine.com, a Hong Kong gambling site, to circumvent U.S. laws against on-line gambling.

The machines in Norman were programmed to detect extraordinary, or fraudulent, charges. But their artificial intelligence routines, supported by neural network software which *learned* how to filter good transactions from bad, could be lulled into a false sense of complacency. Many similar transactions in the past had proved authentic. The new charges were approved by the computers, and jamaicaprocessing.com moved the funds immediately to a player account on PokerPlayerOnLine.com—where they were converted to Hong Kong dollars. Several days later, PokerPlayerOnLine.com was instructed, by the player, to wire the funds denominated in Euros, to an account at Deutsche Bank in Frankfurt.

• • •

Alex Spinoza slammed the accelerator to the floorboard. The trees along the side of German Autobahn 8 blurred as his speed increased to 200, then 220 kilometers per hour. Exits for Augsburg flew by, and then Ulm, as he raced toward Karlsruhe and the road to Baden-Baden. Spinoza mentally computed the speed of his brand new black BMW M5 in miles per hour—132. His math was good. It had to be for a fledgling embezzler and identity thief.

Spinoza, fifty-nine, was a successful accountant. He was the managing partner of a small CPA firm in lower Manhattan. To reduce his commute to Westchester, he'd purchased a small apartment in Battery Park City—it was also an excuse not to go home during the workweek. He'd been married thirty years, and couldn't stand his wife. More than once he'd considered leaving, but he was repelled at the thought of sacrificing half his wealth—New York was a community-property state. That was before he came up with a scheme to steal substantially more than half of what he would have owed his wife—enough money so that the unthinkable, divorce, had become thinkable. The desire to dump his wife now raged in his gut.

Spinoza had studied identity theft methods for months before he put his plan to a test. It was great, he thought, the perfect victimless crime. The only ones that would get screwed were the banks and the credit card companies. Funny, he thought, if his wife only knew the trouble he was going to—which might give her *all* the family money—she'd love him all the more for it. Well, that was unless they came after her for the money. But Spinoza didn't give a damn about that. By then he'd be free!

He'd researched conventional schemes for hustling identities: counterfeiting checks, rifling mailboxes for credit card applications, and stealing credit card numbers from restaurant and bar charge slips. He'd discovered that social security numbers were a dime-a-dozen on the Internet, along with birth and marriage data, death certificates, residential histories, and credit reports. Spinoza also learned how to launder funds through on-line poker websites. The M5, fetched just yesterday from BMW headquarters near the *Olympia Zentrum* in Munich, and a remaining bank balance of almost $72,000 in Germany, proved his system worked. Oh, he'd had to pay for the car. That still would generate a load of bullshit from his wife, of course. And he had to return the rest of the money. But the test was successful, and the pump was primed. After this experiment he was going for the jugular—the entire $7 million in the line of credit.

He smiled as he looked over at his passenger. Jutta Becker's long, red hair fluttered in the wind, which whipped through the car from the open sun-roof. She didn't seem to mind; her eyes were glazed with excitement as the M5 approached 250 kilometers per hour. Gorgeous, thought Spinoza—and smart. Jutta, thirty-six, was a German national he'd met on the flight to Munich; she spoke five languages and was a graduate of the University of Heidelberg. She'd grown up in the *Schwarzwald*, the Black Forest, and promised to give Spinoza a tour after they spent the weekend at the Brenner Park Hotel in Baden-Baden. It made for a promising adventure, he thought, except for that rotten little dog in her lap. It was furless, and stared at him with black, oval eyes filled with hate.

"How's the dog doing?" he asked over the howl of the wind.

"Sigmund? He's fine but we're going too fast to let him stick his head out of the window."

Too bad, thought Spinoza. Maybe the wind would suck Sigmund right out of the car. "Isn't there something we can do about him? He always climbs onto my back when we make love."

"Don't be silly. Sigmund just wants to be loved, too."

Spinoza felt like throwing the dog out the sun-roof. That would make for an interesting sight in his rear view mirror, he mused. But he nodded and kept his silence—better not to be distracted at those speeds. Although the autobahns had long stretches of road with unrestricted speeds, there were periodic speed limits and construction zones that demanded a driver's attention.

When Spinoza turned south onto Autobahn 5, he reflected on his grand plan. Stealing identities was nothing, he thought—the twist was to steal your own identity. That was class! He was going to steal from himself, and give the money back to himself. He'd created a duplicate Alex Spinoza, based on the death of a young boy, Alejandro Spinoza, in Springfield, Illinois, in 1950.

The plan was brilliant. Construct a duplicate identity with a valid social security number mined on-line from death certificates; establish an address through a mail drop in Europe; get an overseas bank account for the new identity; and build a pattern of charges on his existing credit cards in shady establishments where credit card knock-offs were not uncommon. He also moved large amounts of funds through on-line poker sites that used credit card servers to mask their real identities. He didn't even have to gamble—just deposit funds, and then move the money.

As Spinoza slowed to drive through an *Umleitung* (diversion), he recalled his meeting at Deutsche Bank in Frankfurt.

"So, Herr Spinoza, you wish to open a Eurocheque and Eurocard account?" the bank officer had asked. He'd been a *Graf*, a member of one of the landed family aristocracies in Germany.

"I need the account so I can write checks in Euros, Pounds, or Danish Crowns, and a Eurocard to draw upon the funds at ATM machines."

"And the amount of the initial deposit?"

"One thousand in cash, American dollars. I expect to make several large deposits by wire over the next year."

Spinoza, at that time, did not know the amounts he would deposit. But he knew there would be only two sets of transactions: the funds for the test with real money, and then the grand finale. Later, he'd arranged a wire deposit of $173,000 which more than covered the cost of the M5, including shipping to the U.S. The remaining funds would go towards retiring the credit card charges. He laughed at his scheme. Hurley and the credit card companies would be aghast if he didn't refund the money. He imagined the conversation.

Hurley would ask, "What do you mean that's not your signature?"

"That's right. It's not my signature." Concern would be plastered on Alex's face. "Someone stole a batch of checkbooks out of my mailbox, and I have no idea who wrote the check."

"Did you report it to the police?"

"Well, the super reported that my mailbox was broken into, but he didn't know what was stolen. I was traveling; I just returned yesterday." Spinoza smiled. If that were the only sting, he'd have paid some drunk to take a sledgehammer to all the mailboxes.

Visa and the other credit card companies would be incredulous. They'd contact the police. Three bogus $35,000 charges would be too large to swallow. It would be touch and go when he dealt with the people in Westchester County's Office of Consumer Fraud. But eventually they'd agree—after all, it would be a case of identity theft. And all the credit card charges would be reversed.

But this was only an experiment. Jesus, he thought, they might drop dead when he makes the big hit. And they'll never find him after he scores the $7 million.

Spinoza returned his attention to the road and saw the sign for the turn-off to Baden-Baden.

• • •

The phone rang in room 35 at the Hotel Brenner Park.

Spinoza picked up the receiver.

"Hello, is Jutta there? This is Ingrid, her sister." With an inquisitive look, he handed the phone to Jutta. She mouthed, "I called her from Munich to tell her where we'd be staying."

"*Gruss Gott.*" As Jutta listened, her face blanched. Jutta turned to Spinoza. "Ingrid says my husband is on the way here—and he has a gun!"

"Your husband? You're married? How'd he find out?"

"Ingrid must have told him."

"But why would she do that?" Spinoza's first reaction was fear, then disbelief, followed by suspicion.

"She's always been jealous of me! You better leave, right now!"

"But a gun? Don't they have laws against guns in Germany?"

"He's a policeman in the *Bundeskriminalamt*, the German Criminal Police. He has a temper. You better get going!"

Spinoza wondered if he was being scammed, but Jutta seemed scared. Still flustered and nervous, he threw his clothes into his bag and ran for the elevator. Descending, he wondered if he would escape the hotel before Jutta's husband arrived. When the doors opened, he gasped. In front of him was a man breathing hard and excited. Spinoza felt his stomach churn but, after a moment of panic, realized it was his own reflection in a mirror.

Goddamn it, he thought, he had to get control of himself. It was time to get out of Germany. Spinoza drove to the autobahn and headed north and west for Antwerp, a drop point for shipment of cars to the U.S. He wondered if he'd ever see Jutta again. Was she working him? Still, he reflected, it had been a wild time—except for that dog.

• • •

Spinoza returned to New York and closed out the books on the test. $101,000 had already had gone to BMW for the car, and he wired $68,000 to Chase Manhattan Bank to cover the last check he'd written. He combined his remaining funds in Germany with the deposits from the poker accounts, and retired the $105,000 in debt with the three credit card companies—thus reinforcing the computers' senses of security on each of the bogus accounts. With those transactions, he was out only the cost of the car, $4,000 in currency exchange fees, and the pending expenses for the trip to Germany. The title and registration for the car had been assigned to his duplicate identity since he'd decided transfers to his real identity would incur sales taxes in New York. There was some risk if he got stopped by the cops. But that would only last a few months and besides, he had his New York State drivers' license in the same name.

Four weeks later, the car arrived. Spinoza took his wife, who'd been unusually distant, for a ride. His plan to steal the $7 million was afoot, but he needed a few more months to pull it off. He figured he may as well keep peace during the interim.

"So what do you think of it?" He hoped he sounded concerned, but Spinoza really didn't care if she liked it. He was simply covering his tracks on the trip to Germany. "I had to wait several days to pick it up at the factory."

"How much was it?" asked his wife. "It's beautiful, but I thought we'd agreed we were going to save for the children. What did you need another car for, anyway?"

Spinoza didn't care whether he left his kids a dime, but Dolores had always been anxious to build them a nest egg. Still, when he glanced at her, she was looking out the window. He began to talk again, but she wasn't listening. "What is it, Dolores? You've been a bitch since I came home from Europe."

"Me? You're in Europe screwing your brains out, and you're accusing me?"

"Screwing? What are you talking about?"

"Alex, spare me your bullshit. I know you also did it with that banker's assistant."

"What?" Spinoza was stunned. "What do you mean?"

"I signed the line-of-credit, remember? I saw how you looked at her—what's her name, Kathryn?"

"I just looked, that's all. But I thought we had an understanding—what I do overseas doesn't count."

"Well, sure—except now I have an understanding, too—what I do when you're overseas doesn't count, either."

"What do you mean? You went out? With who?"

"Oh, Alex, you're such a fool. I've been dating Fred Kappler for months—ever since you started banging Kathryn ... and spending all your time with that silly on-line poker."

"Fred, the car dealer? That asshole?"

"Yes, that asshole—but he's more a man than you are. We met at that party at the Stags. I bought my Prius from him, remember?"

Spinoza down-shifted his M5 into second gear, hit the "Sport" button, and pushed the car up to one hundred miles per hour on the Saw Mill Parkway, red-lining the engine. His hands clutched the steering wheel while he slowly calmed down. Funny, he thought, he was leaving her as soon as he could, but he was going to get Kappler, too. His lips curled.

• • •

Fred Kappler owned a Toyota agency on the West Side of Manhattan and belonged to the Fraternal Order of Stags, just like Spinoza. Kappler was serious about the order, but Spinoza had joined just to troll for customers. Kappler loved the Stags and enjoyed the comradeship and health club facilities. He dined at the Manhattan lodge twice a week. The rage for fuel-efficient cars, such as the Prius, had made him a small fortune, and he'd volunteered to run for office as a trustee. The trustees controlled the assets of the Order, and Kappler hoped he would make a significant contribution to Stags management. But Kappler worried about his relationship with Dolores Spinoza. She struck him as volatile, and he feared Spinoza, or worse, his own wife would discover his duplicity.

To make it up to his wife, after the election Kappler planned a vacation trip to his ancestral home in Bad Herrenalb, not far from Baden-Baden. His uncle was the day manager at the Hotel Belle Epoque, and Kappler thought his wife would enjoy some time in Germany; she'd been raised in Flensburg, just below the Danish-German border. But first, he had to win the Stags' election, which was scheduled for the following month.

• • •

At first the campaign went well. Kappler played handball with a bunch of guys, and they all agreed to vote for him. The bridge and gin-rummy players signed on as well. The gang in the bar was more distant; Kappler wasn't much of a drinker, and the bar was mostly unfamiliar territory for him. He resolved to spend more time there. For a while the campaign seemed to go well. Then, someone began to post flyers for Kappler's competitors on the lodge walls, bulletin boards, and inside and outside the front and rear doors. Some of the flyers proclaimed Kappler was a poor manager, or too young. Some said he was too old. Others argued he had insufficient experience, and a few said he carried too much political baggage. One particularly nasty flyer claimed Kappler drank too much, wasn't social enough, and made too much noise rolling dice for drinks in the bar. All in all, it was a hate recipe for everyone.

On the night of the election, one of Kappler's friends saw Alex Spinoza handing out crib sheets which instructed Stags how to vote. Kappler was pretty sure the stuff violated the Stags' rules, but the older members he'd asked had told him that all the elections were rigged. Still, Kappler thought that such campaigning was *déclassé*.

The Stags' lodge sat the corner of Eighth Avenue and Seventieth Street. It incorporated an old brownstone, built in 1935, and an adjacent warehouse, which had been converted and now housed a health club, basketball, racquetball, and handball courts, an indoor pool in the basement, and a banquet hall. The brownstone had a magnificent old mahogany bar on the ground level; it was crowded with members the night of the election. Kappler saw a bunch of his cronies at one of the side tables and ambled over.

"Fred," said a past president (PP) of the Stags, "good luck in the election."

"Right on," said Barry Wright, the Stags' vice president. Wright was a close friend who knew about Kappler's liaison with Dolores Spinoza. "You'll need it! Alex Spinoza is passing out crib sheets telling people how to vote."

"So it's Alex, huh? You can imagine what I'd call him if it wasn't Conduct Unbecoming a Stag." Kappler bluffed; he worried that if he made a scene, his wife would hear about Spinoza. She might wonder what the problem was. That might point her at Dolores Spinoza.

"Hey," said Wright, "Spinoza also had some wild adventure with some gal in Germany. Did you see that photo he showed around of him and a redhead at a fancy hotel in Baden-Baden? He said he picked her up on the flight to get his new car."

"But he's married," opined the PP.

"Yeah," said Wright, "but when did that stop some people?" He looked at Kappler with a wry look. "Besides, Spinoza must be as dumb as a stone to brag about it."

"Did you see all the new members here?" asked Lloyd, one of the oldest members of the Stags. "I haven't seen any of them since they were initiated. I heard they're here for the election—someone sent them an email telling them their votes were essential to preserve the order of things."

"Shit! Who sent the email?" asked Kappler who felt a twinge of guilt over Wright's comment.

"I don't know. I just heard rumors. Apparently it was a confidential message."

"My money's on Spinoza." Wright looked at Kappler again, shook his head, and smiled.

"Tammany Hall," muttered Kappler, "could have learned something from this asshole, bringing outside issues into the election." He walked through a gauntlet of Stags who passed out crib sheets in the lobby.

• • •

Fred Kappler lost the election: eighty to thirty-five. He figured about fifty of the voters were new members who'd been enticed to the meeting by the email—otherwise it would have been a close election. Two days later, Wright forwarded him an attachment to an email message:

> From: Barry Wright (barwrt@earthlink.net)
> To: Fred Kappler (Kappler.fred@aol.com)
> Subject: FW: email in election
> Attachments: ¤ WE NEED YOUR VOTE. txt (30 KB)
> Attached is the email that was circulated to the new members in the Lodge. It turns out I was right. Spinoza was the author. Have you considered poking it somewhere else? Take care. Barry.

Kappler read the attachment and saw red. It contained an exhortation to vote if the voter wanted to keep the things he deserved, like a pool. The missive went on to explain that Fred didn't have enough experience, and that the recipient should spread the word. But, with twisted logic, it asked the recipient to keep the message confidential. Kappler clenched his fists. This was too much—he wondered how a philandering jerk like Spinoza could get so resentful over the same thing. Kappler swore he'd get even with the S-O-B.

First, he checked out Spinoza's credit ratings. For that he needed Spinoza's social security number. No problem, he thought. Dolores Spinoza had purchased her Prius at Kappler Toyota, and Kappler had all the data. He pulled up the website for IGC Credit Data Bureau. When he keyed in Alex Spinoza's name, the website listed two Alex Spinozas. That, Kappler thought, was curious. Still, he needed the social security number to get into the files, so he keyed in Spinoza's number. On that account, three charges for $35,000 had recently been processed and then settled. A $68,000 check, drawn on Chase Manhattan Bank, also caught Kappler's attention.

Spinoza had an excellent credit rating of 775—not surprising he was a wealthy man. But a series of payments to jamaicaprocessing.com were interesting. He picked up the phone and called Barry Wright.

"It's me. Did you ever hear of jamaicaprocessing.com?"

"Where is it, Jamaica?"

"It's incorporated in the Isle of Man in the English Channel, some place with tight banking restrictions about privacy. But listen, Alex sure seems to like Germany. Do you remember where he stayed in Baden-Baden?"

"Yeah," replied Wright. "He bragged about the Brenner Park. It's very expensive. Why?"

"I'm doing a little research. Brenner Park, eh? I know the manager at another hotel there; I want to check him out."

"Looking for revenge? Be careful. Maybe he rigged the election for the same reason."

"Barry, I'm gonna get him. I just don't know how yet."

"Good luck. Give him one for me."

"I'll try. My wife and I are going back to Germany for a vacation. We'll spend some time in Offenburg and Bad Herrenalb. Then I'm dropping into Baden-Baden for some research. I'll let you know what happens."

• • •

Kappler drove from Bad Herrenalb into Baden-Baden. The road twisted as it crossed the Murg River, and he entered town from the east. His uncle, Manfred Kappler, the manager of the Hotel Belle Epoque, awaited him in the hotel's restaurant. The Belle Epoque sat in a "New Renaissance Village" south of the central district of Baden-Baden, only 400 meters from the Hotel Brenner Park.

Onkel Manfred waved Kappler over to his table. After the usual greetings and a magnificent lunch of *Blutwurst* and *spaetzle,* the uncle pulled an envelope out of his jacket.

"At your request, I asked the manager at the Brenner Park to make a copy of Herr Spinoza's bill. This is highly irregular considering Germany's privacy laws—you must keep this confidential." He handed it to Kappler.

"*Vielen dank.*" Kappler examined the statement and saw that it had a large room service charge and a huge transfer to the Casino Baden-Baden cashier, charged against a Eurocard issued by Deutsche Bank. That card had to be on the second account that had popped up when he ran the credit report on Spinoza.

"What's this charge to Deutsche Bank? I know it's possible for Americans to get Eurocards, but they're unusual, and the balances in overseas bank accounts must be reported to the U.S. Treasury."

"I was surprised, too. I called *Herr Direktor* Mannig, at Deutsche Bank—I went to school with him in Karlsruhe—and he sent me this document." *Onkel* Manfred produced a faxed page that listed detailed transactions on Alex Spinoza's Eurocard account. "This is even more sensitive, so you must be very careful with it."

Kappler smiled at his uncle's initiative and studied the document. It listed one deposit, $173,000, from an unspecified financial organization on the Isle of Man. Kappler reached for his beer and did a rapid calculation in his head: three times $35,000 plus $68,000 equaled $173,000. But there were large current charges of $287,065, based to a large extent on funds transferred to the Casino Baden-Baden, incurred at the Brenner Park. So Spinoza *had* established a virtual second identity, and he was a gambler besides being an asshole.

"Many thanks, *Onkel.* You've made my day."

• • •

Kappler pondered what to do about Spinoza. What, he wondered, would be just revenge? At the least, he could get him kicked out of the Stags—Spinoza's surreptitious email in the election alone would be considered ample grounds. Or, Kappler could exact some other penalty, something more satisfying on a personal basis. Driving to the Frankfurt airport on the return trip it struck him—the perfect twist. He'd turn the tables on Spinoza.

• • •

Three weeks later, Kappler pulled into the parking lot under the old warehouse wing of the Stags lodge.

Spinoza was just climbing out of his M5. "Fred. You have new wheels?" Kappler, he saw, drove a brand new Lexus LS460L, the top of the line.

Kappler grinned. "You like it? It's a great car. I got it through my agency. It costs a bundle, about eighty-five K at the curb with my dealer discount. But I came into some money from the old country, so I figured it was time to upgrade. See ya!"

• • •

Alex Spinoza sat at his desk in his second floor home study in Westchester. Tiffany, his wife's Persian cat, jumped up. She circled around a few times before she lay spread-eagled on the desktop, in a pool of sunlight that streamed through the open window. He hated the cat almost as much as that goddamn German Chihuahua, Sigmund

Spinoza was ready for the big score. He planned on writing the first check for $675,000 to jamaicaprocessing.com, to be followed by five more of equal amounts, plus credit card transfers. The M5 was packed, ready to go. He cleaned up his last paperwork and rifled through the usual collection of junk mail, searching for something interesting. An envelope with *Luftpost* markings caught his eye. It was his monthly statement for his Eurocard account from Deutsche Bank. It showed charges for $85,350 for a Lexus purchased from Kappler Toyota, and charges of $287,065 for a stay at the Brenner Park Hotel. The balance was in the red over $370,000! Bile rose as he realized the identity he'd stolen from himself had been stolen in turn by Kappler. That prick! Kappler had bagged his wife, and now he'd ripped off a car. But what the hell was the casino charge for over $250,000? He picked up the phone and called the Brenner Park Hotel.

As he listened to the hotel clerk, Spinoza's blood pressure soared, and his nose began to drip blood. He slammed the phone down on the stained bank statement. The bitch in Germany, Jutta, he realized, had ripped him off, too! He'd forgotten that she'd been there when he checked into the Hotel Brenner Park and authorized the desk to advance funds for charges at the casino. Jutta, and probably her husband or sister, had pissed away over a quarter-million bucks playing roulette. He now owed Deutsche Bank big bucks! And there was no way he could chase Fred Kappler—not with that phony second identity. Spinoza grabbed his letter opener, jabbed it into the cat's tail, and then lifted the animal, blade and all, and threw it out the window of his office. The cat shrieked and yowled all the way down to the yard.

Lost in the Velvet Turtle

Jim and Beverly Adams celebrated their first anniversary. Jim had booked an 8:00 PM table, along with special instructions, at the Velvet Turtle in Redondo Beach. En route to the restaurant, traffic was light on the Pacific Coast Highway. But to Jim, it seemed as though he couldn't get Beverly's new Honda to go faster than thirty-five miles per hour. The car was unfamiliar, and the accelerator was stiff. It felt like someone below the floorboards pushed back. Jim cringed, as passing drivers bombarded the couple with angry looks.

He worried about the time. He wanted the evening to be perfect. He looked for his watch, but he'd forgotten it in the bedroom. *At this speed we'll never get there.* "What time is it, hon?"

Beverly pointed at the digital clock display in the radio panel. "The time's on the dash, dear. See?"

He looked, but the numbers seemed blurred and ran together. Outside, the first rain of the season thundered down, and the wipers streaked the windshield. Headlights from on-coming vehicles morphed into tiny Tinker Bells.

He squinted to read the time. "I'm worried we'll be late. This rain and all."

Beverly smiled and grabbed his hand. "Don't worry; we have plenty of time."

He nodded. *That goddamn promise.* Jim's left hand clenched the steering wheel. He hoped Beverly didn't notice that his hands were damp.

• • •

In the Velvet Turtle's parking lot, a young man with an umbrella opened Beverly's door. "Hi! I'm Tommy, your valet. Welcome!"

Jim handed Tommy the keys to the Honda, and the couple entered the restaurant.

"Good evening," said Jim, to the hostess behind the stand. "We're the Adams party. I booked—"

"Mr. and Mrs. Adams, welcome to the Velvet Turtle." The hostess winked at Jim and grabbed two menus. "Happy Anniversary! We've reserved our best table for you. Please, follow me."

Jim and Beverly followed the woman through a labyrinth of crowded rooms and corridors. Delicious aromas filled the air; Jim licked his lips at the sight of an enormous rib eye steak on a patron's plate. In each room, they wended their way through a maze of tables. They passed an attractive salad bar and entered a long corridor. The hostess finally placed them at a table with a canyon view near a roaring fireplace. Outside, trees swayed on a distant ridge line. Large drops of rain sparkled in the restaurant's spotlights. A bouquet of orange blossom and pansy flowers and an ice bucket containing a bottle of Dom Pérignon sat on the table. Two large candles flanked the setting—just as Jim had ordered. The hiss and crackle of the fire added to the cozy ambience. Light cast by the fire flickered and danced across Beverly's lovely face.

The hostess lit the candles, popped the cork with a theatrical flourish, and poured champagne into two crystal flutes.

Beverly beamed. "What beautiful flowers! How sweet."

They enjoyed their champagne. When the waiter arrived, Beverly ordered beef bourguignon; Jim ordered a porterhouse—rare. A bottle of 2004 Stags Leap Cabernet Sauvignon completed their order.

A busboy delivered a pitcher of water. Slices of lime floated on the surface.

Jim was hungry. He pictured himself attacking his steak. "Where's the bread?"

"We have a fresh batch coming out of the oven in a few minutes." The busboy refreshed the flutes of champagne and departed.

"Who's going to the salad bar first?" asked Jim.

"Look, the rain's let up," noted Beverly. "You go ahead. I want to enjoy the view."

Jim nodded. "I won't be long."

• • •

Jim couldn't believe it. He was lost! *How was it possible?* He looked down at his plate. The salad was smothered in Green Goddess dressing, the house specialty. He'd left just a few minutes ago. But now he couldn't find his table. Damn Ed, thought Jim, and that weed they'd smoked two hours earlier. *Boy, they sure make that stuff strong these days.* He realized he never should've taken the second hit. And now, Beverly would wonder where he was. *Rats*!

He turned to retrace his steps. A moment later, he turned in confusion. *Where the hell was the salad bar?* Crowded tables were everywhere. The dining rooms stretched to the horizon. He walked toward another room and bounced off a full length mirror. Some salad fell off his plate. Jim looked around furtively, then he bent down and scooped the droppings onto his plate. He licked his hand clean. Perplexed, he spun around. He spotted another dining room. *Maybe Beverly's in there. Yes, that's got to be it.* Confidence restored, he strode toward the room. But a party waiting to be seated blocked his way, and Jim veered through a pair of swinging doors. He found himself in the parking lot.

The rain had stopped and the mercury vapor lights illuminated puddles on the driveway. Jim felt his socks get wet; his shoes were in an inch of water. *That goddamn dope–*

"Sir, our patrons usually ask for doggy bags."

"Huh?" Jim recognized the valet. "Oh, Tommy. Hi." Jim looked at his salad plate, and grinned sheepishly. More Green Goddess dressing had slopped onto his fingers which he licked again. "I was looking for my table and got confused. Could you point me towards the salad bar?"

Tommy had mirth in his eyes. "Just turn right after the men's room. It'll be in front of you."

Jim thought the boy covered his mouth to hide a laugh. Chagrined, Jim stepped over another puddle and went through the main entrance. *Shit. I got to give that kid a big tip.*

He found the men's room. *Was that turn left or right?* Left, Jim decided, Tommy had said "left," hadn't he? Jim turned and saw a bar. But it was the main bar, not the salad bar. His shoes squished as he walked back toward the entrance, but then he entered another dining room. *What the hell?* By now, Jim's hunger gnawed at him. *I might starve if I don't get to that table soon.* He munched a piece of lettuce and licked a few more fingers.

Time stood still. It raced. It crawled. Jim thought he'd searched for twenty minutes. He began to despair. He knew that Beverly frustrated easily—sometimes she had a hot temper. She might give up and leave. Maybe he should just give up, too, and go home.

Jim turned around. *Ah, the salad bar.* All right, he thought, he'd come in on the side with the croutons. He headed in that direction. As he walked around the bar, he saw a corridor. *That's where I saw that waitress with the hot body.* Jim walked down the corridor.

There! The fireplace—the flowers. Yes, that's where Beverly is. Jim breathed a sigh of relief, wiped his brow, crossed the room, and sat down.

Beverly pointed at his plate. "What happened to your salad?"

"Huh?" Jim looked down. His salad had vanished, just a few traces of the Green Goddess dressing remained.

"I guess I was hungry." Jim noticed his hands were smeared with dressing.

She raised an eyebrow. "You have dressing on your forehead."

He dabbed with his napkin. The green stains startled him. "Sorry I was gone so long."

"Long?" Beverly's lips curled. "You've only been gone a few minutes," she hissed. "Have you been smoking dope again with that asshole, Ed? Damn it, Jim. You promised!"

The chill in Jim's feet crawled up his legs. His hopes for a perfect evening evaporated. Jim shivered and wished he'd taken another hit.

Cesspool Charlie

Cesspool was not the nickname given Charlie by his parents. It was laid on him by a bunch of horny-handed miners—in a moment of questionable judgment on the part of Charlie.

Charlie was a hard-rock silver miner noted for his expertise with dynamite. Folks in Panamint Valley had a high regard for Charlie's skills; it was said he could shape his charges with such precision that he'd blast a pocket of ore a mere fifteen feet from his corn liquor and lunch—knowing full well his stash was safe. When he was sober, such confidence was not misplaced, and Charley's accuracy was unmatched. Three-Fingers McGraw always said he could outperform Charlie. But other miners knew Three-Fingers would never risk a precious bottle of booze.

Things came to a head when Jack Baggin, proprietor of the Last Chance Mine, built a house. He had a new bride, Annie Rose McGonagle, who'd worked at the Trona Saloon. Annie had dated several of the miners in her day, including Charlie, as she searched for the right man. Jack, with the fortune he'd made mining silver, based to a considerable extent on Charlie's skills, seemed to be that man. Jack built the house on some High Sierra granite in a nice part of town. He stuffed it with new furniture and affixed the latest in lightning rods. With the house complete from A to Z, Jack and Annie announced a house-warming party. They invited miners from Inyo and San Bernardino counties—all the way from Lone Pine in the north, down through Trona, and west to Lake Isabella. The miners and their women assembled. Liquor flowed.

Now this may seem improbable, but it was discovered shortly after the party commenced that someone had erred—the house had no cesspool. And the house wasn't sitting on nice, soft, easy-to-dig Illinois loam. Annie, of course, was out of sorts. One would expect a house to have a cesspool. Jack proposed a new outhouse to Annie, but she stormed away. The marriage was too young for her to nag, but Jack knew that the outhouse idea was a dog that couldn't hunt. He called Charlie over and gave him the assignment. As special compensation, he offered Charlie a bottle of bourbon—with a real label on the bottle.

Perhaps Jack's reason to gift a bottle of the devil's brew to Charlie was to ease his toil, or to wet his whistle, or it was just an act of generosity. Those who were there that day weren't sure—but they all agreed it was a mistake on Jack's part.

No one knew how it happened. Maybe Charlie was seized by a mischievous imp or a jealous devil. Maybe it was an accident, or caused by the brew itself—although Charlie could chug a quart of rye and still walk a straight line. In any event, Charlie knocked off the bottle and went to work. He sized up the job, ran his hands over the granite, tapped here and there, put his ear to the stone, and drilled a few holes. He planted his charges, lit the fuses, and "BAM!" Besides the rather oversized hole for the cesspool that appeared after the dust had settled, the explosion shattered all the windows in the new house and blew out half the other windows in the neighborhood. It lifted Jack's roof six inches off the rafters. The explosion was ringing in everyone's ears when the roof slammed down, and shattered tiles went airborne, showering the partygoers Even worse, it launched an enormous boulder which smashed the keg of bourbon that Jack had ordered for the party. Charlie had the good sense to take to the hills. Out of whiskey, the party wound down.

• • •

Several years later, a hiker came upon a prospector in the hills beyond Beatty. The man was camped with two burros tied off to a bush. The animals bore shovels, a pickaxe, and other prospecting gear.

The prospector was brewing a pot of coffee on an open fire. "Name's Charlie. Sit yourself down and have a cup."

"Wow. You wouldn't be Cesspool Charlie by any chance—would you? They tell stories about you in the Trona Saloon."

"Yup, that's me." Charlie added red whiskey to two cups of coffee.

"What happened that day at Jack Baggin's? How could you make a mistake like that with all your demolition experience?"

"Weren't no mistake!"

"Were you drunk?"

"I was sober as a durn Mormon."

The hiker shook his head. "Then I don't understand. From what I heard, the cesspool was three times bigger than it had to be."

"Jack Baggin is full of shit, and I figgered he needed a big one," replied Charlie.

"Do you think you deserve that name, Cesspool?"

"Sure I deserve it," conceded Charlie. "It was too bad about that keg of whiskey." He smiled and stirred the campfire with a stick. "That explosion weren't no mistake but for the boulder missed Baggin. It was damn close, too. Just a foot off."

Charlie smiled wistfully and poured some more red whiskey into his cup. "Let me tell ya what with Annie, her momma and six kids, that cesspool is filling up. Baggin, that cheap bastard, like as not ain't never had it pumped out. Someday I'm gonna sneak up there after dark with some dynamite and a long fuse. That redneck's never gonna forget Cesspool Charlie.

Coolidge Said

Sloan answered the phone.

"Hey, is that you? The Feds are on to us. Get rid of all the data!"

Sloan gulped. "All of it, the files and the emails?"

"Don't waste any time! If they get that shit, we're all going to jail—for life! Enron was a joke compared to what they'll do to us."

Sloan was a neophyte when it came to computers. Scared, he hung up and called the *Geek Squad*.

An hour later, he saw an orange and black Volkswagen pull onto his driveway. He watched as a young woman grabbed a flash memory stick off the rear seat of her car. She walked up to his door. He answered before the knock.

"Mr. Sloan? Hi! My name's Lizzie. I'm from the *Geek Squad*. I believe you called us. You need some help with your computer?"

"Lizzie, it's nice to meet you," said Sloan. "Come in, come in, please. I got to erase some files and email messages—you might say that I need to get rid of some incriminating data, ha-ha!"

Sloan checked the street for strange cars. He closed the door and chained it.

"Don't concern yourself, Mr. Sloan," said Lizzie with a smile. "We don't care what's in the files. Can you show me to the computer?"

"Yes, it's a Dell something. I have a connection to the Internet—whatever that is. I don't really know how it all works. But I can write Word documents and do email."

"Well, that sounds like a useful system, Mr. Sloan. I take it you run Windows on it?"

"I think so. Let me show you the stuff that I need to get rid of. Erase it, right?"

Lizzie frowned. "Mr. Sloan, although we can erase that stuff—as you call it—you do understand, don't you, that just deleting the files won't make them go totally away?"

"What? Jesus! I thought all I had to do was delete them, and the computer would work its magic. I only called you guys because someone on that TV show, *CSI*, mentioned that hard drives held backup data. I figured I might have one, too."

"That's good thinking, Mr. Sloan. When you delete a file it releases the memory, does away with pointers to it, and makes it difficult to retrieve. That means the programs, or, if you prefer, the things that use the file, like your printer, can no longer access it. But it doesn't literally erase the information."

"What's a pointer?" Sloan felt blood pounding in his ears and wiped his forehead with a handkerchief.

"That's not important," she said. "The computer's memory still retains the original information. It'll continue to retain that information until that part of memory is overwritten."

"I thought you said it releases the memory. Shit. Doesn't it go away forever?"

"Well, then, eventually all your computer memory would disappear. That's not how it works."

"So what do I have to do to get rid of the information?" Sloan felt he was on the verge of a spontaneous nosebleed.

"We find a way to overwrite the memory with ones and zeros."

"Can you do that?" he asked nervously.

"No problem. We have software tools for that."

"And these software tools you're going to use—are they different than hardware?"

"Yes, I have some here in my flash memory."

"That looks like hardware to me. It's hard, isn't it?"

"Mr. Sloan, perhaps you can just give me some time, and I'll delete those Word files for good for you."

• • •

Lizzie inserted her flash memory stick in a USB port on Sloan's computer. She spent a few moments typing furiously on the keyboard.

"Okay, Mr. Sloan. Those files have been deleted and overwritten."

A glimmer of hope passed through Sloan's mind. "Thanks. Now, can we move on to my email messages? They're much more dangerous … er … I mean important. I have about 200 I need to destroy—half sent, half received."

"It's the same problem, only worse," declared Lizzie. "We can destroy the messages on your computer. But you understand, don't you, that there are still copies of the messages out there in the ether?"

"Huh? What's ether? What do you mean? How can there be copies? Someone sends me a message; I receive it—and that's it, isn't it?" Blood trickled out of Sloan's nose. He dabbed at it with his handkerchief.

"No, I'm afraid not," said Lizzie. "Do you know how a packet-switched network works?"

"What's a packet?"

"Perhaps I can explain using layman terms. When someone sends you an email message, it gets broken up into little pieces—we call them packets—and those packets get sent over the Internet to your Internet service provider, or ISP."

"So, what's the problem?" Sloan's handkerchief had a large crimson splotch.

"Well, as the packets move through the Internet, some of them are stored and forwarded a number of times on different servers. It depends on your distance from the sender and lots of other things."

"Like what?"

"Well, to give you an absurd example, it could depend on sun spots."

"Who gives a shit about sun spots?" Sloan's nose was bleeding, and this crazy broad was talking about sun spots?

"Anyway, eventually your ISP gets the message, reassembles it, and sends it to your computer. In this whole process, there are many copies made of the message. Not to mention that the original email message might still be on the sender's machine—"

"Lizzie, I'm confused. You're telling me those copies are still out there? But there must be billions. How can they keep all of them? Can't we just delete them on my machine, and send a message to delete them on all those—what'd you call them—servers?"

"No, we can't do that. We can only delete them on your machine."

"What if I send a new email message with just ones and zeros? Can't that overwrite those messages out there?" Sloan's shirt was drenched in sweat; he needed a drink.

"That's a novel thought, Mr. Sloan. But it won't work. You see, that new message would just get stored in a new place—well, actually, in many new places and with new pointers."

"Goddamn pointers, whatever they are. So let's see if I understand you. I can erase my computer, overwrite the memory, beat the crap out of the box with a sledgehammer, and the Feds can still read my emails?"

"There's no need to be crude, Mr. Sloan. But, alas, that's true. The only way to protect the words is to not create them in the first place."

"You don't understand. Oh, Christ, never mind—"

• • •

Flashing red lights bounced off the Dell's screen. The room was awash with men in uniforms.

"That's right, officer," said Lizzie. "Mr. Sloan pulled a large handgun out of his desk drawer and shot himself. It was horrible. Blood splattered all over his desk and printer. I called you immediately."

The policeman looked at a large Smith & Wesson .357 Magnum revolver on the floor. "What happened to cause this tragedy?"

"He had a problem understanding the concept of erasing computer memory."

"I don't understand it, either. But why's that a problem?"

"He said he had some emails and files that he wanted to delete permanently. I tried to explain how it worked, and I paraphrased President Coolidge. Perhaps if Mr. Sloan had been a student of history, this wouldn't have happened."

"What did President Coolidge say?"

"He said, 'If you don't say it, they can't ask you to repeat it.'"

"Can you give me a copy of what's on the machine?"

"The email files are right there, and we can print them. We'll have to put new paper in the printer, of course. Unfortunately, I overwrote the Word files. But, wait … Damn, I forgot the backup files, so, sure, we just have to restore the information from the hard drive."

My Favorite Bar

Hviids Vinstue, my favorite bar in the world, sat below street level in an old brick building at the southwest corner of Copenhagen's Kongen Nytorv, a grand square near the Nyhafn (New Harbor). Hviids' waiters purveyed food from a limited menu as well as beer, wine, spirits, and digestifs. Some of the beers, like Carlsberg Elephant, were aptly named. Two such *heavy* brews could floor a mammoth.

The bar's décor was northern European: massive oak bars, large round tables, beat-up chairs and stools, and a wooden floor littered with peanut shells. The crowd was composed of ravishing Danish blondes punctuated occasionally by long-legged redheads and brunettes, a plethora of students and artists, an occasional family with children, businessmen and bums, plump opera stars, and grizzled sailors. The ages ranged from eight to eighty. During a previous visit, I'd shared a table with a tugboat captain, a former Danish World War II resistance fighter, two students from Sweden, and several anarchists from Germany. As usual, the crowd had been noisy and spirited.

My wife was along on this trip. I must admit I had mixed feelings about taking her to Hviids. Alas, she was curious about it. Lacking judgment, I'd raved about the bar after previous trips—how friendly the people were, the relaxed fun-loving attitude of the Danes especially when compared to the rest of the Scandinavians … and, of course, the great beer.

I wondered if it was a good idea to expose her to the other things I'd experienced: coarse drunk banter and repartee, the sights of sagging rafters in the ceiling, and the lingering smells—from dank dreary peeling walls, decades of spilled beers, tobacco mixed with a little marijuana smoke, and the urine drenched toilets. And then, of course, there was the real reason I hesitated—the women who frequented Hviids. They were liberated, engaging, inquisitive, and sometimes aggressive. Indeed, in the old days, wags would have labeled Hviids a meat market. Since everyone under the age of eighty-five spoke English, I couldn't rely on the crowd using Danish to insulate my wife from that fact. It was a bad idea to take her to Hviids, I decided. It might be my favorite bar, but I shouldn't take my favorite person.

That morning my wife and I took our daily run north along the wharves toward Copenhagen's famous Little Mermaid.

When the pace relaxed, my wife asked, "Are you going to take me to Hviids? We're staying just a block away, aren't we?"

I gulped. Although there were three different rooms in the wine bar, nowhere would we be safe from the suggestive smiles and winks of women who treated men like prey. I equivocated too long.

"C'mon, David. We've been here three days. I want to see the place."

I was trapped! I stepped up the pace again, but my wife was a stronger runner. Seeing no way out, I mumbled, "Okay." I steeled myself for some awkward moments.

That evening, we sat at a table in Hviids' smallest room as far from the corridor to the toilets as possible, in a corner where I could watch the traffic. I'd worked out my strategy earlier. If it became necessary to divert my wife's attention, I'd sidetrack her with questions about Danish museums.

As we finished our second round of drinks—French Premier Cru Chablis for my wife, Carlsberg Elephant chased with ice-cold Jägermeister for me—the attack began. Two lovely women strolled up and inquired if they could share our table. Like a friendly American tourist, my wife invited the women to join us.

One of them said, "Americans, eh?" Then she looked at me. "It's nice to see you again."

I nodded miserably and saw a flash of jealousy in my wife's eyes.

The women ordered Tuborg beers while my wife seethed. In my beer-induced haze, I decided it wasn't prudent to bring up museums. Instead, I studied the puddle under my beer in calculated silence.

The second woman asked, "So who is this pretty woman with you?"

"Yes," said the first woman. She placed a hand on my wife's arm and gave a gentle squeeze. "We thought she might like to join us for a drink. Would you, dear?"

My wife raised an eyebrow and gave me a wicked grin. "I don't think so," she said. "I'm flattered, but I prefer men."

The women looked disappointed. They grabbed their beers and departed.

I was stunned—the women had hit on my wife. I was extra baggage. Salvation had arrived from an unexpected direction. I decided on a third Elephant.

Later, as we stumbled up the stairs to the Kongen Nytorv, my wife said, "What a neat place. You can come here anytime you like."

My favorite bar was safe again!

Street Creds

The Deputy U.S. Attorney studied the FBI Special Agent across his desk. Outside, the San Francisco fog swirled around the Federal Building. It was July, and the fog barreled down the east-west streets and enveloped hills. In John Logan's opinion, it headed directly for his window. He scowled as he sneaked a peek at the gray skies. "So," he said, "do you have any ideas? L.A. is putting a lot of pressure on us to bring down the Cicerone drug operations."

"I do," opined FBI Special Agent Bill Cooley. "But I need some time and a war chest."

"You sure you can pull it off? How you gonna do it?"

"I think it's possible, but you don't want to know how."

"Uh-huh." Logan couldn't care less how it was done, as long as it brought down the Cicerones and stood up in court. "How much?"

"I think we can start small, say five or ten K of task force money. But I got to set up some things. Can we get some assistance from the east coast?"

Logan's head hurt. $10,000 was chump change, but it would turn to dog poop if the deal went south. He'd have to explain his failure to prosecute to the task force in L.A. He popped an Advil and nodded. "Tell Emily what you need. I'm gonna rely on you, Bill."

Cooley smiled. "Just leave it to me, John. I know a guy …"

• • •

The Sheraton in Menlo Park sat on Ravenswood Avenue, next to the El Camino Real, the historic route between Los Angeles and San Francisco. It was known to movers and shakers as an oasis of good food and comfortable rooms, and it had a popular bar. If someone wanted to talk to a venture capitalist on the San Francisco Peninsula, he did it at the Sheraton.

George Mason, fifty-three, shook hands with the venture capitalist (VC) from Boston. Bill Cunningham's business card stated he was the technology manager at Back Bay Investments located on Commonwealth Avenue. The VC wore an off-the-rack gray suit and a narrow dark tie. He sported a short haircut. George sensed it was unusual grooming for an investor. But what the hell—the man represented money. Cunningham had told George that he had appointments with several IT and networking companies in Silicon Valley—spinoffs of firms like Facebook, Google, and Twitter, and hi-tech start-ups with atypical ideas.

"You're interested in unusual business models?" asked George.

"That's why I'm here," Cunningham said. "You have an unusual idea."

That sounded hopeful to George. He knew he had a great idea, but no financing yet. The management team was composed of just him. Hell, he mused, he was the entire team if he didn't count his deadbeat junkie roomer who'd helped build the Beta website for the business.

George wondered if Cunningham knew about his pesky history of failed start-ups. It wasn't helpful that some of those deals had been well-financed. George pushed the thought out of his mind.

"So, how'd you find me?" he said. "I didn't send any documents to Boston."

"Actually, some colleagues told me about it. They were impressed with the idea, the *raison d'être*, of your website."

"Really? Who referred you?" George thought people who could speak another language were cool. And he was curious about Cunningham's interest. George had bounced the idea around, but not everyone thought it had potential. Most agreed it was unique, but this was the first positive response from any people with money. It was about time. George needed the cash.

"I really can't say," replied the VC. "But they're based in the City." George knew *the City* meant San Francisco.

George nodded. He shifted his body on the chair and reached for his beer. George was a large man, about six foot two and seventy pounds overweight. Red-faced and with a runny nose, he wished he'd sat with his back to the window. George suffered from a candy habit—nose candy—and he was light sensitive.

He rubbed his eyes. George knew that damn habit had cost him his job, and he was desperate. He'd ploughed through the $50,000 saved on his last marketing job in the electronics business; it was easy to piss it away at $1,000 a week for cocaine. He barely got by with unemployment (thank God Congress had extended the benefits) and his share of a small pension fueled by royalties from his father's old mineral rights in northeast New Mexico—a pittance, really.

George had abandoned his medical insurance, switched from wine and whiskey to beer, drove a clunker without insurance, and occasionally ate dog food. He'd managed to keep his cheaply-built two bedroom home on West Remington Drive in Sunnyvale, but he was three months behind in mortgage payments. Several letters from the bank demanded a minimum payment of $2,000 to avoid foreclosure. George's roommate, Joe Toomey the junkie, owed George rent money. He wanted to throw Joe out, but then he'd lose the back rent for good.

The VC said, "So describe your business plan, please, in your own words."

George shook off his funk. The idea was great! George's website, www.revolutionarygoodies.com, was almost ready to launch.

"Okay," said George. "The world's drowning in revolutions. The Middle East and North Africa are in chaos. People are demonstrating in Madison, Wisconsin. Labor's going nuts throughout the Midwest. Look at the Tea Party rallies. Every one of those demonstrators is a prospective customer for my new website."

"What do you mean?" asked Cunningham. "My people in the City said it was a big cash flow business, but they didn't give me details."

George straightened his stained tie. He pulled his old jacket down and leaned forward. He looked around. George was a little hesitant, concerned Cunningham might steal his idea. Maybe, he thought, he should have prepared a non-disclosure agreement—but that just would have slowed down any money.

He whispered, "Revolutionaries, anarchists, and just plain demonstrators all need the same stuff: placards, posters, banners, flags, face paint, tents, dummies to burn in effigy, used tires to burn, empty bottles for Molotov cocktails—I'd offer gasoline if I could ship it. I intend to be the single source for the props needed by the people in the streets. My tagline is 'Your Revolution Starts Here!'"

"Interesting. But how do you make money? What about marketing?"

"That's easy! Marketing 101. Word-of-mouth. I'll use viral marketing—the Internet's perfect for that. My website supports a blog, so these guys can pass on their know-how to others. I don't have to maintain an inventory. I just take orders, collect money, and ship directly from the suppliers."

"So what else would you offer?"

George thought Cunningham stifled a smile. But the question itself expressed interest. George looked over his shoulder again and dropped his voice further.

"Loudspeaker systems—these are high margin. Especially when I supply recordings of shotguns, automatic weapons, dogs barking, and armored vehicles clanking down the street. Then there're videotapes of riots, which can be used anywhere and never go out of date. It's a no-brainer—the list is endless."

"Any violent stuff?"

"No, just bogus materials. If they need blood, I have bottles of cows', lambs', and pigs' blood—depending on whether the buyer's Hindu, Jewish, or Muslim. Christians will take any kind of blood. To help stage scenes, I also offer Palestinian scarves, stained dirty bandages, gas masks, and smoke bombs.

My flags include swastikas, hammers and sickles, rising suns, and *Don't Tread on Me*. I'll also sell fist-sized stones—these might be the closest thing to weapons. And, for the intellectuals, books by Mao, Che, and Trotsky."

"How do you identify new markets?" asked Cunningham, who had to lean forward to hear George.

"Not tough. I read the papers and I have a meeting scheduled with the *Wikileaks* folks next week in San Francisco. I figure they'll provide a good heads-up on any upcoming exposé—those always fuel riots."

"It sounds like you've given this a lot of thought. How much are you looking for?"

George realized it was the moment of truth. But he hadn't really worked up the numbers. His business plan was four pages of chicken scratchings, a draft assembled in a coke-induced haze. Who knew how much he really needed? This was a start-up, after all. George hated management. He was an inventor now. Once he got some money, he would hire a chief executive officer (CEO) and concentrate on developing the intellectual property. Let the CEO work the numbers.

Still, at the moment he was on point. He couldn't ask for too much, or it might look flakey. Heck, it would look flakey if he asked for too little. He mumbled, "$250,000."

"What's the return on investment?"

George knew these VC guys were formula-driven. They liked to make six-to-eight times their money in three-to-five years. "You ought to see about $2 million in four years—when we do the initial public offering." George hoped Cunningham wouldn't ask for financial details but then again, he hoped he would because it would signal more interest.

"Okay," said the VC. "I'll get back to you."

"Is there any way we can advance some of the funds on a letter agreement. I'd like to get started on the marketing."

"As I said, I'll get back to you. Send me a draft." Cunningham smiled, shook hands, and departed.

George wondered if the guy was serious. Did he give the man too much information? Cunningham just didn't seem to have the bearing and presence of Silicon Valley investors—even if he was from Boston. George drove back to Sunnyvale. Maybe, he mused, he should get some trade secret protection.

• • •

Joe snored on George's hide-a-bed, which doubled as a couch in the grungy living room. A crack pipe lay on a cluttered coffee table. Ash trays filled with cigarette and cigar butts adorned the table next to a Crème Brule torch the men used as a cigar lighter. A few marijuana roaches lay in a tray next to a pack of ZigZag cigarette papers. George rubbed at some white powder on the table and licked his finger clean. He decided to work on the letter to Cunningham.

George went into his bedroom and booted up his computer. He was just wondering how much information he should provide when Joe came into the room.

"George, did ya get the money for the website?"

"Maybe I can get an advance next week if we're really lucky."

"What about this week? I need some money. We need—"

"I know what we need," snarled George. "Ain't you got any ideas of your own?"

"Well, yeah, I do. You want to make a fast five grand?"

George's mind spun. That amount of money could bring the mortgage current, give him time to work with Back Bay, put some real food in the refrigerator, and provide a bag of coke. "Hell, yes. What's involved? Is it legal?"

"Of course. You remember Amit Singh? Our old dealer in San Mateo? He got busted by the Feds. His mother called me last night. The government wants $100,000 bail. She said if you put up your house as bond, she'll pay you $5,000 cash—all she's got. And it's only for three weeks until the trial."

"But my house ain't worth that much. I mean, sure, maybe it's worth four hundred, but I owe three-fifty."

"She said she's got a guy that'll appraise the house at four-fifty. Maybe more. Interested?"

George pondered the deal. It was hard to believe someone would appraise his house for $450,000. It sounded too good to be true. Except for the land, the place was a tear-down—leaky roof, mildew in the closets, rotten sun-bleached siding, serious plumbing problems, saggy ceilings, and a 1960s kitchen with appliances that barely worked. But five K in cash? And then … if he could launch the business …

"Damn right. Call her back."

Joe smiled and produced a raggedy half-a-joint. George abandoned his writing project.

• • •

The next day George received a call from a phone in the 617 area code. He remembered that was in VC Cunningham's Boston location. He snatched the phone off the cradle. "Revolutionary Goodies."

"Mr. Mason," said a woman, "I'm Bill Cunningham's executive assistant at Back Bay Investments. Do you have a moment?"

George felt his heart thump. A chill ran up his calves and lingered in the back of his knees. Maybe he was going to get the money! He just had to last a few more weeks. George willed himself to calm down. "I have a few minutes."

"Mr. Cunningham is traveling. He asked me to tell you that Back Bay is very interested in your business model. He requested a letter proposal and draft Ts and Cs (terms and conditions). Mr. Cunningham said it might take about a month to put the money together, and it would come in five tranches of $50,000 each—assuming, of course, the Ts and Cs are acceptable."

George's mind raced. Fifty K in a month! The five grand from Amit's mother would fill the gap. A letter proposal was simple. It didn't require more than some top level numbers which he could conjure out of the air. Damn, he should have started that letter yesterday.

"That's wonderful. Please tell Mr. Cunningham that I'll email the documents today."

After working up an email message and attachment, George had a restless night. His coke supply was almost exhausted. He wasn't certain how long he could keep it together. The trial was three weeks away. Still, he looked forward to his meeting with Singh's lawyer, which had been arranged by Amit's mother.

The next morning, he drove to San Francisco. He took an elevator to the tenth floor of the Embarcadero II building on the edge of the financial district.

Mrs. Singh was a small woman with a dot in the middle of her forehead. She was dressed in what George assumed was traditional Indian garb, a saffron- and orange-colored sari. She looked about sixty and had a nervous smile, which George attributed to her concern for her son. She introduced Mr. Lee, Amit's attorney.

"Good morning, Mr. Mason," said Lee. "I understand you're prepared to post bail for Mr. Singh."

"That's right, but I'm not a certified bondsman," said George. "Does that matter?"

"No problem," said Lee. "It's not required. We're in federal court. The state courts have more stringent licensing requirements."

George smiled but was uncomfortable. Dealing with authorities always made him nervous. He told himself to calm down and think about the money.

"Well, that's great. Will the court accept the net value of my home as a bond?"

"It's more than enough," said the lawyer. "I've secured an appraisal. It places a value of $600,000 on your home."

"How'd you get it so quickly? I only agreed to do this deal two days ago. No appraiser came by the house."

"Please, Mr. Mason, just leave it to me. As I said, it's all taken care of."

"So what's next?"

Mrs. Singh and the men descended in an elevator and climbed into a taxi for the Federal Building on Golden Gate Avenue.

"The court's on the ninth floor," said Lee. "We'll see a magistrate. We don't go up before a judge unless the bail is contested."

• • •

Lee introduced a man standing in front of the courtroom to Mrs. Singh and George. "This is John Logan, Deputy U.S. Attorney in San Francisco. He represents the government in the bail hearing. I just need a few moments alone with him."

Mrs. Singh went into the courtroom. Lee and Logan stepped down the corridor. To George, it looked like the men had a friendly conversation. At one point Logan laughed. A few moments later, they shook hands and Lee returned. "Okay, it's all set. He says the paperwork's in order, and the government won't contest the bond."

"What about the appraisal?" said George. It seemed awfully high to him, and he was unsettled by that friendly relationship with the Deputy U.S. Attorney.

"No problem. Trust me. Now, listen. When I nudge you, just say 'Yes.'"

The men went into the courtroom and joined Mrs. Singh in the front row behind the railing.

George's nose was running by the time the bail hearing was called. He moved to the defendant's table with Mr. Lee. Amit was delivered to their table by a marshal. The dope dealer sat on the other side of Mr. Lee and sported an orange prisoner's suit. George felt shaky; he could use a little snort. He looked back over his shoulder at Mrs. Singh. She sat directly behind her son. Mrs. Singh smiled encouragingly and nursed the edge of an envelope out of her purse. Damn, George thought, he needed that money. He decided to shake off the unease he felt about the whole deal. Just another month and he'd be swimming in cash.

Magistrate Irving Landesman called Mr. Lee and the Deputy U.S.

Attorney to his bench. After a brief conversation and the exchange of a few documents, the men returned to their respective tables. The magistrate said, "Er, Mr. Mason?"

George rose.

"Do you understand," asked the magistrate, "that you're posting $100,000 as a bond for the bail of Mr. Amit Singh?"

George was tongue-tied with stress, adrenaline, low blood sugar, and his body's demand for cocaine. After a brief pause, Mr. Lee prodded him.

"Ah, yes, Your Honor."

"I see. Do you understand that this bond is the government's surety that Mr. Singh will present himself for trial? That if he does not, your bond is forfeited to the government and that it can place a lien on your home?"

The word *lien* slammed into George's head. A wisp of caution and fear surged through him. But he needed money. Confused, he bleated, "But I'm not—"

Lee nudged him again.

Money fought with fear and fear lost. "Yes," mumbled George.

Magistrate Landesman pounded his gavel. "Okay, see the clerk for the paperwork. The prisoner is released pending his appearance at trial set for this department at 9:00 AM three weeks from today."

George turned around, and Mrs. Singh slipped him the stuffed envelope. "Don't worry," she said. "He'll be here."

• • •

George and Joe spent a few days stoned. They celebrated with rib eye steaks and pizza. They worked on the website and established a PayPal account to collect payments from the flood of revolutionaries that George expected when the site went live. Another call from Boston confirmed that George's letter proposal had been received. Cunningham was still on the road. George was thanked for his patience.

Time passed. After sending $2,000 to the mortgage company, George got nervous. The $5,000 from Mrs. Singh had evaporated. The trial date was the next day, and he still had not received a signed letter agreement from Cunningham.

On the day of the trial, the drive north was tense. An unusual summer thunderstorm passed through the Bay Area. George took it as a bad omen. It didn't help that his left windshield wiper flew off when he turned up the wiper speed to cope with the deluge. Then George dismissed the defective wipers from his mind. As soon as he got the money, he'd lease that new Jaguar he'd lusted for at British Motors in Burlingame.

When George arrived at the courthouse, he looked for Amit and his mother. Neither were present. The Deputy U.S. Attorney was preoccupied with paperwork. Mr. Lee nodded at him.

George leaned forward to get Lee's attention. He said, "Where's—" just as Judge William Kennedy entered the courtroom.

"Ladies and Gentlemen," declared the judge, "please be seated. Are we ready to proceed? Where's the defendant?"

"Uh, Your Honor," said Lee, "I've been informed the defendant has fled the state. His whereabouts are unknown at this time."

"Mr. Logan?" asked the judge.

"In the defendant's absence, Your Honor, please issue a bench warrant for his arrest and an order to forfeit the bond."

"The bond was secured by a home; is that correct?"

"Mr. George Mason's home, Your Honor," said Logan. "The government will place a lien on the property as soon as you issue your order."

"So ordered." Judge Kennedy banged his gavel, rose, and left the courtroom.

George sat, stunned. He could lose his home. The government would enforce the lien. He'd have to place the house on the market at a terrible time—and the appraisal would never stand up. He was underwater! Where the hell was the Boston paperwork? George could barely breathe.

He returned to Sunnyvale. His message light blinked. He picked up the phone in the kitchen and listened to a message. "*Mr. Mason, this is Mr. Cunningham's executive assistant. I'm afraid Mr. Cunningham has decided to place funds elsewhere. He does thank you for your interest in Back Bay Investments. Have a nice day.*"

The dirty linoleum floor flew up as George slumped forward. On the way down, he banged his head on the sink, and moaned in misery.

Joe ran into the kitchen. "What happened?"

George opened one eye. When he stopped hyperventilating, he said, "What happened is you just lost a place to live. Get out!"

• • •

Months went by as George struggled with his catastrophic finances. He worried every day about the lien, but the government had not yet enforced it. He found a menial job at the McDonalds on Castro Street in Mountain View. His mother sent him a check for $1,500, and he managed to stay no more than two months behind on his mortgage. Any day, he expected a letter from the government or the bank.

George searched for Amit Singh on the Internet. He hired a bounty hunter. The bounty hunter said he'd take twenty percent of the bail as a commission, if successful. But George had to pay out-of-pocket search expenses. The advance wiped out George's dope budget for a month.

One day, George noticed a headline in the *San Francisco Globe.* It read, "CICERONE DRUG MOB BUSTED." Jesus, thought George, that'd drive up the price of coke. The article said the preliminary hearing was set for a few weeks later.

At the end of the month, the bounty hunter visited George.

"Any success?" asked George.

"Have you paid attention to the Cicerone hearing?" replied the bounty hunter.

George, who'd abandoned his own search for Singh in despair, shook his head. "I been too busy."

"I found Singh's name in the transcript of the preliminary hearing. Apparently he's a C-I."

"A what?"

"Confidential informant. The government tried to seal the transcript, but the judge refused. It seems your friend Singh was a dope dealer and worked his way into the Cicerones."

"Well, that's great. Now that you found him, go get him!"

The bounty hunter shook his head. "I don't think so. They got him buried in a witness protection program. The Feds need him to testify at the actual trial. You'll never find him."

George was astonished. The government knew where Amit was, and they didn't remove the lien on his home? "But—"

"Look, buddy, you're shit out of luck on this one. I'm out of here. And here's my final statement for expenses."

George resolved to go to the Cicerone trial. When Singh appeared, George planned a citizen's arrest.

• • •

George pushed his way through the crowd in front of Judge William Kennedy's courtroom. Reporters and students from a law school class filled the hallway and most of the seats. George breathed a sigh of relief when he found an empty seat in the back row. He could see Logan, the Deputy U.S. Attorney, at a table. Sitting next to him was a man in a gray suit. Damn, George thought, the guy looked like Bill Cunningham, the VC from Boston. Goddamn, it *was* him. What was he doing there?

The bailiff escorted Paul Cicerone into the courtroom. The judge first discussed some bookkeeping matters. Then the lawyers introduced the parties. George was stunned when Logan introduced Cunningham as Bill Cooley, an FBI Special Agent from an Organized Crime Task Force. For a while, George's mind went blank. As awareness returned, he stirred anxiously and waited for the morning recess. When the gavel dropped, he sprang to his feet and hovered near the door.

As Cooley walked by, George blurted, "Hey, Bill. Making an investment? In Cicerone?"

Cooley turned. He blanched a little, looked over his shoulder, and grabbed George's arm. "Come with me," he demanded.

Cooley led George down the hall to a small conference room. When the door closed, Cooley patted George down. "You're not wearing a wire, are you?"

"A wire? What are you talking about?"

Cooley insisted George open his shirt and turn around as the agent inspected him for a recording device or transmitter.

"Sorry," Cooley said. "You can button up. What can I do for you?"

"I want to know what you're doing here. And you guys have a confidential informant who owes me $100,000."

Cooley smiled. "Sorry, George. I'll never admit it outside this room, but you're the patsy. It was Singh's idea. We busted him for possession with intent to sell a key of cocaine; he offered to give up the Cicerones if we let him go."

"So what did that have to do with me?"

"It's not complicated," said Cooley. "Singh needed to be released from custody. We couldn't drop the charges. We needed someone to post bail who had nothing to do with the government. Otherwise, Cicerone would have learned about our involvement before Singh hit the streets. What better than a zonked-out junkie desperate for a bag of blow? It was a simple thing; the man needed street creds."

"But why me?" raged George. "How the hell did I get involved?"

"Singh knew about your website. I have to admit that at first I didn't believe it was possible. That's why I visited you as an investor."

"Huh? What was possible?" George's jaw dropped—fury replaced by bewilderment.

"I didn't think it was possible for anyone to have such a stupid idea. As soon as I realized you were dead serious, I knew we could pull it off."

The Letter

Snow blanketed South Haven, Michigan, driven over the eastern shores of the lake by strong westerly winds. Neon lights in a café window reflected off glazed streets and cast red and yellow glows on the façade of Brower Vacuum Cleaner Company's building on the north side of Water Street. At 2:00 AM, the café lights sputtered out. Across the street, a man dressed in black chinos and a heavy windbreaker hid in shadows cast by the Brower company sign. A Michigan State Police cruiser turned onto North Shore Drive and headed for the Interstate. After the cruiser disappeared, the man stepped out of the shadows and crept down a narrow passageway to the side entrance to Brower. He tapped at an electric keypad; gloves and cold fingers rendered him clumsy. He swore several times but kept the gloves on. He tapped repeatedly at the keys, growing frustrated. Finally, a green LED switched on, and the man slipped inside the building. A small pencil flashlight highlighted a ream of company stationery and envelopes on one of the desks. The man grabbed several letterheads and envelopes and stuffed them in his parka. He turned to the door, reengaged the alarm, and made his way back to Water Street.

• • •

Lawrence "Larry" Powell smiled as he parked his dirty Toyota Tundra pick-up on Water Street at the intersection with Kalamazoo Street. He had a good feeling. It was the day Joe Appleby, Brower's vice president, would appoint a new sales manager. Larry sensed he was the favorite. It was important—he needed the promotion if he wanted to keep his new girl friend happy. She liked fine dining, expensive clothes, and lusted for a romantic stroll on a tropical beach. It had been touch and go financing all the expensive meals with her—a few times Larry had to fabricate charges on his expense account. Larry, cocky as was his style, also had promised the girl a trip to the Bahamas.

Fortunately, Buddy Smith, Larry's principal competitor, didn't do well under pressure. And Jim Seagel, just out of the army, was too young and inexperienced. Neither were a serious threat. And Larry had a weapon, a clever subterfuge. No way, he gloated, would anyone figure it out.

The morning temperature had dropped as a weather front moved off Lake Michigan. The mercury stood at five below zero when Larry climbed out of his truck. The snow had stopped, and the streets were thick with ruts filled with churned snow and ice. Despite the cold, Larry felt warm, comfortable, and confident as he strode towards the Starbucks next to the front door of the vacuum cleaner company. As he walked, he thought about his ex-high school English teacher. Mr. Dodge would be proud of Lawrence Powell if he knew how proficient his former student had become at writing anonymous letters. And Larry was gifted; he wrote well and had an excellent vocabulary—honed by years of nasty, sneak attacks and hate mail directed at his perceived enemies.

He'd started in fifth grade writing letters to the parents of the kids who'd bullied him on the playground; he used his dad's typewriter to send the principal complaints about alcohol abuse by a teacher who'd insisted Larry do his homework. Later he'd spread rumors of sexual misbehavior by a high-school coach who'd had the nerve to make Larry run laps. When Larry was eighteen he spread rumors about that bitch, Allison, that she slept around—after she wouldn't sleep with him. It was more difficult in the Army, but he had managed to plant complaints about his drill instructor into the company files one night when Larry was CQ (Charge of Quarters). Unfortunately, he was caught on that one and served a little stockade time. Still, Larry thought, it amazed him how many idiots actually believed the crap in anonymous letters. The missives could be written by anyone, for any reason, and the sanctimonious fools who received the letters eagerly accepted the allegations. And sexual harassment and domestic abuse were no-brainers—everyone believed those charges.

Larry took his non-fat decaf latte to a table. He had a half-hour to kill before the meeting with Appleby. Several patrons had their laptops open, working on the café's wireless Internet connection. Larry wondered if they also wrote anonymous letters. Even blogs were useful weapons to destroy people. But this time, he gloated, he didn't need the Internet. His plan was perfect—it was, he marveled, pure genius! Larry had written an attack letter about himself. He would be the aggrieved party and he planned to exploit it. Of course, the letter had to be detected as a forgery, but that would not be a problem. Appleby was a fanatic for security; he'd mount an investigation to determine who'd written the letter. And Larry's patsy was Buddy Smith! Larry sipped his coffee and perused a *Chicago Tribune.*

• • •

In the conference room, Buddy Smith was flabbergasted. He stared at the letterhead Mr. Appleby had placed in his hands.

"I didn't write this," protested Smith. "I don't believe in anonymous letters."

"I wonder why you thought you could get away with it," said Appleby. "I had security do an investigation and your fingerprints are all over the document and the envelope."

"But anyone could have stolen the envelopes or paper off my desk."

"Come now, Smith," chided Appleby. "Fess up. It's clear you wanted the job." Appleby took the document back and read aloud, "*The officers and directors of this company need to know that Lawrence Powell abused his ex-wife and was arrested for drunk driving. He also slept with Mona, the teenage girl in the mailroom. Is this the kind of person you want representing Brower Vacuum Cleaner Company?*"

"But I didn't write it," argued Smith. "I never saw Larry with Mona. I don't even know where he comes from." Smith looked through the conference room window and saw Larry enter the building. "I never met him before I worked here. I don't even know his family."

"Sorry, Smith," said Appleby. "We don't promote sneaks. I'm not firing you, but I am placing a memo in your file. You've been placed on notice. You can leave now."

"Someone set me up!"

Appleby waved Smith out of the room.

• • •

Smith's shoulders drooped as he exited the conference room. Larry saw a look of disappointment—were those tears?—in Smith's eyes. Larry kept a straight face and opened the conference room door.

"Take a seat, Larry," said Appleby.

"Say, Joe, have you heard this one? If a Brower vacuum cleaner sucks and sucks and never fails, what does the Swiss Navy do?"

"What's this, a joke?"

"It fucks and fucks and never sails—a good one, huh?"

Appleby grimaced. "We need to talk about this sales manager position."

"Did you give the job to Smith? He's very qualified, and I can work with him," said Larry, proud of his devious praise for Smith.

"Well, er … there was a problem."

Larry stared at Appleby and enjoyed the moment. He didn't expect Appleby to take him into his confidence, but it was fun to ask. "What kind of problem?"

"Buddy's not getting the job, Larry. Let's leave it at that."

Larry shifted in his chair. "That's too bad, but … does that mean I get the job?"

Appleby reached for a folder on the table. "Well, that's a problem, too." Appleby slid a document out of the folder and handed it to Larry. "This was faxed to me this morning."

Larry wondered what was in the fax. It was a copy of a letter prepared on an old typewriter with misaligned and spotty keys. "Should I read it?"

"You can if you want. It's pretty damning," said Appleby. "It appears you served time in the army stockade for malingering and making false accusations, and you were dishonorably discharged. Is that true?"

"Where did this come from?"

"It was sent to the chief executive officer (CEO) in Lansing last week. The writer said he knew your drill instructor. He said that you've never accomplished anything on your own, even in civilian life, and that your specialty was character assassination."

"Who wrote it?" demanded Powell.

"It wasn't signed."

"But—"

"Larry, you know that it takes a really dedicated and strong person to send an anonymous letter. And we both know what happens to whistleblowers. So he had to protect himself. This guy did us a big favor."

"But how can you believe something that's not signed? It could have been written by a fifth grader."

"It's done all the time, Larry. You should know. By the way, the CEO ordered an audit of your expense account and found irregularities—bogus entertainment charges. You're quite the piece of work. We're giving the position to Jim Seagel. Now clean out your desk and get out of here."

Larry went back to his desk and sank his head in his hands. Out of the corner of his eye, he saw Seagel enter the conference room. Seagel had a smirk on his face. Larry noticed that Seagel had large shoulders and a ramrod straight back. Damn if Seagel didn't look just like his old drill instructor. Was he the DI's son? Was that it? How come he'd never made the connection before?

Larry grabbed his parka and stormed outside. The cold penetrated to his bones as he crossed Water Street. He'd forgotten how cold Michigan was in the winter. Well, he could forget about the new girl friend and the Bahamas, too. Son-of-a-bitch. Who'd ever thought there'd be two anonymous letters?

Consultants

Alan Kaplan, the forty-year-old senior director of marketing and sales for Carruthers Chemical Company, whistled as he fetched his boarding pass at O'Hare International Airport. Alan was en route to Cincinnati for an extramarital tryst with Allison McDaniels. She worked as a buyer for Proctor & Gamble, Alan's largest customer.

Alan cleared security with his hand baggage and stopped at a bar near his gate. He ordered a Mojjito and looked forward to the evening. Allison was hot and thinking about her aroused him. He knew balling the customer was frowned upon but damn, Allison was worth it. She'd said she loved him. Alan's mind soared as he remembered an evening in Tucson, when they'd both attended a consumer products conference.

His wool-gathering was disturbed when two men sat next to him.

"Where's Jerry?" asked the first man dressed in blue.

"He's on the phone," replied the second who wore gray. "They're negotiating."

"Fantastic," said Blue. "How much?"

Alan saw Gray smile. "We asked for $140,000. It's a one-month consulting gig. With our multipliers and after M and S, we net about seventy grand"

Alan knew M and S meant Materials and Services, like out-of-pocket expenses.

"What do they want us to do?" asked Blue.

"Ask Jerry for the details. It's some management problem," replied Gray.

"But Car—"

Gray interjected. "No names, damn it. You know the client. Remember, the walls have ears."

Alan watched a third man greet Blue and Gray. He carried a garment bag over his shoulder and hovered behind the men. He ordered a beer.

Blue turned around on his stool. "So, Jerry, did we get it?"

"The chairman jewed me down to $100,000."

Alan, a Jew, hid his distaste. He looked at Jerry who appeared mournful.

"Hey, that's not bad, said Gray. We usually overbid by a factor of two. We'll still net a cool $30,000."

Jerry smirked. "I wanted the $70,000."

"So what're the details?" Blue asked.

Jerry reached for his beer. "They need to dump someone in senior management. He's got a sexual harassment problem."

"What's his name," inquired Blue.

"I don't think we should—" cautioned Gray.

Blue seemed curious. "Is he sticking his pen in the company inkwell? Some retarded woman in the mail room? Is it really serious?"

"Hey, they don't hire GDO Associates for one hundred long for nothing," joked Jerry. "But no, he's banging a customer."

Alan put his drink down.

"Who's the customer?" demanded Blue.

"Proc—"

"Listen, you guys," whispered Gray, "you got to stop using names."

Whoa, thought Alan. That *Proc* sounded ominous. Were these guys talking about him? He was in senior management and he was screwing a customer. Further, his board often retained GDO as management consultants. Alan listened more carefully.

"So what's the plan?" asked Blue.

"There are photos—from Tucson. We corner the guy in Cincinnati, confront him, and make him resign—"

"What if he won't?" demanded Gray.

"Then we apply our leverage, go to P&G, and nail the babe. After that, well …" Jerry smiled.

Gray waved a finger at Jerry. "No names, damn it."

My God, thought Alan, they *were* talking about him. Photos! From Tucson! P&G! Alan's arousal deflated and he put his head in his hands. How could he explain it to his wife? Alan considered resignation, but he had to save the girl. He'd have to lie about changing jobs, of course. But, maybe, if his wife didn't find out about Allison, he still might get some action.

As the men prepared to pay their bill, Blue commented, "It don't sound like leverage to me. Why would he care about the girl? She's probably only interested in him because he's a mucky-muck at Carruthers."

"You got it," said Jerry. "It's an old story."

"What don't you guys get?" admonished Gray, who shook his head. "For the last time, don't use names. I can't believe you guys think you're professionals."

Alan's mind froze. It felt surreal and hazy—as though passengers strolled down the concourse in slow motion. An announcement for the flight to Cincinnati seemed to trickle, word-by-word, through his head.

Blue, Gray, and Jerry gathered their belongings and departed.

Tears sprang to Alan's eyes. Of course, those guys were right. Allison had used him—all those discounts. How could he believe she loved him? What a shmuck! He could kiss off his job, Allison, and probably his wife.

Alan tore up his airline ticket and ordered another Mojito.

The Body

Spring, 1983, Columbus, Ohio

Jason Mendel studied the small fragment of a paper towel and a baggie a girl had handed him in the bar at the Hyatt Regency Columbus. The towel was impregnated with Lysergic Acid Diethylamide (LSD) and laced with speed; the baggie contained two psilocybin mushrooms. Jason knew that LSD was a rather pedestrian hallucinogenic compared to the 'shrooms. Buttressed already with beer and spirits, Jason wondered whether he should indulge. Then he looked at Jennifer—she was hot and sultry—he figured what the hell. Better the mushrooms, he decided. They would spice up the party he planned to attend that evening. He popped the two fungi—a rather generous amount—in his mouth and threw away the baggie and acid.

Jason was twenty-three, tall, and thin. He shaved once a week and looked like a high school sophomore. A graduate student at Wayne State University in Detroit, Jason was in town to attend the annual Computer Engineering Conference (CEC). The meetings were at the Hyatt Place Columbus situated near Ohio State University. The conference was organized by the American Computing Society (ACS).

The conference was for graduate students just like Jason. The students presented their theses, attended technical workshops, had birds-of-a-feather meetings with others in their specialties, met senior members and professors from ACS, and attended a job fair.

Jason had already presented his thesis and looked forward to a private cocktail party called the Special Interest Group for Booze (SIGBZE). The society had many special interest groups dedicated to technical specialties, but SIGBZE was off-the-radar, self-financed, informal, and devoted to drink. Jason had heard it was a great place to meet girls—at least the damn few women who attended computer conferences. Jason's walked away from the bar. He was disappointed Jennifer chose not to go with him; he'd heard that if you brought a girl to the party, admission was free. His head began to spin when he climbed into a taxi.

• • •

John Strong studied his reflection in the mirror. He was in one of the bathrooms of a two-bedroom suite reserved for this year's SIGBZE at the Hyatt Place Columbus. John and four other ACS members were the founders of the soirée. The party was not-for-profit. Admission was $4 for males; women were admitted free, and all the revenue went to cover the cost of the booze and the suite. John wondered if they should go for-profit; after all, there was almost always a surplus, which they either gave to the maids for clean-up afterwards, or stockpiled for the following year.

John liked what he saw in the mirror. His normal 5 foot 4 was extended by three-inch heels, a long blonde wig covered his closely cropped brown and gray hair, his collection of scars from playing rugby for years was masked by make-up, and his short, squat legs were covered with sexy mesh nylons. He wore a tight, red, thigh-high dress and his lips sported bright red lipstick. This year SIGBZE was a costume party. The theme was *Mardi Gras,* and John was going as a transvestite. John, straight as an arrow, had experimented before with such a costume; he'd discovered that there was always an empty toilet in a gay or lesbian bar. His epiphany had come during an earlier SIGBZE in New Orleans. From then on, John dressed as a transvestite for costume parties. And costume parties at ACS were his favorite. The society counted among its members an astonishing number of effete snobs. The costume, mused John, would shock and startle them—perfect.

John heard the other guys bantering in the suite. Alex Hunter, an aerospace engineer, was dressed as Chico Marx, with a toy trumpet; Ben Greene, a mucky-muck in New York City's IT department, played Harpo, complete with bike horn in the pocket of a an old, gray raincoat; and Joe Battle, a Northrop employee in accounting, played Groucho with thick eyebrows, a fake mustache, pith helmet, and a fat, long cigar. The fifth SIGBZE founder, Al Jones, a professor from the University of Toronto, was dressed as a Spanish Fly with a serape, Mexican sombrero, and two large wings made out of clothes hangars and clear plastic—ripped from a dry cleaning garment bag and held in place with Scotch tape.

Harpo prepared bowls of peanuts, dip, and chips. Groucho mounted a sign on a tripod that announced "Admission $4." The sign further declared that women were free as well as men who brought a bottle of wine or spirits. Another sign proclaimed: "SIGBZE—NO MINORS!" John sprinkled some Gucci by Gucci, the fragrance for men, on his clothes and left the bathroom to check the inventory. The men expected about one hundred fifty people, and the stock included four cases of beer, one liter each of bourbon, VO, and rum, four liters of Scotch, three liters of vodka, and eight gallons of cheap white wine. Sixteen gallons of mixes and six pounds of nuts, chips, and dip and salsa completed the accoutrements.

• • •

Guests began to arrive. A gaggle of giggling girls trotted in dressed as Egyptian belly-dancers. Male graduate students poured into the suite dropping $4 each in the collection basket. A few came with dates. Most of the students wore street clothes; some of the senior ACS members wore elaborate costumes. Drinks poured. Glasses clinked. Cleopatra arrived with two bare-chested attendants who sported turbans. Spiderman jumped in. Two Star Wars characters came through the front door dueling with fake swords. Kermit, the frog, hopped in and hovered at the wet bar.

Harpo, monitoring the front door, smiled when Dr. Peter K. Lemming, a small, slight man with gray hair and a professorial air, exited the elevator. He wore a gray suit and tie and made his way to the suite. Lemming, president of the society, was a White House appointee to the Office of Science and Technology Policy—an advisor on information technology (IT). He served on several National Science Foundation committees as well.

Harpo knew Lemming and thought of him as an arrogant ass who trafficked in his White House connections. Lemming had once claimed, in a grass-induced haze and in Harpo's presence, that he had the best body in ACS. Rather pompous, Harpo had thought, for such a little man.

"How much?" asked Lemming.

"Four bucks," replied Harpo.

"Even for me, the president?"

"Especially for you, Mr. President," Harpo grinned. He wished he had his bike horn—so he could blow it in Lemming's face, but it was in the suite, on a table next to the dip.

"No way—I should be admitted free," declared Lemming.

The men stared at each other. Harpo shook his head and stuck his hand out.

Lemming said, "But—"

"Four bucks," repeated Harpo.

After an awkward moment, Lemming turned and sauntered back towards the elevator.

"Asshole," muttered Harpo.

Jason Mendel floated down the corridor with two crumpled $2 bills in hand. He needed Harpo's assistance to free the bills from his clenched, sweaty fist. With every step into the suite Jason felt as though his feet sprouted roots. Tinker Bells danced in his eyes. His hand brushed a half-empty beer bottle on an end table. Without thinking, he grabbed and swigged it. The peanuts in a bowl jumped into his hands. He saw a giant frog. As the frog hopped towards him, he blinked and his eyes blurred. He couldn't focus. But the swirling images were a kick. They reminded him of the dancing hippos in *Fantasia*. Then his stomach gurgled and he felt ill.

Jason went into the bathroom. He puked into the sink and sat on the toilet seat. He felt light-headed, dizzy, his image in the mirror twisted, the ceiling looked dangerously close. The walls closed in. He had to lie down. He looked around. A large bathtub on a raised step shimmered in the distance. Jason dropped to his knees and crawled towards it. It seemed to recede as he struggled to close the distance. He gasped when he hit his head on the white porcelain sidewall. He lifted a knee onto the step, reached for the lip of the tub, and pulled himself over the edge. He sprawled face-down with his nose at the drain. Jason passed out.

The transvestite announced an *Animal Crackers* skit. The crowd was cleared out of a small area next to the couch. Groucho, playing Captain Spaulding, the famous African explorer; Chico, playing Emanuel Ravelli, a musician; and Harpo, playing himself as another musician, assembled. Cleopatra was pressed into service to play a grand dame hosting a welcome party for the explorer.

• • •

The grand dame entered the stage.

Captain Spaulding entered and walked up to the grand dame.

"Hello," said the explorer to the grand dame, "I must be going. I'm sad to say I cannot stay, but no, I must be going."

Emanuel Ravelli with his trumpet under his arm, and Harpo with horn, walked up to the grand dame and the famous African explorer.

Ravellli looked at the grand dame. "How do you do?"

"Are you the musicians?" asked the grand dame.

"Say," said Captain Spaulding, addressing Ravelli, "I used to know a fellow that looks just like you. His name's Emanuel Ravelli. Are you his brother?"

"I am Emanuel Ravelli."

Harpo squeezed his horn, "Honk. Honk."

"You're Emanuel Ravelli?" asked Captain Spaulding.

"Yes, I'm Emanuel Ravelli."

"Honk. Honk."

"Well, all right," said Captain Spaulding,

twirling his cigar in his mouth and wiggling his eyebrows, "but I still insist there's a resemblance."

Harpo jumped around the stage delighting the audience with his bike horn.

• • •

The crowd roared with approval. Cleopatra bowed and the transvestite threw a rubber chicken into the crowd. Spiderman dropped crushed ice from a bucket down some girl's dress. Someone spilled a beer on the couch. A couple went into the closet. The two bedroom doors were locked. The wastebaskets overflowed with empty wine and beer bottles and plastic glasses. Time passed. About 11:00 PM, the clamor reached new levels. But the party hushed when hotel security arrived. Guests in the adjoining suite had complained about the noise. John, the transvestite, solved the problem; he went next door and invited them to the party. The consumption of beverages increased.

• • •

The transvestite climbed onto a chair.

Harpo squeezed his horn and banged on a metal bowl, scattering potato chips. "Attention, attention," he yelled. "It's time for our awards."

The crowd formed a pulsing circle around John.

The transvestite smiled and pursed his red lips into a big circle. "Ladies and Gentlemen, and students, welcome to SIGBZE. It's time for the 'John Strong Good-Taste Award.'" Chico handed John a blow-up, naked, female doll. John waved the manikin over his head. "This may not be a programming tool," said John, "but I'm sure it'll be a useful tool to our winner!" John presented the doll to the winner—one of Cleopatra's bare-chested attendants with a large penis painted on his chest—amidst wild and drunken applause.

Loud banging on the door startled the partygoers. The Spanish Fly opened the door and was confronted by two policemen. "That's it!" one said. "The party's over. Go on, all of you—take off." The police stood there for ten minutes until the crowd dispersed. The cops left shaking their heads in disgust at the bizarre behavior of (mostly) adults.

• • •

The men cleared up as best they could and left a $64 surplus in an envelope for the maids. Groucho went into the bathroom and pissed. He turned to the sink and found traces of vomit in the basin. He began to tear his mustache off when he noticed a body in the bathtub. He leaned over and poked at it. It looked like a kid and didn't move. Shit, thought Groucho, this kid's dead. He panicked. He figured they'd served booze to a minor and the sucker had died! Groucho ran into the suite. "Hey, we're in deep shit. There's a body in the tub."

The Spanish Fly investigated. He rolled the body over and checked for a pulse. The kid's pulse was ninety-five. The Spanish Fly called out, "Bullshit. This kid's just drunk as a doornail. What do we do with him?"

"Let's throw him over the railing," said Harpo as the other men filed into the bathroom. The Hyatt had a large atrium, and the doors to each room opened on corridors with waist-high walls. "It won't take much to get him over the wall."

"You're not serious, are you?" asked Chico.

Harpo smiled. "I just want to go; I got a date with that babe from Southern Methodist."

The transvestite checked the kid's pockets. He said, "It's all right. He's got a wallet and a Hyatt cardkey in his pocket." The wallet yielded a driver's license. "His name's Jason, Let's see if we can wake up Jason."

Harpo threw a glass of water in Jason's face. The Spanish Fly gave him a few light slaps.

Jason's eyes fluttered open. "Huh?" Jason saw the Marx Brothers, a squat, ugly transvestite, and some kind of an angel with wings looking down at him. He moaned. Oh, God, he thought, the Marx Brothers were dead and he was in a coffin. The guy with the sombrero must be the Angel of Death. Jason closed his eyes, and curled his body into a fetal position. Then he remembered the transvestite. Jason wondered what that weirdo was doing in Heaven. Maybe he was in Hell. He opened one eye.

"Kid, what's your room number?" asked the Angel of Death.

Jason's mind soared. They wanted his room number. He wasn't dead! "Uh … 1218."

"Okay," said the transvestite. "I'll drag him down there." John picked up Jason, threw him over his shoulder, and headed for the hallway.

"Hey, John," said Chico, "you gonna go like that? You'll scare the shit out of anyone on the elevator."

"That's the idea."

• • •

On the twelfth floor, John propped Jason against his shoulder and pounded on the door to 1218.

"What'ya want?" squeaked a voice.

The voice sounded scared. Damn right, figured John. Shit, it was 1:30 in the morning. John saw someone in the room looking through the little peephole in the door. He pictured the guy—he'd see some weird looking transvestite with somebody hanging on him that looked dead. John smiled. Maybe the guy would think John was a vampire.

"Open up," shouted John. "This guy belongs to you,"

"No fucking way," said the voice which had steeled. "Beat it, or I'll call the cops!"

"What?" John got pissed. He let Jason drop to the floor.

"Jason, Goddamnit, what's your room number?"

Jason muttered, "Wrong … hotel. I'm … ah, at the Hyatt … Regency."

John shook his head in disgust. He felt like leaving Jason in the corridor, but the guy in 1218 might get curious. The last thing they needed was another visit from the police. John took Jason downstairs. They stumbled through the lobby and revolving door. John dragged Jason over to a taxi, opened the door, and shoved him into the back seat. John threw a $20 bill through the driver's window.

"Take this drunk to the Hyatt Regency."

The cabby stared at John. He looked over his shoulder at Jason, back at John, and gulped, "He paid *you*?"

John laughed and walked back into the hotel through the revolving door. He was startled when he saw Dr. Peter K. Lemming. John knew Lemming but he suspected the ACS president didn't recognize him in his costume. Still, he didn't want to deal with the asshole. Lemming made eye contact but John ignored him and turned to go towards the elevators. Lemming followed him.

John turned around. In his three-inch heels he towered over the diminutive Lemming. "Hey, big fellow, you want something?"

Lemming looked furtively over his shoulder. "How much?"

John decided to play along. "$200," he said, suppressing the biggest laugh of the night. Even so, a high pitched giggle escaped.

Lemming reached into his pocket. He counted his money. He frowned. "I only have $120."

"Sorry, I ain't desperate," said John.

"But," protested Lemming, "I'm the pres—"

"Yes?" said John.

Lemming's shoulders slumped and he walked back to the lobby.

So goes America's IT policy, thought John. He pressed the elevator call button and worked his way back to the suite. Upon arrival, he took $20 out of the maid's envelope. No way was he paying for Jason's taxi.

John thought ACS might be not-for-profit, but with all this crap, maybe it was time for SIGBZE to go for-profit.

Part IV

Fantasy, Science Fiction, and Witchcraft

Special Orders 191

Tensions were high in Washington the summer of 1862. The peace wing of the Democratic Party, the *Copperheads,* sought an armistice with the Confederacy. The Democrats were prepared to sacrifice the Union. President Lincoln, whose generals lacked enthusiasm for battle, worried about possible war with Great Britain, or perhaps worse—British recognition of the Confederacy. That would seal the collapse of the Union. France also weighed recognition while Spain, resentful of the Monroe Doctrine, continued to meddle in Cuba.

Friday, September 12, 1862

Artillery thundered on the Northern Virginia horizon as Juan tumbled onto the soil next to an open dispatch case. Pancho and Luis landed next to him. The army orders that accompanied them had spilled out of the case and lay under the Cubans. Juan watched their escort gallop north towards Frederick.

The Cubans were on the edge of a large field of clover, surrounded by elm, beech and sycamore trees. The knee-deep Monocacy River, a tributary of the Potomac, passed several hundred yards to the east. Smoke drifted across the water. Remnants of smoldering campfires and mules' manure littered the field; a Confederate artillery unit had recently evacuated the site. Empty canteens, dirty bandages, and several abandoned six-pound cannon balls lay in the clover. It was late and the moon was nearly full, illuminating the field. A picket fence to the north cast a long shadow over the agents.

"Pancho," said Juan, "*¿cômo estas?*"

"*Bueno.* But Luis is stunned. His leg has a gash."

"The orders—are they intact?" Juan was concerned. The papers had to reach Major D. H. Hall, a division commander in General Lee's forces in the Army of Northern Virginia.

"They're all here," answered Pancho. "But what can we do. We're in the middle of a battlefield—Union forces could discover us at any moment."

"Let me think." Juan looked around. Late summer heat and humidity poured in from the Chesapeake Bay and enveloped the Cuban spies.

Pancho asked, "How important are these orders?"

"I saw General Lee dictate them to Colonel Chilton, the adjutant-general. If they fall into the wrong hands, it will be a disaster for the South."

Juan noticed some movement in the trees to the west.

Luis began to moan.

"Wrap something around that fool's leg and tell him to shut up," whispered Juan. "There are Union soldiers in a skirmish line coming out of the trees."

The agents hunkered down, and Juan hoped they wouldn't be seen in the shadows. It was common knowledge that justice was swift in the field; spies were tried and hung—or burned to death—the same day.

Juan thought about the orders. During the summer months, the South had dominated the fighting. Although most of the casualties were Union soldiers, Juan knew the most serious test for the Confederacy was yet to come. Lee needed to win the battle for Maryland. It was essential if the South intended to wheel into Pennsylvania and menace Philadelphia. And Major Hall needed the orders to plug serious gaps in the disposition of Lee's forces: in fact the army of Northern Virginia was split into five forces, with some units separated by as much as eight miles.

"Juan," groaned the wounded Luis, "the general consigned these orders to us for safety. Perhaps we should destroy them before they fall into the hands of the enemy."

Juan considered retrieving a glowing ember from the fire pit closest to their position. But the movement might attract the attention of the Union soldiers. He decided it was too late. "*Silencio.* If we're lucky, these troops will move on. Or, perhaps our escort will return before we're discovered."

• • •

Corporal Barton Mitchell, F Company, Twenty-Seventh Indiana Voluntary Infantry Regiment, of the Union forces was tired and scared. His unit had fought at Bull Run and suffered appalling losses. Mitchell was grateful when his lieutenant ordered the men to camp for the night. They were in a former Rebel encampment and quickly stoked a plethora of dying embers into fires. The men settled down, ate rations, and dropped off into restless sleep. Something yellow, under a picket fence near Mitchell, flickered in the firelight. But he was too tired to investigate.

The next morning Mitchell opened his eyes. He saw a sheath of yellow documents tied together in a bundle. He crawled out from under his field blanket and stumbled around the campfire. Mitchell picked up the papers, and three cigars with Spanish writing on their labels slipped out of the bundle and dropped onto the clover. Mitchell thought he saw a look of alarm flash across the head of one of the cigars, but shook off the thought. One cigar had a long tear in its wrapper under the label. Mitchell looked around furtively, picked up the three cigars, and stuffed them into his shell jacket. He studied the documents.

The corporal was stunned. Special Orders Number 191, dated September 9, 1862, was addressed to the commanders of the Confederate Army of Northern Virginia and gave the entire plan of battle for Lee's army, including marching orders for the next four days. By noon, Juan, Pancho, and Luis—the last drawing poorly because of the tear in his wrapper—had gone up in smoke. Lee's orders were passed by Corporal Mitchell up the chain of command through F Company to the Twenty-Seventh regimental commanders, and then ultimately to the chief of staff of Major General McClellan. Earlier, Union intelligence reports had suggested that Lee had divided his forces; these orders confirmed it. General McClellan acted with uncharacteristic dispatch, marshaled his forces, and struck at the gaps in Lee's positions. Lee, stymied in battle at Antietam, abandoned his attack on Maryland. Shortly after the attack on Maryland failed, President Lincoln felt confident enough to issue his Emancipation Declaration, which further cooled European interests in recognizing the Confederacy.

President Lincoln's and the War Department's fears were abated when the North's most influential newspaper, *Harper's Weekly*, reported on Saturday, September 20, 1862:

EUROPEAN POWERS STAY OUT

(New York) McClellan's victory at Antietam stunned the world. Acting upon surprise intelligence, extracted under torture from three Cuban spies working for the Spanish crown, the Army of the Potomac proved victorious. Confederate forces have retreated. The Cuban spies, after a swift trial, were beheaded and their bodies burned. Britain and France withdrew their feelers to Richmond and transmitted *démarches* to Spain over its meddling in the American Civil War …

(N.B. General Robert E. Lee's Special Orders Number 191 *was* discovered in the field by Union forces on September 13, 1862, wrapped around three cigars. History did not record the provenance of the cigars.)

Day of Infamy

Kochira wa Nagano-san desu ... Excuse me. Hello, my name is Satoru Nagano. I forgot I was writing to an English-speaking audience. My American friends asked me to tell you what happened on that day in Japan so long ago.

It was late. War had erupted and wild rumors spread throughout the country. I heard some people say it was a sneak attack. Others thought it was inevitable—that we'd been forced into it by the global competition for resources. Professor Goto, of *Todai* University which you know as the University of Tokyo, was interviewed on NHK radio. He pronounced: "It was due to the world's Robinson Crusoe economies, in which each nation trades off its desires and wants with limited available resources. War is the natural consequence of such forces."

American radio said the war was provoked by human cravings for power. European stations talked about world domination. Brussels scoffed. Germany was not upset—it, of course, already had deals with Japan. The Soviets said it was a provocation. But otherwise, in most capitals, resolve was called for. Most people were somber, anticipating hardships and casualties.

At the Fujitsu factory in Numazu we were very concerned. It was a different day in Japan than in America. If I recall, it was late on a Monday when we learned about the hostilities. We'd assembled for dinner. Earlier, I'd watched the sun set over Suruga Bay. A baseball game had just ended when the radio alerted us that a National Pronouncement would be broadcast in fifteen minutes. That was exciting; few of us had ever heard the emperor's voice. All the shifts assembled in the dining room. The room was fraught with tension. A manager predicted we would have to expand the assembly lines in order to manufacture more equipment. It was war, and we would become profiteers!

As we waited for the pronouncement, I reflected on the state of the world. I could understand how many people in the west would be confused and threatened. This was a turning point; things were going to change. On one hand, it was a very exciting time. The Arpanet—precursor to the Internet—was launched. Janis Joplin entertained enthusiastic crowds in America, and a new Chief Justice of the United States Supreme Court was sworn into office. But not everything was positive. That day, the Cuyahoga River in Cleveland caught fire; there were cyclones in Asia and intense floods in Tennessee; in Italy the Vatican removed forty saints from its liturgical calendar; and in France the government of Couve de Murville resigned. Globally, the omens were not auspicious. The new conflict would leave old industries and nations—those that couldn't adapt—in smoking ruins. People would lose more than their jobs.

In Japan, no one knew how it would turn out. This was breaking new ground. It would establish a new order of things, new co-prosperity spheres. But there was doubt, too. Economists were divided. How would the people react? Would they understand? How would the markets react? Would the history books tell the truth? Did they ever?

The people looked to the throne for guidance. The emperor had summoned the Foreign Minister and the Minister of Industry and Trade to his chambers. After twelve hours of intense discussions the emperor issued his National Proclamation: "*To Our good and loyal subjects: We crave only peace and justice for the peoples of the world. We shall weather this storm together, and through strength, determination, a common sharing of the burden, and faith in* Shichi-Fuku-Jin, *the seven gods of good fortune, we shall prevail.*" Later, our factory received an enthusiastic and encouraging letter from the Chrysanthemum Throne.

Things were complicated around the world that day, June 23, 1969, a day that will live in infamy. The Software Wars began the day IBM unbundled and separately priced its applications software from its hardware—software was no longer free.

Nagano Satoru
Fujitsu Systems Engineer, Retired
Yokohama, Japan

A Deed Without a Name

Marcus Bloom, author and retired professor of English literature, grit his teeth as an ER technician pushed a Foley catheter through his urethra and into his bladder. Marcus groaned in pain and squeezed his wife's hand. Tusia held his hand limply, her attention riveted on the blood from Marcus' prostate that trickled out of the catheter.

The staff in the ER room called it post-surgical bleeding. Marcus wondered if they were out of their minds. The original surgery, a transurethral resection procedure (TURP)—the common folk called it a rotor-rooter—had been three years earlier when he was fifty-six. How could it still bleed? Nevertheless, the TURP had been the right thing to do. Afterwards, he'd urinated like a young stallion. Marcus smiled at the memory of the pretty nurse who'd sneaked a peek while he'd filled a specimen bottle—his only regret that he couldn't swish a tail, like horses did on the riding trails.

While his legs quivered from the procedure, Marcus thought about his other problems. He'd been plagued by a mysterious hair loss, a precipitous drop in weight, and a persistent low-grade flu. Blood tests were negative and the doctors bewildered. In Marcus' professional life, a spate of publishers and his agent had defected.

Tusia offered little sympathy. She was an attractive woman with streaked blonde hair at forty-six—who'd also changed over the past few months from a loving partner to a distant stranger. She was concerned not at all with his maladies. Instead, she obsessed over strange herbs and spices. Tusia claimed they were for experiments with Indian cooking. She'd purchased a large black cast-iron pot and used it to brew foul-smelling concoctions.

The ER discharged Marcus, and he waited for Tusia at the curb. The catheter bag, strapped to his leg, felt warm—the probe uncomfortable. He watched Tusia pull her new red Miata convertible onto the hospital's driveway. She leaned across the passenger seat and pushed the door open. Marcus climbed into the car, grimaced, and eased his way into the bucket seat. The catheter pressed against his sphincter.

He moaned, "This thing hurts! You could've helped."

"Oh, you'll be all right."

Marcus fastened his seatbelt. He looked at her. "Belt?"

"I gave it up. It's a stupid law."

Marcus retreated into his seat. Tusia backed up, dropped the gear into first, and peeled out of the driveway. It seemed to Marcus that she aimed at every pothole. A little later, they pulled up in front of their home in Mountain

View. Tusia turned off the engine and looked at him. "I'm going shopping. There's a new market on Grant Road with oriental vegetables. I'll get some take-out for dinner."

Marcus struggled to climb out of the Miata. He feared the strain would aggravate the bleeding. Finally, he managed to roll out of his seat and climb slowly out of the car. He watched Tusia restart the engine and drive off without a wave. He staggered into the house, popped a pain-killer, and crawled into bed.

Dinner that evening was a strange Indian eggplant dish that reminded him of gruel in Poe's *The Fall of the House of Usher*. He ate it with reluctance, drained the catheter bag, swallowed another pain killer, and returned to bed.

After a deep sleep, Marcus found some blood stains on the sheets. The catheter must have leaked. He drained the catheter bag into the toilet bowl again. The urine flowed crimson red. Marcus knew the color was not the problem; it took very little blood to color the urine deep red. It was blood clots that caused mayhem, and Marcus' urine was red-peppered with large and small clots. The doctor in the ER had insisted upon the catheter to prevent those clots from jamming him up. Marcus shook his head in frustration.

He washed his face. He wasn't inclined to take a shower with a hose hanging out of him and a bag on his leg. He brushed his teeth and rooted in one of Tusia's drawers for a Q-tip to clean his ears. Lately, it seemed he generated enough wax to make candles.

He looked up when Tusia walked into the bathroom. "I'm going out," she declared. "Coffee at Peet's with Josephine. We'll probably do a movie. See you later."

"You're going now? Leaving me like this?"

"Don't be a baby. Take an aspirin. Besides, the cleaning lady will be here later. I'll bring some dim sum for dinner."

"What about lunch?"

"Open a can of tuna." Tusia threw a black cape over her shoulder and walked down the hallway to the front door.

Marcus wondered when she'd purchased the cape. It looked new and jogged a distant memory that danced just out of reach in his drug-induced state. He heard the front door slam. He shrugged off the thought and returned to his search for the Q-tip. He pushed aside a small box in the drawer and discovered a tray of hair fragments and fingernail clippings. The fragments looked like the little cuttings that swirl down the drain in the bathtub after haircuts. He picked one up and studied it. Goddamn, it was his hair! But the nail clippings? Were they his? He racked his brain and thought back—they *were* his. He remembered how surprised he'd been when Tusia had offered, so sweetly, to manicure his nails a few weeks back. Why'd she save this stuff?

Marcus decided to check the rest of the house. In the closet under the stairs, he found a shoebox containing a dead sparrow and a worm. Two Tupperware bowls in the pantry yielded a snake's head and some strange herbs; in the wine cellar he found a knee-high ski-sock stuffed with dead frogs.

What the hell? When had this weird behavior begun? They'd been married seventeen years, and Tusia had never shown any interest in witchcraft or voodoo. She'd always been a solid, well-grounded, law-abiding woman—nothing like her mother! That old lady mumbled chants all the time. She'd stared at Marcus with green eyes that penetrated to the warts on his soul, and smiled at his discomfort. And, she'd worn a cape. That's it, he remembered—no wonder Tusia's cape unsettled him.

Marcus felt a chill. He limped into the kitchen and brewed a cup of Prince of Peace Premium Oolang tea. As he sipped, he reflected on Tusia's background. She was of Slovakian descent, born in the Carpathian Mountains, a region well known for its witches, werewolves, and vampires. Her mother had brought her to America when she was three. Marcus reckoned that was kind of young to be a witch.

The mother had stopped her frequent visits only after Marcus, in despair after two years of marriage, consulted old reference books on the occult in the university's library. He'd found an ancient German text, *Der Kampf Gegen Die Zyganerzauberinen* (The Fight Against the Gypsy Witches), which suggested witches could be denied entry to a forest hut. The book recommended the same defense that the Jews had employed in Egypt against the Angel of Death. Marcus had experimented with a few drops of lamb's blood on the front door, and it worked. It kept the woman at bay. Still, he realized, Tusia could have mastered spells from the old hag before or even during their marriage. And there *was* a book on voodoo that Marcus had found in a drawer.

Marcus looked out the kitchen window. The fruit trees were flowering. His hair loss had begun when they'd harvested their Satsuma tangerines, about four months earlier. That was just about the time Carmelita was hired to clean the house. Marcus smiled. Carmelita, twenty-two, was a stunning woman with long legs, an enchanting Mediterranean complexion, breasts for which Apollo would chase Daphne, and long, lustrous, black hair. She was hot and irresistible; they had rutted like dogs in heat every time she came to the house. Funny, he thought, how he'd never noticed that his wife always went for coffee with Josephine on cleaning day. Maybe Tusia had a lover, too?

He blinked. Marcus doubted she had cheated. She lacked that serene and cheerful mien that came from sexual satisfaction; on the other hand, she burned with restless energy. But perhaps Tusia knew about Carmelita? Could she? They'd been so careful. Carmelita washed the sheets every time she and Marcus made love, and she carefully cleaned the bathroom after showering.

Marcus rummaged further. In the refrigerator he found a Claussen dill pickle jar filled with blood, urine, and a few blood clots. His blood! She must have drawn it out of the catheter bag while he slept—that explained the blood stains on the sheets. What was it that Shakespeare wrote in *Macbeth?* It had come up often in his lectures:

> "*Cool it with a Baboon's blood,*
> *Then the charm is firm and good.*"

Suddenly it all came together. She'd gone too far. He had wasted away for weeks and now she was trying to kill him with witchcraft! Because of a little sex with Carmelita?

Angry, he dumped the tea-bag in the compactor and saw a dead gecko. What was that doing there? He waddled into the bedroom with the catheter bag on his leg squishing. On a nightstand was Tusia's copy of *Macbeth.* He opened it to a dog-eared page and read the lines that she'd highlighted with a yellow marker:

> "*Double, double, toil and trouble,*
> *Fire burn and cauldron bubble.*"

Well, that explained why she'd bought that black pot. He scanned down the page. Tusia also had marked "*Tongue of dog*" followed by "*Lizard's leg.*" Jesus! That morning, when he'd looked out the window, he'd seen a dead dog lying in a pool of blood. Tusia must've run down the poor beast and cut out its tongue. And geckos were lizards! Was the one in the compactor missing a leg?

Marcus' eyes watered as he read the next highlighted phrase:

> "*Liver of a blaspheming Jew!*"

How the hell was she going to get that? Suddenly Marcus clutched his side; he wasn't religious—but he *was* Jewish.

Never mind! He was going to get the bitch. He retrieved Tusia's book on voodoo spells and scanned the index for the section on dolls. He smiled grimly as he read the chapter. It wouldn't take much.

Marcus opened the laundry hamper and grabbed a pair of Tusia's used panties. They weren't her usual color, but Marcus was in no mood to be picky.

He limped back into the bathroom and snatched her hairbrush. He trudged into the garage and lowered his HO gauge model railroad system which was mounted on a plywood platform. Turning to a cupboard, he dug out Tusia's doll which she'd brought to America from Slovakia. He slipped the panties onto it, pulled some long, streaked blonde and black strands off the hairbrush, and twisted them into the doll's hair. He mounted the doll on his Bachmann locomotive and placed it at the end of a long stretch of straight track. He ripped a model mountain tunnel off the sheet of plywood and set it cross-wise at the other end of the track.

Marcus admired his work. Spells could work both ways. He plugged in the transformer, pushed the dial to maximum voltage, and watched the engine accelerate. The locomotive reached its top speed and rammed into the side of the model mountain. The doll shuddered and fell into a puddle of oil on the garage floor. Marcus felt better already. If the spell worked, maybe Carmelita wouldn't have to wash the sheets after they made love. He hoped it was just a matter of time. He went into the kitchen, turned on the radio, and brewed another cup of tea.

• • •

Flashing lights blanketed the northbound lanes of U.S. Highway 101. Four lanes of traffic merged painfully into one and inched past an accident scene. A CHP cruiser, fire truck, a tow truck with a long flatbed, and an ambulance blocked three of the lanes. Paramedics and firemen milled about. A small blackened car—so mutilated and burned that its make and color were not apparent—rested on twisted wheels and the remains of burnt tires. Fire retardant foam draped parts of the car. Its hood was crumpled and jammed into the concrete abutment of the Rengstorff Avenue overpass. A stained sheet covered a body on the side of the road. The body lay in a pool of oil speckled with the fragments from a shattered windshield and broken headlights.

A Mountain View police car parked on Rengstorff Avenue. A policeman half ran, half slid down the embankment.

"What happened?" he asked the CHP sergeant.

"Witnesses reported the car was going over a hundred miles per hour straight down the shoulder when it slammed into the overpass. The driver went through the windshield, bounced off the abutment, and landed spread-eagled on the road. The car burst into flames."

"No seat belts? Suicide?"

"You know," said the sergeant, "that's what I thought. But the damndest thing; the victim, a woman, wasn't wearing any panties. She was out there—

for the whole world to see! Don't suicides usually want to die with some dignity?"

"That's what I've read. Any ID?"

"Everything burned in the fire. The note too, if there was one."

• • •

Marcus heard a KCBS radio traffic report. The reporter said there'd been an accident with a fatality on U.S. Highway 101. Traffic was squeezed down to one lane in the northbound direction at Rengstorff Avenue; the backup extended three miles south to Mathilda Avenue. Marcus grinned—maybe the spell had worked! The front door bell rang. That had to be Carmelita! Marcus felt himself becoming aroused—probably not a good idea with a catheter. He willed himself to calm down and whistled as he walked to the door. He wondered if he could remove the catheter himself and make love despite the bleeding. No matter. It would stop soon—if the witch was gone. He opened the door with a smile.

Sunlight skimmed the roof across the street, and highlighted streaked blonde hair on the woman at the door. A red Miata sat in the driveway. Marcus' grin evaporated. Realization flooded in—the hair on the brush—he'd twisted blonde strands into the doll's hair, but there were some black ones, too. And the panties! How did they …? He remembered Carmelita had showered in that bathroom and she'd been in a hurry. They had made love longer than usual. How could she have been so careless? It must have been *her* panties. Oh, my God, he thought. He'd killed Carmelita!

"You asshole!" shouted Tusia. "Where is she? I'm going to kill her and then I'm going to cut out your liver." Tusia brandished a long knife and charged into the house.

Baggage

Ed Axelrod, an attorney, was traveling from Washington D.C. to Toledo, Ohio, for an important deposition when it happened. He first flew National Airlines from Reagan Washington Airport to Cleveland. Then Ed connected to National Express for the short flight to Toledo. The trip required a plane change as well as carrier, although National Express was a subsidiary of National Airlines. Ed worried his luggage might miss the connection, so he first checked his bags to Cleveland. During the layover, he fetched them in Cleveland and rechecked the bags at the National Express counter to Toledo.

"Are you sure the bags will make the flight?" Ed wiped his forehead with nervous energy. The bags contained critical exhibits for his firm's big legal case.

"Oh, yes, Mr. Axelrod," said the agent. "No problem. Here's your boarding pass and two baggage checks. You leave from Gate 2."

Ed passed through security and went to his gate. His airplane, a Brazilian Embraer 130 commuter with eighty-five seats, was ready for boarding. The gate area was empty, and Ed wondered where the rest of the passengers were. *Maybe they're already on-board, or this is an interim stop and I'm the only passenger boarding.* But, when boarding was called and he stepped into the cabin, Ed saw he was the only passenger.

An attractive flight attendant stood inside the door. "Mr. Axelrod? Hi. I'm Cindy. You're our only passenger today. The captain asked me to seat you in 21C, to balance the load, if you don't mind."

"Did my bags make it?"

"I'm sure that's no problem, Mr. Axelrod. Relax and enjoy your flight. Would you like a drink before takeoff?"

Ed smiled and accepted a Bloody Mary. He'd noticed, as he walked to his seat, several empty miniature bottles of gin lying in the galley sink. He hoped it wasn't the pilot who'd been nipping.

• • •

At Toledo's Express Airport ten miles west of the city, the National Express gate agent, Betty Marx, was on the phone with her supervisor, Phil, in Newark.

"Look, Phil, damn it! Cindy said she personally sat this guy in 21C. But, when they landed he wasn't on the plane. The pilot had reported radio problems—apparently lots of sunspot activity—and landing was delayed an hour. All the seats in row twenty-one, both sides of the aisle, were slightly scorched, too."

"Did you check the head?"

"Phil! C'mon."

"Okay. Okay. Did the passenger's bags arrive?"

"Two bags arrived. That's what so strange. Usually we misplace a bag, especially when there are only a few passengers on board. But we're not used to misplacing passengers."

"Cindy must be into the sauce again," pronounced Phil. "Send the bags to the lost luggage depot in Denver."

"What if someone asks about the passenger?"

"Well, he wasn't on the plane. I guess he never made the connection. They must've screwed up in Cleveland and keyed in his boarding pass as though he boarded. Go into the computer and correct the record."

"Okay, I've got to run; I have to turnaround the Cincinnati flight."

• • •

Ed Axelrod was shaky. He'd just awakened. Sweat poured down his face. The air was unusually humid. *Why is it so bloody hot?* Ed was sitting in an airport, and bags slid down a chute in front of him onto a rotating carousel. The building was not enclosed, and a tropical breeze surged through the baggage area. *Where the hell am I? This sure don't look like Toledo to me.* Ed stood and walked over to the carousel. He looked at the tags on the bags—Destination Airport: GUM. *Where the hell is GUM*?

"Excuse me, sir. May I help you?" Ed looked up and saw a man with a jacket sporting an Air Pacific emblem. "You seem lost."

"Where am I?" said Ed. "I was flying to Toledo."

"Toledo? Sir, this is Guam. We get bags sent to Toledo. You're the first passenger."

Guam? What the hell am I doing in Guam?

"What about my bags?"

"They probably went to Toledo."

"Is there a courtesy phone to Air Pacific?"

The man pointed Ed at a wall near the men's room.

Ed strode to the wall and picked up a white courtesy telephone.

• • •

"Good afternoon. This is Air Pacific. My name's John. May I help you?"

"You bet, John," said Ed. "I seem to be in the wrong airport, and my luggage went astray, too. There are critical documents in—"

"Did you say the wrong airport? Air Pacific delivered you to the wrong airport?"

Ed explained that he last remembered boarding a National Express plane in Cleveland, supposedly headed to Toledo, and now he was in Guam.

"Sir, that's ridiculous. If you really flew on National, please call them. The TSA does not take jokes lightly!"

"But—"

The Air Pacific agent hung up.

Ed went to a payphone and dialed an 800 number for National. He worried about making his breakfast meeting in Toledo the next morning. *And where were those bags?*

After four minutes, the phone was answered. "Good morning, this is National Airlines. My name's Josephine. May I help you?"

"Yes," said Ed. "It seems you flew me to the wrong airport. I have to get to Toledo immediately."

"Please, sir. With the way airport security is these days, it's simply not possible to get on the wrong airplane. Did your baggage go to the wrong airport, too?"

"I don't know where my bags are. There're very important papers in them. But I'm in Guam now."

"Well, we fly to Guam, but our flight doesn't leave from Los Angeles International for two hours. What are your ticket and baggage check numbers?"

Ed read the numbers on his boarding pass and his baggage tags to the agent.

"Let me see, according to the computer … Excuse me, you're Mr. Axelrod?"

"That's right, Ed Axelrod."

"According to the computer, Mr. Axelrod, you never made the flight from Cleveland to Toledo."

"But I checked my bags in Cleveland."

"Yes, and Toledo reported two bags arrived. Since they were unclaimed, the bags were forwarded to our lost luggage depot in Denver. But you never boarded the plane."

This is nuts. "But, damn it, I'm in Guam now. How'd I get here?"

"I can't help you, Mr. Axelrod. Would you like to speak with my supervisor?"

"You bet your sweet ass I would."

"Now, now, Mr. Axelrod. There's no cause to be rude. I'll transfer you."

• • •

"This is Laurie, reservations supervisor. May I help you?"

"Laurie, you people have flown me to Guam when I wanted to go to Toledo. Not only that, your computer's all screwed up. It says I never got on the plane, and now my bags are going to Denver."

"What's your name? I'll just look at my terminal."

"Ed Axelrod, damn it."

"Yes, Mr. Axelrod, the record says you never boarded the flight to Toledo."

"But how did I end up in Guam? Look, check my earlier flight from Washington to Cleveland."

"Okay, let me check … Yes, apparently you did board the flight that originated in Washington. It's a mystery, all right. Let me call Operations. Please hold."

Twenty minutes later, Laurie came back on the line. "Mr. Axelrod, are you still there? Sorry for the delay. Thank you for your patience."

"Where do you think I am now, in Minneapolis?"

"Mr. Axelrod, I re-checked the computer, and someone must have changed your record for the Toledo flight. But Operations can't explain this mishap. They did say that there was unusual sunspot activity during the flight to Toledo. Communications were disrupted, and there was some damage to some of the seats on the plane."

"So how'd I get to Guam?"

"Operations said it might be a modified cosmic infidibulum. Kurt Vonnegut wrote about them in *The Sirens of Titan*. An infidibulum is a space wave function, or some thingee like that, where people can appear on several planets or moons simultaneously—when those bodies' orbits are in phase with the space wave. But in this case, it seems you only appeared in one place at the same time. Operations said that if you wait you just might go back to Toledo automatically—uh, when the physics change."

"Look, I can't wait for physics. I have to be in Toledo for a morning meeting. And I need my documents."

"Well, okay, Operations said I could give you a complimentary seat on our next flight to Los Angeles from Guam. It leaves in ninety minutes. From LAX, I can connect you to a nonstop to Cleveland and then on to Toledo. How's that sound?"

"What about my appointment?"

"It's tomorrow in Guam. With the date change, you should make it back in the morning."

Ed frowned. He didn't like the idea of going through Toledo again. Still, he was desperate to make his meeting. He said, "Okay."

"Great, you have seat 37C on National flight 12. I'd upgrade you, but the flight is full. I did upgrade your flight from LAX to Cleveland. The ticket counter in Guam will give you a complete set of boarding passes. Meanwhile, I'll ask Denver to ship your bags back to Toledo. Have a nice flight."

Ed hung up the phone. He went to the ticket counter and fetched his tickets. An hour later, he boarded National 12.

• • •

That afternoon, there was another solar eruption. Fourteen passengers were missing when National 12 landed at LAX.

The Great Race

"Here he comes," said Hare. "Are you going to do it?"

Beaver nodded. "Don't worry. I promised. It's in the brownies."

Billy Tortoise banged on Beaver's door. "Trick or Treat!"

"Don't let him see you," said Beaver to Hare.

Hare hid behind a stool.

Beaver opened the door. "Well, goodness me! Who are you being tonight?"

"Mr. Toad," said Billy, who wore a frog costume over his shell. "See my new motorcar?" He waved a model 1928A Bentley Roadster.

Beaver smiled. "Okay, Mr. Toad. I baked brownies. Here's one for you, and one I wrapped just for your dad. Tell him it's for breakfast."

"Thanks, I will." Billy placed the brownies in his basket.

Beaver closed the door. He looked at Hare. "See? The fix is in. Now don't get distracted tomorrow. You've lost, what, twenty-five years in a row?"

"That's why I needed you to take care of it," said Hare.

"It's all set. I'll wager five shillings on you. Have some more cider."

Hare grinned and sipped.

• • •

The morning dawned fair and bright. Banners hung on willow trees announcing the Great Race. Weasel, the bookmaker, collected bets. Badger, the judge, smoked his churchwarden pipe and brandished a starter pistol.

Beaver placed his bet with Weasel. Hare and Tortoise shook hands at the starting line.

The forest folk cheered. Shouts of "Hey-hey-hare" and "To-to-tortoise" filled the air. Tortoise smiled sheepishly. Hare, in fashionable shorts, crouched.

"On your mark. Get set. Go!" shouted Badger as he fired the gun.

Tortoise began to waddle. Hare sprinted off but stopped when he saw a beautiful flower. Its colors drew him near and captivated him. Meanwhile, Tortoise plodded down the track. Hare was startled when Tortoise passed him. How could that be, Hare wondered. He'd only studied the flower for a second. Hare sprinted again and overtook Tortoise. Hare paused again when another flower sang to him. Then Hare investigated a carrot that seemed to rise up out of the ground. He lingered once more when a pretty girl-hare, with long, floppy ears smiled at him. Tortoise continued.

When Tortoise crossed the finish line, Hare lagged far behind, performing pirouettes in a field of petunias.

Weasel sighed and looked at Beaver. "That was fifty shillings on Tortoise?"

Beaver smiled shrewdly and collected his winnings. He counted out three shillings for the payoff to Billy Tortoise. The fix had been in, all right—except it was the cider which had been doped, not the brownies!

Illegals

Getting into America was not easy. United States naval forces patrolled the nation's waters to prevent those of us, from Cuba as well as elsewhere, from reaching their shores. When I joined the others assembled at the Havana docks, I knew it would be a complicated journey. I never dreamt that I would find myself involved in a criminal case brought by the United States Government.

The smugglers bundled us into groups according to our family names and packed us in shipping containers. The children were scared when they were separated from us, but at least they were with their brothers and sisters.

Our destination was San Francisco. That meant we had to travel through the Panama Canal. During the journey time blurred and the air became stale. We worried about the little ones, but the older children sang songs to keep them occupied. Fortunately, the Central American weather was cool, and it didn't get too hot in the containers. Every now and then the smugglers would renew our water.

When we arrived at San Francisco's Pier 13, the smugglers continued to segregate us. First they took the children away. We sensed their bewilderment and heard shouts of desperation when they thought they'd never see us again. But what could we do? We were still trapped in the containers.

A few hours later, they came for us. They took away our clothes and gave us flimsy wraps from Sumatra. My sister and other family members went in one batch. I went in another. All of us were trucked to various establishments to work or to be sold—so some despicable man could have his way with us.

I was in a shop called Sandy's Shop of Pleasures on Battery Street for several days. Many customers looked me over. The man who purchased me admired me from many angles. He appreciated my figure. I wasn't too tall or too short, or even too fat. Apparently, he liked me even without decent clothing. I imagined that he intended to fool around with me in front of his friends—so they could admire him and be jealous.

Can you imagine my surprise when we left the shop, and a flock of federal agents swooped down and arrested us? They dragged us to the lock-up in the old Federal Building on Golden Gate Avenue.

The man was booked, fingerprinted, and allowed to make one phone call. I was carried off to another room where a Deputy Assistant United States Attorney looked me over. She said, "You'll be the jewel in the crown in my case against that man and the shop that sold you. Trafficking in illegals is the charge. It's an open and shut case."

Of course, as an illegal they detained me. I could tell you tales of the horrors about the federal prison system. People lusted after me all the time. Perhaps my prayers to San Salvador were what saved me.

Later, I learned that the man who'd bought me was a San Francisco lawyer from the firm of Gurth and Gurth in the Russ Building on Montgomery Street. His name was Jack Boone. He practiced immigration law and planned to defend himself. The shop, also charged, was represented by Gurth and Gurth.

• • •

After several months, the case went to trial in the U.S. District Court for Northern California. A senior judge named Giuseppe Zirpoli, who was close to retirement, presided. The trial had been underway for several days. The court was in recess when federal marshals brought me into the courtroom. It looked like the media had latched onto the case; the room overflowed with reporters, onlookers, other attorneys, a law class from some university, and a TV camera crew.

At the end of the recess, the judge returned to the courtroom. I trembled when I saw him. He was one of the men who'd examined me earlier at the shop. Nevertheless, I maintained a discreet silence.

Judge Zirpoli called the courtroom to order, and the Assistant Deputy U.S. Attorney moved towards her peroration.

"Your Honor," she said with confidence, "the government has presented evidence that Sandy's Shop of Pleasures on Battery Street trafficked in illegals. Despite the counterfeit packaging, which suggests the illegals are from Sumatra, we have DNA tests that prove conclusively they're from Cuba. They are in fact the legendary Cohiba *Robustos*!"

Yes, I am, I thought—and proud of it!

The Deputy Assistant U.S. Attorney cited her authorities. "As you know, Your Honor, President Kennedy signed an Executive Order which directed the Federal Trade Commission and the United States Customs Service to prohibit the importation and sale of Cuban cigars. Sandy's Shop of Pleasures sold, and Mr. Boone purchased, such prohibited merchandise! He was arrested with the contraband still in his possession." She closed with a Latin expression. "*Res ipsa loquitor*, Your Honor. It speaks for itself."

Judge Zirpoli nodded, although I could tell from the way he rolled his eyes that he had little enthusiasm for the case. He stared at me for a while. I wondered if he recognized me. Then he said, "What do you say, Mr. Boone, to that comment? The U.S. Attorney's office seems to think it has an easy conviction."

I wondered how Mr. Boone would slither out of the charge. I waited breathlessly for his reply, and hoped I would not have to testify.

Mr. Boone rose. "Your Honor, it's true that the importation and sale of Cuban cigars has been prohibited by President Kennedy's Executive Order for over forty years. However, according to the 1980 Refugee Act, any Cuban nationals that leave Cuba legally—and who land successfully on American soil—are automatically granted permanent residence and asylum in the United States. Even if they leave Cuba illegally, and that has by no means been demonstrated by the government, they are granted the right to apply for asylum. In neither case are they detained. This cigar is a Cuban national. The government itself certified that fact with DNA tests. This Cohiba *Robusto* clearly has satisfied either the statutory requirement for automatic asylum, or has qualified for permission to apply for asylum. Hence, by definition, it is legal. That's Black Letter Law, Judge. The government had no right to detain this cigar. I submit that federal law, approved by Congress, holds sway over a Presidential Executive Order. Further, should there be a clash between the powers of the president and the powers of the Congress, it is long-standing precedent that the courts resolve the conflict. I move, therefore, for an immediate dismissal of all charges against myself and Sandy's Shop of Pleasures."

The Deputy Assistant U.S. Attorney's face turned red with rage. She sputtered and rose with clenched fists to argue against this clever manipulation of legal intent. "Objection, Your Honor. Mr. Boone—"

Judge Zirpoli smiled wryly. "Please, Madame Prosecutor, keep your seat. Mr. Boone's argument seems quite persuasive to me."

At that, a lawyer from Gurth and Gurth jumped up. "Your Honor, we agree. Mr. Boone's argument is compelling. We've prepared this brief in support of his motion." He waved a seven-inch thick document over his head.

Judge Zirpoli recoiled at the sight of such a substantial brief. "You can keep your supporting brief—I've decided the case—but, perhaps in the future, and in the interests of judicial efficiency, your briefs will be brief."

The judge dismissed the case with prejudice—on the spot. He invited Mr. Boone to join him in his chambers and adjourned the courtroom. Reporters jammed the entrance to the courtroom as they raced out, intent upon scooping their rivals with news of this startling ruling—which in effect legalized Cuban cigars in the Northern District of California. No one in the courtroom expected the government to appeal. The United States Ninth Circuit Court of Appeals, also headquartered in liberal San Francisco, was unlikely to reverse the decision. A lost appeal would be costly to the government, since it would extend the legalization of Cuban cigars to all nine western states that comprised the Ninth Circuit.

• • •

In the judge's chambers, the marshals returned me to Mr. Boone. As I wondered what would happen next, I was dismayed to see the judge produce another cigar from inside his gown. It was my sister! That was just before he pulled out a cigar cutter and a book of matches.

Help!!

The Witches

Lisa Agnesi stared at her twin, Agnes. They sat in a small café on the *platz* in Waltennhoffen, on the shore of the Forgensee in southern Bavaria. Ludwig III, the Grand Duke of Hesse, maintained his old castle, Hohenschwangau, in nearby Schwangau (Swan District).

Thank the Devil, mused Lisa, she and her twin weren't identical. Lisa was a lovely woman for a witch—in her mid-thirties, with long, raven-black hair and a delicate nose, framed by high cheekbones, and a dimple on the left side of her expressive lips. Agnes looked like a witch; she had a long horse face, pronounced ears, a twisted nose with a wart at the tip, and large feet. She had poor vision and wore thick, unsightly spectacles with wooden frames. A long conical witch's hat with a wide brim topped her tangled patch of brown hair. If it were not for both sisters' slightly slanted eyes—there was some central Asian blood from an ancient migration in their lineage—and the deformed ring finger on both their right hands, one never would guess the two were sisters.

"So," said Agnes, "you've made up your mind? It's been a long time."

"The woodcutter," said Lisa. "He's a simpleton, and he has two children. I've enchanted him, and it should be easy."

"Two would be wonderful. I can smell the roasts cooking already."

Lisa smiled. As long as she could remember, she'd served as the huntress for the pair, providing fresh meat for the oven. Unfortunately, they'd exhausted the supply of homeless waifs in the Füssen area on the border with Austria. They'd turned to snatching school children from the streets whenever they became desperate. But the kidnappings had stopped when Grand Duke Ludwig, after the receipt of multiple reports of missing children, had launched patrols. So far, no one suspected the witches had stolen and eaten the children.

"When will you take the next step?" asked Agnes. She reached for a pitcher of juice. It sat on a barrel which served as a table in the dirty square.

"The woodcutter has been paid for his labor. He collected wood for the bonfire to celebrate Ludwig's new castle, Neuschwanstein. The fool thinks he can afford me now, and the village priest will marry us next week, after the Sabbath."

"And the children? How will you handle them?"

"The daughter is the problem. She doesn't like me, but the son, Hansel, thinks he's getting another mother."

"Well, hurry up. *Barmecide* has been visiting lately."

Lisa grimaced. Agnes had referred to a *Barmecide's Feast*—a feast without food.

"Just make sure you coat the outside walls of your hut with *Shokolade*, and put icing along the edge of the roof. Bake a new gingerbread door. And don't forget to brush the chimney three times after the Sabbath."

Agnes nodded. Both witches practiced the old custom of running their brush up the chimney at midnight after the Sabbath.

"Will you brush the chimney at the woodcutter's?"

"Of course."

The witches finished their juice.

• • •

Two weeks after the marriage, Gretel kicked her brother under the table. "I don't like Stepmother."

"Why not?" said Hansel. "Father needed a wife to help raise us, and she never yells at us."

"She's mean. I heard her tell Father that there's not enough food, and he has to take us to the forest. And her finger scares me."

Hansel was perplexed. The forest was cold and dark, and witches lived there. "The forest? To do what?" He munched on a lone chicken bone served by his stepmother.

"*Dumkopf*! Father's going to leave us there. I don't know what's happened to him, but he's different now."

"Don't worry, Gretel. If he takes us, I'll bring us home again. Finish your dinner."

The conversation disturbed Hansel. He'd hoped he would get a substitute mother. But Stepmother was distant and selfish, and Father *had* changed since the marriage. Previously warm, friendly, and always concerned with the welfare of his children, Father was now aloof, distracted, and less caring. In case Father took them into the forest, Hansel knew he must be ready. He was the youngest, but he'd felt responsible for his sister ever since Mother had died. To prepare, Hansel went to the dry creek bed behind the woodcutter's hut and scrounged in the gravel. He collected a pile of pebbles and placed them in his pocket.

That night the children were awakened by their father. The fire had died down in the kitchen, but Father's eyes glowed a distant red. He mumbled, "You must come with me. Put on your warmest clothes."

"But Father, where are we going?" asked Gretel while Hansel rubbed the sleep out of his eyes.

"No questions. I must do this. Now come along."

The children dressed silently. "She made you do this, didn't she?" said Gretel. "I don't like her."

Father said nothing. His had a vacuous look on his face. He stuck a loaf of bread under Hansel's arms, and led the children into the forest. Hansel said nothing, but as they trudged along he dropped a pebble every twenty paces.

Father led them deep into the forest along snow-covered trails occasionally swallowed by bushes and trees. Hansel and Gretel had never strayed so far from home. When the moon was high in the sky, Father said, "You will remain here. I must leave now."

The children protested, but Father simply waved a hand and departed.

Hansel hugged Gretel as they watched Father disappear into the birch trees.

"See?" said Gretel. "She did this."

"I guess he's bewitched," said Hansel.

It was cold, and the children looked for some shelter. Gretel pointed at a cave, but Hansel said bears might dwell there.

"In the morning," he said, "maybe Father will be better. We'll follow my pebbles home."

As the sun began to rise, the children located Hansel's last pebble and followed the trail with frequent missteps back to the woodcutter's hut. Exhausted, the children crawled under their blankets on straw mattresses next to the wood-burning stove and quickly drifted to sleep.

• • •

Stepmother's shriek jolted Hansel awake. Tears sprang to Gretel's eyes as Stepmother screeched at them, "What are you doing here? How did you come home?" She turned to the woodcutter, "I told you to take them to the River Brunnen near the Foggersee. Now take them again, and do it right this time!"

"Father," pleaded Gretel, "don't do this. You're not thinking right. Why do we have to leave?"

"There's not enough food," hissed Lisa. "Now that Grand Duke Ludwig has dedicated Neuschwanstein, there's no extra work for your father."

Hansel grabbed a half-loaf of bread off the table. "At least let us have this bread." He eyed a large hunk of cheese. "How about the cheese, too?"

Stepmother swept the cheese into her apron and pointed at the door.

Once more the woodcutter led his children into the forest. He headed northwest towards the River Brunnen. As they walked, Hansel had a clever idea. He decided to use bread crumbs like little pebbles. He dropped crumbs every twenty paces. Only a small hunk of bread remained after they had walked for hours, much further than the previous night.

The River Brunner roared with runoff from the Bavarian mountains. Water tumbled and rushed forward, splashing against large rocks that lay in the riverbed. Birds fluttered noisily from the trees, but they settled down after the woodcutter departed.

Gretel cried, "I told you she's evil. That finger is just not normal. What are we going to do?" Gretel wrapped her arms around her body and shivered.

"Don't worry. I left a trail of crumbs," said Hansel. "We'll follow them."

"But what about Stepmother? She'll just throw us out again, and Father no longer loves us."

"I believe she's cast a spell on Father. This time we'll ask the village priest for help. Let's go."

But alas, when Hansel searched for the crumbs, he discovered the hungry birds had devoured the bread. "We're lost," he said. "We need to do something else."

Hansel sat in the dirt along the riverbank and studied the forest. "Look Gretel!" He pointed at smoke rising downriver. A well-worn path led along the bank in the direction of the smoke. "Maybe someone lives there who can help us."

• • •

The children trudged along the path. They could see bones scattered everywhere. A vixen chewed on a small set of bones that looked like fingers. The children held hands as they followed the riverbank. Fresh piles of dirt were scattered randomly inside the tree line.

"I don't like this, Hansel. I'm so scared."

"I'm more hungry than scared."

After a while, the children discovered the smoke came from a wood-thatched hut nestled in a small glade not far from the river. The roof came down to their shoulders and had a creamy-looking white covering along the edge. There was one window with shutters, and the dark brown walls looked like *Schokolade*. Gretel ran her finger through the creamy substance and tasted it. It was sweet frosting. She picked at the shutters; they were made out of *Schokolade* just like the walls. Both children laughed and nibbled at the sweets.

Hansel reached for the door, which looked like gingerbread. It flew open and a small woman beckoned to them.

"Well, well," said the woman. She was dressed in black with a black hat and had an ugly wart on her nose. "Don't you children have a sweet tooth? Come in, there's more inside."

Hansel walked into the hut and discovered he'd triggered a trap. He was in a cage. "You're nothing but skin and bones," said the woman. "I'll fatten you up, and we'll have a real feast." The woman slammed the door behind Gretel.

"Hansel," exclaimed Gretel, "look at her finger. It's just like Stepmother's. They must both be witches."

The witch said, "My name is Agnes. You," she said addressing Gretel, "will do the housework, and then I'll make a meal out of you, too."

• • •

Days went by. The witch fed the children bread and soup and roasted pieces of wild boar. One day, when Gretel cleaned the kitchen, she found Agnes' spectacles on the table. She smeared grease on them. Agnes didn't notice the grease, but mumbled often afterwards that she needed new spectacles.

Hansel began to gain weight. Every day Agnes would demand to feel Hansel's fingers to see if he was getting plumper. To confuse Agnes, Gretel, in a clever and sly way, slipped a thin chicken bone into Agnes' hand whenever she reached for Hansel in the cage.

"You're still too thin," moaned the witch.

One day Agnes grew tired of waiting. "Light the oven," she said to Gretel. "We're going to have a tasty, roasted boy today. He may be a little lean, but I can't wait any longer."

An hour later, she told Gretel to check if the oven was hot.

Gretel returned whimpering. "I don't know if it's hot enough."

"All right," said Agnes, "I'll check myself." She opened the oven and peered inside where a fire roared. Gretel sneaked behind the witch and shoved her into the oven. The bottom of the witch's large feet stared at Gretel and then disappeared as she slammed the door. The children heard her scream for a minute—then there was silence as black smoke poured out the chimney. Gretel smiled and ran to release Hansel from his cage.

The children finished the rest of the roasted wild boar, and spent several days eating the *Schokolade* and other candies they found in the hut. As luck would have it, they discovered a giant *Schokolade* egg stuffed with Bavarian gold coins.

"We should take the gold to Father," said Hansel.

"But how will we find him? And what will we do with Stepmother?"

"We'll think of something."

The children packed the gold coins into a small rucksack along with several kilos of candy. They left the hut and began to walk. Hansel reasoned that they should keep the river to their back, and they wandered in an easterly direction. The forest was thick, but they managed to find a path; after a while they no longer heard the rushing water.

Suddenly, they heard a man in the forest. He was shouting, "Children! Where are you?" Hansel and Gretel moved in the direction of his voice and from a distance saw the man sitting on a rock. Tears poured out of the man's eyes. It was Father. "Hansel, Gretel, where are you?" he shouted. "I am so ashamed. Please come back to me."

"Father, here we are," yelled Gretel. "Promise you'll never abandon us again."

Father threw his arms around the children. "I don't know what I was thinking. But your stepmother is dead—I must have been bewitched. Come home with me, and we'll be happy again."

Hansel looked at his father. He decided to wait before he spoke about the treasure. He whispered into Gretel's ear not to mention the gold: "Maybe later we can surprise him."

Father led the children back to their hut.

• • •

When they returned home, the children discovered Lisa, dressed in black and quite alive.

Lisa was furious. "What did you do to my sister, you monsters? How did you escape?"

"Father, you lied. You said she was dead," said Gretel.

Father looked bewildered. "I thought—"

"She's still bewitching you," yelled Hansel. Before Lisa cast another spell, Hansel decided to act. "Gretel, help me!" he cried. He grabbed an apron off a chair and rushed at Lisa. He wrapped the apron about her arms, and Gretel stuffed a rag in Lisa's mouth.

The two children pushed Lisa into the oven and slammed the door. "Quick, Father, put more wood on the fire," said Hansel.

"But—"

Gretel raced to the woodpile and retrieved several logs. She returned and Hansel inched the door open. Gretel threw a log in the oven and Hansel slammed the door closed again. Lisa screamed a long time. When she at last became silent, Father collapsed. After Gretel patted his face with a damp rag, he returned to consciousness. "What happened? Where's my new wife?"

"Father," said Gretel, "you've been under a spell. Your new wife was a witch. She and her sister wanted to eat us."

Father blinked. "I feel like I've been sleeping. Eat you, eh? That explains the missing children in Schwangau. We must report this to the Grand Duke."

Hansel looked at his father. If the Grand Duke was involved, they better be quiet about the gold coins.

The three hugged each other and lived happily ever after. Especially Hansel and Gretel, who kept the gold stash for themselves and became rich landowners when they grew up.

Gravity

Joe, an inveterate inventor, burst with enthusiasm when someone knocked on his garage door. He waded through a maze of empty cartons, skipped over a few puddles of spilled liquids, and opened the side door.

Joe grinned. "Don, you came!"

"What else? Your call sounded urgent."

"It was—"

Don wrinkled his nose. "What's that smell?"

"Oh, nothing. I had a goat in here for a day."

"A goat?"

Joe closed the garage door. "Never mind. I'm telling you, Don, I turned the damn box on and I could feel it pulling me."

"Sure, sure, that little box has gravity! What have you been snorting?"

"Look, put that ball over there near the box. I'll turn it on again."

Don couldn't believe he was going along with the farce, but he walked dutifully over to the workbench, put a red handball on a brick about a foot away from Joe's Rube Goldberg box, and stepped back.

Joe grinned. "Now watch this." He plugged an extension cord into the wall.

Don heard a motor rev up. The brick quivered, and the handball rocketed over to the side of the box. Empty cans of coconut syrup and WD-40 skittered across the floor. Don also felt a tug in the direction of the box.

Joe pulled the plug out. The ball dropped off the side of the box, bounced on the workbench, and dribbled away. The tug on Don disappeared.

"Well, I'll be damned," marveled Don. "How's it work?"

"It's based on some Einstein stuff. He said that light bends in a gravitational field. I figured maybe it would work backwards—you know, bend light and create gravity. The more light you bend, the more gravity you get—at least that's my theory."

"But how do you bend it? You can't use a mirror, can you? Doesn't that absorb all that gravity stuff?"

"Right," said Joe. "I tried all kinds of different ways to bend light—mirrors, magnets, smoke, prisms, everything. I finally figured out that you had to use something mechanical. Finally, I tried spinning a Folgers coffee can with an erector set motor and bouncing light off of a rotating fluid. When I used a red spotlight, it worked. It even works with a red flashlight. But I thought plugging the spotlight into the wall would be, you know, more dramatic."

Don was impressed. "What kind of fluid did you use?" He saw empty bottles and cans stashed on the shelves, under the workbench, and scattered around the floor. A half-full bottle of Dewar's White Label Scotch whisky and empty bottles of wine stood on a card table along with several yellow and green light bulbs.

"Boy, talk about problems," replied Joe. "I started with water and then I went through apple juice, V8, coconut syrup, goat's milk, Clorox, Campbell's Chicken Noodle soup, Scotch, vodka, and half-a-dozen different Chardonnays. It finally worked when I used dog piss."

Don was incredulous. "You're using dog piss?"

Joe nodded.

"How'd you figure to use that?"

"I saw the next door neighbor's dog licking his … aw, what's the difference? It's a long story. The hard part was finding out what kind of dog piss to use—it has to come from a Tiny Toy Chihuahua."

"You have to be kidding. How do you keep it in the can? Doesn't it spill out?"

"That was another engineering problem. I solved it with Saran Wrap and duct tape."

"That's fantastic. Have you tried bouncing the light twice?"

Joe shook his head. "I'm afraid to. I'm concerned it might double—or even quadruple—the force."

"Well, if it does that," said Don, "you'll get the Nobel Prize in physics. Let's try. Do you have another motor and coffee can?"

The men scrounged around for more erector set parts. They fabricated a second housing and installed a second motor.

"How much dog piss does it take?" asked Don.

"I used half a cup."

"Let's use a pint this time."

Don was excited as he poured a pint of Tiny Toy Chihuahua dog piss into another Folgers coffee can. He sealed it with Saran Wrap and duct tape.

The men took the can and mounted it inside Joe's box. They aimed the second can at the first can.

Don wondered where all the dog piss came from. "Hey, it's a good thing you had more dog piss."

"Yeah, it cost a bundle. Are you ready for me to plug the box in again?"

"Just a minute, Joe, they didn't know what would happen at Yucca Flats either, when they tested the A-bomb. We might get an earthquake or something. Maybe we should take good notes."

"Good idea, Don—get ready to write. I'm plugging the sucker in."

Joe's gravity pump powered up, motors began to spin, the red beam bounced back and forth between the two Folgers coffee cans at the speed of light, and the gravitational force was magnified exponentially on every other bounce by the extra pint of dog piss.

FLASH!!!

Two years later, astronomers on a small planet circling Draconnis 3, a star in the Crab Nebula Galaxy, were startled at the formation of a new black hole. It sat at the edge of the Andromeda galaxy, formerly called the Milky Way, in the same position as a blue-green planet that had suddenly disappeared. The black hole was slowly swallowing its neighbors—a third-class star and seven planets and their assorted moons.

The Elephant Queen

I meant what I said
And I said what I meant
An elephant's faithful
One hundred percent!
—Dr. Seuss

As Old Gray watched, a train of cows, bulls, and calves trampled the tall Savannah grass which separated the old watershed from the new forests. Old Gray had counted almost sixty rainy seasons. She knew she was old for an African Forest Elephant. But this exodus was a new experience.

It was hot as the western sun hovered over the departing herd. Old Gray flapped her rounded ears to dispel heat. She stared at the dust kicked up by the herd on the African plain. She listened as Sheba proudly trumpeted her political victory. Old Gray rested on her haunches and thought back on her years as herd matriarch. She'd been abandoned now, like the Old Ones. But those had been glorious years …

Gray had been twenty when the herd cows selected her matriarch. Like all the young cows, she'd been tutored by the older elephants. But she was surprised when they'd ignored herd protocol—which dictated that only older elephants be appointed matriarch—and encouraged the younger generation of cows to support her. The senior elephants had said she was wise beyond her years, brave, and resourceful.

Old Gray smiled as she remembered the council meeting. But it had been curiosity that had resulted in her herd's admiration, not resourcefulness. One day Gray had wandered in the bush nibbling at some plants. She'd heard a loud gong and a sound of alarm from the two-legged's village. She'd gone deeper into the bush and discovered a pride of hunting lions. The big cats had carried off a little two-legged calf, and Gray had charged the pride with her tusks. African female elephants, unlike their Asian cousins, also had tusks. The cats had abandoned their prey and retreated. The two-leggeds had been grateful. They'd offered baskets of millet and other grains to the herd. Over a few weeks Gray had learned, that by mounting a defensive patrol around the village, the two-leggeds would offer daily food.

The Old Ones, who no longer had teeth with which to chew, finally had a regular food supply—they could eat the more digestible food provided by the two-leggeds. African elephants ate hundreds of pounds of vegetable matter a day, but little of it was digested—the high-yield grain from the village meant that starvation was no longer the fate of the Old Ones. Thus had the herd honored Gray's resourcefulness with the leadership.

Gray had assigned the entire herd defense duties. All bulls and cows over twelve years old, with the exception of the Old Ones, were organized into patrols to drive off predators. The African elephants were fast; they could run at speeds up to forty miles per hour. They were ordered to pursue the lions for great distances, and to push the big cats out of the watershed. The young adults and adolescents complained that it was too much work; they wanted the two-leggeds' food, too. But Gray had persisted—the food was only for the Old Ones. The watershed provided plenty of water, and the lush bush and trees in the forest generated more than enough food for the rest of the herd which could chew its food.

Old Gray still stood ten feet tall and weighed 8,000 pounds. But that would change now that her teeth were worn out. She'd already gone through five sets of her molars and the last set was worn down. When it fell out, she'd become one of the Old Ones, unable to forage for food.

As she watched the dust fade on the horizon she pondered how the herd had changed. At first the cows had argued that only those cows who'd calved should vote in herd councils. Then, after ten years of plenty, the cows argued that all cows—even those who had not calved—should vote. "After all," they said, "our sisters deserve the right to vote, too."

It had seemed reasonable to Gray. Then, twelve years later, the expanded electorate of younger female elephants had argued that all elephants, bulls included, should vote. "The bulls work also, defending the two-leggeds," they'd argued.

Now any elephant over the age of twelve could vote. It was a young electorate, reflected Old Gray sadly—inexperienced and easy to manipulate.

Sheba, thirty-eight, a large gray-brown female with sensual twisted tusks, had been ambitious and clever. She was a beautiful African Forest Elephant, with an unusually long tail with a deep black tip. Her ears were rounded more than usual. Sheba's trunk was long and shapely. Her lyrical trumpet brought some of the bulls to their knees in orgiastic pleasure. She'd sensed an opportunity with the young bulls and, to gain power, she spread her sexual gifts among many. She told them that they should get their share of the two-leggeds' food, that it wasn't fair that the herd did all the work and received none of the food. Sheba said that the Old Ones exploited them. To pander to the young elephants, she pulled the trees down for the young elephants, so that they could reach the rich leaves; she pushed logs out of the way for the youngsters when they played; and she talked of how the herd could expand simply by moving to richer lands.

Old Gray had argued in the councils that the two-leggeds were essential to the health of the Old Ones, that the herd had a symbiotic relationship with the two-leggeds' village, and that the defense duties were critical. But over time, resentment had grown in the herd, and loyalty shifted to Sheba.

The end came when Sheba argued that the watershed was drying up, that there were richer forests, and that by moving and expanding the herd they could eat and drink without the hard work of protecting the two-leggeds. "Besides," she'd snorted, "only the Old Ones benefited."

One of the young cows, encouraged by Old Gray, had asked, "But who will protect the two-leggeds' village? How will the Old Ones get food?"

"Nothing will change," said Sheba. "I promise that nothing will change. Why should it? The predators have been driven away. Why should you work when you get no benefit from the work? Come with me over the hills where we can eat and drink without work."

"Are you sure?" asked the cow. "It would be terrible if the Old Ones could not get food. They have no teeth; they cannot chew."

"Yes," argued Old Gray. "Someday you, too, Sheba, will be old."

"But I'm not now!" trumpeted Sheba. "Trust me! Nothing will change. The two-leggeds will still give you food. We need to go now. Make me your Queen and come with me over the mountain to the new forest. We will gather more elephants and become the greatest herd in Africa. We will have all the food and water we need and no work. We can do it!"

"We can do it! Yes, we can!" thundered the herd.

The setting sun flashed off the yellow eyes of the big cats in the bush. Old Gray spat out her last set of molars, ground down to flecks and useless to her. She heard a gong in the two-legged's village and cries of alarm.